AN
ARIZONA
CHRISTMAS

WILLIAM W. JOHNSTONE

with J. A. Johnstone

AN ARIZONA CHRISTMAS

PINNACLE BOOKS
Kensington Publishing Corp.
www.kensingtonbooks.com

PINNACLE BOOKS are published by

Kensington Publishing Corp.
119 West 40th Street
New York, NY 10018

PUBLISHER'S NOTE
Following the death of William W. Johnstone, the Johnstone family is working with a carefully selected writer to organize and complete Mr. Johnstone's outlines and many unfinished manuscripts to create additional novels in all of his series like The Last Gunfighter, Mountain Man, and Eagles, among others. This novel was inspired by Mr. Johnstone's superb storytelling.

All Kensington titles, imprints, and distributed lines are available at special quantity discounts for bulk purchases for sales promotions, premiums, fund-raising, educational, or institutional use. Special book excerpts or customized printings can also be created to fit specific needs. For details, write or phone the office of the Kensington sales manager: Kensington Publishing Corp., 119 West 40th Street, New York, NY 10018, attn: Sales Department; phone 1-800-221-2647.

ISBN-13: 978-0-7860-4058-2
ISBN-10: 0-7860-4058-0

First Kensington hardcover printing: July 2017
First Pinnacle mass market printing: November 2017

10 9 8 7 6 5 4 3 2 1

Printed in the United States of America

First electronic edition: November 2017

ISBN-13: 978-0-7860-4079-7
ISBN-10: 0-7860-4079-3

Belgium, December 1944

Gun-thunder filled the forest. Artillery shells screamed overhead, machine guns chattered, and rifles cracked, all punctuated by the occasional boom of a pistol. It was a terrible symphony of death and destruction, accompanied by the near-constant flashing of muzzle flame that made the forest almost as bright as day.

When the shooting stopped, as it always did sooner or later, an eerie, echoing silence settled down over the war-torn landscape, along with the thick gloom of the cold night.

Corporal Wallace leaned back from the M1919A4 .30 caliber machine gun and breathed heavily as he tried to calm his galloping pulse. Beside him, Private Bexley, the assistant gunner, cursed softly, over and over.

He finally eased up on the profanity "The Krauts nearly settled our hash that time, didn't they?"

Before Wallace could answer, a deep, calm, steady voice came from behind the two machine gunners.

"Wasn't even close. We've got the bastards right where we want 'em."

Wallace glanced over his shoulder. "That's right, Sarge. When there's so many of them and so few of us, and they're all around us, you don't even have to worry about aimin'. Just point a gun and shoot, and you're bound to hit a German."

Sarge moved up beside the .30 cal, hunkered on his heels, and chuckled. "Now you're thinkin', Wallace."

Thorp, a private from Indiana, called from behind the tree where he had taken cover. "If we've got 'em on the run, Sarge, how come we ain't out there chasin' after 'em?"

"Well, we're tryin' not to take advantage of them. Wouldn't hardly be fair. No, we'll stay here and let 'em come visitin' again when they're good and ready."

"They're gonna kill us all," another voice said.

Sarge's head swung around sharply toward the private who had spoken. "Can that talk, Mitchell! Our orders are to hold this position, and that's what we're gonna do. That means stayin' alive. Nobody in my squad is gonna disobey orders, so get this through your head right now. *The Krauts are not gonna kill you, and they're not gettin' through here!*" Sarge blew out his breath in a dismissive sound. "Simple as that."

Silence hung over the woods for a moment, then the squad's sixth and final man, Hogan, said, "Sarge is right. We don't have to worry about the Krauts. Now, starvin' or freezin' to death, that's a whole other matter entirely, right, Sarge?"

The noncom had to laugh at Hogan's dry tone. "I can't argue with you there, Private."

The half-dozen men were quiet. It was unlikely the Germans would attack again in the night, but it was a good idea to keep an ear open since it was hard for men to move through the woods in the dark without making some noise. The thin layer of snow on the ground could muffle their steps.

After a while, Wallace said quietly, "It sure is cold." From Florida, he wasn't accustomed to frigid weather.

"That's the way it gets in December in this part of the world," Sarge said. "For what it's worth, I don't much cotton to it either, Wallace. Back in the part of Arizona where I grew up, we usually don't get weather like this, even in December. Hardly ever even got down to freezin'."

"Must not have seemed much like Christmas," Thorp said. "Hell, back home in Indiana, nearly a foot of snow was always on the ground when Christmastime rolled around."

"Yeah, at least here we've got snow on the ground for Christmas," Hogan said. "And lots of little Santa Clauses waitin' out there in the woods to deliver presents to us."

Mitchell said, "We'll never live to see Christmas."

"Damn it," Sarge rasped. "What'd I tell you about talk like that, Mitchell? Stow it!"

Mitchell was stretched out behind a deadfall where he had kicked some snow out of the way. Propped up on his elbows, he could shoot over the log. He twisted around and said, "There are too many of them, Sarge, and they've got us surrounded! You can joke about it all you want, but that's the truth! We're almost out of rations and ammo, and as long as this overcast holds, they can't drop in any more to us. It's only a matter of time until the Germans overrun us and slaughter us all."

Sarge let him spew the words. Dogfaces had to bitch. That was just the way it was. He was hearing more than the usual griping, though. Mitchell's near-hysterics could ruin morale. When the private fell silent, Sarge said in scathing tones, "You got it all out of your system now, Mitchell?"

"I don't see why the brass doesn't just surrender," Mitchell said bleakly.

"Because they don't have any backup in 'em," Sarge said, "and neither do I. I learned a long time ago, listening to my grandpa talk, that you don't give up, no matter how bad the odds may seem. As long as you're drawing breath, you keep fightin', because you never know what's gonna happen. Things can take a turn you never expect."

"Your damn grandpa never had to fight off thousands of Nazis!"

Sarge straightened and took a quick step toward Mitchell, but he stopped himself before he completely lost control of his temper. The tension in his voice revealed how he was trying to rein in his anger. "Maybe not, but he was in a few mighty tight spots in his time, and he got out of every one of 'em because he never gave up. Sure, he had some help from his friends, but none of us are alone here, either. If we stick together and keep fightin' and never give up, we'll come through this just like Gramps did back in Arizona one Christmas when all hell broke loose."

"Sounds like a good story, Sarge," Wallace said. "Why don't you tell it?"

"Yeah," Hogan chimed in. "Maybe it'll keep us from thinkin' about how cold and hungry we are."

Sarge thought for a moment and then nodded. "It just might. It all happened a long time ago. Almost sixty years ago, when Arizona was still a pretty wild and woolly place."

"Were there cowboys and Indians?" Bexley asked. "Back in Brooklyn, I went to the movies every Saturday, and I always loved them cowboy pictures."

"Yeah, there were cowboys and Indians and a bunch of other folks," Sarge said, moving over to sit on another log. An artillery shell had landed a few yards away, back in the opening days of the German offensive, and knocked quite a few trees over. "The whole thing actually got started before Christmas, and it wasn't in Arizona, either. That was in Colorado, in a settlement called Big Rock . . ."

CHAPTER 1

Smoke Jensen dropped to one knee and fired twice. Flame licked from the muzzle of the Colt in his hand.

On the other side of the main street in Big Rock, Colorado, the man Smoke had just shot staggered back toward the plate-glass window of a store. He pressed his hand to his chest. The palm was big enough to cover both bullet holes. Blood welled from the wounds and dripped between his splayed fingers.

He went over backwards in a crash of shattering glass.

That didn't mean the danger was over. A slug whipped through the air only inches from Smoke's left ear. He dived forward, off the boardwalk, and landed behind a water trough. Bullets thudded against the other side of the trough. A few plunked into the water.

Smoke had seen four other outlaws besides the

man he had shot. From the sound of the guns going off, all of them were trying to fill him full of lead.

Hoofbeats pounded in the street. A man yelled, "I got the horses! Come on!"

They believed they had him pinned down, Smoke thought. They figured if they kept throwing lead at him, he couldn't do a thing to stop them from getting away.

They were about to find out how wrong they were.

No doubt spooked by all the gunfire, the horses stomped around in the street, making it more difficult for the outlaws to mount up.

Smoke thumbed more cartridges from his shell belt into the .45's empty chambers. Then he rolled out into the open again, tipped the Colt's barrel up, and fired.

The outlaws had managed to swing up into their saddles. Smoke's slug ripped into the chest of the man leading the gang's attempt at a getaway. He jerked back in the saddle and hauled so hard on the reins that his horse reared up wildly.

The man right behind him tried to avoid the rearing horse but was too close. The two mounts collided and went down, spilling their riders.

Smoke pushed himself up and triggered again. His bullet shattered the shoulder of the third man in line and caused him to pitch out of the saddle with his left foot caught in the stirrup. As the horse continued galloping down the street, the wounded outlaw was dragged through the dirt past Smoke.

The fourth man fired wildly, several shots exploding from the gun in his hand. Smoke didn't know where the bullets landed, but he hoped no innocent bystanders were hurt. To lessen the chances of that happening, he took a second to line up his shot and coolly put a bullet in the outlaw's head.

That left one man in the gang who wasn't wounded or dead, the one who had been thrown when the two horses rammed into each other. He scrambled to his feet as soon as he got his wits back about him, but as Smoke's gun swung toward him, his hands shot in the air, as high above his head as he could reach.

"Don't shoot!" he begged. "For God's sake, mister, don't kill me!"

Smoke came smoothly to his feet. He was only medium height, but his powerfully muscled body, including exceptionally broad shoulders, made him seem bigger. His ruggedly handsome face was topped by ash blond hair, uncovered because his brown Stetson had flown off when he threw himself behind the water trough.

The gun in his hand was rock steady as he covered the remaining outlaw. From the corner of his eye, he saw his old friend Sheriff Monte Carson running along the street toward him. Monte had a shotgun in his capable hands.

"One in the store over there," Smoke said, nodding toward the building with the broken front window. "The others are all here close by, except for the one whose horse dragged him off down the street."

"I'll check on them while you cover that hombre," Monte said. "Not much doubt that they're all dead, though."

"How do you figure that?" Smoke asked.

"You shot 'em, didn't you?" A grim smile appeared on the lawman's weathered face.

Smoke knew the question was rhetorical so he didn't answer. He told the man he had captured, "Take that gun out of your holster and toss it away. Slow and careful-like. You wouldn't want to make me nervous."

The idea of the famous gunfighter Smoke Jensen ever being nervous about anything was pretty farfetched, but not impossible. He had loved ones, and like anybody else, sometimes he feared for their safety.

Not his own, though. He had confidence in his own abilities. Anyway, he had already lived such an adventurous life, he figured he was on borrowed time, so a fatalistic streak ran through him. If there was a bullet out there somewhere with his name on it, it would find him one of these days. Until then, he wasn't going to waste time worrying about it.

The surviving outlaw followed Smoke's orders, using his left hand to reach across his body and take out the iron he had pouched when he mounted up to flee. With just a couple fingers, he slid the gun from leather, tossed it aside, and thrust his hands high in the air again. Then he swallowed hard. "No need to shoot me, Mr. Jensen. I done what you told me."

"How do you know who I am?" Smoke asked with a slight frown. Although he had spent quite a few years with a reputation, first as a notorious outlaw—totally unjustified charges, by the way—and then as one of the fastest men with a Colt ever to buckle on a gunbelt, he was still naturally modest enough to be surprised sometimes when folks knew who he was.

"Who the hell else could you be?" the captured outlaw asked. "You shot four fellas in less time than it takes to tell the tale. I warned Gallagher we shouldn't try it right here in town. I *told* him. I said, Monte Carson's a pretty tough law dog to start with, and Smoke Jensen lives near Big Rock and we'd be liable to run into him . . . into you, that is, Mr. Jensen . . . and I said that's just too big a risk to run, and sure enough—"

"What's this varmint babbling about?" Monte asked as he walked back up to Smoke with the scattergun tucked under his arm.

"Claims he didn't want to pull this job and warned the boss they shouldn't do it," Smoke explained with a trace of amusement in his voice.

"Well, he must not have argued too hard. He's here, ain't he?"

"In the flesh," Smoke agreed.

The frightened outlaw looked at both men. "You reckon I could put my arms down? They're getting' sort of tired."

Monte shifted the Greener and covered him. "All right, but if you try anything funny, this buckshot'll splatter you all over the street."

"No tricks, Sheriff. You got my word on that." The man licked his lips. "I just want to take what I got comin' and get outta this without bein' hung or shot."

"Behave yourself and you won't get shot. As for being strung up, well, that's up to a judge and jury, not me." Monte glanced over at Smoke. "The other four are dead, by the way, just like I figured. The one you shot in the shoulder might've lived if he hadn't gotten dragged down the street with his head bouncing until it busted open."

Smoke was reloading the Colt. He left an empty chamber for the hammer to rest on then slid the gun back into its holster. "Bad luck tends to dog a fella's trail when he starts riding the owlhoot."

"What were these varmints after, anyway?"

"Don't know," Smoke replied with a shake of his head. "I saw them come running out of the freight company office while I was on my way down to the train station." He nodded toward several canvas bags the outlaws had slung on their saddles as they tried to make their getaway. "I'd check those bags."

Monte squinted over the shotgun's barrels at the prisoner.

"Or I could just ask this varmint, and if he knows what's good for him, he'll answer."

"Money, of course," the outlaw volunteered quickly. "We got a tip that a fella named Reilly was having a payroll brought in by freight wagon, rather than on the train. He figured it'd be safer that way, since nobody would know the money was hidden in some sacks of flour."

Monte frowned. "Jackson Reilly, the rancher? He's sort of an oddball. That sounds like something he'd do. You know him, Smoke?"

"Met him once or twice," Smoke said in his usual laconic fashion. "Wouldn't say I know him all that well. He's been in these parts less than a year."

"I've heard him say he doesn't trust banks. Appears he doesn't trust the railroad, either."

Now that the shooting was over, quite a few of the citizens who had scrambled for cover earlier were coming back out to gawk at the sprawled bodies of the outlaws and stare at Smoke, Monte, and the prisoner. A ripple of laughter suddenly went through them. The man walking toward them was covered in white powder that clung to his clothes, his hair, and his mustache.

Smoke recognized Angus Mullen, one of the clerks from the freight office. He smiled and said, "Angus, you look like you got caught in a snowstorm."

"There'll be snow soon enough," Mullen said as he slapped at himself and raised a little floating cloud of white. "This is flour! Those scoundrels were cutting bags open and throwing them around the office."

Smoke nodded. Now that he took a closer look, he could see that some of the bandits were dusted with flour as well, although not nearly to the extent that Mullen was.

"Who the hell had the bright idea of hiding money in flour sacks?" the clerk went on.

"You should check your manifests," Smoke suggested. "I'll bet those sacks were being held for Jackson Reilly."

Mullen grimaced and scratched his jaw. "Yeah, now that you mention it, I reckon that's right," he admitted. "I'll have to have a talk with Mr. Reilly. The freight company has rules about this sorta thing, you know!"

"You do that, Angus." Monte jerked the shotgun's barrels in a curt gesture to the prisoner. "You march on down to the jail now. Smoke, thanks like always for lending a hand. You sure keep the undertaker busy."

"Not by choice," Smoke said. "I'm a peaceable man."

Monte just snorted and prodded the prisoner into marching toward the jail. Smoke returned to the errand that had brought him to Big Rock. He had come to meet the westbound train, which would soon be delivering his wife Sally to him.

He'd been early, so he had parked the buckboard at the station and walked back up to Longmont's Saloon for a cup of coffee and a visit with his old friend Louis Longmont. As the time for the train to arrive had approached, Smoke had said his good-byes and started for the depot again.

He had spotted the outlaws and recognized trouble in the making right away. When he'd called out for them to hold it, a man across the street, who had probably been posted as a lookout, opened fire on him.

Smoke hadn't wasted time asking any questions. Anybody shot at him, he regarded it as a declaration of war and proceeded accordingly.

And anybody not prepared to back it up hadn't ought to slap leather in the first place, as far as Smoke Jensen was concerned.

A thin overcast hung in the sky, thickening into darker clouds over the mountains. Avery Mullen was right. There would be snow soon enough. But that was expected in the fall in the Colorado high country. Smoke had seen plenty of snow and never minded it. The brisk nip in the air felt pretty doggoned good, in fact.

The shoot-out with the would-be thieves had delayed him some, but the train still hadn't rolled in. As he walked out onto the platform after crossing the station lobby, he heard the locomotive's shrill whistle in the distance, heralding the train's arrival.

A few people on the platform were waiting to board, others looked more like they were there to meet someone . . . like Smoke was. He smiled and nodded pleasantly to several he knew.

It was impossible not to notice a few folks whispering to each other behind their hands. Smoke wasn't so full of himself that he assumed they were talking about him, but given the recent ruckus, it made sense if they were.

Smoke knew he was famous—or infamous, depending on how you looked at it—but it wasn't anything he had ever set out to be. All those years ago, in the hardscrabble days right after the war, when he and his pa Emmett had left the farm in Missouri and headed west, all young Kirby Jensen had been interested in was getting by from day to day. That was before he'd met the old mountain man called Preacher, who had dubbed him Smoke because of his speed with a gun, and before he'd set out on the vengeance quest that had changed the course of his life forever.

Smoke preferred not to dwell on that.

Anyway, the train was pulling in, with smoke puffing from the diamond-shaped stack on the big Baldwin locomotive, and as it came to a stop he looked toward the passenger cars, eager to catch a glimpse of the woman he loved.

There she was! Sally stepped down from one of the cars, graceful as always. She looked up as Smoke came toward her, and a smile appeared on her face, making her more beautiful than ever.

Then she was in Smoke's arms and his lips were on hers, and he wasn't going to waste one bit of time or energy thinking about anything else for a while.

CHAPTER 2

"I've had an idea," Sally said a few minutes later, turning in her seat as Smoke lifted her valise and carpetbag into the back of the buckboard.

Some men might feel uneasy when their wives said something like that, but not Smoke. Sally was as intelligent as she was lovely, and any idea she had was liable to be a good one.

He swung up beside her and reached for the reins hitched to the pair of horses. "What's your idea?"

"Where are Matt and Luke these days?"

Smoke thought about the question. His brothers tended to travel around quite a bit. Luke was a bounty hunter, so his work took him all over. Matt was a drifter as well, holding a variety of jobs in as many places.

"Last I heard, Matt was in Nevada, working as a guard on shipments from a silver mine in the Comstock Lode. Luke was in northern California, on the trail of some outlaw, I suppose. Why? What did you have in mind?"

"Well, Christmas is coming up in a couple months . . ."

Smoke tried not to wince. Christmas had become sort of a sore spot with the Jensen clan. Every time it rolled around, so did all sorts of trouble. Gun trouble, usually, and often accompanied by some sort of natural disaster.

"You think we ought to ask them to come to the Sugarloaf again?" Smoke asked as he twitched the reins and got the team moving. "That didn't work out too well last time."

"On the contrary, we're all still alive, and we did some good for those orphans. Anyway, I wasn't thinking about having them come to the ranch. To be honest, I'm not sure I'm up to throwing a big Christmas fandango again."

"So what did you have in mind?"

"I thought maybe we could take a holiday trip and meet Matt and Luke somewhere. And Preacher, too, of course."

"I have no idea where that old pelican is. You know Preacher. He's not much for staying in touch. So he might be anywhere." Smoke paused. "I suppose I could send letters to most of his old haunts, though. Saloons and trading posts and, uh, certain other places where he always stops in whenever he's passing through the different areas."

"Certain other places," Sally repeated as a smile played around her mouth. "Houses of ill repute, you mean."

"He says he enjoys the piano music most of 'em provide in their parlors. Or so I've heard tell."

Sally laughed. "You don't have to dance around the subject with me, Smoke. I know you had a life before you met me."

Smoke sobered, and so did Sally. Their banter had led them into memories of a dark time in Smoke's life when he'd had a wife and a son, both murdered by brutal enemies.

Having left Big Rock behind, Smoke flicked the reins and got the team moving a little faster. The wind had picked up, and he wanted to get back to the ranch before it started to rain.

To lighten the mood, he turned the conversation back to the idea Sally had proposed. "Just where would this Christmas trip take us? Where would we meet Matt and Luke and Preacher, if we can get word to them in time?"

"What about somewhere in Arizona? If they're in California and Nevada, and we're in Colorado, that's sort of a central meeting place, don't you think?"

Smoke considered the suggestion and nodded. "Tucson, maybe. Been a while since I've been there." He chuckled. "Wouldn't have to worry about getting caught in a blizzard or an avalanche."

"See, you're warming up to the idea."

"Pearlie and Cal and the rest of the crew would be able to take care of things at the Sugarloaf."

"Of course they would."

"I kind of like it," Smoke admitted. "I reckon I'll sit down tonight after supper and write some letters, see if I can round up the boys in time."

Sally squeezed his arm and leaned against him. "I think we'll have a fine time."

"Any time I'm with you, darlin', it's always a fine

time," Smoke said as he slipped an arm around his wife's shoulders and held her.

He was getting too old for this, Luke Jensen thought as he ducked lower behind the overturned table and listened to the bullets thudding into it.

Almost a quarter of a century had gone by since he had ridden off from the Missouri farm to join the army and send the Yankee invaders back where they came from. That hadn't worked out too well, and ever since, violence had dogged his trail.

Of course, a lot of that was his own fault. Nobody had forced him to take up bounty hunting after the war. Some might say fate had led him to it, but he could have walked away from it if he'd wanted to badly enough. Turned his back on a life of gunplay and spilled blood—some of it his own.

There had been tranquil moments now and then. Some women he'd grown fond of, even though he couldn't stay with them permanentlike. The reunion with his brother Smoke, whom he regretted avoiding for years. Getting to know their adopted brother Matt and that crusty old mountain man Preacher. Even those two young hellions Ace and Chance Jensen, who shared a last name with Luke, Smoke, and Matt but weren't related as far as any of them knew. Luke had enjoyed his meetings with them.

But mostly his time had been spent with outlaws and killers who wanted to put bullet holes in his hide.

Quint Barclay, for example, who was behind the

bar at the moment, shooting at the table Luke had kicked over and then dived behind.

The tabletop was nice and thick and had stopped all the slugs so far, but sooner or later one of those hunks of lead would punch through the wood and lodge itself in Luke's body . . . unless he somehow stopped Barclay before then. Luke had hoped to get close enough to buffalo the son of a bitch before Barclay even knew he was there, but like a wild animal, the outlaw was too watchful for that. As soon as he'd caught a glimpse of Luke in the mirror, the outlaw had vaulted over the hardwood bar, knocking over a nearly full bottle of whiskey.

He was fast with a gun, too. Luke had gotten behind the table barely in time. As it was, he heard bullets whispering in his ears as they went past.

He risked a look, spotted a flash of muzzle flame, and felt the wind-rip of a slug an inch or so from his face. That located Barclay for him. Luke triggered three fast shots with the long-barreled Remington in his hand. The bullets whipped over the bar and smashed several bottles of whiskey sitting on a shelf, spraying glass and liquor over the area where Barclay crouched behind the bar.

The contents of the overturned whiskey bottle glugged out and formed a puddle on the hardwood. Luke looked above it to where an oil lamp hung from the ceiling. He drew a bead, fired again, and busted the chain holding up the lamp.

It fell and shattered, the flame igniting the spilled liquor. That set off the reservoir of oil in the lamp, and the ball of flame spread to the whiskey that had splattered behind the bar.

All of it combined in a *whoosh!* of fire that set Quint Barclay ablaze, too.

Screaming, Barclay jumped up and started swatting at the flames leaping around his torso and his hair. He forgot all about Luke, who rose up high enough to aim the Remington.

He didn't hesitate as he slammed a bullet through Barclay's head, killing him.

Barclay had murdered at least two men up in northern California, just to make it easier to rob them, and during his getaway from a bank holdup, he had gunned down a woman and a little girl just because they'd gotten in his way. Actually, a bullet in the head was more mercy than he deserved, the way Luke saw it.

Should've let him burn for a while. Would have been a nice foretaste of what he had coming to him in Hell.

But Luke wanted the carcass to be identifiable so he could collect the reward. He stood up, grabbed a bucket of sand that stood near the bar, and started throwing it on the flames. The bartender, who had crawled down to the end of the bar and hunkered there while the shooting was going on, hurried to join in the firefighting efforts. He slapped at the flames with a wet bar rag.

In a matter of minutes the fire was out, but the sickening smell of burned flesh and hair hung in the air. Nobody but Luke and the bartender were left in the place for the stink to bother, though. Everybody else had lit a shuck out of there as soon as the lead started to fly.

"Sorry about the damage," Luke told the bartender as they stood and surveyed the grim scene, including the charred corpse. "I would have preferred to take him without anyone being hurt."

Luke was a tall man pushing middle age, with a face too craggy to be called handsome. Dark hair and mustache and black clothing did nothing to relieve his generally stern appearance. He was a well-spoken man, though, self-educated but highly intelligent and quiet for the most part.

The bartender said, "You two fellas, uh, had a grudge against each other?"

"Not personally, no. But I've been chasing him all the way from up near the Oregon border down here to Bakersfield, and he knew it. We've traded a few shots before, at long distances. When he saw me this close, he knew it would be a fight to the finish."

"You're a lawman?"

"Of sorts," Luke said with a faint smile.

"Oh. Bounty hunter."

One of Luke's shoulders rose and fell in a semblance of a shrug. No point in putting face paint on a pig. He was what he was.

"Good Lord in Heaven, what happened here, Clanton?" a voice asked from the saloon's entrance.

With the Remington still in his hand, Luke looked around to see a man in a brown suit and tall white hat coming in with a rifle in his hands. A star was pinned to his vest under the suit coat. He swung the rifle so it pointed in Luke's general direction.

"I'm going to holster this gun, Sheriff," Luke said. "I'm telling you so your trigger finger doesn't get itchy when you see me move my hand."

"All right, but do it slow and easylike," the lawman warned.

Luke pouched the iron in the cross-draw rig where it usually rode. He didn't like leaving it with empty chambers. He was in the habit of reloading a gun as soon as he was done using it . . . but it was probably more important to settle things down. "My name is Luke Jensen."

"He's a bounty hunter," the bartender added helpfully.

"The dead man lying behind the bar is Quint Barclay. He's wanted on multiple counts of murder, robbery, and assault. I suspect you have posters on him in your files, Sheriff."

The lawman used the rifle to motion Luke back, then came over and peered behind the bar. "Good Lord," he muttered again. "Did you have to set him on fire before you shot him?"

"It just sort of worked out that way," Luke said.

"Well, he's dead, all right. No doubt about that. You say there's a bounty on him?"

"Eight hundred dollars, at least. The reward may have gone up while I've been chasing him the past couple weeks. He killed a woman and a child during a bank robbery."

The sheriff grunted. "That so? Reckon he had some burning coming to him, then."

"The same thought crossed my mind."

The sheriff finally lowered the rifle. "All right. I'll have the undertaker deal with this, and I'll check on your story. You can be sure of that, Jensen."

"Of course," Luke said.

"I reckon there's no chance of you leaving town before you collect that bounty, so I don't have to worry about that. If you're telling the truth about all of this, though, I'll expect you to be on your way as soon as you've got that blood money in your hand."

"That was my plan. Since I'm this close, I thought I might ride on down to Los Angeles. It's been a while since I've been to the city of angels."

"They can have you." The lawman added grudgingly, "No offense."

"None taken," Luke said. After all the years of killing, what would be the point?

CHAPTER 3

Matt Jensen had to hang on to the wagon seat with one hand and shoot with the other. It wasn't easy to start with, and the way the wagon jolted and swayed as it careened down the steep mountainside trail made accuracy even more difficult.

Even so, he was pretty sure he had winged at least one of the bastards shooting at them from the rocks on the slope above the trail. "Can't you get that team going any faster?" he yelled to the driver, Buckshot Taylor.

The old-timer didn't take his eyes off the trail as he shouted, "We start goin' any faster and them mules'll sprout wings and fly right offen this mountain!" He knew what he was talking about. He'd been driving ore wagons up and down those Nevada mountains for a long time. He was a short, squat, mostly bald man with two tufts of white hair sticking out from under his pounded-down slouch hat. Thickly muscled forearms pistoned back and forth as he worked the reins attached to the mule team.

The hammer of Matt's Colt fell on an empty chamber with a resounding, frustrating *click*. With no time to reload, he bit back a curse, jammed the gun back in its holster, and grabbed the shotgun from the floorboard at his feet. Since he couldn't fire the shotgun one-handed, he had to let go of the seat and hope he wouldn't go flying off the next time the wagon hit a big bump in the trail.

A man with a bandanna tied over the lower half of his face stood up from behind a slab of rock, leaped on top of it, and fired several rounds toward the wagon as it careened closer. Matt lifted the Greener and touched off one barrel.

The load smashed into the robber's chest, shredded clothes and flesh, and flung him backwards off the rock. That was one of the sons of bitches Matt wouldn't have to worry about anymore. He swung the shotgun toward another outlaw.

The hombre wasn't foolish enough to stand out in the open, but he had raised up too much from his cover. The charge from Matt's second barrel shattered his jaw and tore off his right ear. He fell back, howling and spraying blood.

Matt broke open the Greener, dumped out the empty shells, and thumbed in fresh ones from a pocket in the long duster he wore. He snapped the shotgun closed just as the wagon bounced so hard he flew up off the seat.

He let out a startled yell. A second later he came down on the back of the seat and rolled over it to land on the ore shipment, latching on to the tied-down sheet of canvas that covered the ore. He still had hold of the shotgun with his right hand.

A bullet tore the canvas near his head and whined off the ore. Matt rolled onto his belly and splayed out his legs to steady himself and keep from falling off. He propped himself up on his elbows so he could use both hands on the Greener.

A bullet thudded into the wagon's sideboards. Matt raised the shotgun's twin barrels and fired one of them toward another masked man crouched beside a boulder.

Between the booming of the shotgun and the rattle of the wagon's wheels, Matt couldn't hear much, but he heard Buckshot Taylor's startled oath. Luke turned his head to look toward the seat.

Up ahead on the slope to the left, dust rose. Buckshot whipped up the team and shouted, "The low-down sons o' polecats started a rockslide!"

Matt understood the strategy. The bandits had set up the ambush along the mountain trail hoping to kill him and Buckshot and grab the silver ore. But if the wagon successfully ran the gauntlet of bushwhacker lead, the outlaws were ready to cause an avalanche that would block the trail.

Since the falling rocks might bury the wagon, too, making it more difficult for the thieves to dig out the loot they were after, that method was used only as a last resort.

The time for last resorts had arrived, Matt supposed. "Can you beat it?" he shouted to Buckshot.

The old-timer threw a startled, wide-eyed glance over his shoulder. "Beat it? We gotta stop!"

"We do that and they'll be swarming all over us! They'll kill us, anyway! Make those mules run, Buckshot!"

Buckshot muttered something but started using the whip with more enthusiasm. The mule team leaped ahead.

More bullets zinged around the wagon, but the real threat came from the tons of rock tumbling down the slope. Some of the smaller stones, bounding out ahead, flew through the air and smacked against the wagon. Matt ducked his head and put his arms over it . . . although what good that would do if the avalanche caught them, he didn't know.

The rumble grew into an overpowering roar that slammed painfully into Matt's ears. He couldn't withstand the impulse to raise his head and look up. The leading edge of the slide was practically on top of them, pushing out a cloud of dust that rolled around the racing vehicle. The stuff was choking and blinding.

At least if he was about to be crushed, he wouldn't be able to see that grisly fate coming. That was mighty cold comfort.

They broke out of the swirling dust as the rocks swept down behind them. A boulder that must have weighed several tons missed the back of the wagon by scant inches. More of the smaller stones pounded down around them, but Buckshot kept the team moving and suddenly they were in the clear.

Matt pushed himself up on the ore shipment and let out an excited whoop. "You did it, Buckshot! You beat that damn avalanche!"

Buckshot glanced back over his shoulder again.

Blood seeped from a cut on his cheek where a flying rock had nicked him. "I sure as blazes don't see how we did it! It's the most flabbergastin' thing—" He let out a sudden grunt, rocked back, and twisted on the seat in obvious pain.

Matt spotted a crimson flower of blood blooming on the front of the old-timer's shirt. "Buckshot!"

Matt clambered forward and threw himself over the back of the seat as Buckshot sagged toward the edge. Matt grabbed him to keep him from falling off and pulled him more upright. The bloodstain was still spreading. No rock had done that.

Buckshot had been hit by a bullet, and it had come from somewhere ahead of the wagon.

Matt looked down the trail and saw three riders spurring up toward them. Powder smoke and flames jetted from their guns as they fired.

The back of a running horse was no place for accuracy, and the way the wagon was swaying back and forth made it an even more difficult target. The gap between the wagon and the would-be killers was closing by the second, but that wasn't the only danger.

The wagon kept veering perilously close to the edge of the trail. If the wheels on the right side slipped off, the vehicle would tip and roll toward the valley a couple hundred feet below, pulling the mules down with it. Matt and Buckshot would be smashed to pieces and likely crushed as well.

Matt looked around for the reins Buckshot had dropped when he was hit. Grimacing, he saw that the reins had trickled off the floorboard and fallen down alongside the wagon tongue.

Rolling along on flat, level ground, Matt might

have slid down to the wagon tongue and retrieved
the reins or even jumped on the back of one of the
mules and taken control of the team that way. Up on
the rough mountain trail, either of those things
would just get him killed.

Of course, once those three bandits closed in, they'd
probably shoot him to doll rags. So what would he be
risking, really?

Before he could attempt anything, the wagon's
rear end came around some and the vehicle began
to slew sideways. They were going over.

"Son of a—" Matt grabbed Buckshot again.

The wagon's right rear wheel broke apart under
the pressure and dropped the heavy bed on the edge
of the trail, snapping the rear axle. With a grinding
sound, the wagon tilted and slid along the trail, its
back end sticking out over empty air. That caused the
harness to jerk back heavily against the mules and
they came to a staggering halt.

The wagon stopped, too, half on and half off the
trail.

Matt and Buckshot were still on the seat. Somehow, they hadn't been thrown off by the violent
crash. More dust coiled around them, making Matt
cough.

A bullet whined past his ear.

The three outlaws were still coming, their guns
blasting as they closed in. Matt had the shotgun in
his left hand. He swung it up to his shoulder and
fired the remaining barrel. The charge swept down
the trail and struck the two outlaws in the lead, as
well as their horses. Men and animals went down in a
bloody welter of flailing limbs.

"Here," Buckshot gasped out. "Take . . . this!" He pressed into Matt's hand the butt of the old cap-and-ball pistol he carried.

Matt dropped the empty shotgun and raised the percussion revolver with its long, octagonal barrel. His thumb looped over the hammer and drew it back, and as soon as the sights settled on the chest of the third bandit, he squeezed the trigger.

The gun went off with a dull boom, almost like a cannon, and recoiled heavily against Matt's hand. Smoke from the black powder coiled from the muzzle. The heavy ball smashed into the chest of the outlaw and drove him back out of the saddle. He flew through the air, arms and legs flinging out in four directions.

One of the men who'd been downed by the shotgun blast made it back to his feet and triggered a couple shots at the men on the wagon seat. Matt returned the fire with Buckshot's old hogleg, hitting the man in the shoulder. It packed so much punch, the ball almost blew the man's arm off his body. It wound up hanging by a few strands of muscle as blood fountained from the wound. The outlaw crumpled, screaming as his life pumped out.

The other man was still down, so Matt hoped he was out of the fight.

A couple slugs thudded into the sideboards to Matt's left. He jerked his head around and saw a couple men climbing over the rocks heaped on the trail. They carried Winchesters and paused to throw more lead at Matt and Buckshot.

"We gotta get . . . off this wagon!" Buckshot grated.

"If we do, it's liable to slide the rest of the way off the trail."

"Don't matter . . . We're sittin' ducks here!" The old-timer was right about that.

"You jump one way. I'll jump the other."

"Better . . . make it quick!"

"Go!" Matt leaped to the left while Buckshot quit the wagon seat to the right. The wagon slid another foot or so and Matt thought it was going over, but it ground to a halt again.

Matt wound up on his knees with bullets kicking up dust around him. He lifted the old pistol and thumbed off a couple rounds. Neither found their target, but they came close enough to make the two outlaws dive for cover among the rocks left by the avalanche.

Matt surged up and ran around the mules to put them and the wagon between him and the bandits. Buckshot sat on the ground, bloody but still conscious.

Matt dropped to a knee beside the wounded man. "How bad is it?"

"Don't rightly know, but I reckon I'll live a while longer, anyway."

Matt handed the revolver back to him. "Here, you may need this."

"What about you?"

Matt glanced down the trail. The horses he had wounded had managed to get up despite their injuries. The third man's mount hadn't fallen in the ruckus. Rifle butts stuck up from saddle scabbards on all three horses. "I'll be back. Hold those varmints off!"

"Damn right I will." Buckshot grabbed hold of the front wheel and started pulling himself upright.

Matt dashed down the trail toward the outlaws' horses.

The animals were spooked and skittish, but as they danced around he was able to leap and snag one of the rifles. As he dragged it out of the saddle boot, he hoped it was loaded.

Buckshot's old iron boomed a couple times as Matt turned back toward the ore wagon. As he lifted the Winchester to his shoulder, he yelled, "Keep your head down, Buckshot!" then cranked off several rounds as fast as he could work the lever.

One of the bandits trying to climb over the rock-slide reared up and dropped his gun to paw at his bloody throat where a .44 slug had ripped through it. He collapsed, twitching.

The other outlaw whirled around and tried to scramble for cover as the bullets flew around him. Matt hesitated only long enough to make sure of his aim, then he drilled a slug into the bandit's back. The man threw out his arms and flopped forward on his face.

Matt lowered the rifle slightly and waited as the echoes of the shots bounced back and forth from the slopes of the surrounding peaks. No more shots sounded. He didn't know how many of the gang were left alive, but evidently they had decided to cut their losses and had given up on the ore shipment.

Either that or they were working their way around for another try from a different direction now that the wagon was crippled and stranded.

CHAPTER 4

Matt hurried over to Buckshot, who was leaning against the wagon and fumbling with the revolver as he tried to reload it—not as easy with a cap-and-ball weapon as it was with a more modern revolver.

"Let me do that for you," Matt offered.

"I can reload my own damn smoke pole," Buckshot said.

"Yeah, but you're hurt."

"This?" Buckshot looked down at the bloody front of his flannel shirt. "Ain't nothin' to worry about. I reckon what hit me was a ricochet, 'cause I could tell it didn't have as much punch as a reg'lar round. Chewed up some meat and spilled some blood, but it didn't go far enough in to do any real damage." A wry grin stretched across the old-timer's face. "Reckon havin' a nice thick layer o' fat comes in handy sometimes."

"Yeah, you can hibernate in the winter like a bear."

Matt turned his head to search the slopes around them. "I don't see anybody moving."

"The rest o' those ol' boys lit a shuck, I'll betcha. They just didn't know what a pair o' ring-tailed terrors they'd be takin' on when they decided to jump this wagon."

"You might be right about that. But even if they're gone . . . how in blazes are we going to get this ore to Virginia City? We can't repair this wagon by ourselves, especially with you hurt."

"I told you, I ain't hurt all that—" Buckshot stopped short, swayed, and had to grab the wagon seat to hold himself up. "Well, maybe I lost a little bit too much blood. I'm feelin' a mite lightheaded."

"Sit down," Matt told him. "But don't lean against the wagon. It could still slide over. I'm going to unhitch the mules just in case it does. No point in letting them get killed for no good reason."

"Durn right. They're stubborn ol' jugheads, but they done a good job of pullin' this wagon for a long time."

Matt had a hunch that he and Buckshot might have to abandon the wagon and its cargo and ride a couple mules on into Virginia City, which had been their destination when they'd started out from the Double Slash Mine early that morning. Buckshot would argue about that, claiming he had a responsibility to see the load through, and even though he'd be right, Matt still wasn't going to let the old-timer bleed to death. He would tie Buckshot onto the back of a mule if he had to.

As it turned out, by the time Matt finished unhitching the team, he heard the sound of hoofbeats floating up from somewhere lower on the mountain. The way the trail twisted around, he could see bits and pieces of it a few hundred feet below, and as he watched he spotted a group of half a dozen riders coming in his direction.

He thought one of the men was Ambrose Macauley, the owner of the Double Slash. No surprise, since Macauley wasn't just a rich man who owned a mine. He was also an engineer and supervised a lot of the operation himself. It wasn't unusual for him to ride up to the mine with some of his assistants and a handful of guards.

"I think maybe help's on the way," Matt told Buckshot, who was sitting cross-legged on the trail.

"Good to hear. I'm feelin' a mite puny." The old-timer spat. "How many o' them thievin' scoundrels did you kill, anyway?"

Matt thought about it. "Six or seven, I calculate. Wasn't time to keep count while the ruckus was going on."

"And there wasn't a one of 'em but what had it comin'."

A half hour later, the group of riders from Virginia City reached the stranded wagon. By then, Matt had rounded up the three horses that had belonged to the dead outlaws, reloaded the Winchester, and filled his pockets with .44-40 cartridges from the thieves' supplies. He had refilled the cylinder on his Colt and had slid fresh shells into the Greener.

If the newcomers *weren't* friendly, they would find a mighty warm reception waiting for them.

The rider in the lead was unmistakably Ambrose Macauley. Matt would have recognized the mine owner's broad, florid face and thick black mustache anywhere. Macauley cut a fancy figure at the balls he threw in his Virginia City mansion, but up in the mountains on the way to the Double Slash, he wore a brown corduroy jacket and trousers and a round-crowned brown hat. He reined in at the sight of the dead outlaws, the crippled wagon, and the rock-covered trail. "Was there a war?"

"Close to it," Matt said with a weary grin. "Buckshot's hurt."

Macauley motioned curtly to a couple of his men. "See to him," he ordered, pointing to Buckshot. "Patch up that wound as best you can and then get him to the doctor in town."

"Sure thing, boss," one of the men said.

"It ain't as bad as it looks, Mr. Macauley," Buckshot said.

"We'll let the doctor make that decision." Macauley told the other men to see if the wagon could be repaired, then to Matt, he went on. "Obviously, someone tried to hold you up."

"Eight or nine somebodies," Matt said.

"How many of them got away?"

Matt shrugged. "A couple, I'd say."

Despite the grim subject they were discussing, Macauley threw back his head and guffawed. "I knew I was doing the right thing by hiring a Jensen to ride herd on my ore shipments. I'm going to hate to lose your services."

"Lose my services?" Matt repeated with a frown.

"You're not firing me because the wagon got wrecked, are you?"

"Not hardly." Macauley reached inside his jacket, felt around in the pocket, and brought out a folded envelope. He leaned down slightly from the saddle to hand it to Matt. "This letter came for you. It was sent from Big Rock, Colorado, and that's where your famous brother lives, isn't it?"

"Yeah, Smoke's ranch, the Sugarloaf, is near there," Matt replied as he took the envelope from his employer. "But just because he sent me a letter doesn't mean I'll be leaving these parts."

"Unless he needs something. In which case, I know you'll waste no time rattling your hocks out of here."

"That's true, I reckon." When one member of the Jensen family sent out the call for help, all the others answered. And all the Jensens gathered together were a pretty formidable bunch.

As Matt opened the envelope, took out the letter, and began to read, a grin slowly appeared on his face.

"So it's not trouble after all?" Macauley asked.

"Nope, not exactly. Smoke wants me to meet him down in Tucson for Christmas. He says he's trying to get in touch with our other brother, too, and this old mountain man who's sort of our adopted uncle."

"I suppose you're going?"

"It won't be too much longer before the snows set in and you won't be shipping any ore until spring. You won't really need me. Anyway, maybe I'll drift back in this direction in a few months."

"You know you're always welcome, and you'll always have a job with the Double Slash Mining Company." Macauley smiled. "I don't blame you for not wanting to miss a chance to visit with your family."

"Yeah. Somehow those holidays usually wind up being sort of special."

Los Angeles had been little more than a village surrounded by farms and ranches the first time Luke had been there, a few years after the war. It had grown slowly, so that on his subsequent visits the place really hadn't changed that much.

With the arrival of the railroads and all the immigration they brought, the sleepy little country town had become a city. Luke wasn't sure he liked that. He had never cared much for crowds.

He brought his horse to a stop in front of a four-story brick building with the word HOTEL painted in big letters at the top of the side wall. He wouldn't have wanted the job of climbing up there to paint that sign.

He went inside, rented a room from a clerk who didn't seem to care for the layer of trail dust on his clothes, then took his horse to a nearby livery stable. The hostler there scratched his head and frowned when Luke asked him about Diego's.

"A restaurant, is it? There's some of them Mexican places a few blocks from here."

"It's a cantina," Luke explained. It suddenly occurred to him old Diego could be dead. He'd been getting well up in years the last time Luke was there, and that was a long time ago.

"Lemme ask one of the other fellas. There's one of 'em who's been around these parts for a long time. He'd know if anybody would." The hostler went out to the corrals behind the stable and came back with a wizened old-timer in a straw sombrero.

The old man's face lit up in a toothless grin at the sight of Luke. "Señor Smith!" he exclaimed.

The last time Luke was in Los Angeles, he had been calling himself Luke Smith for reasons he'd considered good at the time.

"Is it really you?"

"It's me," Luke said as he searched his memory for the old-timer's name and came up empty. "But it's Jensen now."

"*Que?*" The old man waved the question off, even as he asked it. "It is of no importance. You are still Señor Luke. You remember old Pedro?"

"Of course I do." Luke clapped a hand on the man's bony shoulder. "I was asking about your cousin's place. The city has changed so much I'm not sure where it is anymore."

"The same place as always, by the river, but there are buildings all around now. The cantina no longer sits by itself next to the grove of trees. Go two blocks west, follow the river toward the sea, and you will find it."

"Thank you, Pedro."

A mournful expression appeared on the wrinkled old face. "You will not find Diego there. My cousin passed on several years ago. His granddaughter runs the cantina now. You remember her?"

"Not really, but I'll stop by and pay my respects. The beer is still good?"

Pedro licked his lips. "Of a certainty, *mi amigo.*"

It was a beautiful day with white clouds floating in the deep blue sky over the mountains to the north. In most of the rest of the country, people were waiting for winter to arrive and wondering when the first snows would fall. In southern California, the likelihood of that happening was so small, most folks never even considered it.

Luke enjoyed the walk along the Los Angeles River. As Pedro had said, things had changed. Businesses and houses lined the banks of the stream, but a few of the trees from the grove were left, and next to them was the familiar adobe building. Luke smiled when he saw it.

The inside of the cantina was dim and cool, a welcome break from the sun after a walk of several blocks. In the middle of the afternoon, the place wasn't very busy. Only a few men stood at the bar, and a single table was occupied. The customers were split evenly between Mexicans and gringos.

Behind the bar stood a women with flawless olive skin and a mass of thick, midnight black hair. She wore a low-necked blouse that displayed the lush curves of her body. She looked at Luke, her dark eyes widening with what seemed like recognition. "Señor Luke?"

"That's right," he said in Spanish. "I'm surprised you know me. The years have been long ones, with many lonely miles."

"You are older, but there is still no doubt you are Señor Luke." Mischief twinkled in her eyes. "The ugly ones, they do not age so quickly."

He laughed, recalling her name. "Bonita, you always had some sharp-tongued comment for me when

I came here. Your grandfather scolded you, but I told him I enjoyed it. In those days, though, you were like this." He held out his hand about four feet off the floor.

"I have grown since then," Bonita said.

"Indeed you have." Under different circumstances, he might have been tempted to see just how much she had grown, but he had known her since she was a little girl and knew nothing like that was going to happen during this visit. However, he could still compliment her. "You have grown very beautiful."

"My thanks," she said, looking down at the bar. "You would like a drink?"

"Very much so."

She drew a beer and set it in front of him. "When you were last here, you were a manhunter. You still follow this line of work?"

"I do." Luke took a swallow of the beer and found that Pedro had been right. It was still very good and went down cool and smooth. "I'm a little surprised I've survived at it this long, to be honest."

"I am not surprised at all. You were always a brave, tough hombre. That is one reason I am very glad to see you, Señor Luke."

He frowned a little. "I'm not sure I understand."

"I am glad to see you because you were always my grandfather's good friend . . . but also because there is a man here I think you will want to kill."

CHAPTER 5

"He fancies himself a legendary bandit, like Joaquin Murrieta was supposed to be," Bonita said a short time later as she and Luke sat at one of the tables in the rear of the cantina, well away from the other customers. "His name is Alejandro Ruiz. He has held up trains and stagecoaches, but mostly he robs stores and lone travelers. He claims to have killed eleven men, but I do not know if that is true." Her voice hardened as she went on. "What I *do know* is that he has set his sights on me and is determined to marry me. If I will not comply . . . he says that he will take me, anyway."

Luke nodded slowly. "He does sound like he needs a stern talking-to."

"No. He needs killing."

Luke wasn't so sure about that. This Alejandro Ruiz might well be a thief, but hombres who boasted of how many men they had killed often lied about that. It was possible Ruiz hadn't been responsible for anyone's death.

On the other hand, he might be every bit as bad as Bonita painted him.

There was only one way to find out, Luke supposed. "Where will I find him?"

"Here. He will be in tonight. He promised—or rather, *threatened*, as far as I am concerned—that he would be here to see me."

Spending more time at the cantina in the company of the beautiful young Bonita appealed to Luke. Having collected that $800 bounty in Bakersfield, his finances were in good shape for the time being. Even if Ruiz didn't show up that night, Luke could afford to linger in Los Angeles for a while and take care of the problem for the granddaughter of his old friend . . . whatever that solution turned out to be.

The afternoon passed pleasantly, with Luke and Bonita sharing memories of old Diego and earlier times when Los Angeles had been a sleepy little village instead of a bustling town. Bonita remembered those days, although she had been very young at the time.

She also kept Luke's mug full of excellent beer, and after a while she retreated to her living quarters in the rear of the cantina and prepared a plate of tortillas, frijoles, and highly spiced beef for him.

"Keep feeding me like this and your other customers will get jealous," he warned her. "Also, I may never want to leave."

She grinned. "That might not be a bad thing."

He thought there was a faintly seductive note in her voice and reminded himself again that he had no intention of getting romantically involved with her. He wasn't old enough to be her grandfather, but he was certainly old enough to be her father!

He paced himself so the beer didn't get him drunk. The food helped with that, too, keeping him clear-headed as evening fell softly over southern California. The cantina had gotten busy enough that Bonita had to work at the bar serving drinks, along with her bartender, a stocky, middle-aged man who worked efficiently despite seeming to be half-asleep part of the time.

Luke stayed where he was at the rear table, turned in his chair so he could stretch his legs out and cross them at the ankles. He leaned back and tipped his hat down a little over his eyes, but not so much that he couldn't see everyone who came in. His eyes partially closed, he remained watchful.

After an hour or so, Alejandro Ruiz came in. Bonita had described him, but Luke didn't really need that to recognize him. The young man's air of casual cruelty and arrogance was enough.

Ruiz was lithe and lean, dressed like a vaquero in tight trousers that flared at the bottom, a loose, colorful silk shirt, and a flat-crowned hat. He carried a pearl-handled revolver in a low-slung holster on his right hip. He was a bit of a dandy, and often men like that weren't really the dangerous hombres they made themselves out to be.

Luke had a hunch that wasn't the case with Ruiz. His cold-eyed gaze that swept around the cantina was as flat and deadly as that of a snake. His eyes didn't linger on Luke. The dark, well-worn trail clothes, the old hat, and the casual attitude marked the gringo sitting in the rear corner as nothing more than a saddle tramp. From where Ruiz had paused just inside the entrance, he couldn't see the pair of Remingtons Luke wore.

Luke glanced at the bar. Bonita stood behind it, her expression a blend of anger and fear as she watched Ruiz swaggering toward her. Her eyes flicked toward Luke as if to let him know this was the man she had told him about. He nodded his head just enough to tell her he understood.

The men sitting at the tables watched Ruiz nervously as he crossed the room. Those at the bar moved aside to give him plenty of room, but Luke noticed they tried to be unobtrusive about it . . . as if they didn't want him to notice and get angry.

Ruiz had thrown a scare into those folks, all right.

"Bonita, *muy bonita*," the self-styled bandit greeted her with a cocky grin. "Have you thought about my proposal? I told you I would come tonight for your answer."

She hadn't mentioned that part to him, Luke thought, but he supposed it didn't matter.

"I've already given you your answer, Señor Ruiz," she said stiffly. "I have no interest in being your wife . . . or anything else to you."

"But I can take you away from this squalid little cantina and give you a rich life!" He waved his hands at their surroundings.

"I grew up in this squalid little cantina, as you call

it," she snapped. "This is my home. I have no wish to leave it . . . especially to live with a man as cruel as you."

"Cruel?" Ruiz's mouth tightened. "I do not believe you know anything of true cruelty, little one. But I can teach you if you wish."

Luke stood up without moving the chair back and causing its legs to scrape on the floor, uncoiling smoothly and silently. Ruiz, thinking no one in the cantina would dare to defy him, was ignoring everyone except Bonita. He didn't know anyone had moved up behind him until he heard a soft footstep.

That footstep was quickly followed by Luke saying, "The señorita told you she's not interested, fella. Maybe you should listen to her and get out of here."

Ruiz stiffened but didn't turn around. After a couple heartbeats, he said, "I think I hear a little Chihuahua dog yapping. That little dog should run away while it still can."

"There's only one dog here," Luke said, "and it's a dirty yellow mutt."

Ruiz's pride couldn't stand that. He whirled around, hand stabbing toward his gun. For all he knew, the man behind him already had a gun drawn, but Ruiz's confidence was such he believed he could turn, draw, and fire before his enemy could get a shot off. He was fast—fast enough to clear leather with that pearl-handled gun before both of Luke's Remingtons centered on his chest and belched flame.

At that relatively short range, the .44 slugs that slammed into Ruiz's body drove him against the bar with such force that he almost bent double backwards over the hardwood. As he tried to straighten, the gun in his hand went off and smashed a bullet into the floor at his feet. He turned, caught at the bar with his free hand in an attempt to hold himself up and failed, sliding down to lie in a crumpled heap at the brass rail along the bottom.

Luke kept his thumbs on the Remingtons' hammers, ready to cock and fire again. He stepped closer and kicked the pearl-handled gun out of Ruiz's limp fingers. It slid away. Ruiz gasped and coughed and looked up at Luke with blood trickling from the corners of his mouth.

"I hope there really is a bounty on you, amigo," Luke said. "I just spent two whole bullets on you. But even if there's not . . . like a friend of mine told me, you needed killing."

Ruiz's eyes started to turn glassy. His head slumped to the floor.

Everyone in the cantina stared in awed silence at Luke and the man he had just shot. Even the sleepy bartender seemed wide awake. Excited murmurs began to rise.

Bonita found her voice. "Everyone saw him draw first, Luke. There will be no trouble with the law. And although I do not know for sure, I believe there are several rewards for Ruiz. As I told you, he has robbed trains and stagecoaches. The men who own such things do not take robbery lightly."

"No, they don't," Luke agreed. He holstered one of the Remingtons and began replacing the expended round in the other.

Bonita reached under the bar, brought out an envelope, and placed it on top. "I have this for you, as well."

Luke frowned. "What's that?"

"It looks like a letter that came for you, addressed to you in care of my grandfather."

"How long has it been here?"

"It arrived only last week, from a place in Colorado called Big Rock."

Big Rock! That meant Smoke. But why had his brother sent a letter to him here?

The answer came to Luke as he reloaded the other gun. The last time he'd written to Smoke, he'd been up in northern California. Smoke would know that Luke seldom stayed in one place for very long, so if he wanted to get in touch he might have sent notes to several places Luke had mentioned in the past, thinking that he would stop at one of them sooner or later.

It was a pretty haphazard way of getting in touch, but when somebody was on the move as much as he was, it was just about the only way.

He picked up the envelope and tore it open. What he read confirmed his hunch. Smoke explained that he was sending several letters in the hope of one of them finding Luke. The purpose of the message was to extend an invitation. It seemed that Smoke and Sally were taking a trip to Tucson for Christmas, and they wanted Luke to join them there if he could, and if the letter reached him in time.

"What is it?" Bonita asked. "Trouble?"

"No. At least I hope not." He thought about the times he and Smoke had gotten together over the past few years. A couple visits had involved holidays, and some had come at other times of the year, but the one thing they all seemed to have in common was that hell had a tendency of busting loose whenever two or more Jensens found themselves in the same vicinity.

Despite that, after having been estranged from his family for so long and finally realizing how much he had missed, Luke was no longer avoiding Smoke and Matt, their adopted brother. Smoke's letter had also mentioned old Preacher.

It would be good to see all of them, Luke decided, and there was no reason in the world for him *not* to take a ride over to Tucson.

And maybe there *was* a good reason for him to get out of Los Angeles as soon as he settled things with the law regarding the dead bandit lying a few feet away. Luke saw the way Bonita was looking at him with a mixture of hero worship and something else in her eyes, and he figured the sooner he got out of there, the better.

He was only human, after all, and there was only so much temptation he could withstand . . . especially when it came in such a beautiful package!

Bonita looked at him and sighed sadly. "You are leaving, are you not?"

"I reckon I am."

CHAPTER 6

Preacher hadn't been in San Antonio for a good number of years. The first time he'd visited the city, Texas had still been part of Mexico. Not long after that, however, those contrary Texicans had gotten tired of putting up with the Mexican dictator Santa Anna and decided to hell with that. A lot of dead folks later, it was the Republic of Texas.

Of course, there were some who said that Sam Houston and the other leaders of the revolution had been angling to become a part of the United States all along, and a few years later, that was what happened. Texas was the Lone Star State and had been ever since.

Preacher ambled along past the chapel of the old mission where a relative handful of Texans had stood off Santa Anna's whole army for almost two weeks, back in '36, before falling to those overwhelming odds. A part of Preacher would have liked to have been there, fighting alongside those doomed devils, but then he never would have had all the adventures that had come his way since then.

He never would have met Emmitt and Kirby Jensen, either, or dubbed the boy Smoke. Yeah, his life would have been a hell of a lot different.

He was thinking about Smoke because he had a letter from the youngster in the pocket of his denim trousers. It had caught up to him where he was staying at the Crockett Hotel, having been forwarded from Fort Worth, where Preacher had been previously.

The letter explained that Smoke and his wife Sally were going to be making a trip to Arizona for Christmas and were planning to get together with Matt and Luke in Tucson, if word reached them in time and there was no other reason they couldn't make it. Smoke wanted Preacher to come, too, if he could.

Preacher didn't see why he couldn't. Yeah, he was getting on up in age, but he was still spry enough and could take care of himself. He'd been drifting for most of seven decades and didn't plan to stop any time soon.

True, he couldn't fork a horse and stay in the saddle for days on end like he once could, but trains and stagecoaches would take a fellow almost anywhere he wanted to go.

At the moment, Preacher wanted to go to the Buckhorn Saloon . . . so that was where he was headed.

"Hey, old-timer." The soft-voiced call came from the mouth of an alley about halfway between the Menger Hotel and the Buckhorn. Preacher paused and looked in that direction. He couldn't spot whoever had called to him.

"I need some help," the unseen man continued. "Some sons o' bitches jumped me . . . beat me up . . . I'm in bad shape here."

"I'll go find one o' them new-fangled policemen they got here now," Preacher said.

"No time . . . for that . . . You gotta . . . help me . . ."

Preacher—a tall, lean man in boots, denim trousers, buckskin shirt, and a battered old brown hat—walked toward the alley. He looked scrawny at first glance, but that was because the whipcord strength in his body wasn't apparent. His face had a permanent dark tan and a weathered, slightly squinty look. He was clean-shaven, but silvery stubble dotted his angular jaw.

"What is it you want from me?" he asked as he entered the alley. His steps echoed from the building walls looming on both sides. "I ain't no damn saw-bones. If you're hurt, you need to see a doctor to patch you up."

"You can help me," the man said, closer now. "I reckon all the money you've got on you would fix me right up."

Two burly shapes appeared out of the shadows in front of Preacher. He heard the soft scrape of boot leather on paving stones behind him and glanced over his shoulder to see that two more men had closed in from that direction. The four men had Preacher pinned between them.

"Let me get this straight," he said. "You fellas are fixin' to rob me?"

"That's right, you old fool," said the man who had lured him into the alley. "Are you soft in the head or something?"

"Are you gonna hurt me?"

"Afraid, are you, Gramps?"

Ugly laughter came from a couple of the men.

"Maybe you should be. We're gonna give you a good beatin' so you can't get up and start hollerin' for help any time soon. At your age, you decrepit old bastard, it might just be too much for you. You might not ever wake up."

"I figured that might be what you had in mind," Preacher said. "Gives me a good reason for what I'm about to do, so I can tell the law later."

"Wait a minute," said the second man in front of him. "What the hell's he—"

Preacher reached behind him and pulled out the .38 caliber Colt Double Action Lightning revolver he had tucked behind his belt at the small of his back and concealed by the buckskin shirt hanging over it. Small enough, the Lightning was easy to carry that way, and while Preacher preferred a .44 or .45, the .38 was potent enough for close-range work.

"Look out!" one of the men behind him cried. "He's got a—"

The gun's roar drowned out anything else he might have been saying. Flame spurted from the revolver's muzzle as Preacher squeezed the trigger again. The two shots were so close together they almost sounded like one, but there was just enough of a gap between them that Preacher had been able to shift his aim and put one slug apiece in the two men in front of him.

Boot soles slapped the pavement behind him as the other two men tried to rush him. Preacher whirled and darted to one side of the alley. Muzzle flame licked from the Lightning a third time. One of the men cried out, stumbled, and fell to his knees.

"You old bastard!" the fourth would-be robber yelled. He had a club of some sort in his hand and swung it at Preacher's head.

Preacher ducked to let the bludgeon sweep over him with a faint *whoosh*. He thrust his arm out, jabbed the Lightning's barrel against the man's belly, and pulled the trigger twice more. Flesh muffled the booming sound of the shots.

The man screamed, reeled back, doubled over, and collapsed. "You . . . you shot me!" he cried.

"And I'll sure as hell do it again, too, if you don't get down on your belly and stay there without movin' until the law gets here." Preacher pulled back the Lightning's hammer so it made a grim, metallic cocking sound.

The thief yelled, "Don't shoot, don't shoot!" and sprawled facedown in the muck of the alley.

No point in explaining to the fella that he *couldn't* shoot, Preacher thought. Not without reloading.

The Lightning was empty.

But the no-good skunk who'd been bent on robbing and probably beating to death an old man didn't know that.

He hadn't known that some old-timers still had all their teeth . . . and knew how to use them, too.

San Antonio de Bexar had always been a mite on the wild and woolly side, but even so, five gunshots and a bunch of screaming and yelling right downtown, just a few yards from the fancy Menger Hotel, was plenty to bring the law running. They showed up just a few minutes later, four uniformed policemen toting riot guns.

One of them had a bull's-eye lantern, too. He shone its light down the alley, revealing some scrawny old geezer pointing a gun at another man lying on the filthy pavement while three other gents sprawled around in various stages of bloody distress.

"Drop that gun, Grandpa!" one of the officers shouted.

"No, sir," Preacher said. "This here's a fine pistol, and I ain't gonna throw it down and maybe damage it. Howsomever, I *will* set it on the ground and back off so one of you fellas can come get it. It's empty, anyway."

"Empty?" the man on the ground gasped.

"Hell, yes. No man with any sense 'd tote an iron with the hammer restin' on a live round. Didn't your mama ever teach you that?" Preacher bent over, placed the revolver on the ground out of the robber's reach, then backed off a couple steps, holding his hands out in plain sight. He didn't know how cool-nerved those officers were, and since they all had shotguns, he didn't want them getting antsy. Too easy to tickle a trigger a little too much and touch off one of those loads of buckshot.

"You there," an officer said to the thief as he advanced along the alley, "stand up."

"I . . . I dunno if I can. I'm shot!"

"Well, you'd better be able to. I want you against

the wall over there while we're sorting this out." The man snorted. "Sounded like Santa Anna had come back to town and started the war all over again!"

"You must not be from around here," Preacher said, "or you wouldn't joke about it."

Groaning, the wounded man struggled to his feet, then lurched over against the closest wall and leaned against it with his face toward the bricks and his hands resting on them to hold him up. One of the policemen covered him while the others used the lantern light to check on the three men lying in the alley.

The two Preacher had shot in the chest were dead. Even in near-darkness, the old mountain man had planted his slugs in their hearts.

"This one's still alive, but he'd better hope he won't be for much longer, gut-shot the way he is," was the report on the fourth robber. "On the other hand, he seems to have passed out already, so I guess he's beyond hurting."

"What happened here?" one of the officers asked Preacher.

"One o' the varmints pretended to be hurt to lure me in here, and then they figured on robbin' me. They said they was gonna beat me to death so I couldn't raise the alarm."

"That's a lie!" The exclamation came from the man leaning against the wall. "My friends and I were just walkin' along this alley, usin' it as a shortcut, you know, when this crazy old coot showed up and started shooting at us!"

Preacher let out a contemptuous snort. "Why in blazes would I do that?"

"He's crazy, I tell you! That's why he did it!"

"I might believe you, Miller, if I hadn't recognized you and these other three," said the officer with the lantern. "You've all been in and out of prison for robbery, assault, and attempted murder. You're probably to blame for a good number of the dead bodies we've found in alleys like this. We've just never been able to catch you at it . . . until now." The officer turned to Preacher. "What's your name, mister?"

"They call me Preacher."

"You're a reverend?"

Preacher snorted again. "Not hardly. It's a long story that goes back a hell of a long way. Has to do with a bunch o' Blackfeet who figured on burnin' me at the stake. I've done told it so many times it wearies me to go through it again, it purely does."

"Well, never mind," the officer said. "You're not from around here, are you?"

"I'm from all over. Stayin' at the Crockett Hotel right now."

"You plan on leaving town any time soon?"

"Fact of the matter is, I was fixin' to take a trip on out Arizona way. Stop by in Colorado first, though, and meet up with some friends o' mine."

"We'll need you to stay around for the inquest on the two you killed."

A grotesque, choking rattle sounded from the man Preacher had shot in the belly.

The police officer grunted and went on. "Make that the three men you killed, since that gent just breathed his last."

"I reckon I can hang around for a few days,"

Preacher said. "Best make it quick, though. I'm too old and feeble to linger in one place any longer 'n necessary."

"Yeah, about as old and feeble as a mountain lion, from the looks of it," said one of the other officers. "Where are you headed right now?"

"Soon's you fellas give me my gun back so I can reload, I'm goin' on over to the Buckhorn and have me a drink. Whiskey's the best preservative for a fella's innards, you know."

The one who seemed to be in charge picked up the Lightning, checked it in the lantern's glow, and then handed it back to the old mountain man. "San Antonio's a modern city now. We frown on people packing guns. I have a hunch you're not going to shoot anybody accidentally, though."

"This here iron o' mine goes off, it'll be a-purpose," Preacher said. "You can bet ol' Davy Crockett's coonskin cap on that."

CHAPTER 7

The Buckhorn Saloon was famous for just that—horns. If an animal sported any sort of antlers, chances were a pair was mounted somewhere on the saloon's walls.

Even though it had been years since Preacher had been there, he recognized one of the bartenders working behind the hardwood. The man's face was a little rounder and softer, and the pale hair on his head was considerably thinner, but Preacher knew the man had been working in the Buckhorn the last time he'd been in San Antonio. After a moment he was even able to come up with the bartender's name. "Howdy, Darby," he greeted the drink juggler.

The bartender's sparse eyebrows rose. Clearly, at first glace he didn't know Preacher . . . but then realization came into his eyes "Preacher? Is that really you?"

"Why wouldn't it be?" the old mountain man asked.

"Well, I figured—" Darby stopped short.

Preacher laughed. "Figured I'd done kicked the bucket years ago, didn't you?"

"Oh, no," Darby said hastily. "Of course not."

"No need in denyin' it. I know I'm pert-near 'bout as old as Methuselah."

"Not at all. Why, you, uh, don't look a day over seventy, to be honest."

"I've got that beat by a mite. Hell, bein' old is just a matter of how you feel, ain't it? And I feel fine." Preacher cocked his head to the side. "Might feel a little better, though, with a shot o' your best who-hit-John inside me."

"Sure. Coming right up." Darby reached for a bottle on the shelf behind the bar, then changed his mind and reached *under* the bar. He brought out a bottle and a glass and poured an inch of amber liquid in the glass.

"Put about twice that much," Preacher suggested. After the bartender complied, Preacher took a sip, said, "Ah," and licked his lips.

"What brings you to San Antonio?" Darby asked.

"You know me. I never can stay in one place for too long. This was just the next place on the way to wherever I'm goin' next"—Preacher paused—"although for one o' the few times in a good long while, happens I *do* know where I'm goin' next. Headed up to Colorado to see Smoke and his pretty lil' missus and take a trip out to Arizona to see some other folks."

Darby's eyebrows waggled again. "Arizona?" he repeated. "You remember Lije Connolly?"

"Why, o' course I do. Fella used to scout for the

army. Did some buffler huntin', too, if I recollect right."

Darby nodded. "That's the man."

Preacher stroked his chin. "What's Connolly got to do with Arizona? Last I heard of him, he was up in Dakota Territory, tryin' to see if there was any gold left in the Black Hills."

"Somebody was in here not that long ago and mentioned him. Said Connolly had moved out to Arizona for his health. He's in a pretty bad way, I think. The fella said he didn't have much longer."

Preacher frowned. "I'm mighty sorry to hear that. Connolly and me got ourselves chased by a bunch of Sioux one time, back when the railroad was first buildin' a line up through their huntin' grounds. Barely made it to a little knob where we was able to fort up. Stood off those varmints for more 'n eight hours 'fore they got tired of it and decided we'd knocked enough of 'em off their ponies with our rifles." Preacher took another sip of the whiskey. "Spend that long with a fella at your shoulder, both of you breathin' the same gun smoke, you don't soon forget him."

"If you're going to Arizona, maybe you should look him up. From what the gent who mentioned him was saying, Lije settled down in Tucson."

"The hell you say! That's where me and Smoke and Sally are goin'. You're damn right I'll look him up and say howdy, if he's still alive and kickin'."

Darby started polishing a glass. "Say, you should have been around a little while ago. There was a big gun battle not far from here. People were talking about it. Sounds like two groups of thieves shot it out. Dead bodies were lying everywhere, from what I heard." He shook his head. "You don't see things like that very often anymore. San Antonio's gotten civilized."

"A place is only as civilized as the folks who are there, I reckon."

"Maybe. What's your point?"

Preacher threw back the rest of the whiskey and wiped the back of his other hand across his mouth. "Anywhere I go, I've still got civilization on the run."

Smoke grinned as he leaned on the corral fence and watched Calvin Woods struggling mightily to stay on the back of a bucking horse. The horse was black as sin and twice as nasty, but Cal was making a valiant effort.

Pearlie, Smoke's foreman on the Sugarloaf, had a booted foot propped on the fence as he also watched the young cowboy battle the horse. He thumbed back his battered old black hat. "I don't think he can do it. I think the world and all o' Cal, but he ain't gonna be able to stick on that loco cayuse."

"Would you be interested in a little wager on that?" Smoke asked as he continued to smile.

A dozen more cowboys from his crew were gathered around the corral, whooping and hollering encouragement to Cal. Smoke enjoyed seeing the fellows who worked for him having such a good time.

Pearlie glanced over at him. "What sorta stakes did you have in mind?"

"If you win, I'll ask Sally to fix you up a big batch of bear sign before we leave for Arizona next week."

Pearlie almost started to drool. There was no food in the world he liked better than the doughnuts Sally fried up. Those delicious, sugary, greasy treats could make him almost pass out with enjoyment.

A suspicious frown suddenly creased Pearlie's forehead. "And what if *you* win?"

"Well, I've had my eye on that new saddle of yours." Despite his habit of wearing dusty range clothes and working right alongside his men, Smoke Jensen was one of the richest hombres in Colorado, thanks to a gold claim he had owned since he was a young man and the highly successful ranch he had built. Smoke could afford to buy ten saddles if he wanted to.

Pearlie's frown deepened. The lure of bear sign was well nigh irresistible. He had already worried some about how he was going to get by while Smoke and Sally were gone. She made sure the men of the Sugarloaf ate better than any ranch crew west of the Mississippi.

"I'll risk it," Pearlie said.

At that moment the other cowboys around the corral let out a pained "Ohhhh!"

Smoke and Pearlie looked into the corral in time to see Cal seemingly suspended in midair for a second before he came crashing down to earth several yards away from the horse that had just thrown him. A couple cowboys scrambled over the fence and dived into the enclosure to keep the stallion away from Cal by yelling and waving their hats at it.

Smoke chuckled. "Well, it didn't take long to settle that bet." He didn't mind losing. He wouldn't have taken Pearlie's prized new saddle away from him anyway, even if he'd won. Mostly the wager was just an excuse to rib the lanky foreman about his fondness for bear sign.

There had been a time when Pearlie was a gunman and had ridden the owlhoot trail. He'd even been part of a gang given the task of running Smoke to ground and killing him. When Pearlie found out more about what was going on, he had changed sides in the conflict and had been one of Smoke's best friends and most loyal employees ever since.

That loyalty ran both ways.

Smoke saw Cal picking himself up and recognized the burning intensity and determination in the young man's eyes as he took off his hat and used it to slap some of the dust from his clothes. "Why don't we switch it around and go double or nothing?" he suggested to Pearlie. "Cal looks like he's gonna get back on that horse, but I've decided there's no way he can ride it."

"That boy can plumb do whatever he sets his mind to," Pearlie said with a stubborn look on his face. "I ain't got two saddles, though, so I can't go double or nothin'."

"Forget the saddle," Smoke said, enjoying the bantering with one of his oldest friends. "If you win, I'll ask Sally to make a double batch of bear sign. If you win, they might get a little stale before you could finish them off—"

Pearlie grunted. "Not much chance o' that. I'd have all them buzzards in cowboy hats swarmin' around me, beggin' me to share. But what if *you* win the bet?"

"Then no bear sign for you."

Pearlie's eyes widened in horror. "You mean—"

"I mean you'll have to give me your word of honor

you won't eat any doughnuts until we get back from Arizona."

"But that . . . that just ain't fair! You can't ask a fella to give up somethin' he loves so much, 'specially at Christmastime!"

Smoke's broad shoulders rose and fell in a shrug. "It's up to you."

Pearlie glanced into the corral, where Cal was taking a deep breath. The young puncher strode toward the big black horse. The cowboys who had jumped into the corral had caught the horse and were holding tightly to its harness.

"Let me back on there," Cal said.

"Better not, kid," one of the men said. "This devil's liable to kill you if you try to ride him again."

"No, he won't. I'm gonna get the best of him this time."

"I'll take that bet, Smoke," Pearlie said.

Smoke nodded to the punchers, who were looking at him to see if he wanted Cal to take another crack at the horse. They continued hanging on tightly to the animal's harness as Cal put his foot in the stirrup and swung up into the saddle.

"Come on, Cal! You can do it!" Then the foreman added under his breath, "I got a hell of a lot ridin' on this."

The cowboys let go of the harness and stepped back hurriedly.

Instantly, the horse started pitching and swapping ends. Cal clamped his knees against the horse's flanks and hung on for dear life.

It was a wild ride, and with every bone-jarring, tooth-rattling maneuver by the horse, the men around the corral shouted encouragement to Cal. Smoke thought the youngster looked a little green around the gills, although it was hard to say for sure with so much dust in the air.

Smoke had been to several cowboy contests called rodeos that had sprung up in recent years. In those competitions, a man had to ride a bucking bronc for a certain amount of time in order to qualify for a prize. There was no such time limit on the Sugarloaf. Cal would have surpassed it several times over already. No matter how long the ride seemed to Smoke, he was sure it felt a lot longer to Cal. The young puncher was the one who was taking the pounding.

Only two possible outcomes existed for that battle of man against horse. Cal might be thrown again, or the horse would give up and turn gentle. Despite the bet Smoke had made with Pearlie, he honestly figured Cal was going to emerge victorious. He hoped so.

The horse began to look like it was weakening. Cal looked like he was about to be sick or pass out. Which of the combatants would give up first?

The horse's gyrations slowed. Its head drooped. It gave a couple more halfhearted bucks, then came to a stop. A shudder ran through its powerful body. Cal slumped in the saddle, but wasn't letting his guard down. The horse could be trying to trick him into relaxing, then the animal would explode into action again.

That proved not to be the case. When Cal pressed his heels against the horse's flanks, it started walking slowly around the corral. After a few steps, its head came up, but it continued to cooperate. Smoke was glad to see that the horse's spirit wasn't broken. It had just decided the smart thing was to be on the same side as its rider.

Several of the men whooped in excitement.

Pearlie slapped Smoke on the back. "He done it! I knew the boy could stick! And I get a double batch o' bear sign outta the deal!"

Smoke laughed. "I happen to know Sally's planning on frying up a big mess of them anyway, bet or no bet."

Pearlie stared. "You was just funnin' me?"

"That's right."

Pearlie looked at him for a moment longer, then threw his head back and guffawed. "You sure enough know my weak spot, Smoke. When I thought about losin' out on them bear sign, it plumb give me the fantods."

Smoke clapped a hand on Pearlie's shoulder. "Why don't you go congratulate Cal on that ride?"

"I reckon I'll do that."

While Pearlie climbed over the corral fence, Smoke turned toward the ranch house. He stopped short at the sight of a man sitting several yards away on a big gray stallion. With all the commotion in the corral, Smoke hadn't heard the rider come up. That wasn't good. He had too many enemies to be letting anyone sneak up on him, ever.

It was no enemy, though. A grin creased Preacher's leathery face as the old mountain man said, "I got your letter, Smoke. Headin' out to Arizona for Christmas sounds plumb nice!"

CHAPTER 8

There weren't many things in life Tom Ballard liked better than being in the newspaper office late at night with the work all done, the press running in the back room, and the satisfying knowledge that in the morning a new edition of the *Courier* would be on the streets of Tucson. If he was the sort of man who smoked, he would have propped his feet on the desk, fired up a cheroot, and sighed in contentment.

That feeling lasted all of ten seconds or so.

He thought about Avery Tuttle and his good mood vanished. Ballard scowled. Thinking about Avery Tuttle roused all sorts of feelings in him. First was resentment at the way Tuttle lorded it over other folks in town, including Ballard. Some men felt like having more money made them better than everybody else. Avery Tuttle definitely fell into that camp.

Then there was anger. Tuttle had started his own newspaper, in direct competition with the *Courier*, after

Ballard began editorializing about how one man shouldn't own half the businesses in town and have his greedy eye on the others. So far, Ballard had been able to stave off Tuttle's attempt to put him out of business, but there was no denying that Tuttle had a lot deeper pockets than he did.

Next came worry. Ballard knew he might not be able to withstand having Tuttle as an enemy forever. Tuttle had a reputation. He claimed he was just a sharp businessman, but everybody in town knew he was downright ruthless.

That thought led to fear . . . not fear for himself. He knew what he'd been letting himself in for when he had decided that Tuttle had been getting everything his own way for long enough.

No, Ballard was afraid for his wife Louise and their two children. What might Tuttle do to them if he got tired of the annoyance that the *Courier* had become? Some of Tuttle's enemies had disappeared from Tucson in the past. It was rumored they had packed up and left town in the middle of the night, but Ballard wondered if they'd had some help with that . . . and if they had only gone as far as a shallow grave in the desert.

He didn't want to believe that Tuttle would go so far as to strike at an innocent woman and children, but in his darker moments—like the one that had just come over him—Ballard couldn't swear that wouldn't happen.

And if it did, it would be his fault for making such a powerful, vicious enemy.

As Ballard sat at his desk, he became aware that

the press's clanking and clattering had stopped. In its place, he heard profane muttering from Edgar Torrance.

Ballard stood up and went to the open doorway between the office and the press room. "What's wrong, Edgar?"

"One o' the damn gears is stripped." Torrance was a stocky man around sixty with sparse, graying red hair and a beard of the same shade.

"We have some replacements, don't we? You can fix it."

"Yeah, but it'll take me half the night. The paper'll be late gettin' out in the mornin'."

"It can't be helped," Ballard told his assistant with a shake of his head. "People will just have to wait a few hours longer to read the news."

Torrance grunted. "Maybe it's a good thing. It'll be that much longer 'fore Tuttle sees that you're breathin' fire about him again and sends his gunnies after you."

"We still have a free press in this country, and Tuttle knows it. He's not going to send any gunmen after me."

"You sure about that? I've seen Smiler Coe lookin' at you on the street. He was practically lickin' his chops, like a dog eyein' a big ol' steak. Only time Coe looks like that is when he's fixin' to kill somebody."

"The law's never arrested Coe, at least not around here," Ballard pointed out.

"That's because he's smart enough to do all his killin' outside 'o town where there's no witnesses."

Edgar might have a point there, Ballard thought.

He'd heard rumors connecting Coe to some of Avery Tuttle's rivals who had dropped out of sight. But the law still required proof, or at least witnesses, and there weren't any.

He thought about Louise and Tom Jr. and Alice, and then he thought about Smiler Coe leering that killer's grin at them, and his blood seemed to turn to ice in his veins.

But he had gone too far in his opposition to Tuttle for him to back down. For one thing, Tuttle would never believe it and would remain suspicious of him. The only alternative that might actually work would be to leave Tucson and go far, far away.

The thought of running away stuck in Ballard's craw. He didn't know if he could bring himself to do it, even for his family's sake. And they wouldn't want him to, he was sure of that. Louise had always supported him in everything he'd done, all the way.

Ballard nodded toward the press. "Just get to work on that, Edgar. I'll give you a hand if you want."

"Naw, ain't necessary. You just spend your time tryin' to figure out how we can afford some more modern equipment around here that don't break down all the time."

That would be a good thing, all right, Ballard thought. If he had some capital, he could turn the *Courier* into a more up-to-date newspaper . . . The sound of the office door opening broke into his musing. No great loss, he thought, since those dreams were hopeless, anyway.

He turned, wondering who could be coming in that late at night. Technically, the *Courier's* office had been closed for hours, although he usually didn't lock the door as long as he was there. He began to feel a little apprehensive as he swung around.

Late-night visitors usually didn't bode well for anyone.

He saw instantly that his hunch was right. Three men stood just inside the office. Ballard recognized them. Sam Brant, Nelse Andersen, and Phil Deere. They didn't have quite as bad a reputation as Smiler Coe, but they were friends with the gunman and, like Coe, worked for Avery Tuttle.

"How can I help you men?" Ballard asked, keeping his voice carefully neutral. It was possible they weren't there to cause trouble. Not likely, but he supposed stranger things had happened.

"Thought we'd come by and see if we could get an early copy of the paper." Andersen was a lean, wiry man with such pale hair, eyes, and skin he could almost be taken for an albino.

"Yeah," Brant added. He was shorter and rounder than Andersen, and as hairy as an ape. "The boss is eager to see what you've got to say about him this week."

"The paper will be on sale tomorrow." Ballard almost added *At its usual time,* but then he remembered the stripped gear on the printing press and the delay it was going to cause. No point in explaining that, though.

"Mr. Tuttle wants to see it tonight." Deere was almost as pale as Andersen, but his hair and the beard stubble on his cheeks and jaw were black as midnight and seemed even darker because of the contrast with his skin.

Ballard shook his head. "I'm sorry I can't accommodate Mr. Tuttle, but he'll just have to read the *Courier* at the same time everyone else does."

A harsh laugh came from Brant. "You think folks actually read that rag o' yours, Ballard? From what I hear, they just use it for cleanin' their boots."

Ballard kept a tight rein on his temper. "If that's the case, then Tuttle shouldn't mind if he can't get a copy until tomorrow."

As a matter of fact, Edgar Torrance had run off quite a few copies before the press broke down. Ballard had seen them stacked on the big worktable in the back room. He could have gone back there and gotten one of them for Tuttle's men. But he wasn't going to give them the satisfaction, and he certainly wasn't going to cooperate with Avery Tuttle's highhanded demands.

Andersen was probably the most cunning of the trio. He cocked his head to the side a little. "I don't hear the press running. Usually it is on the night before you publish a paper, isn't it?"

"The paper will be out tomorrow. You don't have to worry about that." Ballard didn't want to tell them about the mechanical difficulty. He knew that would please Tuttle, and he was stubborn enough not to want to do that.

"What I'm worried about," Brant said as he eased toward Ballard, "is that that big mouth of yours is gonna get you in bad trouble one of these days."

Ballard knew the man was trying to intimidate him. He was determined not to let the tactic work, but apprehension stirred inside him anyway. "On the contrary, I've always considered myself rather soft-spoken," he managed to say.

"A man can have a big mouth in what he writes, too," Andersen snapped. "And when he writes lies and spreads them around for all the world to see, he can expect trouble because of it."

"I print only the truth, and if anyone can prove otherwise, by God I'd like to see it!" Despite his nervousness, Ballard was getting angry. He didn't like it when anyone challenged his journalistic integrity.

All three men moved close. Ballard started to feel crowded.

"Tell us what's gonna be in tomorrow's paper," Phil Deere said. There was a definite warning tone in his voice.

Edgar Torrance stepped into the doorway between the office and the press room. He had a shotgun in his hands, the twin barrels pointed in the general direction of Anderson, Deere, and Brant. "Thanks for letting me take a little time to clear this old scattergun of mine, Mr. Ballard. It's loaded and in perfect workin' order now. I'll get back to the press in a minute." Torrance looked at the three toughs as if he were just noticing they were there. "What are you boys doin' here in the middle of the night?"

Each of the three packed a handgun, but the irons were holstered and even the fastest draw would have a hard time beating a finger already on the trigger. Andersen, Deere, and Brant weren't even the fastest who worked for Avery Tuttle. That honor belonged to Smiler Coe.

"Thought we'd see if we could get a paper," Andersen said tightly.

"Tomorrow," Torrance said. "But I reckon the boss has already explained that to you."

Brant's lips drew back from his teeth so he looked like a snarling beast, especially with the hairy pelt he sported. "I don't like people pointin' guns at me."

"I ain't pointin' it at you," Torrance said. "I only point guns at things I intend to shoot right away. Is that what I'm gonna be doin' here?"

Andersen jerked his head toward the front door. "Come on, fellas. Let's get out of here."

"You can get your paper tomorrow," Ballard couldn't resist saying as the three men left the office with surly looks on their faces.

When the men were gone, Torrance lowered the shotgun. "That bunch don't have the brains to figure their way out of a paper sack. If they did, they might be dangerous."

Ballard blew out a breath. "They felt sort of dangerous to me."

"That's what they wanted you to think. When you're scared of 'em, you've done half their work for them."

"I know. Anyway, it's not like any of them are Smiler Coe."

"If Coe had been here, I might not 've come out with this Greener," Torrance admitted. "He's pure hell on the shoot."

Ballard leaned against his desk. "Actually, I'm sort of glad they came here and tried to scare me. It shows that Tuttle is taking me seriously. He thinks if I can get enough people to pay attention, I might pose a real threat to him."

"Yeah . . . or maybe he ought to just wait a while."

Ballard frowned. "What does that mean?"

"It means I'm pretty sure I can get that press goin' again in a little while, but later tonight, or next week, or sometime soon, it's gonna break down again. You can count on that, boss. It ain't a matter of *if*. It's a matter of *when*."

"So you're saying—"

"I'm sayin' that if you can't get some better equipment in here, you won't be a threat to Tuttle because you won't be publishin' a newspaper anymore."

Ballard sighed. "I was afraid of that. I knew this day was coming."

"Then I hope you've got a good plan figured out."

"Oh, I have a plan. I'm just not sure it's a good one."

CHAPTER 9

Louise Ballard was the most beautiful woman her husband had ever seen. He had thought that the first time he'd laid eyes on her twelve years earlier, back in Kansas City when she was still Louise Montgomery, the daughter of a successful merchant, and he was a brand-new reporter without a penny to his name. Her golden hair, her blue eyes, her exquisitely inviting lips had taken his breath away. She had shocked him by agreeing to let him court her. He had been even more surprised—but grateful and very, very happy—when that courtship had turned into love.

A lot had changed in the dozen years since then, but not Louise's beauty or the way Tom Ballard felt about her. His breath still caught in his throat when she looked up from the chair where she was sitting and reading by the light of a lamp while she waited for him. She always sat up and waited for him on the nights when the paper was being printed.

"The paper's put to bed already?" she asked as he came into the parlor of their neat little adobe house three blocks from the *Courier* office.

"No, there was a problem with the press. Edgar's working on it." Ballard bent over to kiss her and felt a quick stirring of desire as he viewed the top of her breasts not covered by the dark blue dressing gown she wore. Good for a man to still feel that after so many years of marriage, he thought.

"Is he going to be able to fix it?" she asked as he pulled a straight-backed chair over closer to the armchair where she was and sat down.

"This time. At least he claims he can. But he warned me that we can't continue as we have been. We need better, more modern equipment."

"I've been telling you that for quite a while, Tom."

Ballard sat forward and clasped his hands together between his knees. "The problem is we can't afford it. It takes a considerable amount of money to make improvements like that."

For a moment, Louise didn't say anything. Then, "My father would loan us the money."

Ballard was shaking his head before all the words were even out of his wife's mouth. "I wouldn't give your father the satisfaction of going to him and begging for money."

"You wouldn't be begging. It would just be a business proposition."

Ballard grunted. "Some people might look at it like that, but he wouldn't. You know that. Anyway, I'm not sure he'd go along with any such deal. He's never forgiven me for moving you and the children all the way out here to Arizona Territory."

"You don't know that." She smiled faintly. "But I'll admit, he *can* hold a grudge." She set the book aside on a small table next to the armchair. "I still think it would be worth asking him. The *Courier*'s circulation is growing. You know there are plenty of people here in Tucson who like the way you've stood up to Avery Tuttle."

"That's another thing," Ballard said. "Three of Tuttle's men came into the office tonight."

A look of alarm sprang into Louise's eyes. "Not that horrible Smiler Coe, I hope. Did they threaten you or try to hurt you?"

"Not really, and Coe wasn't with them. They were his friends, though—Andersen, Brant, and Deere. They said they wanted an early edition of tomorrow's paper, that their boss was curious what I was going to say about him this week."

"I can imagine! You tell the truth about Mr. Tuttle, and he doesn't like that."

"Cockroaches never like it when the light shines on them."

"That's good," Louise said with a smile. "You should put that in next week's editorial."

"Anyway, their visit, and the problem with the press, both drove it home to me that things can't continue the way they are. Something has to change."

She frowned. "You're not thinking about . . . leaving Tucson, are you, Tom? You know how much I like it here, and the air is so good for Tommy."

Ballard nodded. When he was two, their son—now ten years old—had come down with a serious illness that had weakened his lungs. Over time his condition had worsened back in the Midwest, until one of the doctors they had seen had recommended they try moving to an area where the air was drier. The move to Arizona Territory had indeed done wonders for Tommy's breathing.

"No, we're not leaving Tucson," Ballard reassured his wife. "Well . . . *I* am, but you and the children aren't."

Louise stared at him. "What in the world are you talking about? I know better than to think you'd abandon us, Tom!"

"Of course not," he said with a shake of his head and a slight laugh. "But I am going to the territorial capital in Prescott to have a talk with the governor."

"Do you think he can help?"

"He might. I happen to know that when the governor was appointed, Tuttle used his influence to try to get someone else into the post. That was one of the few times Tuttle didn't get what he wanted, thank goodness. If he had the governor in his pocket, he really could run roughshod over the whole territory. But things like that aren't easily forgotten. The governor knows Tuttle opposed him . . . and he knows it'll probably happen again in the future."

"What are you going to ask him to do?"

Ballard leaned back in his chair and stroked his chin. "Tuttle's been careful not to do anything to bring the law down on his own head. I could ask the governor to send in troops, but there's really no legal justification for that and I doubt if he'd do it. But we can fight Tuttle in other ways. A number of businesses in town are struggling. Tuttle would love to see them go under so he could take them over or at least have them out of his hair . . . like the *Courier*. We could keep that from happening . . . with some cash."

"The governor can't just give you money," Louise pointed out.

"No, but he wields considerable influence with the banks. He could help arrange for a loan . . . a big loan that would help some of Tuttle's opponents stay afloat and keep fighting him."

"Like the *Courier*."

Ballard inclined his head in acknowledgment of her point. "That's true. I'm not being totally selfless here."

"You won't take a loan from my father, but you will from the governor."

"I didn't marry the governor's daughter," Ballard said dryly. "Anyway, your father couldn't swing a big enough loan to accomplish what Tucson needs."

"No, I suppose not," she admitted. "When are you going?"

"As soon as I can."

"Tom"—she leaned over and put a hand on his knee—"it'll be Christmas in less than two weeks. You don't want to be away from your family for Christmas."

"I won't be. Enough spur and branch lines exist that I can take the railroad all the way to Prescott and back. I won't be gone more than a few days."

"You're sure?"

"I would never miss Christmas," he promised

solemnly. "Of course, this is all contingent on the governor agreeing to see me. I'll wire him first thing in the morning and ask for an appointment."

"You can't handle the whole business by telegraph?"

Ballard shook his head. "I wouldn't want to ask a man for such a big favor without doing it face-to-face."

"I suppose that makes sense. I just hate for you to be leaving at this time of year. Tommy and Alice are already starting to get excited about Christmas."

"I won't be gone long." Ballard stood up and stretched, easing muscles in his back that would be even wearier by morning. "I really ought to get back down to the office and see how Edgar's coming along with that repair job on the press. I just wanted to talk to you about this idea."

"For the trip to see the governor, you mean?"

"That's right."

"It sounds like the only thing you can do, Tom. I worry about what Mr. Tuttle will do when he finds out about it, though."

"That's why we have to be careful. Tuttle can't know anything about it until something's already been done and it's too late for him to stop it. I wouldn't put much of anything past that man."

"Neither would I."

To lighten the mood, Ballard bent, kissed her again, and smiled. "That's the other reason I walked over here from the office. It's going to be a long night, and I needed something to help me get through it."

She returned the smile. "Are you sure that's

enough?" she asked with a touch of boldness in her voice.

"Unfortunately, it'll have to be," Ballard said with a sigh of regret. "For now." He carried the memory of his wife's smile and the taste of her lips with him as he left the house and walked back toward the newspaper office.

At the late hour, Tucson was mostly quiet, although some music and laughter would still be coming from the saloons. Ballard didn't intend on going anywhere near them, however. He still had work to do.

Reaching the office, he walked in hoping to hear the press running. That would mean Torrance had finished the repair and the paper was being printed. Instead, silence greeted him.

The silence was worrisome. If Torrance was still working on the press, there should have been a steady stream of muttered profanity accompanying his efforts.

"Edgar?" Ballard said as he stepped into the doorway of the press room. "Having any luck with that balky contraption?"

Torrance wasn't there. The press was partially disassembled. The faulty gear had been removed, and the new one put in its place, but everything still needed to be put back together.

He looked around, suddenly worried that something bad might have happened. Tuttle's hired toughs could have returned to cause some real trouble, instead of just issuing vague threats. But there was no sign of a struggle, and thankfully, no blood on the floor or anywhere else. It looked like Edgar Torrance had just . . . vanished.

A chill went through Ballard as he remembered how some other citizens of Tucson had dropped out of sight after standing up to Avery Tuttle. He didn't believe anyone would have been able to drag Torrance out of there without leaving some evidence of it behind, though.

Ballard's worried gaze landed on the closed rear door. "You're just getting ahead of yourself and borrowing trouble, Tom," he muttered to himself. He went over to the door, opened it, and looked out toward the outhouse in the dim and shadowy alley, thinking Torrance had probably just stepped out there. He didn't see anyone, so he called softly, "Edgar?"

A low moan came from somewhere to his right.

Ballard stiffened in alarm. He stepped out into the alley and swung in that direction, said again, more urgently, "Edgar! Are you there?"

His right foot bumped against something. He knelt, fished a match out of his pocket, and struck it against the wall. He winced from the sudden flare of light and from the scene it revealed.

Edgar Torrance lay on his back in the alley, close to the back wall of the newspaper office. Blood from half a dozen cuts covered his face. His lips were smashed, his nose was broken, both eyes were swollen almost shut, and bruised knots had ballooned up on his forehead and cheeks. He had been beaten brutally.

But he was alive. His moan had told Ballard that much.

As he knelt beside Torrance, he heard the bubbling rasp of air in the older man's busted nose. He got an arm around his printer's shoulders and struggled to lift him into a semisitting position, hoping it would be easier for him to breathe. "Edgar, what the hell happened?" Ballard thought he already had a pretty good idea.

"T-Tom . . . ? That you?"

"It's me. You're going to be all right, Edgar. I'll get the doctor—"

"Did they . . . did they do any damage . . . inside?"

"In the office? No, not that I could see. What happened to you?"

"I come outside . . . in the alley . . . to smoke a stogie . . . Just takin' . . . a little rest from the work . . . on the press . . . Somebody jumped me . . . started whalin' on me . . ."

"Tuttle's men," Ballard said bitterly.

"Dunno . . . I never got . . . never got a look at 'em . . . I figure . . . you're right, though. Had to be . . . some of that bunch."

Since Torrance hadn't seen them, he couldn't testify to that in court. And so Tuttle's hired hardcases would get away with their violence once again.

Torrance clutched feebly at Ballard's sleeve. "I tried to . . . fight 'em. Keep 'em from . . . goin' inside."

"It looks like you did. You must have raised enough of a ruckus that they took off rather than hanging around to cause more trouble. Thank you, Edgar. You may have saved the newspaper."

"If you'll . . . help me up . . . I'll get back to work . . . on that press."

"Not tonight. I'm getting you to the doctor, and

then I'll come back and finish the job. I'll get the rest of the paper printed, too."

Torrance summoned up a grin and then grimaced at the pain it caused in his swollen and bleeding lips. "Not gonna let 'em . . . get away with it . . . are you?"

"You're damned right I'm not."

CHAPTER 10

"I really figured you'd meet us in Tucson, Preacher," Smoke said as he and the old mountain man sat on the front porch of the ranch house after enjoying a fine supper prepared by Sally.

"I was in San Antonio when your letter caught up to me, so it would've been easier to do that, sure enough. Comin' all the way up here to Colorado is more than a mite out of the way."

"So why'd you do it?" Smoke asked as he propped his booted feet on the railing along the front of the porch.

"Just figured it'd be more pleasurable to travel with you and Sally. How do you plan on gettin' there?" Like most frontiersmen, Preacher was always interested in the various routes and how somebody planned on getting from one place to another. An extensive knowledge of where the trails ran and what lay along them could mean the difference between life and death. Because of that, whenever two old-timers got together, a discussion of where they had been and how they had gotten there was quite common.

Smoke wasn't an old-timer in years, but he had packed several lifetimes of experience and adventure into the two decades that had passed since he and his father had headed west. In answer to Preacher's question, he said, "It would be easy enough to take the train down to El Paso and then head straight west on the Southern Pacific."

"But you had somethin' else in mind?"

"I've been reading about a new railroad that's opened up from Albuquerque over west into northern Arizona Territory. We could take it through Flagstaff and Williams, and then it turns south to Phoenix. There are branch lines from there to Tucson."

· Preacher thought about it and then nodded. "Be a mite more scenic that way, if you give a hoot in hell about scenery. All of it looks better from the back of a horse, if you ask me."

"Yeah, but I'm not gonna ask Sally to sit a saddle all the way to Tucson."

"Don't reckon I blame you there. We probably wouldn't make it by Christmas, neither, especially if any storms blew in along the way. You sure all the passes will be open the way you're talkin' about goin'?"

"I'll check on that," Smoke said. "I expect they will be, though."

The two men sat in companionable silence for several minutes, then Preacher said, "You recollect hearin' me talk about a fella name of Lije Connolly?"

"The name's familiar. Old friend of yours, isn't he?"

"Yep. I been told his health took a turn for the

worse and he moved on down to Arizona to live out his days where it's nice and warm. While we're out there, I plan to look him up and say howdy, if he's still kickin'."

"Well, shoot, Preacher, in that case you should've gone straight on out there instead of coming all the way up here."

Preacher's bony shoulders rose and fell in a fatalistic shrug. "If Lije's time is up, he'll cross the divide whether I been to see him or not. If it ain't, he'll still be there. It don't pay to make too many plans in this life, nor to worry about how things are gonna turn out. Life's got a way of happenin' the way it wants to. A fella said to me once, time wants a skeleton. Took me a while to figure out he meant that's where we're all headed."

From the doorway, Sally said, "Well, it seems I got here just in time to keep you from descending into doom and gloom, Preacher."

"You're sure right about that," the old mountain man said as she came out onto the porch and leaned back against the railing near where Smoke had propped his feet. "Havin' a gal as sweet and pretty as you around makes it plumb difficult for an old cuss to get down in the mouth."

"She always puts a smile on my face," Smoke said.

"What was that about an old friend of yours, Preacher?" she asked. "I only caught a little of what you were saying."

He explained again about Lije Connolly. "I got to admit, it'll be good to see the old pelican again, if that's how things turn out. We backed each other's play in two or three little dustups a long time back.

He'll remember me, though. I took a bullet outta his brisket once. Saved his life. A fella don't forget that."

"I hope it'll be a good reunion for you," Sally said. "And a nice peaceful Christmas for all of us."

"A nice peaceful Christmas with family and friends is about the best present anybody could get," Smoke said.

Tom Ballard had been nervous before his meeting with the territorial governor, but the man's warm, friendly smile and hearty handshake put him more at ease.

"Tom, it's good to see you again," the big, bluff, gray-haired man greeted him. "How are Louise and the little ones?"

To the best of Ballard's recollection, he had met the governor exactly once and exchanged little more than a dozen words with him. Either the governor had a politician's knack for names and families of anyone who might someday be in a position to help his career—or he had somebody find out those details in a hurry. It didn't really matter which of those was true.

"They're fine, sir," Ballard replied as he shook the governor's hand.

"And how are things in Tucson?" the governor asked as he waved Ballard into a chair in front of the big desk. "Is the *Courier* still holding the feet of those in power close to the flames?"

"When it's needed."

The governor grunted as he sat down. "I can think of one fellow who could do with a hotfoot."

"Avery Tuttle," Ballard said.

The governor leaned back in his chair. "He did his dead level best to see to it that I never occupied this office. I suspect that was because he knows I'm an honest man, unlike him and his cronies."

"Tuttle's the reason I've come to Prescott to see you, sir."

The governor frowned. "I try to keep up with things going on in the territory, and from what I hear, Tuttle's managed to skirt along just inside the law. I wish it were otherwise, so I could press the local authorities to throw him behind bars, but—"

"Tuttle's been really good at hiding his trail," Ballard said. "Several of his business rivals have disappeared in recent months. Nobody knows if they just left town, or if . . . something else happened to them."

"That's a pretty serious accusation to make," the governor said as his frown deepened. "Especially since you're not offering me any proof Tuttle had something to do with their disappearances."

"That's because there *isn't* any proof," Ballard admitted. "Like I said, he's good at hiding his trail. That's not all, though. He's been pressuring some of the businesses in town to sell out to him. He made me an offer for the *Courier* a while back. I turned him down flat, of course."

"So if he can't shut his enemies up, he'll just buy 'em out, is that it?"

"That's part of it. He's also hired a gunman, Smiler Coe, and has several other hardcases working for him. Some of them beat up my assistant, Edgar Torrance, a few days ago." Ballard lifted a hand to forestall the governor's question. "And before you ask, no, I don't have any proof of that, either. Edgar never got a good look at the men who attacked him. But three of Tuttle's men had been at the office just a short while earlier, making some veiled threats."

"The law can't do much about that, and neither can I."

"No, sir, I know. But I'm coming to the point where you might be able to help the honest citizens of Tucson. Tuttle has one more weapon in his arsenal. He's trying to take over the bank so he can foreclose on folks who have opposed him. The bank's had some reverses and is in a bit of a precarious position. The president, Race Dobson, has been holding off Tuttle's attempts to take over, but he may not be able to keep it up for much longer. The bank needs a fresh infusion of cash, and so do quite a few of the other businesses in town. Otherwise . . . it won't be long before Avery Tuttle owns Tucson, lock, stock, and barrel."

While he thought about that, the governor opened a humidor on his desk and took out a long, fat cigar. He offered the smoke to Ballard, who shook his head and murmured a no, thanks.

Without lighting the cigar, the governor chewed on it for a moment and then said, "I'll be honest with you, Tom."

"I appreciate that, sir," Ballard said, thinking that when a politician declared he was about to be honest about something, chances were just the opposite was true.

The governor surprised him, though, by saying bluntly, "I can't afford to have Avery Tuttle get his hands on that much power. He'll try to tie my hands on everything I do, and sooner or later he's liable to worm his way into this job. You came here to ask me for enough cash to shore up Tuttle's enemies down there, didn't you?"

"That's right."

"I can't give it to you under the table. I *won't* do that. I won't claim to be any sort of angel, but so far I've managed to do things pretty much proper and legal, and I intend to keep on doing that. But I *can* get in touch with some of the bankers I know and see if they can arrange for a large loan. The money would come from several different sources, but it could be consolidated here in Prescott and sent back to Tucson with you on the train."

"Do you think you could get things done that fast? I didn't want to have to wait here for too long, what with Christmas coming up soon . . ."

"Don't worry," the governor said with a wave of his hand. "The process will move pretty quickly once I've thrown my weight behind it. We'll get you back to Tucson in plenty of time to enjoy the holiday with your family."

"Thank you, sir. You don't know how much this means to the town, and to me, too."

"What it means is throwing a wrench into Avery Tuttle's plans, and I'm all for that!" the governor said as his teeth clamped down on the cigar in his mouth.

The governor called in his secretary, Gerald Saxby, and explained the situation to him, rattling off a list of names, all of them bankers or other prominent financiers he knew could be counted on for assistance. "Write notes to all of them, Gerald, and stress that speed is of the utmost necessity. We have to move quickly on this."

"Yes, sir. You'll sign them before I have them delivered?"

"Of course. In fact, why don't you just write one note and then have Ford use the typewriter to make a copy for each man?" The governor chuckled. "We ought to get *some* use out of that new-fangled machine after we went to the expense of buying one."

"A good idea, sir. I'll have the notes typed up and ready for your signature before the end of the day."

"Thanks, Gerald. I knew I could count on you."

As a matter of fact, Gerald Saxby was very loyal and very efficient. It took him only a few minutes to write an effective note appealing for financial help for Tucson. Then he passed over the handwritten copy and the list of recipients to Raymond Ford, the assistant secretary. "Type a copy for each of these men, Raymond."

"Certainly, Mr. Saxby."

Within moments, Ford had the typewriter clattering. The racket filled the outer office. Saxby didn't know how to use the machine, and the governor definitely didn't, but Ford had taken right to it. He could type swiftly and accurately, and he didn't even really have to think that much about what he was typing.

That was good, because his brain was full of the debts he owed from IOUs signed during various games over the past few weeks. The men who held those IOUs weren't the sort to sit around waiting forever for their money. Ford had already been told more than once to cough it up or he'd wind up in a dark alley some night, being pummeled and stomped into senselessness.

Luck might not have been on his side during those poker games, Ford reflected as his fingers flew over the typewriter keys, but he had been fortunate in other ways. Now he had some valuable information in his hands, and he knew just who he was going to sell it to, as soon as he found out exactly what the results of these notes were going to be.

Whenever Raymond Ford knew what that was, Avery Tuttle would know as soon as possible after that. And Ford was certain that Tuttle would be very grateful . . .

It might turn out to be a much better—and less violent—Christmas than he'd expected after all, Ford thought with a smile.

CHAPTER 11

Smoke, Sally, and Preacher got on the train at the Big Rock station on a crisp, cold day a week before Christmas. Smoke hadn't heard from Luke and Matt, but he hoped his letters had found them and that his brothers would meet them in Tucson sometime during the next week. With the train changes and layovers, it would take a couple days for Smoke, Sally, and Preacher to reach their destination in Arizona Territory.

Pearlie and Cal had come into Big Rock with them to see them off on their journey. Monte Carson was at the station, too, along with Louis Longmont and several more of Smoke and Sally's friends. Plenty of waving and calling good-bye went on between the group on the depot platform and the trio of travelers inside one of the railroad cars.

"That's a whole lot o' carryin'-on, if you ask me," Preacher said.

"It's just our friends being . . . well, friendly," Sally told him as she smiled and waved through the window glass.

"Yeah, but you'll be back in a couple weeks or less. It ain't like you're goin' off to Timbuktu or one o' them other foreign places. Shoot, it's just Arizona. I hear tell it's almost civilized down there, leastways when the Cherry Cows ain't out on a rampage."

With a blast of the locomotive's whistle, a huge puff of smoke from its diamond stack, and a rumble of rods and drivers, the train surged into motion.

As the platform and the well-wishers dropped behind, Sally settled back on the seat beside Smoke and looked at Preacher, who was riding in one of the seats across the aisle. "Cherry Cows?" she repeated. "What in the world is that, and why should we be worried about them? Surely you're not talking about actual cows!"

Preacher just chuckled.

Smoke explained. "He's talking about the Chiricahua Apaches. Old-timers sometimes call them Cherry Cows."

"Do we have to worry about running into trouble from them?" Sally asked.

"Probably not. The army's been down there fighting them and the other Apache tribes for quite a while, and most of them are on reservations now. But from what I hear, there are still a few bands holding out in the mountains here and there, not just Chiricahuas but Mescaleros and White Mountain Apaches and a few others." Smoke paused. "Geronimo and his warriors are still out there somewhere. It never pays to underestimate tough hombres like that, but the chances of them trying to stop a train these days are pretty slim."

"Well, then, I won't worry about it," Sally said. "Anyway, I have you and Preacher with me. What person in their right mind would be nervous with you two around?"

"I dunno as I'd say that," Preacher drawled. "Ain't you ever noticed how often trouble crops up when Smoke's around? I think he attracts it like one o' them magnets draws metal to it."

"And you just bring peace and harmony with you wherever you go," Smoke said as he directed a wry grin at the old mountain man.

Preacher sniffed. "I never claimed to be nothin' but what I am."

So far, the area east of the Front Range in Colorado had had only a few light dustings of snow, although it was thick at the higher elevations. The train had no problems making it through the passes, and at Denver the travelers switched to a southbound headed for Albuquerque. They could have taken that train all the way to El Paso, but in Albuquerque they switched to a line running east and west.

A day and a half after leaving Big Rock, they were in Williams, Arizona Territory, the next stop west of Flagstaff. The railroad line split there, one leg going on west toward California and Nevada, the other turning south toward Prescott, Wickenburg, Phoenix, Casa Grande, and ultimately Tucson. It would take most of a day to cover the remainder of the distance.

Smoke was glad he wouldn't have to ride the train for any longer than that. While it was true that a fellow could get from one place to another a lot faster by rail than by riding horseback, he wasn't used to it. He didn't mind a horse's regular gait, but the swaying and lurching of a railroad car got old in a hurry. Also, when a fellow was in the saddle, he could breathe fresh air instead of smoke and cinders, so from time to time Smoke had to get up and stretch his legs.

He walked to the platform at the front end of the car and stood there with his hands resting on the railing, enjoying the sight of tree-covered, snowcapped peaks in the distance. It was cold, but better than the stuffy air inside the passenger coaches.

The vestibule door of the passenger car directly in front of him burst open, and a boy emerged from it at a run. As he bounded over the gap between platforms, a stout, gray-haired woman appeared in the open door behind him and called, "George! George, stop!"

Smoke turned and grasped the boy's arm, stopping him without being too rough about it. "Whoa there, son. A train's sort of a dangerous place to be running around like that."

"Lemme go!" the boy cried. He was about ten years old, with reddish-brown hair and a scattering of freckles. He tried to pull away from Smoke's grip. "You got no right to hold me, you son of a bitch!"

"George!" The woman's eyes widened in horror as she came to a stop on the other platform.

Smoke's fingers tightened on the boy's arm, but not enough to actually hurt him. With a stern expression on his face, he said, "I know a fella up in Wyoming. Any time somebody calls him a bad name he says, 'When you call me that name . . . smile!' You're not smiling, son, so I'm liable to think you meant that seriouslike. I don't cotton much to that."

The youngster swallowed hard as he looked up at Smoke towering over him and seemed to figure out that maybe he should've watched what he'd said. "I'm sorry, mister," he managed to get out.

"Don't let it happen again." Smoke looked over at the woman. "Is this hombre supposed to be with you, ma'am?"

"Yes, and thank you for stopping him, sir. I was so afraid he was going to hurt himself." She was a well-dressed woman, probably in her fifties, with a few touches of what had once been lustrous brown hair among the gray under her stylish hat.

Smoke looked from her to the boy and back again and thought he saw a slight resemblance. "Your grandson, ma'am?"

"That's right. His name is George. George Bates. I'm Mrs. Violet Bates."

Smoke reached up and ticked a finger against the brim of his Stetson. "Smoke Jensen, at your service."

The name didn't seem to mean anything to her, which was all right with Smoke. He glanced at George, who seemed to be the sort of boy who read dime novels. Of course, *most* boys read dime novels . . . when they could get away with it. However, George didn't appear to recognize Smoke's name, either.

That was good. Smoke got tired of explaining to

folks that the dime novels about him were usually wildly exaggerated fantasies written by fellows who didn't know much about the frontier and rarely sobered up. A few of those scribblers knew what they were talking about, but they were the exceptions that proved the rule.

Smoke put those thoughts aside, frowned down at George, and put his hand on the boy's shoulder. "Now, why were you charging around like you had a pack of wolves chasing you?" He had been able to tell right away that George wasn't running because of the sheer exuberance of youth.

The boy had been running to get away from his grandmother.

"I want to go home! I don't wanna go to damn—I mean, darn—Tucson." George relaxed a little under Smoke's hand.

Mrs. Bates said, "George, I want you to stop talking like that right now. Such language is rude and unacceptable." She paused, and Smoke heard a considerable strain in her voice as she added, "Besides, you know perfectly well that we can't go back to Flagstaff."

"Ma'am, I don't mean to pry," Smoke said, "but if there's some sort of trouble—"

"Thank you, Mr. Jensen, but other than keeping George from hurting himself like you did, there's really nothing you can do. You see, my son and his wife . . . George's parents—"

"They're dead," the boy said.

Smoke felt a pang inside. Even as old as he was, he remembered his folks and how neither of them had come to a good end. "I'm sure sorry." He looked at the boy's grandmother again.

"They were both taken by a fever," Mrs. Bates said. "It happened fairly quickly, which I suppose is the only blessing about the whole thing. That and the fact that they had only one child—"

"Only one stinkin' orphan for you to take care of, right?" George said with his lips curling in a sneer that looked out of place on one so young.

"That's not what I meant and you know it. I'm just glad no one else has to suffer the sorrow and grief that you and I are going through." Mrs. Bates looked up at Smoke. "George and I, we're the only family that each of us has left."

"Well, at least you've got each other, ma'am," Smoke told her. "You're right. That's something to be thankful for."

"Oh, dear. Here we've gone on about our problems, and I haven't even thought to inquire about your trip, Mr. Jensen. Is it for business or pleasure?"

"Definitely pleasure," Smoke replied with a smile. "My wife and an old friend and I are on our way to Tucson to spend Christmas with some other members of my family."

"They live there?"

"Nope." He chuckled. "Jensens tend to wander around a lot. You could say I'm the only one who's put down roots. Tucson's just a handy spot for us to gather."

"Well, I hope you have a wonderful journey." Mrs. Bates held out her right hand. "Now, come along, George. We need to get back to our seats."

"But I don't want to go to Tucson," the boy protested. "That ain't where I live."

"It is now," Mrs. Bates said, her tone growing

firmer. "That's my home, and now it's yours as well, and nothing is going to change that."

"It will if I run away!"

Smoke tightened his grip again, just a little. "You don't want to do that, son. The world's a mighty lonely place for a fella on his own. I had to learn that the hard way, back in my earlier days. Besides, if you run off, it's going to make your grandmother mighty sad, and I can tell just by looking at her that she's a good woman. You wouldn't want to hurt her, would you? Hasn't she always treated you good?"

"Yeah, I guess," George said with obvious reluctance.

"And as sad as you are about your folks, I can promise you that you'll feel even worse if you're out there on your own. I learned that, too."

George cocked his head to the side and squinted up at Smoke. "You've had a lot of trouble in your life, mister?"

"More than my share. I try not to let it get me down because I've got the prettiest wife in the world, a couple of fine brothers, and the best bunch of friends any man could ever hope for. I tell you, sometimes I feel like the richest man in Colorado."

"You mean you've got a bunch of money, too?"

"You weren't paying close enough attention, George. Money doesn't mean a thing to a man who doesn't have loved ones and friends."

"You should listen to Mr. Jensen, George," Mrs. Bates said. "He sounds like a very wise man."

Smoke laughed. "I know some folks who would argue with you about that."

George shuffled his feet a little. "So you're goin' on to Tucson, too?"

"That's the plan," Smoke said.

"So I might see you again, here on the train."

"Sure. Come look me up any time you want to."

The youngster drew in a deep breath and blew it out. "All right. I'll go."

"And you won't give your grandmother any more trouble."

"I reckon not," George said, but he wore a dubious frown on his face that testified he wasn't sure about that.

Smoke squeezed his shoulder and gave him a little push toward the other car. George stepped across the gap. Mrs. Bates bent over and gave him a brief hug, which he accepted with a pained tolerance. "Thank you for your help, Mr. Jensen."

He tugged on his hat brim again. "Any time, ma'am." He turned and went back into the car.

As he sat down next to Sally, she looked over at him. "You were gone for quite a while. That must have been a pretty big breath of fresh air you took."

"I made a couple new friends out there on the platform and was talking to them," Smoke explained.

"And they didn't try to shoot you?" Preacher asked from across the aisle.

"I don't think they were even packing iron."

"Things is lookin' up then," the old mountain man said. "Just don't expect it to last."

CHAPTER 12

Avery Tuttle didn't look like a monster. He was a medium-sized man who tended to dress in plain gray suits. His squarish, clean-shaven face was topped by brown hair starting to go gray. From time to time, depending on what he was doing, he needed to wear spectacles, but he was just vain enough that he tried to avoid doing so in public.

He was wearing them at the moment to study several telegrams he had received from the territorial capital in Prescott. He had put them in the order he had received them, from the first to the most recent, then read them over again several times as he thought about his options. He was a deliberate man, Avery Tuttle was, and that was the secret to his success. Whenever a problem arose, instead of jumping right in, he considered all the possibilities. And he never took quick, violent action himself.

He paid men for that.

Having made up his mind, he set the telegrams

down on the desk in his office, took off the wire-rimmed spectacles, folded them, and put them in a drawer. Then he called through the open door, "Mrs. Perkins, come in here, please."

A moment later, Amy Perkins appeared in the doorway. Most businessmen who needed a secretary hired a man for the job, but Mrs. Perkins was every bit as efficient and competent as a male would have been. More so than a lot of men, Tuttle sometimes thought. And as a widow, she needed the job and was grateful for it.

The fact that she was stunningly beautiful was a bonus of sorts, he supposed, but truthfully, her looks didn't matter all that much to him. As long as she did her job, she could have been as plain as mud and he wouldn't have cared.

"Mrs. Perkins, send a boy to find Mr. Coe and tell him to come here as soon as possible."

"You want him to come here to the office?"

"That's right." A crisp edge came into Tuttle's voice as he added, "Did I not make that clear?"

"Yes, sir, of course," she said quickly. "I'll take care of it right away."

"Thank you." Tuttle looked back down at the papers on his desk, a signal that the conversation was over for the moment.

Mrs. Perkins wasn't in the habit of questioning his orders. He supposed she had done so because whenever he met with Smiler Coe, it was usually in his suite at the Territorial House. Coe didn't come to the office very often.

Maybe she was afraid of Coe. The gunman certainly provoked that reaction in a lot of people.

Tuttle put those thoughts out of his mind. That was another element of his success. Whenever he could do nothing about a situation, he simply didn't waste time and energy thinking about it. He concentrated on other matters.

He wasn't sure exactly how much time had passed when Coe sauntered into the private office without knocking. Tuttle found that annoying, but tolerated it because the gunman was so good at his job.

"I hear tell you want to see me, boss," the tall, lean gunman drawled. The habitual grin that had given him his nickname curved his mouth, revealing a single gold tooth.

With his build and his sharply angled face, Coe looked a little like an ax. He wore gray-striped trousers tucked into high boots, a dark green vest over a faded red shirt, and a flat-crowned black hat cocked at a rakish angle on his thick dark hair. He was one of those men who seemed to have beard stubble five minutes after shaving.

He was also a two-gun man, which was something of a rarity. A pair of gun belts crossed around his hips and supported twin holstered Colts with black, hard rubber butts.

Tuttle placed both hands flat on the desk and nodded toward the chair in front of the desk. "Please close the door and have a seat, Mr. Coe."

The gunman moved with a casual grace and ease, an indication that he could strike as swiftly and deadly as a snake. He shut the door, sat, cocked his right ankle on his left knee, and draped his left arm over the back of the chair. "What can I do for you?"

Tuttle tapped a blunt fingertip on the stack of

telegrams. "Thomas Ballard is proving to be a considerable thorn in my side."

"Some of the boys had a talk with him last week."

"And then returned later that night to beat his pressman, Edgar Torrance."

Coe's shoulders rose and fell slightly in a negligent shrug. "I wouldn't know anything about that."

Tuttle nodded. Both men were perfectly aware of what had happened to Torrance and everything else that went on in Tucson, but some things they didn't talk about. It was a way of keeping a barrier between Tuttle and the things that were done to benefit him.

"So what's Ballard done now?" Coe went on. "Seems like I heard a rumor he'd left town."

"Only temporarily."

"Yeah, I didn't figure he'd leave that pretty wife of his."

"He went up to Prescott to talk to the governor." Tuttle's distaste for that official was easy to hear in his voice.

"What's Ballard got to do with the governor?" Coe asked.

"He persuaded him to do a favor."

Coe squinted suspiciously. "A favor for who?"

"Certainly not for us. The governor used his influence to arrange for a large loan, put together from a number of sources. Ballard is on his way back here with the money. He intends to use it to prop up the businesses of several men who oppose me, including his own newspaper and the bank."

Coe put his right foot back on the floor and sat up straighter. "You say Ballard's bringing the money back here to Tucson? In cash?"

Tuttle nodded solemnly. "That's right."

"Why didn't he just have it transferred to the bank?"

"Because in the time he's been away, he couldn't be sure that I hadn't taken over the bank. He didn't want to take a chance on turning the money over to me."

Coe grunted. "Yeah, that would have scotched his plans good an' proper. But you *ain't* taken over the bank yet, and you probably won't if Ballard gets here with that cash."

Tuttle still had his hands flat on the desk, but the fingers of the right one drummed a little tattoo. "We're thinking along the same lines, I believe."

"Yeah." Coe's fingertips rasped over dark stubble as he stroked his chin. "Something needs to happen to that money before it gets here . . . and it wouldn't hurt if Ballard had some permanent bad luck along the way, too."

"I wouldn't even speculate on something like that," Tuttle said.

"No need for you to, boss." Coe stood up. "I'll do some thinking on it."

"Very well."

Coe had stopped smiling while they were talking, but he wore his usual grin as he left the office and closed the door behind him.

Tuttle leaned back in his chair, satisfied, at least for the moment. He wasn't sure what was going to happen to Tom Ballard . . . but whatever it was, the meddling fool had it coming.

Coe paused in the outer office, glanced at the

door he had just closed, and then turned to Amy Perkins. "I reckon you heard what he said?"

"Of course I heard," she replied. "Nobody listens through a door better than I do, Smiler. You know that."

He moved closer to her, cupped a hand under her chin, and leaned toward her as he murmured, "You do a lot of things better 'n anybody else, darlin'." He kissed her.

As their mouths worked together hungrily, she wrapped her arms around his neck. He reached up with his other hand and pulled them back down. Tuttle had no idea what was going on between his secretary and his chief gun-wolf, and Coe wanted to keep it that way. He could step away from Amy quickly if his keen ears heard the boss approaching on the other side of the door.

Amy was a little breathless as she broke the kiss and stepped back. Her black hair was pulled into a tight bun at the back of her head. When she took it loose and shook it free around her shoulders . . . when she peeled out of those staid, dark dresses she wore in the office . . . she was enough to make any man's heart gallop like a racehorse.

Coe wasn't sure he completely *trusted* her, but he sure was glad they had discovered how much they liked dallying with each other.

"What are you going to do?" Amy asked, keeping her voice low enough Tuttle wouldn't hear. "Ballard will be coming back to Tucson on the train. Are you going to stop it and kill him and take that money?"

"I don't see any need to go into detail—"

"I do." Her tone was sharp. "We're partners, Smiler.

I need to know what you've got in mind, so I can be prepared if there's any trouble."

"There won't be any trouble."

She was a persistent minx, always wanting to know his plans, acting like they were on equal footing. Sure, if the day ever came when he double-crossed Avery Tuttle, Amy's help would come in mighty handy. But Coe was confident he could handle things without her if he needed to. Still, he supposed it wouldn't hurt anything to humor her. Most men had been humoring her ever since she was twelve or so, he suspected.

"Holding up a train ain't as easy as it used to be," he went on. "All the railroad lines have gotten leery of bein' robbed and have put on extra guards, either men they've hired or some of those damn Pinkertons. It's a big job for half a dozen men."

"You can't wait until Ballard's back here with the money."

"I don't intend to," Coe said, suppressing his annoyance. "I'm gonna get Ballard—and that money—off the train."

Amy frowned and shook her head. "How do you intend to do that?"

"Ballard can't ride the train if the train ain't comin' through, now can he?"

"I thought you said you weren't going to stop the train."

"Not while he's on it. I'm going to make sure the train can't get here, and then Ballard will have to come back to Tucson some other way. I don't see a dude like him getting a saddle horse and a pack mule and setting out across country alone. That only leaves one way."

"The stagecoach," Amy said as understanding dawned in her brown eyes.

"The stagecoach," Coe repeated. His smile grew larger.

In those days when the railroads ran almost everywhere, the stagecoach lines that still existed were having a tougher and tougher time of it. The Saxon Stage Line was hanging on, though, running a circle route that included Tucson, as well as Casa Grande, Maricopa, Gila Bend, Ajo, and Sahuarita Ranch. If Coe could stop the railroad from getting through, then the stage would be Ballard's only way home.

With Christmas coming up soon, Coe was willing to bet that Ballard would risk making the journey that way. It would take longer and be a lot less comfortable, but he would put up with that in order to spend the holiday with his wife and kids.

And it would be a hell of a lot easier for six men to stop a stagecoach, kill a meddlesome newspaper editor, and steal a small fortune than it would be to hold up a train.

"It's a good idea," Amy said. "Can you keep the train from coming through?"

"If the trestle at Boneyard Wash is down, that'll do the trick. The train can't cross a wash without a bridge."

"You'd better move fast. According to those telegrams Tuttle got from Prescott, Ballard has already left the capital."

"I'll round up the boys and ride out right now."

She put a hand on his sleeve. "Be careful."

"Don't worry," Coe assured her. "There's no danger in this part of the job. All we've got to do is blow up a trestle." He stroked his chin again. "There was a flash flood in that wash a while back. If we do it right, maybe we can make it look like the flood damaged the trestle, and it just now collapsed. That won't be as likely to make anybody on that train suspicious when it can't get through."

"Dynamite can be tricky stuff."

"Sam Brant's worked with it before. For that matter, so have I. We'll get it down without blowin' ourselves to kingdom come."

"You'd better. Did Tuttle say anything about what you're supposed to do with the money Ballard's bringing back with him?"

"Not a word," Coe said.

"Then I expect most of it will wind up in our pockets." Amy began breathing a little harder at the thought.

His grin got a little bigger. "I wouldn't be a bit surprised."

CHAPTER 13

The sound of loud, angry voices made Smoke pause and look around. He was on the platform of the train station in Casa Grande, where he and Preacher had stepped out to stretch their legs while the train was stopped.

"What's all the commotion about?" Preacher asked.

Smoke shook his head as he looked at the knot of passengers gathering around the blue-uniformed figure of the train's conductor. "I don't know, but maybe we ought to go find out."

"Now, I know you folks are all upset and I don't blame you, but there's not a thing you or I can do about it," the conductor was saying as Smoke and Preacher walked up. "Until that trestle is repaired, this train's not going anywhere."

"What trestle?" Smoke asked.

The harried conductor looked over at him. "The one over Boneyard Wash. Blasted thing fell down.

The fella who reported it said it looked like it gave out because of some flood damage a while back."

Preacher said, "The flood was a while back, but the bridge is just now fallin' down?"

"I've known it to happen," the conductor said with a nod. "Sometimes those timbers will crack so you can't hardly see it. They hold up fine for a while, but eventually the weight of the trains passing over them makes the damage worse, and finally the whole thing just gives out."

A man in a dark suit and a gray felt hat said, "But I have to get back to Tucson! It could be after Christmas before that bridge is repaired."

"I expect it will be," the conductor admitted. "We ought to be rolling again before the new year comes around, though, Mr. Ballard. In the meantime, you can stay at the hotel here in Casa Grande, or we'll take you back up to Phoenix, no charge, and you can stay there—"

"You don't understand," Ballard said. "I have to get home *now*. As soon as possible."

The conductor shook his head. "Well, I'm afraid that's not going to be any time soon."

Angry muttering came from several of the passengers, but even though they were complaining, most seemed resigned to the unexpected delay. The man called Ballard was more upset than anyone else, Smoke thought.

A young woman stepped up to the conductor. "There has to be some other way. My fiancé will be waiting for me in Tucson, and when I don't arrive, he'll be very upset."

"I'm sure he'll understand, Miss Bradshaw."

"He might, but the army won't. He's a lieutenant, you see, and he can be away from his post for only so long." Her hands tightened on the small bag she held. "I'd hate for him to get in trouble if he waits too long for me."

"He won't get in trouble. We've already sent a wire to Tucson explaining what's happened. Your lieutenant will know not to expect you, so he can return to his duty and then come back to meet you later."

Miss Bradshaw sniffed. She wasn't happy with the arrangement, and she didn't care who knew it, Smoke thought.

"Reckon we'd best go tell Sally we're stuck here?" Preacher asked.

"Hold on a minute." Smoke didn't like the idea of Matt and Luke showing up in Tucson for Christmas, only to find that he, Sally, and Preacher weren't there after all. He wasn't going to disappoint his brothers if he could help it. "Is there any way around that collapsed trestle? An old spur line, maybe?" he asked the conductor as the crowd of annoyed passengers was starting to break up.

"No, sir, I'm afraid not. We've got a southbound line and a westbound line from here, but that's all." The conductor suddenly frowned. "But come to think of it, there *is* another way to get to Tucson."

"The stagecoach!" Ballard exclaimed.

"Yep," the conductor said, nodding. "I didn't think of it until just now. I reckon because it's our competition, sort of."

Smoke said, "The railroad has put most of the stage lines out of business, hasn't it?"

"That's right," Ballard said, "but a fellow named John Saxon started one of the first lines in Arizona Territory, back before the Civil War, and he's kept it going all this time. He runs his coaches to settlements where the railroad doesn't go, like Ajo and Sahuarita Ranch."

"The stage road parallels the railroad for part of the way," the conductor put in. "Don't know what the schedule is, but if the coach is somewhere between here and Gila Bend, you could take a westbound train and catch up to it there, then make the circle back around to Tucson." The blue-uniformed man shook his head. "That's a mighty long, dusty trip. Might be bearable this time of year, though I wouldn't want to try it during the summer. That'd be like catching the last stagecoach to Hell."

"I don't have a lot of choice," Ballard said. "I need to get back to Tucson just as soon as I can, not just because of Christmas with my family but—"

He stopped short as if he realized he was about to say too much, Smoke thought. But that was Ballard's business and none of his. He *was* interested in the idea of trying to catch up to the stagecoach, though. Smoke looked over at his companion. "What do you think, Preacher? Do you want to try to make it to Tucson on the stage?"

"I never cared much for them jouncin', bouncin' contraptions." Preacher's bony shoulders rose and fell. "But I'll go along with whatever you and Sally want, you know that."

Ballard said, "If you gentlemen would like to come along with me, I'm headed down to the stage line office to find out if it's even possible."

"I'll walk down there with you," Smoke said. "Preacher, do you mind going back and letting Sally know what's going on?"

"Sure," the old mountain man said. "She's prettier company than you two hombres."

Smoke and Ballard left the depot, with Ballard setting the course since he knew where the stage line office was located and Smoke didn't. As they walked along, the man introduced himself by saying, "I'm Tom Ballard, by the way, editor and publisher of the Tucson *Courier.*"

"Smoke Jensen."

Ballard didn't stop, but his stride had a little hitch in it as he looked over at his companion. "Smoke Jensen the famous gunfighter?" Before Smoke could answer, Ballard went on. "No, wait. It's not very likely there would be *another* Smoke Jensen, is it?"

Smoke wasn't surprised that Tom Ballard, being a newspaperman, had heard of him. He smiled. "You've got the right Smoke Jensen, Mr. Ballard. Or the wrong one, I guess, depending on how you look at it. Some folks tend to think I'm a mite on the notorious side."

"Not me. I've read quite a bit about you over the years, and nothing I've ever read has made me think you're less than an honorable man."

"I appreciate that. Not everybody feels that way."

"I'll bet they do if they take the time to learn anything about you. I seem to recall that you have one of the finest ranches in Colorado and are friends with some of the most influential men west of the Mississippi."

Smoke shrugged. It was true that if he'd wanted to, he could have sent a telegram directly to the president of the railroad they had been riding, but Smoke didn't see where that would accomplish anything. No matter what sort of influence was brought to bear, that collapsed trestle could be repaired only so fast.

They reached the stage line office, a small adobe building next to a pole corral and a barn. A sign hanging from the awning over the door read SAXON STAGE LINE.

"I believe this is the headquarters of the entire line," Ballard said. "Old John Saxon still runs this office himself."

They went inside and found a tall, spare, elderly man with a bald dome and a crisp white mustache leaning over a table with a map spread out on it. He looked up and greeted them by saying in a brisk, nononsense manner to Ballard, "I know you. You put out one of the newspapers down in Tucson."

"Yes, sir, that's right. I'm Tom Ballard of the *Courier*. This is Mr. Jensen."

Saxon shook hands with both of them and asked, "What can I do for you?"

"We were hoping you have a coach coming through here in the near future."

Saxon shook his head. "Afraid not. It left for Gila Bend a few hours ago, so you didn't miss it by much. Won't be another for four days."

"That's still better than waiting for the train," Smoke said to Ballard.

"But not good enough," the newspaperman said with a frown. "Mr. Saxon, I really need to catch up to that coach. If there's a westbound train today, that would beat it to Gila Bend, wouldn't it?"

"Should be able to," the stage line owner said with a puzzled look on his weather-beaten face. "Is it that important?"

"It is to me," Ballard said.

Once again, Smoke had the feeling that there was more to Ballard's eagerness to get back to Tucson than it appeared on the surface. He felt an instinctive liking for the man and wondered if Ballard was in some sort of trouble. That was one more reason Smoke leaned toward going along with the plan that was forming . . . not that he'd ever needed any excuse for doing what he wanted to do.

"I'd like to go ahead and buy a ticket, Mr. Saxon," Ballard continued. "That way there'll be no question about it when I get to Gila Bend."

"I reckon you can do that," Saxon said, nodding. "What about you, Mr. Jensen?"

"I'll need three tickets," Smoke said, going along with his instincts.

"Do you know if any other passengers will be in the coach?" Ballard asked.

"The only folks on board when the coach left here were bound for Gila Bend, so they'll be getting off there," Saxon said. "I couldn't tell you who might get on there. It's not likely you'll be too crowded, though. About half the time there aren't any passengers at all, but seeing as I've got the mail contract for Ajo and Sahuarita Ranch and those other little settlements down there, that's enough to keep me in business." He wrote up their tickets and gave to them. "Appreciate the business."

They paid him and he added, "Have a safe and pleasant trip." The old man chuckled. "Although that part about pleasant might be asking too much. We *are* talking about southern Arizona Territory, after all. It's not what you'd call the most scenic place on Earth."

"The only scenery I really care about seeing before Christmas is my home in Tucson," Ballard said.

CHAPTER 14

By the time Smoke and Ballard got back to the train station, Sally and Preacher were waiting on the platform with their bags.

"When Preacher told me where you had gone and what you were doing, I went and talked to the station manager right away," Sally said. "There's a west-bound train leaving for Gila Bend in less than an hour. I've already arranged for us to use our Tucson tickets on it."

Smoke laughed. "You don't waste any time, do you?"

She smiled sweetly at him. "Being married to you, darling, I've learned that when it's time to take action, it's best to do so quickly."

"Well, I can't argue with that," Smoke said.

Three more people were waiting nearby on the platform, also with their bags, and he recognized all of them. Mrs. Violet Bates smiled and nodded at him, while her grandson George sat next to her on a bench, still looking a little sullen. A few feet away on the same bench was the well-dressed young woman who had been arguing with the conductor earlier. Miss Bradshaw, he had called her, Smoke remembered.

He inclined his head slightly toward the trio and asked Sally, "What about these folks?"

"They've decided they're coming along on the stagecoach, too."

"I don't know if that's a good idea," Smoke said quietly. "A long stagecoach trip can be pretty rough."

"And yet you don't hesitate to take your wife on one."

"That's because I know living with me has toughened you up," he said with a smile.

"And *I* can't argue with *that*."

"I'll have a talk with them."

"It's their decision to make, Smoke."

"I know that. I just want to make sure they know what they'll be getting into."

He walked over to the bench, took off his hat, and nodded politely to Mrs. Bates and Miss Bradshaw. "My wife tells me you folks have decided to take the stagecoach to Tucson instead of waiting for the train to be able to get through."

"That's right, Mr. Jensen," Mrs. Bates said. "The conductor said we might be stuck here for days or even a week or more, waiting for that repair work to be done. I think it would be best to get George back to my home in Tucson as soon as possible."

The boy muttered, "It don't matter. I'll still be an orphan, wherever we are."

"Have you ever ridden on a stagecoach, ma'am?" Smoke asked Mrs. Bates.

"I most certainly have," she replied. "My late husband and I came to Arizona Territory on the old Butterfield Stage Line, many years ago."

"Then you know it'll be a long, rough, dusty ride from Gila Bend on around to Tucson. We'll be on the trail for several days, going that way."

"But at least we'll be making progress toward home, rather than just sitting and waiting."

Smoke sensed that there might be a core of steel underneath Mrs. Bates's placid exterior. She had made up her mind, and she wasn't the sort to be budged from a decision easily.

He turned to the young woman and said, "Miss, this is something you need to consider, too."

"I certainly have considered it," she told him with a little sniff in her voice. "And we haven't been properly introduced, sir."

Sally linked her right arm with Smoke's left and said, "I'm Sally Jensen, and this is my husband Smoke. And you are . . . ?"

"Miss Catherine Bradshaw," the young woman replied. "Soon to be Mrs. Harrison Preston."

"Congratulations," Sally said, smiling. "Is your fiancé with you?"

"He's meeting me in Tucson. He's a lieutenant in the army, and I'll be living at the fort where he's posted. That's why I simply must get to Tucson as soon as possible. Army regulations give Harrison only so much time to handle personal matters, you know."

Smoke thought about how the evidently spoiled, stuffy young woman from back east was going to take to living at a hot, dusty frontier fort while the threat of Apache raids still existed, although they weren't as common as in the past. He hoped Miss Catherine Bradshaw really loved Lieutenant Preston or they might be in for some difficulties.

Sally said, "I think my husband is just trying to make sure you understand—"

"I understand the situation quite well, Mrs. Jensen. Thank you."

Sally's expression didn't change much, but Smoke knew her well enough to recognize the signs of anger.

However, she was too much of a lady to give in to that emotion, so she smiled and said, "Very well, then. I'm sure you know best what you should do."

Ballard returned from talking to the conductor. He was followed by a porter wheeling a cart that held a medium-sized trunk with a carpetbag sitting on top. Since Ballard was traveling alone, Smoke wondered what he had in the trunk.

But again, it was none of his business.

As Ballard came up to the group, he frowned in the direction of Mrs. Bates, George, and Catherine Bradshaw. "What's this?" he asked Smoke.

"These folks heard you talking earlier and figured you'd come up with a good idea," Smoke explained. "They're going to take the stagecoach, too."

Ballard didn't look too happy about that, but he didn't try to convince the others they should wait for the train either in Casa Grande or in Phoenix. Smoke supposed Ballard might have thought that would be hypocritical, since he was obviously in such a hurry to get to Tucson himself.

All the arrangements were made for changing trains, so all the travelers had to do was wait for the call to board the westbound. That came soon enough. Their bags and Ballard's trunk were loaded.

As they started to climb onto one of the passenger cars, Mrs. Bates said, "Since we're all going to be together until we get to Tucson, perhaps we should start by sitting together now."

"That's a fine idea," Sally said. "It'll give us a chance to get to know each other better."

Hanging back a little with Smoke, Preacher said in a voice quiet enough that only Smoke could hear, "By the time we get to Tucson, I reckon these pilgrims may know each other a mite better than any of 'em expected."

As he thought about the cramped quarters inside a bouncing, jolting stagecoach, Smoke could only agree.

The whole scheme hinged on making it to Gila Bend before the stagecoach did. If the travelers failed to do that, they would have to turn around, return to Casa Grande, and wait for the train to be able to make it through.

So as soon as the westbound pulled into the station at Gila Bend, Smoke and Ballard hurried to find the local office of the Saxon Stage Line.

Preacher went with them, saying, "You ain't leavin' me back there in that hen party. That Bates woman can talk a mile a minute when she gets wound up."

"I'm sure Mrs. Bates is disappointed that you're not hanging around, Preacher," Smoke said with a grin. "She seemed to be eyeing you pretty thoroughly during the trip from Casa Grande, and I don't think she was disappointed in what she saw."

Preacher let out an explosive grunt of scorn and derision. "That'll be the day!" he exclaimed.

One of the citizens of Gila Bend was able to direct them right to the stage line office. They found a short, plump, mostly bald man with the face of a cherub working there.

The man introduced himself. "Emile Collier, gentlemen. What can I do for you?"

"Has the stage from Casa Grande been through here yet?" Smoke asked.

"Why, no," Collier replied. "I'm not expecting it for another couple hours."

Ballard let out a relieved sigh. "That's good. We'll be traveling on it."

"Just you three fellows?"

Smoke said, "No, there are three ladies and a boy with us. Two of the ladies and the youngster will need tickets." When Collier pursed his lips, Smoke went on. "That's not going to be a problem, is it?"

"No, no, not at all. There'll be room for all of you. As of right now, there are no other passengers bound for Ajo. But I can't guarantee that situation will remain the same."

"Reckon you'll crowd us all in like sardines if you have to," Preacher said.

"Well, we'd certainly prefer not to have the coach be too crowded . . . but at the same time, the line can't really afford to turn down paying customers."

Ballard said, "As long as there's room in the boot for my bags, I don't care how crowded I am inside the coach."

"There should be plenty of room," Collier assured him. "Where are your things now?"

"At the train station. We can get porters to bring them down here."

"I suggest you do that, then. Scratchy Stevenson is at the reins on this run, and he doesn't like to waste any more time during the stops than he has to."

"Scratchy, eh?" Smoke said. "Sounds like some jehus I've known. They're pretty rough-edged sorts."

"He's a bit of a character, all right," Collier agreed. "I think you can safely say that Scratchy has his share of rough edges."

The three men went back to the depot to see to having the baggage transported to the stagecoach station. The women were going to a nearby café for a meal before the next leg of the journey began.

Smoke saw that George still wore his usual sullen expression and said to Mrs. Bates, "How about letting George help out me and the other fellas for a while?"

"Oh, I don't know if that would be a good idea, Mr. Jensen." Mrs. Bates lowered her voice to a conspiratorial tone, but Smoke had a hunch George could still hear her. "He can be a real handful when he wants to be, you know."

"He'll do fine," Smoke said. "If you're worried about him running off, I don't reckon you have to. I'll keep an eye on him. I've got a hunch he won't give me any trouble."

Mrs. Bates still didn't look convinced, but she turned to her grandson. "George, would you like to go along with Mr. Jensen and Mr. Ballard and Mr. Preacher? They're going to see to it that our bags are taken to the stagecoach station."

The old mountain man grimaced at being called

"Mr. Preacher," Smoke noticed, but he held his tongue.

George seemed to perk up a little. "What would I have to do?" he asked Smoke.

"Maybe carry a bag. The porters will take most of it, but we can tote some of the smaller stuff."

Clearly not wanting to appear too eager, George put on a show of indifference. "I guess I can do that."

"Come on, then," Smoke said with a wave of his hand.

"Time's a-wastin'," Preacher added.

Smoke picked out a small bag of his to let George carry, while he took a larger valise. Preacher just had his old war bag, which he toted himself. Sally had brought along enough that a porter and a cart were required to transport those bags.

The same was true for Catherine Bradshaw. Mrs. Bates and George had little enough that it could be added to the cart with Catherine's things. Ballard supervised as a porter loaded his trunk and carpetbag onto a cart.

Preacher narrowed his eyes and said quietly to Smoke, "He's mighty particular about how that trunk's handled. He's watchin' it like there's somethin' mighty important to him inside it."

"I noticed the same thing," Smoke said.

Preacher scratched his grizzled jaw. "You reckon it's anything that might attract some trouble?"

"I don't know, but if it is, there'll be plenty of chances for it between here and Tucson."

CHAPTER 15

Once all the bags were at the stage station, Smoke and Preacher figured they would go over to the café and join the ladies.

When Smoke said as much, Tom Ballard told them, "You fellows go ahead. I'll stay here, just to make sure the stage doesn't arrive without us being aware of it."

Smoke thought that was pretty unlikely, considering the café was just in the next block and a stagecoach made quite a bit of racket when it rolled into town. He figured a more plausible explanation was that Ballard was getting nervous about leaving that trunk unattended and didn't want to do so anymore.

Emile Collier, the manager of the local station, piped up. "I can send a boy to fetch you when the stage gets here if you want, Mr. Ballard—"

"No, that's all right." Ballard sat down in a ladder-back chair on the station's porch, not far from the stack of bags and trunks, including his. "I'll be fine right here."

As Smoke and Preacher strolled toward the café and George ran on ahead out of earshot, Preacher grunted. "Now *that* ain't suspicious at all. Ballard's got somethin' in that trunk he don't want nobody else knowin' about nor gettin' their hands on. I figure it's got to be either a heap o' money . . . or a carcass."

Smoke glanced over at him. "You mean a dead body? A human body?"

"Well, think about it. Say he killed somebody back up the line, wherever he got on the train, and he don't want the carcass to be discovered 'cause that'll get him hung." The old mountain man gestured animatedly. "So what he does, you see, is he wraps it up in somethin' . . . shoot, maybe he even chops it up into pieces first . . . and then he packs it in that trunk and brings it with him. If nobody finds the body, the law can't get after him for the killin', now can it?"

"Wouldn't it have started to stink by now?"

"Maybe not, if he salted it down real good 'fore he wrapped it up."

"So the newspaper editor is traveling with a trunk full of salted human carcass."

"I ain't sayin' he is or he ain't," Preacher declared. "I'm just sayin' that'd be one reason why he wouldn't want nobody a-messin' with that trunk o' his."

"Well, I don't suppose anybody could argue with that. I don't reckon we ought to be discussing it around the ladies, though."

"No, most likely not. Don't reckon it'd bother Sally all that much. She'll do to ride the river with, that gal, and I've seen her handle a gun and fight like a man. Them other two, though, they could be a mite persnickety about such things."

They went into the café and found George already sitting at a long table with Sally, Mrs. Bates, and Catherine Bradshaw.

Mrs. Bates said, "I hope George was helpful and behaved himself, Mr. Jensen."

"He was a big help," Smoke said, smiling as he took off his hat and set it on the table, which had bench seats running along it on both sides and no cloth covering it. Gila Bend was a good-sized settlement, but it wasn't a fancy one. Life in southern Arizona was too rugged for many frills.

Smoke and Preacher sat down. A pot of stew had been set on the table, along with some empty bowls. The women had already eaten, and George was tucking into a bowl of stew with the gusto of youth. Smoke filled a couple bowls, handed one to Preacher, and kept one for himself.

"Where is Mr. Ballard?" Mrs. Bates asked. "Isn't he joining us?"

"He's over at the station, waiting for the coach to come in," Smoke explained. "He didn't want us to miss it."

Preacher's knee nudged his, and the old-timer chuckled. Smoke didn't acknowledge it, but he knew Preacher was thinking about the gruesome conversation they'd had on the way to the café.

"I wonder if I should take him a bowl of stew," Mrs. Bates said. "He's going to get awfully hungry if he doesn't eat something before we leave. We don't really know when we'll have another meal, do we?"

"Most of the stage stops keep a pot of beans on the

stove," Smoke said, "and there's usually a mess of cornbread, too. It's pretty simple fare, and how good the food is depends on who fixed it, but you won't starve eating at way stations."

"Well, that's good to know. I believe I'll take Mr. Ballard some stew, anyway."

"Make sure you get some o' that salted meat in it," Preacher said.

The entire group had moved back to the station to wait. The stagecoach was a little behind schedule, just enough for Emile Collier to make a worried comment about it. Ballard was tense, Catherine was impatient, and Mrs. Bates fretted.

George sat with Preacher on the porch steps.

"You ever done any whittlin'?" the old mountain man asked the boy.

"Sure," George replied. "Everybody's whittled."

"Well, 'most ever'body, I reckon. You'd be surprised, though. There's prob'ly younkers back east who ain't never had a whittlin' knife in their hand." Preacher reached into his war bag, which was on the step beside him, and drew out a bowie knife in a fringed sheath. As he slid the razor-sharp blade out of leather, he added, "Like this here."

George's eyes grew wide at the sight of the bowie, which glittered in the sunlight. "Can I hold it?" he exclaimed.

"Sure, I don't see why—"

"George!" Mrs. Bates said. "Don't touch that . . . that weapon. Mr. Preacher, please put that away."

"It's just a knife, Grandma," George protested. "I've handled knives before."

"Not like that. That's the sort of knife that might be used to . . . to . . ."

Smoke and Sally were sitting in rocking chairs at the other end of the porch. Smoke knew Mrs. Bates was about to say Preacher's bowie was the sort of knife that might be used to kill somebody. In Preacher's case there was no *might* about it. That blade had drunk deeply of many an enemy's blood.

Smoke didn't figure Mrs. Bates would appreciate her grandson hearing the details, though. "That knife's too big for whittling, Preacher. You could chop down trees and make a raft with that thing."

"Come to think of it, I believe I did just that one time." Preacher slipped the bowie back in its sheath, replaced it in the war bag, and went on to George. "I got a good whittlin' knife stuck in there somewhere. I'll dig it out and show you some tricks later on. Right now, though"—he nodded toward the eastern end of the street—"I reckon the stagecoach is comin'."

Smoke saw the clouds of dust rising outside the settlement and knew Preacher was right. It took a team of eight horses and the four wheels of a stagecoach to kick up those thick columns.

Having heard Preacher, Emile Collier emerged from the building with a look of satisfaction on his face. "Finally! Of course, minor delays are to be expected now and then, so I'm sure this one is nothing to worry about."

A minute later, Smoke heard the thunder of hoofbeats, the rattle of wheels, and the creaking of the broad leather thoroughbraces that ran underneath the coach and supported it. He had ridden many stagecoaches before, so it was a familiar melody to his ears.

As the vehicle approached, it almost appeared to be out of control, careening along the street like it was. But the burly driver worked magic with the reins and shouted to the team, and the coach came to a smooth, perfect stop right in front of the station.

As the slight breeze carried the dust away, the jehu called, "Sorry we're a mite late, Emile. Had to do some harness repair whilst we were stopped at Hendricks Station."

"That's all right, Scratchy," Collier said.

The driver thumbed his hat back on thinning, salt-and-pepper hair that matched his close-cropped beard and looked at the people gathered on the porch. "Are all these folks passengers?" He nudged the bigger, younger man sitting beside him and added, "Looks like we're gonna be full up, Mike."

"I reckon." Mike had the butt of a coach gun propped against his right hip with the twin barrels sticking almost straight up.

Smoke wondered if a shotgun guard rode the coach regularly. It seemed possible, since the route went through mining country and from time to time the stagecoach would be carrying payrolls or silver ore.

Hostlers hurried from the barn to unhitch the team and replace it with a fresh bunch of horses. The driver and the guard climbed down from the box. Both men wore long dusters. The driver was middle-aged, while the guard was around twenty-five, Smoke thought, a big young man with a thatch of blond hair under his hat and a holstered Colt on his hip.

The coach door swung open and a couple men climbed out. Judging by the friendly way they spoke to Collier, they were local businessmen. They got their bags from the boot at the back of the stage after Mike pulled aside its canvas cover, then they walked off to wherever they were bound.

"These folks are going with you all the way to Tucson," Collier said as he nodded toward Smoke and the others.

"It's been a fair spell since we had this many passengers," Scratchy said.

"The railroad bridge over Boneyard Wash is down," Collier explained. "They need to get where they're going quicker than the railroad can repair the trestle."

Scratchy nodded. "That makes sense." He faced the travelers. "Mike and me will get you there, folks. Put your bags back yonder in the boot and we'll be ready to roll soon's we get a fresh team hitched up."

Ballard said, "If someone could give me a hand with this trunk . . ."

"I'll do it." Smoke bent down and grasped the handle at one end of the trunk before the shotgun guard, Mike, could step forward and volunteer.

Ballard took the handle at the other end. The two men had no trouble lifting the trunk, although it was fairly heavy. Smoke couldn't really tell from the feel of it what was inside, though.

Deprived of the opportunity to help with the trunk, Mike turned to Catherine Bradshaw. "Let me get your bags, ma'am."

"Thank you," she said rather stiffly and without looking at him.

Mike didn't seem offended by her coolness. He took her bags to the back of the coach and fitted them in with Ballard's trunk, which would ride on the bottom since it was the largest and heaviest piece of baggage.

Everything else was placed in the boot, after which Mike drew the canvas cover back over it and tied it down. He and Scratchy went into the station to grab a quick cup of coffee before they pushed on.

Smoke turned to Collier. "Who's the guard?" He liked to know who he was going to be traveling with.

"Mike Olmsted," the station manager said. "Comes from a ranching family that has a spread over west of here. Mike never really took to cowboying, though. He was a deputy marshal up at Wickenburg for a while, then started riding shotgun for the Saxon Line a couple years ago. Good solid young man. He can handle any trouble you might encounter."

Preacher grunted, and Smoke knew what the old mountain man was thinking. With the two of them along, Mike Olmsted would have plenty of help if they ran into any problems along the way.

Smoke, Sally, and Preacher took the backward-facing seat in the front, with Sally in the middle between the two men. Tom Ballard was next to the left-hand window on the other seat, directly opposite Smoke. Mrs. Bates was next to him, with Catherine on the right. George perched on the bench between the two seats.

"I could ride on top," he suggested. "See better from up there."

"I don't think so," his grandmother said. "You'd get pitched right off and break your neck."

"Aw, Grandma—"

"Don't 'Aw, Grandma' me. I'm just looking out for your well-being."

George sulked up again. Smoke might have tried to kid him out of the bad mood, but by that time Scratchy and Mike had finished their coffee. They emerged from the station and climbed onto the box.

Scratchy took up the reins. "Last call for anybody who don't want to get their innards shook up!" When none of the people inside the coach responded, he chuckled, popped his whip above the heads of the team, slapped the reins against their backs, and sent the stagecoach rolling out of Gila Bend, bound for Ajo.

CHAPTER 16

Bored of the card game they'd been playing, Smiler Coe, Nelse Andersen, Phil Deere, and Sam Brant sat around a table in the back room of a Tucson saloon passing around a bottle of whiskey, smoking, and talking quietly about their success the night before.

Brant had done most of the work, rigging the dynamite at the top so when it went off, the blasts would weaken some of the thick beams holding up the trestle. To make it look like the damage had been caused by a powerful flash flood that swept through the dry wash once or twice a year, Coe had instructed Brant to keep the blasts small, using as little dynamite as he could get away with.

Once the beams were weakened, Coe's men had tied ropes around them and used the horses to pull them loose. As the beams toppled, the weight of the trestle was too much for the remaining supports. The whole thing had come crashing down, and the wreckage was extensive enough that Coe believed no one would ever be able to tell some of it was man-made. It looked like a natural collapse due to damage done by the flood.

Satisfied, Coe and the other gunmen had returned to Tucson.

In the saloon, they were waiting until it was time to launch the next step in the plan.

Coe glanced at the rolled-up piece of paper on the table not far from his elbow. Amy Perkins had given it to him earlier. It was a map of the circular route the Saxon Stage Line followed, with all the way stations between the settlements marked.

The door to the back room opened and several of Avery Tuttle's men stepped into the saloon. Avery Tuttle owned the saloon—although it wasn't his name on the deed, but that of the man who ran the place—so it wasn't unusual.

The man in the forefront of the group was a dark-faced hombre known as Caddo. Nobody was sure if he had any Indian blood to justify the nickname, and he was proddy enough that no one much cared to ask him. He nodded to Coe. "All right, Smiler, we're here. What's the next job you've got for us?"

Coe threw back the inch or so of whiskey left in his glass, then licked his lips. "Ah." He set the glass aside, reached for the map, and unrolled it "All right, boys, gather around here." He drew his left-hand gun and set it on one side of the map to keep it from rolling up again, then weighted down the opposite corners with his empty shot glass and another one.

With a long forefinger, he started pointing out the

way stations along the stagecoach's route. "I want one of you boys at each of these stations. Your job is to wait for that stagecoach to show up and make sure Tom Ballard is on it. When you see he is, you hurry it back here and let me know. No way of telling exactly how far along that coach is, so we're gonna have to cover as many stations as we can."

"What's so important about Ballard?" Caddo asked. "He just puts out a stinkin' newspaper."

Coe hadn't told any of the others about the money Ballard was bringing back to Tucson with him. Not even his most trusted lieutenants, Andersen, Deere, and Brant. That secrecy was the best way of ensuring that most of the loot wound up with him. Tuttle didn't really need the money; he just wanted to keep it out of the hands of those who opposed his iron-fisted rule. Coe didn't mind spreading around a little of it, but the lion's share was going to wind up in his pocket.

Well, his and Amy's, he supposed. Unless he decided to take the loot and head for Mexico. The border wasn't far away, and while the señoritas down there might not be as pretty as Amy, they were every bit as willing and eager to please a man with plenty of *dinero*.

"Don't worry about why Ballard's important," Coe answered Caddo's question. His sharp tone indicated that he wasn't going to put up with any argument. "All you need to know is how to get back here in a hurry once you've spotted him."

"Fine," Caddo said, scowling at the reprimand. It wasn't enough to make him push Smiler Coe. None of that bunch was going to do that. As tough and fast as they were, Coe was tougher and faster. "You care which one of us heads for which station?"

"Take your pick," Coe said with a casual wave of his hand.

The gun-wolves gathered around the table and quickly split up the assignments.

That settled, Coe told them, "Pick up some supplies and head out right away."

Caddo frowned again. "It's late enough in the afternoon that'll mean ridin' at night. Can't it wait until morning?"

"No, it can't," Coe snapped. "If that stage was to slip by us somehow and Ballard makes it back to Tucson, there'll be hell to pay."

"All right, all right," Caddo groused. "If it's that important." He jerked his head toward the door. "Come on, boys."

When the others had all filed out and the door was closed again, the pale-faced Nelse Andersen said to Coe, "You're gonna have to kill that Injun-looking son of a bitch someday, Smiler."

"Yeah, I know." The customary vicious smile creased Coe's lean face. "And I'm looking forward to it."

It didn't take long for Preacher to start complaining about the stagecoach. "I swear, I don't know how come I let you talk me into this, Smoke," the old mountain man said as he swayed a little back and forth. "This here seat is so hard, and the coach bounces so much, I reckon by the time we get to Tucson, what few teeth I got left will all be shook right outta my mouth!"

"You still have all your teeth, don't you?" Smoke said.

"Well, that don't mean I can afford to lose any of 'em for no good reason. If I didn't want to get there and see ol' Lije Connolly, and if it wasn't Christmas and Matt and Luke might be there, you'd never catch me ridin' in one o' these bone-jarrin' contraptions!"

From the seat facing them, Mrs. Bates asked, "Do you have a friend living in Tucson, Mr. Preacher?"

The old mountain man winced. "Beggin' your pardon, ma'am, but it'd be plumb fine if you'd just call me Preacher."

"But that seems disrespectful."

"No such thing. I been called just plain ol' Preacher for so many years I've pert near forgot what my handle used to be 'fore that."

"You don't look like any preacher I ever saw," George said.

"George, don't be rude," his grandmother admonished him.

"The youngun's right. Nobody'd ever take me for a real sky pilot. And I never claimed to be."

"Then how come they call you Preacher?" George asked.

"Well, you see, a long time ago, a little more 'n seventy years ago, in fact, I went west to see me some mountains and do a mite o' fur trappin'. That weren't long after me and ol' Andy Jackson got in a scrape with a heap o' them British redcoats down yonder in New Orleans."

Ballard said, "You were at the Battle of New Orleans?"

"Yep, I sure was. Quite a tussle, too. But we whipped them bloody British and sent 'em runnin' off through the briars and the brambles just as fast as they could go.

"I done got sidetracked, though. I was tellin' the boy how I come to be called Preacher. Back then, ever'body knowed me as Art, 'cause of my real name bein' Arthur."

"I thought you didn't remember your real name," George said.

"Well, that part of it come back to me. Just don't ask me about the rest of it, 'cause I disremember." Preacher leaned forward, caught up in his story-telling, which made him forget to complain for the moment. "So there I was in the Shinin' Mountains— that's what we called the Rockies back in them days— and I made me some friends amongst the other trappers . . . a few amongst the Injuns, too. But one bunch o' redskins didn't have no use for me atall, and I didn't have no use for them, neither. Them were the Blackfeet."

Mrs. Bates said, "Is this going to be a very violent story, Mister—I mean, Preacher?"

The old mountain man rubbed his chin. "Well, not as violent as it coulda been, but that's sorta the point of the whole story."

"Let him tell it, Grandma," George urged.

Mrs. Bates sighed and nodded. "Go ahead. I just hope it doesn't give you nightmares, George."

"It won't." The boy turned back to Preacher. "What about the Blackfeet?"

"They was a pretty mean bunch, at least where I

was concerned. Fact of the matter is, they wanted to kill me."

The Blackfeet had had good reason to hate and fear Preacher, Smoke reflected. Preacher had killed untold numbers of them, usually in battle. But he had also been known to creep into Blackfoot camps at night and slit the throats of half a dozen warriors, sending them on to the spirit world without ever waking them. And then he would sneak back out, with no one in the camp aware that he had been there until they made the grisly discoveries in the morning.

Those lethal, nocturnal raids had led the Blackfeet to dub Preacher the Ghost Killer. Some called him the White Wolf, thinking that he had to be some sort of supernatural, animalistic creature to carry out those deadly errands.

Smoke hoped Preacher wouldn't go into those particular details. If he did, Mrs. Bates might be too spooked to even ride in the coach with the old mountain man.

Preacher did skip over that part. "So when a bunch of those varmints grabbed me one time, I figured I was done for. A plumb goner. That seemed even more likely when they tied me up to a stake. Come mornin', they planned to heap up some wood around my feet and set it on fire."

"They were going to burn you alive?" George exclaimed.

"Oh, dear!" Mrs. Bates said.

Catherine Bradshaw looked like she found the whole conversation crude and distasteful.

"What did you do?" George asked. "You must've escaped somehow, since you're here now."

"I wouldn't exactly say that I escaped. You see, back in St. Louis, 'fore I ever went off to the mountains, I saw a fella standin' on one of the street corners a-preachin'. He could really sling them words around, and it didn't seem like he ever got tired. He just kept goin'. Seemed plumb loco to me." Preacher paused, then continued. "But that got me to thinkin'. You see, Injuns don't like to kill a fella if they think he ain't right in the head. They believe that the Great Spirit watches over folks like that, and if they hurt 'em, then the Great Spirit's liable to have a grudge against *them.*"

"Those are heathens you're talking about," Mrs. Bates said. "You can't put any stock in their so-called beliefs."

"Well, I ain't arguin' that one way or the other, ma'am," Preacher said. "The only thing important to me at the time was that they believed it. So I figured if I could make 'em think *I* was loco, they might decide not to kill me. Seemed like the best way to do that was to preach at them, the same as that fella I seen back in St. Louis.

"So I started in a-preachin', and I just let them words flow, never worryin' too much about what I was sayin', just keepin' it up without stoppin' 'cept to take a breath ever' now and then. It got dark, and I kept preachin'. The Blackfeet gathered around to look at me, and I could tell they was startin' to wonder if I was crazy. I kept on all night, just a-preachin' away, and by mornin' they was plumb sure I'd lost my mind. Their war chief, who hated me particularlike, wanted to go ahead and burn me anyway, but the rest of 'em wouldn't go along with it. They turned me loose, and since there was a bunch o' them and only one o' me, and since they'd took all my guns and knives and tomahawks away from me, I run off through the woods, still hollerin' whilst I skedaddled. They didn't come after me." Preacher paused again. "Some of 'em mighta had reason to regret that later."

Thankfully, he didn't elaborate on that, either.

"Once word got around about what had happened," the old mountain man went on, "some o' my pards started callin' me Preacher, and the name stuck. I ain't answered to nothin' else for a long time now . . . that's why I ain't *Mister* Preacher."

"That's a great story," George said. "I'll bet you know a bunch more."

"I might. We got a long ride in front of us. I reckon I could spin a few more yarns, like the one about the time when I run into these fellas who dressed and acted like ancient Romans, like the ones you read about in the history books."

Smoke had heard that story. He hoped Preacher would have the good sense to clean it up some if he told it.

The stagecoach rolled on through the late afternoon.

CHAPTER 17

The stagecoach stopped only once to change teams between Gila Bend and Ajo. By then it was pretty late in the afternoon, but Scratchy Stevenson told the passengers they would continue on to the settlement, arriving there after dark. "We'll be stoppin' there for supper and to let you folks get some rest. Then we'll roll on first thing in the mornin'."

Smoke had ridden some stagecoaches that continued on through the night, but in those cases the company had plenty of drivers and could switch them out with almost the same frequency that they switched teams. The Saxon Stage Line, barely hanging on like it was, couldn't afford that luxury. Scratchy and Mike would make the entire run to Tucson, where another driver and guard would take over. They couldn't keep going around the clock, so rest stops had to be taken.

Night fell with its usual suddenness. The moon hadn't risen yet, but Scratchy knew the trail well enough that he was able to drive by starlight without any trouble. It helped that the landscape was mostly flat and the stage road ran straight.

After a while, Smoke saw lights appear ahead and knew the coach was approaching Ajo. The last time he had been through those parts, the place had been a mostly abandoned mining camp.

Since then, several copper strikes had caused the place to grow by leaps and bounds. Some of the richest veins of copper in the whole country could be found in the area, and as the mines grew, so did the need for stores, restaurants . . . and the less savory elements that followed any boom.

"Comin' in to Ajo, folks!" Scratchy called as he wheeled the coach past the adobe huts on the outskirts of the settlement. Most of the buildings in Ajo were made of adobe, although a few frame buildings had been put up. As the coach rolled past, Smoke noted a bank made of brick, evidently the only such structure in town.

Scratchy brought the stagecoach to a stop in front of the line's local office, which was one of those few frame buildings.

"Thank God," Catherine Bradshaw murmured. "I was beginning to think this day was never going to end."

"The trip will start again early in the morning," Ballard told her. "You'd better try to get some good rest tonight."

"I will. Although I'm not sure where in a place like this."

"There's a hotel across the street," Sally said. "It doesn't look too bad."

The building in question was a sprawling, one-story adobe with the simple legend HOTEL written across its front window in an arch of letters.

Smoke opened the coach door without waiting for Scratchy or Mike to do it and stepped out, then turned back to help Sally down from the vehicle. Catherine came next, then Mrs. Bates.

Earlier, George had gotten sleepy and stretched out on the bench in the middle of the coach.

Preacher leaned forward. "Little fella's sound asleep, ma'am. I'll gather him up and hand him out to Smoke."

"Thank you, Preacher," Mrs. Bates said. "And not just for helping with George. Your stories helped pass the time. They were certainly, ah . . . colorful."

"Yes'm, I reckon you could say I've had a colorful life." The old mountain man got his arms around George, lifted him, and passed the boy out into Smoke's waiting arms.

"I'll carry him over to the hotel for you, ma'am."

Preacher climbed out next, leaving Tom Ballard to emerge from the coach last. The newspaperman cast a glance toward the boot at the back of the stagecoach.

He was reluctant to leave that trunk, Smoke thought, but he didn't want to call attention to it by making a fuss about it.

Mike Olmsted hopped down from the driver's box and stood with the short-barreled shotgun tucked under his arm. "Don't worry about your bags and other gear, folks. The coach'll be parked inside the barn, and Scratchy and I will be sleepin' in there, too. Nobody'll bother your things. You got my word on that."

Smoke wasn't sure that would be enough to reassure Ballard, but it seemed to be the best the newspaperman would do.

Ballard brought up the rear as they all headed for the hotel. He looked back over his shoulder a couple times as he followed the others. They went into the hotel to find a short, chubby Mexican man with a ready smile standing behind a counter in the lobby.

"Welcome to the Ajo Hotel, señors and señores," he greeted them. "I am Hector Gonzalez, the proprietor of this fine establishment. We offer special rates to passengers of the Saxon Stage Line, thanks to an arrangement between myself and Señor Saxon."

"We'll need five rooms." Smoke still had George cradled against his shoulder. The boy hadn't budged. He wasn't light, but Smoke's great strength allowed him to carry George as if the youngster weighed almost nothing.

"Could get by with four," Preacher said. "Me and Tom could bunk together."

"We have plenty of rooms," Gonzalez said. "Whatever you prefer is fine with me."

"I, uh, think I'd like to have my own room." Ballard glanced at the old mountain man. "No offense, Preacher."

"None taken. That way I don't have to worry about you snorin'."

Smoke chuckled. "I think you're the one who dodged that particular bullet, Tom."

Arrangements were soon completed. Gonzalez

waved the guests toward the arched entrance of a hallway and told them that their rooms were located along the corridor. "And there is food and coffee in the hotel dining room. Only tortillas and frijoles and beef, but after a long day, it will be filling."

Catherine looked like she found the idea distasteful, but whether or not she ate would be up to her.

"I can't wait," Sally said. "I'm hungry."

Mrs. Bates held her arms out for George. "Give him to me, Mr. Jensen. I'll take him and put him to bed. Once he goes sound asleep like that, you're doing good to wake him in less than twelve hours."

After Smoke handed George over to his grandmother, he, Sally, Preacher, and Ballard went into the dining room. Catherine said she was more tired than hungry and went the other way from the lobby.

An attractive middle-aged woman who told them she was Señora Gonzalez was waiting for them in the dining room. She soon had cups of coffee and plates of food in front of them.

The meal was simple but filling, as Hector Gonzalez had promised, and the coffee was excellent. As they ate, Tom Ballard seemed to relax a little, but Smoke still caught him glancing in the direction of the stagecoach station from time to time.

They were just finishing up with supper when Smoke heard the hotel's front door open. Several sets of heavy footsteps clomped in, accompanied by raised voices. The men who had just entered the hotel weren't shouting, but they were definitely arguing.

Three figures came through the arch into the dining room. Smoke recognized two of them immediately—Scratchy Stevenson and Mike Olmsted.

The third man was a barrel-chested hombre with a shock of white hair and a bushy mustache of the same shade. He was saying, "It's loco, I tell you, and you fellas ought to know that!"

"Won't be the first time in my life I've done something loco," Scratchy responded, "and it probably won't be the last!"

"I wouldn't be so dang sure of that!" The white-haired man stalked past Scratchy and Mike and came straight toward the table where Smoke and his companions were sitting, the only table in the dining room that was currently occupied.

Smoke and Preacher had both tensed, preparing for trouble. As far as Smoke could see, the stranger wasn't armed, just upset.

"You folks are the passengers from the stage?" he asked.

"Most of them," Smoke replied. "A couple ladies and a youngster went to their rooms."

"My name's Jack Cordell, and I run the stage station here in Ajo. I got some bad news for you. The coach ain't goin' on to Tucson."

"What!" Any relaxation Ballard might have achieved vanished in an instant. "That's impossible. The coach has to go on!"

"Not on my say-so, it ain't. Too dangerous. The Apaches are out!"

"You don't know that, Jack," Scratchy drawled. "You got some rumors floatin' around, that's all."

"It wasn't rumors that burned that supply wagon down by the Santa Cordelia mine."

"That's a good ways south of here, nearly clear down to the border," Scratchy argued. "And you don't know for sure what happened. The men who were with that wagon disappeared, didn't they? For all you know, they stole everything valuable and burned the rest so nobody would know what they'd done."

Cordell blew out an explosive, obviously disgusted breath. "You know good and well the reason those fellas vanished is because the 'Paches drug 'em off to torture 'em. They don't believe in killin' a white man quick when they can take twelve hours o' screamin' agony to do the same thing." Cordell jerked a curt nod in Sally's direction. "Beggin' your pardon for bein' blunt, ma'am."

"That's all right, Mr. Cordell," she said. "I've been exposed to a considerable amount of unpleasantness in my life."

Preacher said, "This was down close to the border, you say?"

"Yeah," Cordell replied.

"So if the Apaches are to blame, they could've ducked right back over the line after hittin' that supply wagon."

Cordell's beefy shoulders rose and fell. "I suppose that's true. But it could have been just the start of a bigger raid. They may plan to hit every way station and ranch between here and Tucson!"

"You've got crews at those way stations, don't you?" Smoke asked.

"Yeah, but when the coach don't show up, they'll know somethin's wrong and they'll fort up. Those stations are built to defend. The line may lose some horses, but our men will have a fightin' chance, anyway."

"Wouldn't it be better for us to go ahead and *warn* the fellas at the stations? That way they'll know for sure to be on the lookout." Mike looked at the four people sitting around the table. "You folks wouldn't have to go on. You could wait here until we know it's safe to travel."

"If you're going on to Tucson, then I'm coming with you," Ballard declared firmly. "I'm *not* going to miss Christmas with my family if I can help it."

Cordell grunted. "Christmas. There'll be another Christmas next year, mister. A holiday ain't worth getting yourself caught by those Apaches!" He made a slashing gesture. "Anyway, the coach ain't goin' through, with passengers or without!"

"That ain't your decision to make, Jack," Scratchy said coldly. "I'm the jehu on this run, and I'll decide whether or not we keep goin'."

"Like hell! Old John Saxon would have my hide if I was to let you folks get killed."

"Write out a paper sayin' that I made the decision and the responsibility is all mine," Scratchy said. "I'll sign it. I can sign my name, you know."

"You think that'd be enough to satisfy Saxon?"

"I reckon it would. That old man's fair. He wouldn't blame you if he knew you tried to stop Mike and me."

"And me," Ballard put in. "I'm going, too."

Cordell let out another explosive grunt and threw

his hands in the air. "Why don't we just put it to a blasted vote? Get the rest of the passengers in here, and you can all have your say."

Sally stood up. "I'll get Mrs. Bates and Miss Bradshaw. Maybe they're not asleep yet."

"Even if they are, it'd be a good idea to wake 'em up," Scratchy said. "They've got a right to know what they'll be gettin' into if they decide to come along."

Sally hurried out of the dining room and came back a few minutes later with the other two women. Both of them wore dressing gowns, and their slightly tousled hair indicated that they had indeed been asleep.

Catherine Bradshaw was wide awake now, though, and not happy. "What's this about not going on to Tucson?"

"I run the station here, and I say it's too dangerous," Cordell said. "There are hostiles on the loose."

Mrs. Bates clutched the throat of her robe closer. "You mean the Apaches?"

"Yes, ma'am."

Catherine said, "I thought the cavalry had them under control."

"Most of 'em are on reservations," Scratchy said. "Havin' 'em under *control* . . . well, that might be a bit of a stretch."

"Not to mention the ones that ran across the border and started hidin' in the mountains in Mexico, except when they decide to raid on our side of the line," Cordell added.

Catherine crossed her arms and glared. "My fiancé assured me in his letters that it would be perfectly safe for me to come to Arizona Territory, that there was no real threat from the Indians. I'm sorry, sir, but I'm going to accept his word—the word of a lieutenant in the United States Army—where this matter is concerned."

"I don't understand," Mrs. Bates said. "Is the stage going on or not?"

"I say it is," Ballard told her.

"So do I," Catherine said. "I don't want to postpone my marriage for any longer than is absolutely necessary."

Scratchy said, "You know how Mike and me feel about it. We're for pushin' on. Shoot, I ain't never failed to finish a run, and I'll be da—I mean, I'll be doggoned if I want to start now!"

Cordell looked at Smoke, Sally, and Preacher. "You folks haven't said anything about what you want to do."

"The day I hunker down and hide just 'cause there might be some trouble up ahead is the day you can put me up in a tree," Preacher said.

Smoke knew he was talking about the old Indian burial custom, even if the others didn't.

Sally spoke up. "When the Good Lord made my husband, He didn't put in much backup." She smiled. "I'm afraid being around Smoke has sort of rubbed off on me. If we knew for certain that we were going to run into trouble, it might be different. I can't see sitting around and waiting just because there's a chance something might happen."

Smoke squeezed her hand to let her know he was proud of her. "Scratchy and Mike seem like pretty tough hombres, and Preacher and I have sure seen our share of ruckuses. I think there's a good chance we can get through."

"I give up, then," Cordell said. "Scratchy, if you're bound and determined to start for Tucson in the morning, then more power to you. I'm writin' that paper you talked about, though, and you're signin' it!"

Smoke looked at Mrs. Bates. "That just leaves you and George, ma'am. It's different for you, since you've got the responsibility of taking care of that youngster—"

"Yes, but I want to get back to Tucson as soon as possible, Mr. Jensen. I think the sooner I get George settled into his new home, the better. It'll be his first Christmas without . . . without his folks, and that'll be hard enough as it is. I think it'll be even more difficult if we're stuck in some hotel, even a nice one like this."

Ballard nodded. "It's settled, then. We're all going on as planned."

Smoke thought he sounded uncommonly relieved about that and figured once again it had something to do with that trunk and its contents.

"God help you all," Cordell said, then stomped out of the dining room.

Scratchy looked at the passengers. "I realize you folks are takin' a mighty big chance. Mike and me will do our best not to let you down."

"We sure will," Mike added.

Smoke saw him glance at Catherine Bradshaw. That wasn't surprising. Catherine was a very attractive young woman. She was also engaged to an army lieutenant. Smoke didn't know if Mike was aware of that or not.

Such things would be the least of their worries over the next few days, though. The trip to Tucson would have been arduous enough even if everything went perfectly. With the possible threat of Apache raiders hanging over the rest of the journey, things might just get interesting before they reached their destination.

Smoke smiled grimly to himself.

CHAPTER 18

Scratchy Stevenson went along the hallway pounding on doors as he called, "Rise an' shine, folks! Better start gettin' ready, or we'll be burnin' daylight!"

Smoke was an early riser by habit, so he was up and shaving already when Scratchy roused the others. He looked over at the bed where Sally was still nestled under the covers and smiled as his wife muttered sleepily.

She lifted her head and said, "I don't suppose I could talk you into coming back to bed."

Smoke's smile widened into a grin. "Don't tempt me, woman. We've got a lot of ground to cover today."

"I know, I know. I'm getting up." She sat up, swung her legs out of bed, and went over to Smoke. She stretched up to kiss him on the cheek.

He turned, slipped an arm around her waist, and gave her a proper good morning kiss.

A short time later, they walked into the dining room to find Preacher sitting at one of the tables with Scratchy Stevenson and Mike Olmsted. All three men were drinking coffee.

"Preacher was up before we were," Scratchy said.

"The older you get, the less time you got left, and the more you don't want to waste too much of it sleepin'," Preacher said. "Besides, time you get to be my age, you got enough aches and pains keepin' you comp'ny that sleepin' ain't always easy."

Señora Gonzalez brought cups of coffee for Smoke and Sally. As they sat down with the others, Tom Ballard came into the dining room, stopped short, and frowned at Scratchy and Mike. "If you two are over here, who's keeping an eye on the stagecoach?"

"Jack Cordell and his hostlers are gettin' a fresh team hitched up right now," Scratchy replied. "Don't worry. They're keepin' an eye on your things, Mr. Ballard."

Ballard shook his head. "I wasn't worried."

He was trying to achieve a casual tone, Smoke thought, but he didn't quite make it.

Mrs. Bates and George came into the dining room next.

Señora Gonzalez began serving breakfast, which was bacon, flapjacks, and fried eggs. "You are still missing one passenger," she commented.

"That's right. Miss Bradshaw isn't here," Sally said. "I'll go make sure she's all right."

Mike scraped his chair back. "That's all right, ma'am. You go on with your breakfast. Since I work for the stage line, I reckon it's my job to check on Miss Bradshaw."

Sally shrugged and smiled. "All right." She looked over at Smoke with a twinkle in her eyes as Mike's long-legged strides carried him out of the dining room and across the hotel lobby.

Smoke knew what she was thinking. Mike had been quick to jump at the chance to talk to Miss Catherine Bradshaw. If the young shotgun guard expected anything to come of it, though, Smoke suspected he would be disappointed.

Mike Olmsted was nervous—unusual for him—as he paused in front of the door to Miss Bradshaw's room. From the time he'd been a kid, he had been bigger, stronger, and faster than most of the fellows his age, and as he got older he'd found that he could rope and ride and shoot better than most of them, too.

Despite those talents, he'd never had much interest in being a cowboy. He would have been willing to stay on the family ranch and help out, but his pa had sensed his restless nature and sent him packing, but in a kindly way.

"Go out there and find out what it is you want to do with your life, boy," he had told Mike.

Ever since, Mike had been trying to take that advice. He was confident in his own abilities and so far hadn't run into any trouble that he couldn't handle. At the moment, his heart was pounding heavily in his chest and a few beads of sweat had broken out on his forehead even though it was actually pretty cool inside the hotel's thick adobe walls.

He hadn't expected such a reaction and didn't

like it, so the best thing was to get the job over with, he decided. He rapped his knuckles against the door.

Since he got no response from inside, Mike knocked again, a little louder. He heard a murmur from the other side of the door, but he couldn't make out the words. He leaned closer. "Miss Bradshaw? Sorry to bother you, but it's Mike Olmsted. You know, the shotgun guard from the stagecoach? Everybody else is havin' breakfast in the dining room, and we'll be pullin' out soon."

Again, someone muttered inside the room, but Mike couldn't make heads or tails of it. He didn't like doing it, but he knocked again and called, "Miss Bradshaw?"

The door jerked open suddenly. Catherine stood just inside the room with one hand on the door and the other holding closed a silk robe that gaped a little here and there despite her grip. And where the robe wasn't open, it was molded distractingly to her body.

"I said I'm awake and getting ready," she snapped at him. "Are you hard of hearing, Mr. Olmsted?"

"Yes, ma'am. I mean, no, ma'am!" Mike started to back away. "I can hear just fine. I just didn't understand what you were sayin'."

"Now are you accusing me of mumbling?"

He shook his head a little more vehemently than necessary. "No, ma'am, I'm sure not. And I'm sorry I disturbed you. You just, uh, go ahead and get ready—"

"That's exactly what I intend to do." Her light brown hair was loose around her head, falling in waves around her face and over her shoulders. She was pretty enough to take Mike's breath away, even though she glared at him. "Is there anything else?"

He reached up, tugged on the brim of his hat, and lowered his gaze as he said, "No, ma'am, that's all."

Turned out looking down was a mistake, he realized as his eyes lingered on her bosom under the clinging silk. Looking down even more didn't help matters. Then he was all too aware of the enticing curve of her hips. He swallowed hard and turned away as he felt heat rising in his face. "I'll be goin' now."

She stopped him by saying, "Mr. Olmsted."

"Yes, ma'am?" he asked without looking around again.

"You won't leave without me, will you?"

"No, ma'am," Mike answered instantly. "You can bet that fancy hat you wear on that."

"All right." Her tone was less hostile now. "Thank you."

"Yes'm," Mike muttered, then he hurried up the hallway toward the hotel lobby. He wasn't sure what he'd been thinking when he'd volunteered to make sure she was awake. It hadn't been a proper thing to do at all. She was probably convinced now that he was a rude, lecherous buffoon.

Maybe he was. The way she'd looked in that silk robe was going to haunt his thoughts for a long time.

Tom Ballard left the hotel with Scratchy and Mike when they went to check on the stagecoach and see if it was ready to roll. The sun still wasn't up, but the eastern sky was awash with crimson and gold, heralding dawn's approach.

It had been damned hard for Ballard to leave the trunk in the coach's boot the night before, but dragging it into the hotel would have looked suspicious. He'd been fighting a constant struggle not to draw attention to himself or the trunk that contained the money Tucson needed to survive Avery Tuttle's avaricious grasp.

Ballard wasn't sure he'd been successful in that effort, especially where Smoke Jensen and the old mountain man called Preacher were concerned. Those two were so keen-eyed, it was hard to put anything past them. They had a reputation for getting involved in gunplay, too, which was worrisome.

But as far as Ballard knew, Smoke had always been on the side of law and order. He had been a wanted outlaw at one time, but the way Ballard understood it, those were bogus charges cooked up by some of Smoke's enemies. Not only was Smoke Jensen *not* an owlhoot, he had even carried a deputy U.S. marshal's badge when he was younger, before settling down as a successful rancher.

Ballard wasn't as familiar with Preacher, but he figured if the old mountain man was Smoke's friend, he had to be all right. Actually, having a pair of obvious fighting men like them along on the journey was a comfort.

The newspaperman had even considered telling Smoke just what was in the trunk but ultimately decided against it. Secrecy was his best weapon. If Tuttle got wind of what he was doing, the man would move heaven and earth to stop that money from reaching Tucson . . . although, considering Tuttle's villainy, it might be more appropriate to say that he would summon all the forces of Hell.

In front of the barn next to the stage line, Jack Cordell stood beside the stagecoach with a fresh team in its trace. "I hope you stubborn hombres have changed your minds about this foolhardy venture," he greeted them.

"No such luck, Jack," Scratchy told him with a grin. "We're goin' on through, just like we planned."

"Even though you've had a night to sleep on it?"

"Nothing's changed since last night, has it? No new reports of Apaches raidin' on this side of the border?"

"Well, no, I reckon not," Cordell admitted grudgingly.

"So there's really no proof any Apaches are within a hundred miles of here."

"You and I both know damned well there are," Cordell snapped. "It's just a matter of whether or not they're lookin' for trouble—and I never saw an Apache who wasn't, if he thought he could get away with it."

Scratchy shrugged. "Those are good horses, and I'll have Mike ridin' beside me. We've got some passengers who can put up a fight, too, if need be, like Mr. Ballard here. We'll take our chances, I reckon."

Ballard had drifted over to the boot at the back of the coach while the other men were talking. He tugged at the canvas cover, making it seem like an idle gesture, but really he was making sure the trunk had been loaded. He felt relief go through him when he saw the corner of it.

What he really felt the urge to do was open it up so he could lay his eyes on the bundles of cash it held. But he didn't want to reveal what he planned to do with it unless it became absolutely necessary.

"Here come the others," Mike said.

Ballard turned to look toward the hotel and saw the other passengers approaching. Mrs. Bates didn't look eager to resume the journey, and neither did Catherine Bradshaw. But the little fellow, George, didn't seem quite as sullen, and Smoke, Sally, and Preacher looked ready to meet any challenges that might arise.

Sally Jensen reminded Ballard a little of Louise. She would be at her husband's side, ready to support him or join the fight herself, come what may. He and Smoke were both lucky men, Ballard mused.

A few minutes later, everyone had climbed into the coach and Scratchy and Mike were perched up on the driver's box. Scratchy's shouted command to the team echoed back from the buildings along the street as the coach rolled toward the sun, which was just beginning to peek above the horizon.

CHAPTER 19

According to Scratchy, there were ten way stations between Ajo and Sahuarita Ranch, a settlement directly south of Tucson that served as the final way station on the southernmost leg of the stagecoach route. If the coach could have traveled straight through with fresh drivers as well as fresh teams, the journey would have taken only a couple days. Since Scratchy couldn't drive nonstop, it would be three and a half to four days before the coach rolled into Tucson.

And *that* was assuming they wouldn't run into any trouble along the way.

"We'll be cutting it close when it comes to getting there before Christmas," Ballard said as the passengers discussed what the next few days would bring. "If there are any delays we probably won't make it."

"My brothers are supposed to meet us there," Smoke said. "It'd be a shame if they decided we weren't coming and rode on before we got there."

Preacher said, "You know what you need to do. Talk to that there jehu about givin' you a turn at the reins. Him and the shotgun guard can climb in here and get some sleep, and you and me can get up there on the box, Smoke. We'll drive all night."

"But that would mean any sleep the rest of us got would have to be in here," Catherine said, looking appalled at the idea. "At least when we stop at a way station, we can sleep in a real bed."

"Or a cot or a bunk," Ballard told her. "You won't find any luxurious accommodations at these way stations, Miss Bradshaw. The conditions will be pretty primitive, in fact."

"It would still be better than trying to sleep in here while breathing dust and being jerked around."

"Well, I can't argue with that," Ballard said with a shrug.

"I'll talk to Scratchy about it the next time we're stopped," Smoke said. "It could be that he won't go along with the idea. Mr. Saxon probably has some sort of rule about passengers not handling the reins." He chuckled. "Although Scratchy strikes me as the sort who might bend a rule a little now and then."

Mrs. Bates said, "Can you really drive a stagecoach, Mr. Jensen?"

Preacher let out a bray of laughter. "Ma'am, there ain't many things ol' Smoke here *ain't* done since him and his pa came west all them years ago. You know his real name ain't Smoke, don't you?"

"Well, I figured as much," Mrs. Bates said with a smile.

George said, "Did you get your name because you

smoke a lot, Mr. Jensen, like Preacher got his for preachin'?"

"I never noticed him to smoke hardly any," Preacher answered before Smoke could say anything. "I'm the one who hung that moniker on him, a long time ago. Not long after we met, it was, back over yonder in Kansas. I run up on a couple pilgrims name o' Jensen. There was Emmett, and there was his boy Kirby. Kirby had him one o' them Colt Navy revolvers, a .36 caliber. A bunch o' Pawnee bucks jumped the three of us—"

"I'm not sure you need to tell this story, Preacher," Smoke said.

Sally patted him on the knee and smiled. She knew he was uncomfortable with people fussing over him and making out like he was some sort of legend . . . although he was probably the only one west of the Mississippi who didn't think that was the case.

"I want to hear the story!" George said. "Go on, Preacher, tell the rest of it."

Preacher glanced at Smoke, who sighed and gestured for him to go ahead.

The old mountain man continued. "Like I was sayin', them Pawnee jumped us, and it was a mighty hot fight there for a little while. Kirby had a .52 caliber Spencer repeatin' rifle and used it to down one of 'em, but then two bucks went after Emmett, Kirby's pa, and was a-fightin' hand to hand with him. It was too close to be usin' a rifle, so Kirby, he skinned out that Colt from its holster, faster and slicker than anything you ever saw in all your borned days, and he plunked a .36 slug right in the noggin o' one buck while his pappy got t'other 'un with a Arkansas tooth-pick!"

"Wow!" George exclaimed, his eyes big and round like saucers.

His grandmother wore a worried frown as if concerned that the grisly story might warp George's mind, while Catherine just looked out the window with an expression of haughty disgust on her lovely face. Ballard wore a tolerant and interested smile as he listened.

"When the ruckus was all over," Preacher went on, "me and Emmett both knowed Kirby wasn't a kid anymore. He'd done gone through what you call a baptism of fire, and he was a man. Injuns, they give a boy a new name when he becomes a man, and I spent a whole heap o' time with Injuns in my life, so I figured Kirby oughta have a new name, too. I called him Smoke, on account o' his hair is about the same color as smoke from a campfire. That's what I told him then, but I was a-thinkin', too, about how fast he smoked down that Pawnee buck. 'Smoke'll suit you just fine,' I told him. 'So Smoke it'll be.' " Preacher leaned back against the bench seat. "Has been ever since."

George looked from Preacher over to Smoke. "I hope I get to see you shoot an Indian sometime, Mr. Jensen."

"George!" his grandmother exclaimed. "What a terrible thing to say!"

"If it's all right with you, George," Smoke said, "I'd just as soon not shoot anybody."

But in all likelihood, it wouldn't be up to George,

or to him, either, Smoke thought. It would all depend on what they ran into between Ajo and Tucson.

But . . . if anybody needed shooting—red, white, or any other color—Smoke would do his best to take care of that chore.

The first way station was at a place called Mule Creek, the second at Saddle Blanket Wash. Both were squat adobe cabins with pole corrals and sheds for the horses. The men who worked at them had hard, lonely existences, Smoke knew, but some hombres welcomed that. He had ridden some solitary trails himself, in his time.

The travelers had their midday meal at Saddle Blanket Wash. It wasn't much, just beans, cornbread, and coffee, as much as anybody wanted for fifty cents. Stagecoach fare didn't include meals; the money the station keepers collected for feeding passengers supplemented their meager wages.

The next stop would be at Flat Rock Crossing, Scratchy told Smoke and the others before they set out again. The place partly got its name from a geographical feature—a large, flat slab of rock that looked like someone had dropped it down on the arid landscape for no apparent reason. The *crossing* part of the name came from the fact that an old mule train route angled across the stage road there. Mules had carried ore from the mines across the border in Mexico up to Phoenix along that trail, although it wasn't used anymore.

The landscape had a stark beauty to it. Low, rugged mountains and flat-topped buttes and mesas bordered broad, level valleys dotted with organ-pipe cactus, saguaro, and assorted other thorny vegetation. Small, gnarled trees and clumps of hardy grass sucked enough moisture from the sandy soil to survive in places. For the most part, it was a land of dirt and rock of varying shades of brown and gray. A vast, largely empty country perfect for folks who couldn't stand being crowded.

Like the Apaches, Smoke thought as he squinted against the dust and scanned the horizon from the coach window. Once it had been almost exclusively their domain. You couldn't really blame them for being unhappy when outsiders had come in and tried to push them out.

On the other hand, the Apaches had done the same thing. They weren't the first inhabitants of that part of the country. They had come from Texas, pushed out *there* by the Comanche. They had slaughtered and driven off the peaceful tribes they had found in what was now Arizona Territory.

It was a seemingly eternal cycle of conquest and defeat. Smoke had heard it said that barbarism was the natural state of mankind, that in the end no civilization could stand forever against the forces of anarchy. That was a bleak way of looking at things, but he supposed there was some truth to it.

A lot of folks would consider *him* a barbarian, he mused. Preacher, along with all the other old mountain men, certainly fit the mold, too.

The heat built as the coach rocked on through the afternoon. Even though it was less than a week until Christmas and most of the country was locked in the grip of winter, the weather was still mild and dry and downright hot at times, especially for those who were accustomed to cooler climates.

The dust that swirled in through the windows, even when the canvas shades were drawn, didn't help matters. Catherine Bradshaw looked particularly wan and uncomfortable. Mrs. Bates fanned herself. The heat and the motion of the coach had made George drowsy. Sally rested her head on Smoke's shoulder and dozed.

Smoke was alert, though, and kept watch out one window while Preacher monitored the view on the other side of the coach.

"You two are on the lookout for trouble," Tom Ballard commented.

"Never hurts to be careful," Preacher said.

"Do you think the Apaches are really raiding over here, or that it was just a quick strike across the border and they've gone back to Mexico?"

"You're the one who lives down here in this part of the country, Tom," Smoke said. "You'd probably know better than us."

"Not necessarily. In the time my family and I have been in Tucson, there really hasn't been much trouble. I was hoping it would stay that way."

"I ain't never had many dealin's with them 'Paches," Preacher said, "but I can tell you that just in general, Injuns is the most notional critters God ever put on this green earth. Tryin' to predict what they're gonna do is pert-near impossible. You might make a guess, but you'd have just as good a chance o' bein' wrong."

"Well, then, I'll just hope that they've gone back to

Mexico and we won't run into any of them," Ballard said.

"You can't go wrong hoping that," Smoke said.

By midafternoon, a dark hump had appeared in front of the coach on the eastern horizon. Scratchy leaned over on the seat and called to the passengers, "You can see Flat Rock up ahead if you want to have a look, folks. But to be honest, there ain't that much to see."

George pulled one of the shades aside and leaned out far enough to peer into the distance. When he let the shade fall back and sat down on the middle bench again, he wore a disgusted expression on his face. "It's just a big ol' rock."

"Well, what did you expect?" his grandmother asked him. "Mr. Stevenson warned you."

"Yeah, I know. I just thought it would be more interesting than that."

"You ought to go up to Monument Valley in Utah sometime," Preacher said. "That's some plumb picturesque scenery. 'Course, it ain't a patch on some o' the places I've seen in the Rockies."

The way station at Flat Rock Crossing was virtually identical to the others along the route . . . with one difference, Smoke noted.

Several saddle horses were tied to the corral's pole fence.

More pilgrims than just the ones on the stagecoach had stopped at Flat Rock Crossing.

CHAPTER 20

The station keeper emerged from the adobe building with a couple young Mexican hostlers.

"Howdy, Paulson!" Scratchy called to the man as he brought the team to a halt with dust billowing around it.

Paulson, a tall, lean, mostly bald man with a face that resembled a buzzard, waved a hand in front of his face to clear away some of the dust. He stepped closer to the coach and took hold of a piece of brass trim. "Your passengers might want to stay in the coach today, Scratchy," he said quietly, but not quietly enough to keep Smoke from hearing him.

Scratchy frowned down from the driver's box. "Stay inside the coach?" he repeated. "What in blazes for? Folks like to get out and stretch their legs and get a breath of fresh air. Besides, ain't you got some cool water in there like you usually do?"

"Yeah, but I've also got customers bent on drinking up all my liquor, seems like. They ain't caused any real trouble so far, but"—Paulson craned his neck to look through the coach window nearest to him—"you've got ladies in there."

Catherine proved that by popping her head out through the window beside her. "Mr. Stevenson, what's wrong? Did I hear this man say something about not going inside the station?"

"Yes'm," Scratchy replied. "This here is Ike Paulson. He runs the place. Says there are some fellas inside who might look to cause trouble if they was disturbed."

"Nonsense. This is a Saxon Stage Line way station, isn't it? Passengers on the stagecoach ought to take precedence over anyone who just *rides* up."

While the others were talking, Smoke had been studying the mounts tied to the corral fence. Three horses were together, while the fourth one was tied a little ways off. The fourth rider had come in separately from the other three. That might not mean anything, but it was worth noting.

"Besides," Catherine went on, "didn't I hear something about cool water? I'm very thirsty."

"So am I," George said. "And I need to, uh—"

"That's around back, sonny," Paulson told him. "No need to go inside for that."

"Well, *I'm* going in," Catherine said as she reached out through the window to twist the door's latch without waiting for one of the men to do it. "I want to sit down someplace where it's cooler and not moving."

Scratchy started to say, "Ma'am—"

"It'll be all right, Scratchy," Mike cut in. "I'll go in, too, and take this coach gun with me. Besides"—he angled his head toward the coach's passenger compartment—"that's Smoke Jensen in there, remember?"

"Smoke Jensen!" Paulson exclaimed. "Why in blazes didn't you say so?"

Inside the coach, Sally smiled and told her husband, "Your fame precedes you."

"Dogs my trail is more like it," Smoke said with a grunt.

Catherine had the door open but hadn't climbed out yet.

Mike said hurriedly, "Wait a minute, Miss Bradshaw, and I'll give you a hand." He swung off the driver's box and dropped to the ground.

"Careful. You'll break your neck," Scratchy told him dryly.

Mike ignored the gibe and stepped up to the open door to help Catherine to the ground. George scrambled out next and trotted off around the building in search of the outhouse Paulson had mentioned.

His grandmother followed, calling after him, "George, be careful! There could be snakes!"

Smoke got out next, followed by Sally, then Preacher and Ballard. Catherine and Mike were headed for the station's open door. The hostlers had already started unhitching the team. The schedule didn't call for a lengthy stop at Flat Rock Crossing. Scratchy would want to be back on the way fairly quickly.

As they walked toward the station, his left arm linked with her right, Sally said to Smoke, "Do you think there's going to be trouble?"

"Maybe, maybe not. Depends on what—or who— we find in there. But whatever happens, we'll meet it head-on."

"Just like always."

"Yep."

After the bright sunlight outside, it seemed dimmer inside the station than it really was. Smoke's eyes adjusted quickly, though, and he looked around, instantly taking in everything in the station's main room.

A couple long tables with bench seats were to the left. Passengers would use them whenever they ate a meal. Farther back were two round tables where men could sit and play poker or drink. A short bar was to the right with a few unlabeled bottles sitting on a shelf on the wall behind it. A water barrel with a dipper tied to it stood at the near end of the bar. In the back corner, beyond the bar, was a big potbellied stove, cold at the moment.

The setup with the horses outside was repeated inside. Three men stood together at the bar, while a fourth man sat by himself at one of the round tables.

One of the men at the bar thumped his empty glass on the planks. "Damn it, Paulson, you need to be back here pourin' drinks, not out there chewin' the fat with some damn pilgrims."

Mike walked Catherine to one of the long tables, where she sat down. Still on his feet, Mike frowned and said, "Watch your language, mister. There are ladies present."

The man at the bar bristled with sudden anger. "I ain't never held my tongue on account of no damn woman, and I don't figure on startin' now."

Mike's face hardened as he took a step toward the bar.

Without seeming to move fast, Smoke put himself between the young shotgun guard and the mouthy hardcase. "Go sit down with Miss Bradshaw," he said quietly. He had no authority to tell Mike what to do, but that didn't really seem to matter. The note of command in Smoke's voice was unmistakable.

Mike responded to it. Although he still looked upset, he didn't try to push past Smoke. He moved back to the table and sat down across from Catherine.

Scratchy and Paulson came into the station last, Paulson with a worried frown on his face. That frown deepened when he felt the air of tension that gripped the room.

Paulson had warned of trouble, Smoke thought. It hadn't been long in coming.

But maybe it could be headed off yet. Smoke nodded pleasantly enough to the men at the bar. "Buy you fellas a drink?"

"Now that's more like it," the loudmouth said. He had a foxlike face and long, stringy hair the color of wheat. "Paulson, get over here, take this man's money, and pour some drinks."

Paulson moved behind the bar, looked like he wanted to say something and was biting his tongue to keep from it, and reached for one of the bottles on the shelf.

The fox-faced man squinted at Smoke. "Don't I know you?"

"I don't reckon we've ever crossed trails. Not to speak of, anyway." Smoke had seen men like that many times in the past, though. Too many times. Hard-faced, beard-stubbled men whose clothes carried the dust of long, lonely trails. They would be handy with their guns and have no scruples about using them. There might or not be wanted posters out on them, but either way, they were outside the law.

The fourth man in the room, the one sitting at the table in the back with a bottle and a glass, was cut from a little better cloth but still had a dangerous look about him. He wore a black hat with a flat brim and a slightly rounded crown and a black-and-white cowhide vest over a butternut shirt. His dark, square face might as well have been carved from stone. He didn't seem to want any part of whatever was shaping up, and as long as he stayed out of it, that was fine with Smoke.

When Paulson had filled the glasses, the stringy-haired spokesman picked his up and said to Smoke, "Here's to you, mister." He tossed back the drink. "What do they call you, anyway?"

"My name is Jensen," Smoke said.

The man set the empty glass on the bar and frowned. "From up Idaho way?"

"Colorado."

"Oh." The man relaxed slightly but still wore a suspicious look. "An uncle of mine once had a run-in with a man named Jensen, at a silver mining camp on the Uncompahgre. That was a long time ago." He cocked his head a little to the side. "You ever been up in those parts?"

"A long time ago," Smoke said.

The man's left hand slapped down on the bar. His

lips drew back from his teeth in a snarl. "I knew it! Damn you. You're Smoke Jensen, ain't you?"

"That's my name," Smoke said with a familiar feeling edging into his muscles. Many times over the years, he had run into relatives of men he had killed, and most of the time they wanted to settle that score.

All that wound up doing was getting them killed, too, but that didn't seem to stop them.

It always went one of two ways—either the hombre bent on vengeance grabbed for his gun as soon as he realized who Smoke was or he wanted to talk first, to bluster a little about what he thought was going to happen.

This one wanted to flap his gums. Still sneering, he said, "You killed my uncle, Jensen. Shot him down like a dog."

"He must've had it coming," Smoke said. Sometimes, on very rare occasions, one of those vengeance-seekers could be talked out of throwing his life away. Smoke didn't figure that was going to happen, but he figured it was worth a try. "I never killed anybody who wasn't trying to kill me first."

"That's a damn lie! One of my uncle's pards saw the whole thing. He come and told us how you gunned him with no warnin'."

Smoke shook his head. "I'm telling the truth. You're nursing a grudge for no reason. Smartest thing would be for you to let it go. We won't be here long. We'll be leaving soon, and you can go your way while we go ours. There doesn't have to be any gunplay."

"The hell there don't!" The man glanced at his companions. "You boys'll back my play, won't you?"

The two men began to spread out a little as one of them said, "We always do, Badger."

The fella *did* look a little like a badger, Smoke thought idly . . . although he resembled a fox even more.

"You know, I'm not alone, either." Smoke leaned his head toward the tables. "There's a fella over there with a coach gun, and you might have heard of the old-timer. He's called Preacher, and he's been to see the elephant more than a few times. I suspect Scratchy can use that hogleg on his hip, too."

"Durned right I can," Scratchy rumbled.

"So it seems like you're outnumbered and out-gunned," Smoke went on. "Best thing to do is let it go."

For a second, Badger looked like he was considering it . . . but then he shook his head. "Those other fellas aren't gonna open fire, not with women in the room." An ugly smile plucked at his mouth. "Thing of it is . . . I don't care who else gets hurt, Jensen—as long as you die!"

His hand flashed toward his gun.

CHAPTER 21

Badger was right about one thing—with Sally and Catherine in the room, Smoke didn't want a lot of lead flying around. So there was no time to waste. Faster than the eye could follow, his Colt was out, spitting flame.

The first shot went into Badger's chest, knocking him back a step and widening his eyes in shock and pain. His gun had barely cleared leather.

Smoke's second bullet punched into the midsection of the man to Badger's left, doubling him over. He had gotten his gun out, but it was still pointed at the floor when his finger clenched spasmodically on the trigger. The shot chewed up splinters at his feet.

Smoke had already tracked back to the third man, who was trying to duck to the side. The slug from Smoke's revolver shattered his left shoulder and spun him off his feet. He dropped his gun and collapsed, whimpering and pawing at his wounded shoulder.

Badger was the only one still on his feet. Smoke didn't see how he was even still alive. Hate must have been holding him up. He tried hard to raise his gun.

Smoke shot him a second time, the black, red-rimmed hole springing into existence in the center of Badger's forehead. The bullet bored through his brain and blew out a fist-sized chunk from the back of his skull. He thudded to the floor next to his friends.

In the echoing silence that followed the final shot, George yelled, "Holy cow! They weren't Injuns, but . . . holy cow!" The boy was standing in the open back door with his grandmother behind him, looking horrified.

Smoke glanced at the fourth man, the one sitting by himself at the rear table. "Friends of yours?"

The man hadn't budged during the gunfight. Slowly, he shook his head back and forth. "Never saw them before today, mister. I don't have a single card in this game."

"That's good to hear." Smoke looked at Mike, who had turned on the bench and angled the coach gun's barrels toward the man in the cowhide vest. Figuring that the young man had things under control, even if Cowhide Vest tried some sort of trick, Smoke broke open the Colt and started replacing the expended cartridges.

Behind the bar, Paulson blew out a disgusted breath. "That's what I was afraid might happen. Oh, well. Won't be the first time I've cleaned up some blood and brains in here."

"Oh!" Mrs. Bates gasped. She took hold of George's arm and started dragging him back around the building toward the front without going through the station. "Come along! We're going back to the coach!"

"Aw, Grandma! I want to see what Mr. Jensen did!"

"You've seen enough! More than enough!"

Smoke knew that the only shot any of the hardcases had fired hadn't come anywhere near Sally or Preacher, so he wasn't worried about them. As he closed his reloaded Colt and pouched the iron, he said, "Sorry for the ruckus, Mr. Paulson. I could tell they weren't going to give me any choice, so I figured it was best just to get it over with in a hurry."

"You certainly did that. What was it, four shots in three seconds? Too fast for me to follow, anyway." Paulson leaned forward and looked over the bar, down at the wounded man on the floor. "What'll I do with him?"

"We don't want him," Scratchy said. "He ain't the responsibility of the Saxon Stage Line."

Paulson scratched his bony jaw. "There's an Indian woman who lives up the creek a ways. I'll send one of the hostlers to fetch her. She can patch that varmint up as best she can and then I'll send him on his way. Maybe he'll make it." Paulson's shrug made it clear he didn't care all that much, either way.

Honestly, neither did Smoke. Badger and the other two had made up their own minds to pull iron on him. What happened to them was on their heads.

Over at the table where she was sitting, Catherine swallowed hard and said, "I think I want to get out of here now. The . . . the smell is making me a bit ill."

"The gun smoke, you mean?" Mike said.

"I just want to get out, please."

"Sure." He took her arm and held on to it until

the two of them were back outside. Then he said, "I'll fetch you a cup of water out here."

"Thank you. That would be . . . very nice."

Inside the station, Smoke said to Sally, "Do you want to go, too?"

"I'm all right," she told him. "This isn't the first shooting I've seen, you know. But I wouldn't mind going on as soon as we can."

"Fresh team's almost hitched up, ma'am," Scratchy told her. "I reckon we'll be rollin' again in another five minutes."

That prediction was off, but not by much. It was six minutes later when the stagecoach clattered away from the station at Flat Rock Crossing.

None of the people on it saw the man in the cowhide vest come out of the building, get on his horse, and ride away fast a few minutes after that.

Although the stagecoach would circle well to the south so it could curve around to Sahuarita Ranch, Caddo didn't need to follow that route. He had recognized Tom Ballard, even though the newspaperman hadn't paid any attention to him.

They moved in different circles back in Tucson. Caddo was usually in one of the saloons or whorehouses and seldom saw the light of day. Ballard, being a good family man, didn't patronize such places.

That thought put a faint smile on Caddo's face as he pushed his horse almost due east toward Tucson. Most of the houses of ill repute in the world would probably go out of business if it weren't for the "good family men" who patronized them.

None of that mattered. The only important thing was that Caddo had confirmed Ballard was on the stagecoach. That was what Smiler Coe wanted to know. Caddo was on his way to tell the boss gunman about it. If he rode all night, he could reach Tucson by the next night.

He might just about kill his horse doing it, but Caddo was willing to pay that price. Of course, there was always a chance he might come across some wandering cowboy who'd be glad for Caddo to take his mount . . . after Caddo put a bullet in him.

He might find some isolated ranch where he could get a fresh horse, too, again at gunpoint if necessary.

One way or another, he would make it back to Tucson and deliver his news to Coe as quickly as he could.

Caddo hadn't counted on something, and his only warning was a glimpse of late afternoon sunlight reflecting from the side of a small butte as he approached it. instincts and reflexes allowed him to react instantly. He jerked his horse to the left. At the same time, he heard the whine of a bullet passing close by on his right.

If he hadn't jumped when he did, that slug would have knocked him out of the saddle.

A half-second later, he heard the flat crack of the shot that had already missed him and saw a puff of powder smoke at the base of the butte. He yanked his horse even more to the left, away from the butte, and rammed his spurs into the animal's flanks to make it leap ahead into a gallop.

Several figures on horseback came boiling around the side of the butte and charged at him. Caddo didn't have to get any closer to know they were Apaches.

What the hell? Why hadn't Coe warned them an Apache war party was roaming around that part of the territory? Those redskin bastards would never pass up a chance to jump a white man traveling alone. Despite his nickname and his complexion, Caddo had no Indian blood in him, although he didn't go around explaining that to people.

He didn't know . . . or care that Coe hadn't known about the Apaches. All that mattered was getting away from the red devils.

He urged his mount on to greater speed. The horse was a big, rangy bay gelding. Caddo was confident that it could outrun the scrubby ponies the Apaches rode.

At least, it could have in a straight race. Problem was, the savages had an angle on him. What he should have done, he realized, was turn around and head back the way he had come, toward the stage station at Flat Rock Crossing. That would have taken advantage of the distance between himself and the Apaches, and the station would be a good place to fort up if he could reach it in time.

But that was no longer an option. If he turned around, the Apaches would cut across his trail for sure. All he could do was try to stay ahead of them.

It didn't help that he'd already been pushing his horse pretty hard, trying to get back to Tucson and carry the news to Smiler Coe as fast as he could. Even though the bay had more speed than the Indian ponies, if they were fresher, that would negate any advantage Caddo might have.

As he leaned forward over the horse's neck and urged it on, he turned his head to the right and looked back over his shoulder. The Apaches were still angling toward him, cutting the gap between him and them with every lunging stride of their mounts.

Caddo tried to count them. At least five, he thought, probably more. It could be a scouting party. No telling how many more might be around. They might have already heard that shot and be on their way.

He thought about stopping right where he was, getting off the horse, and making a fight of it. He could pull the bay down on the ground, take cover behind it, and try to pick off some of the Apaches with his rifle. If he downed two or three of them, they might decide capturing or killing him would come at too high a price.

But they had rifles, too, he reminded himself. If he opened fire on them, they would return the shots. Almost certainly, his horse would be killed. Even if the savages turned tail, that would leave him on foot, a long way from anywhere. He might be able to walk back to Flat Rock Crossing, but his feet would be two gigantic blisters by the time he got there.

He wouldn't stop and make a stand just yet, he decided. He kept pushing on.

Close enough behind him, he thought he could hear the Apaches' shrill, exultant whoops over the pounding hoofbeats. That was just his imagination, he knew, but it made chills go through him, anyway.

Caddo was past the butte where the Apaches had been hiding. The area was off the beaten path, with no regular trails going through. Stark desolation surrounded him. Water could be found—unless the weather had been extraordinarily dry—but an hombre had to know where to look for it.

Something loomed up from the mostly flat landscape in front of him. He squinted and saw that it was a pile of rocks. Why those boulders, each of them weighing tons, were sitting there with nothing around them, he had no idea, but he wasn't going to question his good luck. He pointed the horse toward the rocks. "Come on, you bastard. Make it there and we might both have a chance to live through this."

The horse seemed to understand. Its legs stretched out farther as it raced across the rocky, sand-strewn ground.

It was a race, plain and simple, with Caddo's life as the stakes. If he could make it to that nest of boulders and take cover there, he could pick off several of the pursuers. He was a good enough shot with a rifle that he was sure of that.

On the other hand, he had only a couple canteens of water and a little bit of food. Those supplies wouldn't last very long. If the Apaches decided to lay siege to the place, in the end he'd probably die anyway, one way or the other.

What he had to do was kill enough of them to make the others abandon their efforts to capture him. But every Apache he killed might just make the others more determined to have their grisly sport with him.

He was in a hell of a bad spot, no getting around that.

First, he actually had to reach the rocks.

The Apaches had failed to cut him off. The angle they had wasn't quite good enough. They were directly behind him, about three hundred yards back. The boulders were still half a mile away. Caddo thought he could make it, as long as his horse didn't make any missteps.

The few minutes it took to cross that half-mile were the longest of Caddo's brutal life. He forgot all about Tom Ballard and Smiler Coe and Avery Tuttle. His entire universe had boiled down to him, his horse, those howling savages behind him, and the heat and dust that surrounded them all. The sky turned blood red behind him as the sun dipped to the horizon. That crimson hue washed over the Arizona landscape and made it look like something out of a nightmare.

The rocks loomed larger and larger ahead of him, and suddenly he was among them. He hauled back hard on the reins to bring the horse to a skidding stop and was out of the saddle while the animal was still moving. He grabbed the butt of his Winchester and dragged it out of the sheath strapped under the fender. He hit the ground running and stumbling and twisted around toward one of the big slabs of rock so he could start shooting.

He worked the rifle's lever and lifted it to his shoulder. Before he could fire, he heard something behind him and glanced over his shoulder to see a bronzed figure clad only in high-topped moccasins, loincloth, and blue headband lunging at him and swinging some sort of club.

Terror leaped into Caddo's heart as he saw the snarling face framed by long, midnight-black hair.

In that instant, he knew what had happened. The Apaches had played him for a fool. When they first spotted him, they'd sent this man trotting out to the rocks to lie in wait while they herded the foolish white man right to him. And Caddo had cooperated, galloping straight to his death.

He tried to jerk the Winchester around and fire, but he was too late. The club smashed against his head with stunning force, sent his hat flying, and made him drop the rifle as he toppled to the ground. The Apache hadn't hit him hard enough to smash his skull and kill him.

That would have been better.

He felt strong hands on him, heard the swift rata-plan of hoofbeats as the others rode up, and muttered a curse as he tried to force his muscles to work, to fight back. A foot slammed into his groin, doubling him up in agony.

Caddo knew they were ripping his clothes off, stretching out his arms and legs and lashing them to stakes they pounded into the ground. Then the knives came out and he started to scream.

The shrieking went on for a long time as the sunlight reddened more and more and then began to fade away. The screams didn't stop until long in the night.

CHAPTER 22

The stagecoach reached the way station at Hondo Wells a short time after dark. Catherine Bradshaw, Mrs. Bates, and George were all tired, and Smoke could tell they were glad the coach would be stopping for the night instead of continuing on as it would have if a relief driver and guard had been available. Even Sally, who had a core of steel, as Smoke had seen demonstrated many times, looked weary after a day of stagecoach travel.

A man named Whitney ran the station and greeted the passengers. "Got a pot of stew, some fresh-baked bread, and plenty of hot coffee inside, folks. The rooms just have cots, but I promise you, after sitting on those bench seats all day, once you stretch out those cots will feel almost as good as feather beds."

"I doubt that," Catherine muttered sullenly as she and some of the other passengers began to drift inside.

Smoke noticed him sidling over to Scratchy and Mike with a worried expression replacing the smile he had displayed earlier. Smoke drifted closer to hear what the stationmaster was going to say.

"I didn't really expect to see you boys. Couple riders came by earlier, stopped to water their horses, and said the Apaches were out again on this side of the border."

"Just a raidin' party from across the border," Scratchy said. "They jumped a supply wagon . . . maybe. Ain't no real proof even of that."

"Well, there's proof now," Whitney said grimly. "Last night they hit a ranch south of here, burned it out, stole most of the stock, and killed all the folks who ran the place except for one fifteen-year-old boy who managed to get away with an arrow in his shoulder. He made it to one of the other spreads scattered down that way and told the tale."

"He was sure it was Apaches?" Scratchy asked with a frown.

"Certain sure. And that isn't all. There's been reports that some of the bucks have jumped the reservation. They probably heard about the raids from south of the border and decided they want to get in on the sport." Whitney gave a glum shake of his head. "It looks like it might be shaping up to be a general uprising, Scratchy. I'd tell you to turn around and head back to Ajo, but hell, you might be better off just trying to make a run for Tucson. There's no way of being sure where the hostiles are."

"I ain't turnin' back," Scratchy declared. "That ain't the way I do things. I'll stick to the schedule and make the reg'lar run. We can get through all right, can't we, Mike?"

"I reckon."

Smoke didn't think he sounded entirely convinced, though. The young shotgun guard was concerned—as anybody with a lick of sense would be.

Whitney glanced over at Smoke as if just noticing that he'd been listening. "Mister, you don't need to worry—"

"You don't have to try to reassure this hombre, Hal," Scratchy broke in. "He ain't a reg'lar passenger. This here is Smoke Jensen. The old fella who went inside with Mrs. Jensen is that old mountain man they call Preacher. They could lose half the bark on 'em and still have more than anybody else in these parts."

"Smoke Jensen, eh?" Whitney put out his hand. "I'm pleased to meet you, Mr. Jensen. I've heard a considerable amount about you."

"The pleasure's mine, Mr. Whitney," Smoke said as he gripped the man's hand. "I appreciate the plain talk about the dangers we're facing. We wouldn't be heading for Tucson by stage if there was any other way."

By way of explanation, Scratchy put in, "Railroad bridge is out between Casa Grande and Tucson. Likely won't be fixed until after Christmas. These folks didn't want to wait that long."

Mike added, "They didn't know they had to worry about Apaches when they started out, though."

"Anybody who wants to stay here until the army has a chance to corral the hostiles is welcome to do so," Whitney offered. "The station has a lot thicker walls than a stagecoach does."

"The station don't move, though," Scratchy said.

Smoke smiled. "I reckon we'll push on, although I don't speak for anybody but myself. Everybody else seems anxious to get to Tucson, though. I expect you'll still have a full coach tomorrow morning, Scratchy."

"I hope so," the burly driver rumbled. "My job is to deliver all you folks safely to where you're goin', and by golly, I intend to do it!"

Mike was inside the station, headed toward the stove where a pot of coffee was staying warm, when Catherine Bradshaw approached him.

"Mr. Olmsted, I wonder if I could trouble you for a moment," she began.

Instinctively, he took his hat off as he nodded to her. "Sure thing, Miss Bradshaw. What can I do for you?"

"I forgot and left my small bag in the boot. I'll need it tonight. Do you think you could fetch it for me?"

"Why, sure," Mike answered without hesitation. "I'd be glad to get it. Is there anything else I can do?"

"No, that's it. Thank you." She started to open her handbag. "I'd like to give you something . . ."

That sort of pained him. He thought she was just asking him to do her a favor. The sort of thing a friend might ask of another friend. But he was just an employee of the stage line to her, he realized. A servant to be tipped.

He didn't want that. He reached out and laid his

fingers over hers as she fumbled with the bag's clasp. "You don't have to do that. I'm glad to lend a hand whenever I can."

"Of course." She actually looked a little flustered, as if she realized what she was doing and felt embarrassed. She summoned up a smile and added, "Thank you."

"See, that smile is payment enough for any chore. More than enough."

He probably shouldn't have said that, he thought. It wasn't proper, her being a passenger and him being just the shotgun guard, and with her being engaged, to boot.

When her smile widened a little and what he believed was some genuine warmth shone in her eyes for a second, he was glad he'd been so bold. He turned and headed for the station's front door.

As he passed a table where some of the others were sitting, he heard Tom Ballard saying to Scratchy, "Will someone be standing guard over the coach tonight, Mr. Stevenson?"

"Don't know that there's really any need to," Scratchy said. "We're out way the hell an' gone in the middle of nowhere. Shouldn't be anybody around to bother it."

"But you never can tell when those Apaches might come sneaking around."

"If there's Apaches sneakin' around the station, we got bigger worries than anything on that coach, I reckon."

Ballard didn't look like he was convinced of that, Mike thought as he reached the doorway and stepped outside. The newspaperman had been mighty antsy the whole trip, as if he were carrying a king's ransom in that trunk of his.

Suddenly, Mike wondered exactly what *was* in that trunk. It had seemed too heavy to be carrying just the things a man might take with him on a trip to the territorial capital. But it was none of his business what the passengers took with them, he reminded himself.

The sun had been down for more than an hour, but the air was still heavy with heat. It would have a chill to it by morning, though. In the dry climate, the earth and the rocks gave up their heat fairly quickly once night had fallen.

The moon had not yet risen, but the millions of stars provided quite a bit of light. Enough for Mike to spot a figure moving around the stagecoach. The sight made him stiffen as he thought back to the scene inside the station he had just left. In his head, he counted the folks he had seen.

Scratchy and all the passengers were accounted for. Likewise Whitney, the Navajo woman who cooked for him, and the two hostlers. All the horses were in the corral.

Mike heard a horse stamp and blow somewhere on the other side of the coach. He couldn't see the animal, but he had no doubt it was there. He was convinced the man who had ridden up was the one standing next to the coach, as well. The hombre was right beside the boot at the rear and reach out toward it.

Mike had left his shotgun inside the building, but he had a holstered Colt .44 on his hip. He brushed the long duster aside, closed his hand around the revolver's walnut grips, and pulled it out of leather. "Hold it right there, mister."

The stranger froze at Mike's soft-voiced call. If the man tried to run, Mike intended to fire a shot over his head.

If the man reached for his own gun, Mike was going to shoot him, or at least try to. It was too dark to make out any details. The stranger could be a hostile or just a drifting thief.

"Take it easy, mister." The words that came from the shadowy figure identified him as a white man, not an Apache. "I'm not lookin' for any trouble."

"What *are* you lookin' for, then?"

"Huh?"

"Seemed to me you were about to start riflin' through that boot."

"What? You're loco! You mean just because I was gonna lean on the coach for a second before I came on inside? Damn it, man, I've been in the saddle all day. I'm tired."

Had the man really been about to rest his hand on the coach for momentary support? It was possible, Mike supposed, but he wasn't going to accept that story on face value. He had the .44 pointed in the stranger's general direction. He gestured with the gun. "Come closer so I can get a look at you."

"Who in hell are you to be givin' orders?"

"I work for the Saxon Stage Line," Mike snapped. "And that's a Saxon stage you're lurkin' around."

"You're too blasted suspicious," the man muttered as he moved toward Mike.

"Keep those hands where I can see 'em."

"Damn it, don't get an itchy trigger finger! I tell

you, I'm not up to anything fishy. I just saw the lights and came on in to water my horse and maybe spend the night. Gets mighty lonely out there on the desert for a man on the drift."

The man was close enough for Mike to make him out in the light that came from the station. He was lean, dark-faced, wearing dust-covered range clothes. The trail dust backed up his story that he had been in the saddle all day. He wore a holstered gun, but that was nothing unusual.

"Everything all right out here, Mike?" Smoke asked from the doorway.

"Yeah," Mike answered. "Just a fella pokin' around the coach, Mr. Jensen. Claims to be a drifter."

"No claims to be about it," the man said. "Look, if this place is going to be so unfriendly, I'll just water my horse and move on. I don't want people givin' me the skunk eye all night."

"Where are you headed?" Smoke asked.

"Southwest toward the mines along the border. Thought I might get a job at one of them. If not, I reckon I'll drift on across into Mexico for a spell."

That sounded reasonable enough, Mike supposed, but he still wasn't completely convinced. "All right. I guess you can come on inside. We'll be keepin' an eye on you, though."

The man didn't say anything for a moment. Then, "Hell, no. Like I said, I don't want to sit around with everybody bein' suspicious of me. I'd rather rattle my hocks outta here."

"That's up to you, mister," Smoke said as he ambled up alongside Mike.

"I'm just gonna get my horse, give him some water, and move on."

"Go ahead," Smoke said. "You won't mind if we stand here and watch you." His tone made it clear he didn't really care if the stranger minded or not.

The man just grunted and went back around the coach. He reappeared a moment later, leading a saddled horse to the well, where he pulled the bucket up, poured water in his hat, and let the horse drink. He used the dipper to get some water himself, then lowered the bucket and swung up into the saddle. Without a word, he rode off toward the southwest.

As the hoofbeats faded, Mike said to Smoke, "You believe any of what he had to say?"

"Not particularly, other than the part about him being a saddle tramp. I figure he was looking around out here to see if there was anything loose he could steal."

"You think he'll be back?"

"Doubtful. But it wouldn't hurt to post a guard anyway, if for no other reason than because there might be Apache raiders in the area. If there are, you can bet they know the station is here. They might even have eyes on it right now."

That thought made an icy finger drag its nail down Mike's spine. "We'll have to take turns on guard duty."

"I'll take a shift. I reckon Preacher will, too. If Whitney and his hostlers pitch in, you and Scratchy ought to be able to get a full night's sleep." Smoke paused. "You'll need it, since you'll be up on that box all day tomorrow."

"Yeah. I appreciate it, Mr. Jensen."

"Did you come out here for a reason, other than checking on the coach?"

"Yeah. Miss Bradshaw asked me to get her small bag from the boot."

"And you were happy to do that for her."

"Well, yeah." Mike bristled a little. "I'd do that for any of the passengers."

Smoke chuckled. "Yeah, you probably would, but it doesn't hurt when the lady asking the favor is as pretty as Miss Bradshaw, does it?"

"She's betrothed," Mike said.

"Yep, she is. Doesn't make her any less pretty."

Mike didn't know what to say to that, so he just went to the boot, untied the canvas cover, and reached inside to find the bag Catherine wanted.

Smoke leaned on the coach. "You take that on back inside to Miss Bradshaw. I'll stay out here and keep an eye on things for a while. You might tell Preacher we're going to be standing guard."

"All right. Thanks, Mr. Jensen."

"De nada."

Catherine stood up from the table where she was sitting and talking with Sally and came toward Mike as he entered the station. "I was beginning to think you were having trouble finding it."

"Nope, not at all." He handed her the bag. "Just got sidetracked a little."

"No trouble, I hope."

"Nope," he said again. "Nothing I couldn't handle." He wondered what might have happened if Smoke hadn't shown up. Would the drifter have gone for his gun and decided not to only when the odds against him had abruptly doubled?

No way of knowing, Mike told himself, and anyway, the incident was over. The stranger was gone, and Catherine was standing right in front of him, smiling at him. "How about if I get you a cup of coffee?"

"That would be very nice. Thank you again. You seem determined to take very good care of me, Mr. Olmsted."

"Yes, ma'am." He started to add, *It's my job*, then decided not to. Better to leave things just like they were.

Hard to say what the future might bring.

Southwest of the station, the rider brought his horse to a stop and looked back. The lights of the Hondo Wells station were no longer visible, which meant he was well out of earshot. He listened for a moment to make sure no one was trailing him, then turned the horse and headed east.

It would be a long, hard, and possibly perilous ride to Tucson, but once he made it and delivered the news to Smiler Coe, there might be a nice bonus in it for him.

Unless Caddo, who had been bound for Flat Rock Crossing, made it back to Tucson first. That was probably what would happen.

That bastard Caddo had all the luck.

CHAPTER 23

Smoke, Preacher, Tom Ballard, and the station keeper Whitney took turns standing guard during the night, but the hours of darkness passed peacefully, with no sign of the lurking stranger returning. No Apaches came skulking around the Hondo Wells station, either.

At least, not that any of the men were aware of. With Apaches, it was hard to be sure.

Everyone was up early the next morning, before dawn. When Scratchy and Mike went to check on the coach, Smoke walked outside with them. Scratchy stopped abruptly and lifted his head to sniff the air.

"Something wrong?" Smoke asked.

"Dunno," the old jehu said. "Smells a little like rain . . . but not like rain, if you know what I mean. I think what we got is some sand blowin' around."

"You'd expect that in country as dry as this, wouldn't you?"

"Yeah, any time there's a little breeze it blows the

dust around. We'll just have to hope it ain't nothin' more than that."

Mike said, "Do you think we need to lay over here for a day, Scratchy?"

"I wouldn't go that far," Scratchy replied with a frown. "Shouldn't be any reason we can't roll right on through to Tucson."

Satisfied that the coach was undisturbed and in good shape, Scratchy told Whitney to roust out the hostlers so they could get a fresh team hitched up. While that chore was being taken care of, the men went inside the station to enjoy the breakfast the Navajo woman had prepared.

Except for Preacher, the other passengers were looking a little tousled and sleepy. He was bright-eyed as ever and filled with vigor that seemed almost unnatural in a man his age. Any time anyone asked him about his surprising youthfulness, he always attributed it to whiskey and decades of adventurous living. "The whiskey keeps my blood flowin' good, and the rest done worn all the paddin' off of me," he would say. "Ain't nothin' left but the hard center."

Smoke poured himself a cup of coffee and sat down on one of the benches next to Sally, who was eating some strips of dried beef and chilies with a tortilla wrapped around them.

"Everything all right out there?" she asked him.

Smoke took a sip of the coffee, relishing the bite of the strong, black brew, and nodded. "Yeah, nobody else came sneaking around during the night, and it won't be long before the coach is ready to roll." He didn't say anything to her about Scratchy's

mild concern over the weather. Since it would probably come to nothing, there was no reason to worry
her or any of the other passengers.

"Will we reach Tucson today?"

"We might. If we're close, Scratchy will probably
want to push on until we get there, even if it means
traveling at night."

"I don't mind traveling at night. At least it's
cooler."

"Just as dusty, though."

She laughed and nodded. "Unfortunately true."

George's jaw stretched in an enormous yawn.

His grandmother told him, "Stop that or you'll
have me doing it, too."

"Sorry, Grandma. That bunk wasn't very comfortable. I didn't sleep good."

"Neither did I. But soon we'll be home, and things
will be much better."

A sullen expression came over George's face
again. "Tucson ain't never gonna be my home."

"You shouldn't say *ain't*. And you're wrong. It will
be your home."

"It ain't where I grew up," George said stubbornly.

Sally said, "George, do you know where I grew up?"

"No. How in the world would I know that?"

"George, don't be rude," Mrs. Bates said. "You
should respect your elders. Now apologize to Mrs.
Jensen."

"Sorry," George muttered without sounding the
least bit sincere.

"I grew up in New Hampshire," Sally went on. "I
never had any idea that I would wind up living in the

West and loving it out here. Now my home is in Colorado, and I wouldn't want to live anywhere else. It truly is my home and always will be."

"Yeah, but that's because you've got Mr. Jensen."

"That's some of it, of course. But I truly feel I was meant to be out here. I just didn't realize it when I was younger. You have your grandmother, and you'll make friends in Tucson, and someday there'll probably be a girl that you really like—"

"No ma'am!" George shook his head vehemently and declared, "Not hardly."

"Well, you just wait and see," Sally told him with a smile. "Good things will happen. I'm sure of that."

George turned to look at the other young woman at the table. "How about you, Miss Bradshaw? You're goin' to a new place."

"I'm not sure I'm going to like it, either, George," Catherine said. "I have to admit, a large part of me wishes I was back in Philadelphia. But if I'm to marry an army officer, I suppose I'll have to get used to moving around and living in places I don't like very much. And to be fair, there *are* a few things I've discovered that I like about the West." Her eyes darted toward Mike sitting at the other table with Scratchy, putting away a cup of coffee and a plate of food.

Smoke noted it and Sally did, too. He could tell by her smile. From time to time she gave in to a matchmaking urge, but he doubted if she would do that in this case, since Catherine was engaged to the lieutenant who was supposed to be waiting for her in Tucson. Even so, the thought might have crossed Sally's mind.

Whitney came into the station and announced, "The team's hitched up, Scratchy. You can pull out whenever you want."

Scratchy nodded and told the passengers, "Eat up, folks. We need to be hittin' the trail as soon as we can."

A short time later, everyone trooped out of the station, carrying whatever belongings they had taken inside with them the previous night.

As soon as those things were placed back in the boot and the canvas cover was secure, Mike went to the coach door on the side nearest the building and opened it. "Let me give you a hand, Miss Bradshaw," he said as Catherine was the first passenger to board.

"I can—" She stopped midsentence and smiled. "Why, thank you, Mr. Olmsted."

She had been about to refuse Mike's assistance, Smoke thought, just out of the habits her haughty nature had given her, but then she'd changed her mind. She continued smiling as Mike put his hand on her arm to steady her while she stepped up into the coach.

Yeah, definitely a little flirtation going on there. Smoke was glad that, even though he noticed it, it was none of his blasted business.

The sun wasn't up yet, although the eastern sky was red and gold with its approach. A breeze was whipping around this way and that, never blowing in the same direction for more than a second or two, it seemed. That would account for the dusty quality of the air Scratchy had noticed earlier.

The coach rocked on its leather thoroughbraces

as the passengers climbed in one by one. Mike closed the door behind Preacher, who was the last one in, then swung up to the driver's box beside Scratchy.

The old jehu spat over the side and in his rumbling voice told Whitney, "Keep your head down till all the trouble settles." Then he pushed the brake lever forward to disengage it, gathered up the reins, and popped his blacksnake whip over the heads of the leaders. The horses surged forward as Scratchy yelled at them.

The journey was underway again.

Nothing happened during the morning, although each time the coach stopped, Smoke noted that Scratchy still had a worried frown on his bearded face. While they were stopped for lunch and a fresh team at a station called Natty Flat, Smoke approached the jehu as he was staring back the way they had come. The air was hazy in that direction.

"Something wrong?" Smoke asked quietly.

"What?" Scratchy gave a little shake of his head as if Smoke had interrupted some deep thoughts. "Aw, no, it's fine. Nothin' to worry about."

"No offense, Scratchy, but you seem a mite worried. I'm a pretty good judge of things like that."

Scratchy hesitated for a moment, then said, "I don't want to get the passengers all stirred up for nothin', 'specially the ladies. I still don't like how much dust's in the air, and if you look back to the west, it's even thicker. You ever been in a sandstorm, Mr. Jensen?"

"A time or two. They're not much fun, as I recall."

"No, they sure ain't, and in these parts they can be so bad you ain't never seen nothin' like 'em."

"Nothin' like what?" a new voice asked.

Smoke and Scratchy looked over to see that Preacher had come up in time to hear the tail end of the conversation.

"Sandstorms," Smoke said.

"Lord have mercy!" the old mountain man exclaimed. "Once I got caught in one that was so thick, I looked up and seen a prairie dog a-diggin' hisself a hole a hunnerd feet in the air!"

Scratchy laughed, seemingly in spite of himself. "Yeah, I've seen 'em that bad, too."

"You reckon that's what we've got coming today?" Smoke asked.

"Maybe. It's hard to say. Could just be a mite dustier than usual, and that's all it'll amount to. That's what I'm hopin' for, anyway."

"Should we wait it out here?"

"No, I can get us through," Scratchy answered without hesitation. "I been drivin' coaches in this part of the country for a long time. Started on the old Butterfield route as a youngster. Even if it comes a blow, I can get us through."

Smoke nodded. "That's good enough for me, then."

Scratchy looked at Smoke and Preacher. "You won't say nothin' to upset the other folks?"

"Nothin' to say," Preacher replied.

Scratchy seemed satisfied with that.

The coach departed the Natty Flat station a short time later. The last one in line, Smoke paused for a second and glanced up at the sun. It was brassier than it had been earlier in the day. Instead of its usual midday brilliance, its light seemed to have been dimmed somehow, as if a curtain hung over it.

A curtain of sand, maybe?

"Anything wrong, Smoke?" Sally asked.

Smoke wasn't one to lie to his wife, not even little white lies to spare her unnecessary worry, so he said, "I hope not," and stepped up into the coach, shutting the door firmly behind him.

CHAPTER 24

About an hour after leaving the last station, Smoke felt the stagecoach vibrate a little harder as its speed increased. Up on the box, Scratchy's whip cracked as he shouted at the team.

Smoke looked across Sally at Preacher and saw that the old mountain man felt the change as well.

Preacher wasn't the only one. Tom Ballard leaned forward tensely and said, "Is something wrong?"

Mrs. Bates gasped and asked, "Could it be those Apaches?"

"I'll have a look." Smoke reached over and loosened the canvas cover on the window beside him. He took his hat off, stuck his head out, and peered behind the coach as best he could. He didn't see any Apaches, but what he saw made his jaw tighten in alarm, anyway.

Sally saw that, and knowing her husband as well as she did, she said, "Smoke, what is it?"

"Looks like a sandstorm." That was putting it mildly. He had never seen anything like it before.

In the distance behind the stagecoach rose a wall of flying sand that looked like a massive cliff or bluff, but those geographical features didn't move. The towering cloud of sand seemed to be rushing over the landscape, swallowing up everything it came to and obliterating it.

"A sandstorm?" Catherine Bradshaw repeated. "Well, how bad can that be?"

No point in keeping the knowledge from the other passengers, Smoke thought. "Pretty bad," he said as he sat back on the seat again and tied down the canvas curtain. He knew from the way the coach had sped up that Scratchy and Mike were aware of what was behind them, too. Smoke offered no suggestion of turning back. The storm would engulf them long before they could reach Natty Flat.

Their only option was to outrun it to the next station and take shelter there while the storm blew itself out. From what he had heard about some southwestern sandstorms, that might take quite a while. If worse came to worst, they might have to stop and ride it out inside the coach.

With a storm the size of the one following them . . . that might be enough to bury the horses, the stagecoach, and everybody inside it.

Up on the box, Scratchy looked more worried than Mike had ever seen him. In fact, the old jehu looked downright scared. And that scared Mike, who had seen Scratchy face all kinds of trouble without ever flinching.

Mike raised his voice over the clattering wheels

and the thundering hoofbeats. "You reckon we can stay ahead of it?"

"We have to!" Scratchy replied. "If it gets too bad, I ain't sure I can keep the team movin'! Once we stop, we're done for if there ain't no place to get inside!"

Mike's hands tightened on the shotgun. He had faced bandits on several occasions, and even though those had been harrowing incidents, he hadn't had time to be scared, either for himself or for the coach's passengers. With possible disaster closing in behind them, he had more of a chance to think about what it might mean. Like most Westerners, the code he lived by demanded that women and youngsters be protected at all costs. He and Scratchy were paid to risk their lives, but those other folks weren't.

As Scratchy worked the reins and the whip, he kept looking back over his shoulder at the approaching storm. After a few minutes, he suddenly said, "I got an idea!"

With no more warning than that, he hauled on the reins and pulled the team to the left, which sent the coach in a big, sweeping curve that left the road behind. Luckily, the surrounding terrain was still level and hard-packed enough that the coach's wheels were able to roll over it without much trouble. The ride got a little rougher, but it had been far from gentle to start with.

"What in blazes are you doing?" Mike yelled. The coach was heading north by northeast now, which put the massive sandstorm on their left as it closed in.

"We can't outrun the damned thing!" Scratchy replied. "It'll catch up to us sooner or later! But look at it! It stretches farther to the south than it does the north. If we can get to the upper edges of it, maybe it won't be as bad!"

That seemed like a mighty risky plan to Mike, but at the same time, he could understand Scratchy's reasoning. The storm wouldn't be as powerful at its fringes as it was at the center. They might be able to keep moving through it and eventually break out into the clear.

Unfortunately, now that they were traveling parallel to the wall of flying sand instead of moving in the same direction, it was barreling down on them even faster. Mike didn't know what the odds were of them reaching safety before the storm smashed down on them in all its choking fury, but even if he'd been a gambling man, he wouldn't take that bet.

The turn to the north made it possible for the other passengers to look out the windows on the left side of the coach and get a good look at the monster bearing down on them.

"Oh, my heavens!" Mrs. Bates cried out. She recoiled back against the seat as if she had been struck and reached out, groping blindly for George. She couldn't take her eyes off the storm. Her hand found the boy's shoulder and closed down tightly enough to make him wince.

Catherine stared wide-eyed at the wall of sand, her mouth opening in an shocked *O*, even though no sound came out.

Tom Ballard's hands clenched into fists. The bleak expression on his face said that he realized he couldn't strike out at the natural disaster in the making, but the impulse to do so was in him, anyway.

Even Sally, who had more fortitude than any woman Smoke had ever known, clutched her husband's arm for a second. "That looks bad."

"It's a-blowin' up a humdinger, all right," Preacher said.

"What's Scratchy doing?" Ballard asked. "We should be trying to get away from the storm, not traveling at right angles to it."

Smoke had grasped the old jehu's plan as soon as he felt the coach start to turn. "He's going to try to reach the northern edge of the storm before it sweeps over us. He may not be able to make it, but at least on the outskirts the storm shouldn't be as bad."

"That's still pretty risky."

"Not as risky as letting the center of that behemoth overtake us. If it did, we'd all stand a good chance of choking to death."

"That can't happen," Ballard muttered. "I've got to get back to Tucson."

"To be with your family for Christmas," Sally said.

"Yes, ma'am," Ballard said.

But once again Smoke got the impression there was more to the newspaperman's anxiety than that.

George coughed. "It sure is dusty in here."

Even though the main body of the storm was still off to the west, wind gusts were blowing out in front of it with enough force to whip up swirling clouds of dust. Smoke drew a bandanna from his pocket and held it out to Catherine. "You should tie this around your face so your mouth and nose are covered."

"What about your wife?" Catherine asked as she hesitated in taking the bandanna.

"Don't worry. I'm prepared," Sally said as she drew a large handkerchief of her own out of her bag.

"Here you go, ma'am," Preacher said to Mrs. Bates as he extended his bandanna to the older woman. "You better do likewise. You want to keep from breathin' as much o' that stuff as you can."

"You should give it to George!"

"Aw, I'm all right, Grandma," the boy said, but another cough followed the words.

Smoke leaned forward. "Pull your shirt up like this, son." He tugged upward on George's shirt to demonstrate. "Hold it over your mouth and nose. That'll help."

George did as Smoke suggested, then hunkered on the bench in the middle of the coach.

Tom Ballard found a handkerchief and held it over his face as the ladies were doing. Smoke and Preacher persevered the way they were, giving no sign that the dust was thickening in the stagecoach except a slight squinting of their eyes.

The coach hit a rough spot and jolted heavily. Smoke thought the wheels actually might have left the ground for a split second. Scratchy was getting all the speed he could out of the team. The question was whether that would be enough to get them to safety in time.

Seeing that Mrs. Bates looked terrified, Sally lowered the handkerchief she'd been holding in front of her face and said, "Mr. Ballard, would you change places with me?"

Ballard looked puzzled, but he said, "Of course, Mrs. Jensen."

In the coach's close quarters, making the switch was rather awkward, but a moment later it was done and Sally was sitting beside Mrs. Bates.

She took hold of the older woman's hand. "It's going to be all right, Violet. Mr. Stevenson is an experienced driver. I'm sure he's going to get all of us through this just fine."

"Do . . . do you really think so, my dear?"

"I really do."

"But that storm looks so bad, and . . . and we're going so fast I'm afraid we're going to crash!"

George said, "I think going this fast is fun!" He grew more solemn, though, as he added, "I don't like the looks of that storm. We had some sandstorms up in Flagstaff, but never one like that!"

"Oh, George, I'm sorry I dragged you away from there."

"I reckon you had to, Grandma. I couldn't stay there by myself."

Smoke was glad to see that the boy had dropped his sullen, complaining nature . . . at least for a while. Mrs. Bates was already upset enough without having to worry about that.

"I wish we were out of this," the older woman said in a half-moan.

Catherine, on Mrs. Bates's other side, patted her on the shoulder and said in a reassuring tone, "It's going to be all right. Why, I think the air is starting to clear up a bit already."

Smoke was a little surprised to see the young woman exhibiting concern for anyone else. That was encouraging, too. Folks could be petty and self-centered, but when things got bad, most of them were able to put that aside and care for their fellow human beings.

Luckily, only a handful were such skunks they just needed shooting. For varmints like that, Smoke, Preacher, and fellows like Matt and Luke were around to deal with them.

That thought had just gone through Smoke's mind when something thudded hard against the side of the coach and he felt an all-too-familiar sensation as something ripped through the air in front of his face. He jerked his head around and spotted the rough-edged hole in the coach's side next to the window and recognized it immediately for what it was.

He had seen too many bullet holes not to.

"Down!" he shouted over the racket made by the bouncing, careening stagecoach and the howling wind. His hand flashed to the Colt on his hip. "Everybody down on the floor!"

Preacher reacted as instantly as Smoke had, drawing his revolver with his right hand while he reached across with his left and took hold of Catherine Bradshaw's arm. "Get down there next to the bench, miss," he snapped. "Hurry!"

Sally might not have realized exactly what was going on, but she knew Smoke and Preacher wouldn't be acting like that unless something was very wrong. She put her arms around Mrs. Bates and urged her to the floor, joining the crowded huddle there.

Tom Ballard told George, "Get down there with your grandmother, son!" He looked at Smoke. "Is it . . ."

Gun in hand, Smoke was peering out the window, his neck twisted so he could look behind the coach. He had already spotted figures on horseback racing through the haze, trying to overtake the stagecoach. Others were off to the sides, closing in. He saw another spurt of orange muzzle flame, but the bullet didn't seem to hit the coach.

Smoke turned back toward the front of the stagecoach and bellowed, "Scratchy! Mike! *Apaches!*"

CHAPTER 25

Up on the box, Scratchy roared curses as he popped the whip over the heads of the team. The horses were already running at full speed, but he had to keep trying to get more out of them. He didn't look back to see how close the Indians were. That wouldn't help anything.

Mike reached down, placed the shotgun on the floorboards at his feet, and snatched up his Winchester. As he turned on the seat to see behind the stagecoach, he worked the rifle's lever to throw a cartridge into the chamber.

Exposed between his lowered hat brim and the bandanna over his mouth and nose, his bare skin felt the sting of a million needles as the fine grains of sand pelted it. He squinted and made out half a dozen or more figures galloping after the coach on the squat ponies the Apaches favored.

Those horses had plenty of stamina and had

plenty of meat on them for emergencies. Although they weren't built for speed, a few of the riders had managed to draw ahead of the others and were almost even with the coach on both sides. Mike saw a flash of muzzle fire and heard the bullet smack into the coach.

He brought the Winchester to his shoulder and aimed as best he could through the blowing sand. The rifle cracked and kicked against his shoulder. He couldn't see well enough to tell if the bullet found its target or not. As he swung the rifle around, he triggered four more shots as fast as he could work the Winchester's lever.

Spray enough lead and maybe one or two of the shots would knock an Apache off his pony, he thought. If he could bring down a couple, the others might break off the attack.

They must really be on the prod, he told himself. Otherwise they would have headed for shelter when they saw the storm coming. Instead, they had used the flying sand as cover until they were practically right behind the stagecoach, then launched their attack. If they managed to kill any of the horses, the chase would be over before it even had the chance to get started good.

"You hittin' any o' the red devils?" Scratchy yelled.

"Don't know!" Mike replied as he momentarily lowered the Winchester. "I'm sure as hell trying!"

Shots boomed from inside the coach. Some of the passengers—Smoke and Preacher, almost certainly—were using handguns to put up a fight. Mike wasn't sure Colts would do much good in their current

predicament, but if anybody could do damage with
.45s, it was Smoke Jensen and the old mountain man
called Preacher!

Their Winchesters were in the boot at the rear of
the coach. Smoke wished they had the repeaters.
They would be able to get the rifles into action if
Scratchy managed to get to a place where they could
fort up. Until then, they would do what they could
with their revolvers.

The Apaches were at the far edge of handgun
range, and the sand in the air made aiming difficult if
not impossible. Few men had the almost supernatural
ability with a gun that Smoke and Preacher possessed,
however.

Smoke drew a bead on one of the raiders and
squeezed the trigger. The Colt roared and bucked in
his hand. He caught just a glimpse as the Apache
threw up his hands and toppled off the racing pony.
It was enough to tell him that one member of the war
party was down, at least.

Preacher fired from the window on the other side of
the coach, then exclaimed, "Got one o' the varmints!"

"So did I. They're not dropping back, though."

"Not yet, anyway." Preacher's gun slammed out another shot. "Drat! Missed that time!"

From the floor, Mrs. Bates quavered, "We're all
g-going to d-die!"

"No, we're not," Sally said firmly. "This isn't the
first time Smoke and Preacher have fought off Indians. Remember the story Preacher told about the
Pawnees, when he and Smoke first met?"

"I remember," George said. "That's where Smoke
got his name!"

"That's right, and nothing has changed. They'll protect us."

Bent low on the front seat rather than down on the floor, Tom Ballard slid over to the front window on the same side as Smoke. The newspaperman reached under his coat and pulled out a small pistol. "I can help." He angled the pistol's barrel out the window and fired a shot.

"How many rounds do you have for that?" Smoke thought Ballard's gun was probably a .32. It wouldn't pack much punch, especially at that distance.

"A couple dozen," the newspaperman replied.

"Better save 'em in case you need 'em for closer work," Smoke advised. He paused, then added, "And save four of them, for sure."

Ballard looked confused for a second, then understanding etched bleak lines in his face. The four rounds would be for Sally, Catherine, Mrs. Bates, and George, if things got so desperate it was either that or be captured by the Apaches. He nodded solemnly to show he knew what Smoke meant.

Up on the driver's box, Mike Olmsted kept up a steady fire with the Winchester. None of the Apaches were close enough for him to use the shotgun on them. When the rifle ran dry, he reached in the pocket of the duster where he kept extra rounds and reloaded.

Bullets continued to whip around the coach. Every now and then, a slug would thud into the vehicle, and once a bullet struck the brass rail running around the roof of the coach and ricocheted off with a vicious whine.

But the raiders weren't very good shots from the backs of running ponies, and neither Mike nor Scratchy were hit as the fight continued.

Mike, on the other hand, was pretty sure he had knocked a couple Apaches off their mounts. Down in the coach, Smoke and Preacher kept up a withering fire of their own that caused more than one raider to fall.

Preacher whooped immediately after triggering another round. "Got another one! And they're fallin' back on this side."

"Over here, too." Smoke lowered his gun and started reloading while he had the chance. His fingers moved with swift efficiency as he dumped the empty shells and thumbed in fresh cartridges. Considering the many thousands of bullets he had slid into guns, he didn't have to look at what he was doing. He could reload strictly by feel, allowing him to keep an eye on what was going on outside the coach.

And that was a good thing. As he snapped the .45's cylinder closed, he said, "Got some others coming up fast!"

Some of the Apaches' ponies were about played out, but others still had a burst left in them. Since the stagecoach was on the verge of getting away, the raiders had to stop it soon if they were going to.

Blowing sand continued to whip around the vehicle as it careened across the landscape. The main body of the storm hadn't caught up yet, but it was close. As he leaned closer to the door and aimed at the riders drawing even with the coach, Smoke narrowed his eyes as far as he could and still see.

At that moment, the coach hit another rough spot and bounced hard. The unexpected jolt sent him lurching against the door. With a sharp crack, the latch gave way and the door swung out violently. Smoke toppled into empty space.

Twisting in midair, he flung out his left hand desperately and grabbed the door flapping back and forth.

Sally saw him fall out of the coach and lunged after him. Her arms closed around his ankles and she hung on for dear life. Smoke hung there, his wife's grip on his feet and his own tenuous grasp on the door all that kept him from smashing into the ground at high speed.

As he tightened his fingers around the door where the window opened in it, he heard a peculiar sound. He realized it was a high-pitched war cry coming from one of the raiders swooping in toward him. The sight of a white man hanging out of the stagecoach was just too tempting a target for the Apache to resist.

Smoke craned his neck around for a better look and raised his right arm. Even falling out of the stagecoach, he had held on to the Colt. It took more than a brush with death to make Smoke Jensen drop his gun. As the barrel came up, flame jetted from the muzzle.

The Apache's head jerked back as the slug tore into his throat just under his chin. He flung his arms out to the side and went backwards off the pony as if a giant hand had swatted him away from the animal.

More exposed to the wind and sand outside, Smoke's hat flew off. He had given his bandanna to Mrs. Bates, leaving him with no protection as the storm clawed at his face. His mouth and nose clogged with grit. Although his eyes were almost closed, he could see well enough to take aim and loose another shot at one of the galloping Apaches. The raider jerked but didn't fall off his mount. He did begin to veer away from the pursuit, however, so Smoke figured he was wounded.

The rest of the raiders had fallen back on that side of the coach. Smoke jammed his Colt back into its holster and reached for the doorjamb with his right hand. When he grasped it, Catherine Bradshaw caught hold of his arm and heaved. With his feet planted firmly at the edge of the door, Sally let go of his ankles, grabbed his belt, and pulled, too. Smoke fell into the coach much like he had fallen out of it.

Tom Ballard reached across and closed the door, but the latch was broken and it wouldn't stay shut. He gave up and said, "That was close!"

"Too close," Smoke agreed. "Preacher, what's going on over there?"

Preacher fired another shot, then lowered his revolver and leaned back away from the window. "Looks like they're lightin' a shuck," he reported. "I reckon between us and Mike, we done for more 'n half the skunks. That storm's pretty much on top of us, though, so I don't know how much longer we can go on. That might have somethin' to do with those 'Paches pullin' out, too. They don't want to be caught in this any more than we do."

"Smoke, are you all right?" Sally asked. "You weren't wounded?"

"No. Wrenched my arm a little when I caught hold of the door and my weight hit it, but it's nothing to worry about. I probably would have fallen if you hadn't grabbed me like you did."

She managed to smile a little. "I'm not letting you get away from me that easily, mister."

"I'm mighty glad about that." A frown suddenly creased Smoke's forehead. "Wait a minute. Are we slowing down?"

He was right. The stagecoach was coming to a stop.

In those conditions, with the giant sandstorm about to sweep over them, that couldn't be anything good.

CHAPTER 26

Seeing the Apaches begin to peel away and fall back, Mike sent a couple more shots after them, then lowered the Winchester and called to Scratchy, "Looks like they're giving up!"

"Ain't a moment too soon!" the old jehu replied. "I think at least one of the horses was hit!"

That news made a chill go down Mike's backbone. Out in the middle of nowhere, horses meant life, especially with the dual threat of the Apaches and the massive sandstorm. He turned to look and saw that the leader on the right and the horse right behind it were faltering. The animals' gallant hearts kept them moving, but something was wrong, no doubt about that.

"I got to stop and check on 'em," Scratchy said. "Are those heathens still back there?"

Mike twisted around to study the landscape behind them, then reported, "I don't see them! Of course, I can't see very far with all this blowing sand."

"We'll have to risk it," Scratchy said as he pulled back on the reins. "Keep your eyes open, son!" Gradually, he brought the stagecoach to a halt.

As soon as the vehicle stopped, Smoke opened the door and got out. "What's wrong?" he asked as he looked up at the box.

"Got some wounded horses in the team, I'm afraid." Scratchy set the brake lever, wrapped the reins around it, and climbed down.

Smoke had already moved forward, his experienced eyes finding the splashes of blood on the two horses. The leader was hit the worst. He was breathing hard, and blood bubbled from his nostrils with each labored breath. That, along with the blood on the horse's side, told Smoke the bullet must have passed through the animal's lungs.

"I'm sorry, old-timer," he murmured as he rested a hand on the horse's shoulder. He looked over at Scratchy and added, "I'm afraid he's a goner."

"Yeah, I can see that," Scratchy said, grim-faced with anger. "How about the other one?"

"Shot through the neck. He's bleeding pretty bad. Doesn't have long, either."

Scratchy looked up at the box, where Mike was standing and peering around, alert for any sign of danger . . . although the sandstorm would mask any such signs until they were perilously close.

"You see them Injuns anywhere?" Scratchy asked.

"Nope."

"Well, keep watch." Scratchy turned back to Smoke. "We got to get these poor animals unhitched while they're still standin'. It'll be easier and faster that way. Then I can put 'em outta their misery."

Smoke knew Scratchy was right. He could handle hitching and unhitching as well as any hostler, so he and the jehu set to work, knowing they were racing the clock.

"We're going to push on with a four-horse hitch?" Smoke asked as they handled the grim chore.

"It'll be mighty slow, but there ain't much else we can do unless you want to unhitch them, too, and use 'em to ride. I don't figure Mrs. Bates and Miss Bradshaw would be very good at ridin' bareback, and we sure can't ask 'em to walk in these hellish conditions."

"No, we'd probably make better time like you said, using the four horses to pull the coach. We need to look them over and make sure none of them are hurt."

"I don't reckon they are, but we'll make sure."

When the two wounded horses were freed from the team, Smoke and Scratchy led them forward a few yards, the animals taking slow, faltering steps as blood continued to drip from their injuries.

Smoke glanced back and saw Sally leaning out to see what was going on. He told her, "Keep everybody inside the coach."

She nodded in understanding. She had seen more than her share of danger and tragedy over the years. That seemed to go hand in hand with being married to Smoke Jensen.

Smoke and Scratchy drew their pistols. A moment later, two shots rang out so close together they sounded almost like one. Both horses slumped to the ground, beyond pain and suffering.

"We got to move the other leader over and back to

even things up," Scratchy said. "Best get at it, too. If those 'Paches are still close enough to have heard those shots, they're liable to figure out what they mean and come lookin' for us again. With a four-horse team, we can't make a run for it the way we did before."

He and Smoke turned toward the coach to get that chore done, and as they did, the full force of the storm struck with all its fury.

The wind was so strong they stumbled back a step. The sand lashed at them. Both lowered their heads and raised their arms to protect their eyes. Smoke looked up at the driver's box. He could barely see Mike hunkered there, using the coach itself to blunt some of the storm's power.

Staggering, Smoke grasped Scratchy's arm to steady him and leaned close to shout in the jehu's ear, "Do we still try to push on?"

"We got to!" Scratchy replied. "If we sit still, the sand'll bury us!"

Smoke nodded. He had figured that was what Scratchy would say. They were still in deadly danger and would be until they found some sort of shelter.

Of course, in the blinding hell storm, finding shelter would be purely a matter of luck . . . or divine providence.

Less than a week before Christmas, they could sure use a miracle.

By the time Smoke and Scratchy got the uninjured leader moved back to replace the dead horse that had been in second place on the right, Smoke felt like he had breathed in a pound of sand and swallowed a gallon of the stuff. Every inch of exposed skin was covered by a thick layer of grit. He wanted to know how Sally, Preacher, and the others inside the coach were doing, but there was no time to check on them.

At least the Apaches hadn't doubled back and shown up again.

They had too much sense to be out in this, Smoke thought wryly.

At last the remaining horses were hitched so they could pull the stagecoach. As soon as Scratchy had climbed onto the box, Smoke made his way through the yellow, howling gloom to the broken door, which still flapped wildly and banged against the side of the coach.

He grabbed the door and used it to brace himself as he climbed in. All the passengers were huddled on the floor except for Preacher, who was keeping an eagle eye out through the window on the opposite side.

"I told ever'body to stay down, just in case them varmints come back," the old mountain man said. "Figured since we were stopped, there weren't no immediate danger, but you never can tell with Injuns."

"You sure can't," Smoke agreed, his voice hoarse from all the irritation in his throat. "I think they've gone to ground, though, and we're going to try to do the same. The Apaches killed two of the horses, so we're a little crippled. Scratchy and I agree that we can't just sit here and try to wait out the storm."

"It'd be liable to kill the other horses if we did," Preacher said. "Then we'd really be in a fine fix."

"So what are we going to do?" Tom Ballard asked.

As if in answer to the question, the coach lurched

into motion. It rolled forward slowly as the remaining horses strained against their harness.

"We're going to keep looking for shelter," Smoke said.

Catherine Bradshaw asked, "What if we can't find any?"

"We will," Smoke said confidently. But he knew the real answer to Catherine's question, and so did everyone else in the stagecoach.

If they didn't find shelter, chances were very good they would all die.

Up on the box, Scratchy no longer used the whip. He wouldn't be getting any more speed out of the team than he already was. The big draft horses were strong and had all the stamina in the world, but he had already asked a lot out of them.

Not only that. The sandstorm was rough on them, too. The horses could pull the stagecoach and its passengers, but only at a slower pace and for a limited amount of time.

Mike and Scratchy sat with heads drawn down between hunched shoulders. They had tied their hats on so they wouldn't blow away. The bandanna over Mike's nose and mouth helped a little, but the sand was still choking and gagging him. He turned his head from side to side and kept the Winchester ready, but he could see barely twenty feet in the terrible murk.

He was a little surprised it wasn't pitch black. It didn't seem possible any sunlight could penetrate the clouds of sand. Yet there was still a feeble glow in the air to tell them that somewhere the sun was shining.

The horses trudged along. The slow pace and the gentle rocking of the coach might have been enough to cause Mike to doze off if he hadn't been so miserable. His eyelids were drooping anyway over gritty orbs when a flash of movement caught his attention. His head jerked up.

A bronzed figure leaped out of the gloom and landed on the side of the driver's box, clinging to it with one hand as the other drove a knife at Mike's throat.

CHAPTER 27

Mike jerked the rifle up and around, swinging the barrel toward the swiftly descending blade. It was purely an instinctive move, but they came together with a clang of metal against metal as the Winchester knocked the knife aside.

Since Mike already had the rifle raised, he thrust out with the stock and slammed the brass butt plate into the middle of the Apache's face. He felt bone crunch under the impact. The Apache lost his grip on the coach and fell backwards.

"Over here!" Scratchy yelled.

Mike swung around and spotted a raider with a rifle charging toward them from the left. Mike knew he couldn't bring his Winchester to bear in time to stop the Apache from firing.

He didn't have to. The passengers inside the coach were alert. A shot blasted from in there and the charging raider dropped his rifle and fell to his knees. Another slug from a Colt drove him over onto his back.

Visibility was too bad for the Apaches to attack from long range. They had to get close to strike, which meant Mike could use the scattergun. He set the repeater on the floorboards and snatched up the coach gun.

He spotted another figure in the swirling sand, hesitated just long enough to make sure it was an Indian, and then slammed a load of buckshot into the raider. A rifle cracked and a bullet chewed splinters from the seat only inches away from Mike. He twisted more, saw another spurt of muzzle flame, and heard the slug rip past his ear. He triggered the coach gun's other barrel and saw the vague figure fly backwards from the buckshot's impact.

Yipping and howling, more Apaches closed in around the coach. Several guns were going off inside the vehicle. The gun-handling skill of Smoke and Preacher was legendary, and they proved why as an Apache fell with each blast. It was as deadly a display of shooting as Mike had ever seen.

He added to it, stuffing fresh shells into the shotgun and then blowing huge holes in the sandstorm and anything else that got in the stagecoach's way.

"You all right, Scratchy?" Mike asked as he reloaded again.

"Durned near deaf from all the shootin', but I reckon I'll live!" Scratchy answered. "How many more o' them devils are there?"

Mike didn't know the answer to that. He peered around through narrowed eyes, searching for another target as he held the shotgun ready to fire. The

shooting had stopped, though, and he didn't see anything but sand. "Looks like they pulled out again!"

"Ain't no way of knowin' that! There could be a
hunnerd of 'em right out there, fifty yards away, and
we wouldn't know it! We can't see 'em!"

That was true. It was like the only part of the world
that still existed was a small, ragged circle about fifty
feet across, surrounded by flying sand. That was as
far as Mike's vision could reach.

He felt the coach shift and looked around to see
Smoke climbing out. In lithe, athletic fashion, Smoke
put a foot in the window, pushed himself up, and
swung onto the coach's roof.

"Any of the horses hit that time?" he asked as he
knelt there.

"I don't think so," Scratchy replied. "None of 'em
broke stride or seem to be laborin' any more 'n you
expect under the circumstances."

"How well do you know this part of the country?"

"Well, that's hard to say, seein' as I don't really
know where we are! We're a long ways off the reg'lar
trail, though. Ain't much of anything in these parts,
as far as I recollect. Plenty o' sand and rock, some
ridges and a few gullies and dry washes. Here and
there a mesa or a pile o' rock big enough to be called
a mountain."

"If there's any shelter, that's where we'll find it."

Scratchy nodded. "Yeah, there might be a cave in
the side of a hill, maybe an overhangin' bluff, somethin' like that. If it's just enough to break the wind,
I'll sure be grateful for that!"

"Sooner or later it'll be night. We need to find a
place to hole up before that."

"You ain't tellin' me anything I don't already know, Mr. Jensen! We can't travel after dark. Too much chance of drivin' right into a gully and bustin' this ol' coach into a million pieces!"

Scratchy kept the team moving, and Smoke remained atop the stagecoach. Mike was glad to have another pair of eyes to help him watch for more Apaches.

Once again, the raiders seemed to have faded away. Mike didn't trust that for a second. They had broken off their attack before, only to come back and try again. They were certainly capable of showing up a third time.

After what seemed like an endless amount of time, Smoke leaned forward with his head between Mike's and Scratchy's and said, "I think I see something up ahead. There's some sort of . . . dark line."

Mike squinted. "I see it, too, Mr. Jensen. Scratchy, can you tell what it is?"

"Could be a ridge," the jehu said. "It'll be pure luck if there's a cave in it we can use, though."

Smoke muttered something, and Mike asked, "What did you say, Mr. Jensen?"

"Pure luck . . . or a miracle," Smoke repeated.

"I'll sure take it, either way!" Scratchy leaned forward, slapped the reins against the backs of the horses, and yelled, "Come on, you varmints! Not that much farther, and then you'll be stoppin'!" He added grimly, "One way or the other!"

Time really had no meaning inside the storm, but it seemed to drag terribly anyway as the horses plodded on and the coach rocked and creaked. Every joint in its suspension would need oil once the ordeal was over, or the sand might make them seize up.

That was assuming, of course, the coach and everybody in it didn't wind up buried under a mountain of sand.

The dark line Smoke and Mike had spotted thickened and turned into a bluff about forty feet high. The top of it bulged out, but not enough to offer any shelter. The bluff's face was pitted sandstone.

Scratchy hauled back on the reins and exclaimed disgustedly, "Son of a—! So much for a miracle!"

"There might still be someplace we can get out of this storm," Smoke said. "Anyway, we can't get over this bluff, so we might as well drive along beside it."

"Yeah, but which way?"

"Mike, why don't you and I get down and explore a little on foot?" Smoke suggested. "I'll go one way and you can go the other. With the bluff to guide us, we won't get lost as long as we don't get out of sight of it."

"Just don't stray off where you *can't* see it," Scratchy warned. "Then you'd likely never find your way back here."

"I don't much like splitting up like that," Mike said with a frown.

"Neither do I," Smoke agreed, "but we can cover twice as much ground that way. Preacher and Scratchy will still be here to protect the passengers if the Apaches come back."

"Sounds like our best bet, Mike," Scratchy said. "Just be careful."

"All right. How far do we go?"

"No more than half a mile or so," Smoke said. "Can you make a good guess at that?"

"Yeah, I grew up out here. I can tell how far I've gone . . . although this storm might throw me off some!"

"Do the best you can." Smoke climbed down part of the way and then dropped to the ground.

Scratchy and Mike clambered down from the box.

Smoke pulled back the broken door and leaned through the opening to explain to the others what he and Mike were going to do. Mrs. Bates was sobbing quietly as George sat beside her, patting her shoulder every now and then. Catherine was pale and drawn and scared, but she seemed to be fighting to hang on to her composure and succeeding for the most part.

Tom Ballard said, "Is there anything I can do to help, Mr. Jensen?"

"I reckon under the circumstances, you might as well call me Smoke, Tom. No need for formality once fellas have fought side by side. Best thing you can do is stay here and lend a hand to Preacher and Scratchy if they need it. Probably not a good idea to have more than two of us out wandering around in this mess."

Catherine untied the bandanna she had around her mouth and nose and held it out to Smoke. "Here, Mr. Jensen. You'll need this more than I do."

"Thank you, miss," he told her with a smile.

Preacher asked, "You sure you know what you're a-doin'?"

Smoke laughed. "No, but that's never stopped me before, has it?"

Sally leaned closer to him. "You be careful, Smoke. Don't get lost in this . . . this insanity."

"Shoot, I've never been lost in my life."

She raised an eyebrow. "Is that so?"

"Yeah. Sometimes I wasn't sure how to get from where I was to where I wanted to go, but I always knew where I was. That means I wasn't lost."

Sally laughed softly, shook her head, and leaned forward to press her lips against his. It was the sandiest kiss they had ever shared, but that didn't make it any less sweet to Smoke.

He couldn't linger. He straightened and saw Mike waiting beside the horses. The animals' heads drooped with exhaustion. Like the rest of them, the horses were near the end of their rope.

"You ready?" Smoke asked.

"Yeah, I—"

Catherine stuck her head out the door and called, "Be careful, Mike!"

Mike looked like he was about to take a step toward her. He had to be thinking about a good-bye kiss, too, but he settled for nodding. "I sure will. Don't you worry, now. We'll be back soon with good news."

"I'll be counting on it," Catherine said.

Smoke and Mike walked toward the bluff. They didn't have far to go before it towered over them. When they reached it, Smoke asked, "Which way do you want to go?"

"I reckon one way's as good as the other, isn't it?"

"As far as I can tell," Smoke replied with a shrug.

Mike pointed to the right. "I'll go this way."

"Good luck." Smoke held out his hand, and the two men shook.

Then they turned away from each other, started along the sandstone wall, and were soon lost to sight in the storm.

CHAPTER 28

Smoke didn't like being parted from Sally, especially in circumstances where both of them were in danger. He wasn't the sort to brood about such things, though. Action was what would save them.

He stayed close to the bluff as he walked, bent forward slightly to help him push into the wind. The sand stung his face, and he was glad Catherine had given him back the bandanna. He wished he still had his hat, but that was long gone. He kept his eyes slitted as much as he could and still see where he was going, but the grit still got in there. His eye sockets felt like they were lined with the stuff.

After a while, he paused and looked back, but of course he couldn't see the stagecoach. It was long since out of sight. He rested for a moment and then went on.

The sand was starting to drift against the bluff, just like snow would have. The thick layer of it made the going harder. Smoke slogged onward. The air around him was almost the same color as the bluff, so he reached out from time to time to brush his fingers against the sandstone, just to make sure he hadn't wandered away from it.

He was trailing his fingertips along the bluff when suddenly they weren't touching anything anymore.

Smoke stopped and turned toward the rock. He could have encountered just a tiny irregularity. He reached out farther and still didn't feel anything. The bluff seemed darker to his tortured vision, too . . . because it wasn't there anymore.

The entrance to a cave was before him.

Smoke's heart slugged heavily in his chest as he realized it might be the life-saving shelter they'd been looking for. He stepped inside it to explore and find out.

The cave mouth was twelve feet wide and maybe ten feet high. Not big enough for the stagecoach, but that didn't matter as long as the people and the horses could crowd inside. The gloom was even thicker than it was out in the terrible sandstorm.

He fished a lucifer out of his pocket and snapped it to life with his thumbnail. The wind blew out the match almost immediately, but in the brief flare of light Smoke saw that the cave widened out inside the entrance and extended at least several yards inside the bluff, deeper than the match light had reached.

Keeping his right hand on the butt of his Colt, he used his left to strike another lucifer. He cupped it inside his palm to protect it from the wind, and the match burned for several seconds, showing him the cave had no other occupants. He'd been concerned there might have been a rattlesnake den or maybe a cougar or some other wild animal harboring inside. The cave appeared to be empty and about twenty feet deep—enough room for everybody. And even though the air was still sandy, it wasn't nearly as bad as it was outside. A person could breathe in there without choking.

Satisfied that the cave would provide sanctuary, Smoke left it and headed back toward the stage-coach. If Mike hadn't returned by the time he got there, he thought, he would send Scratchy, Preacher, Sally, and the others to the cave while he waited for the young shotgun guard.

He hoped Mike hadn't run into any trouble.

Mike carried his Winchester in his right hand and reached out fairly often with his left to touch the face of the bluff. He could see it, of course, only a few feet away, but his eyes ached so much from the sand that he didn't fully trust his vision. The rasp of the sand-stone against his fingertips was reassuring, even though he felt a little like a blind man fumbling his way along.

He thought about Catherine. In a way, he would have rather stayed back with the stagecoach so he could comfort her and reassure her that everything was going to be all right. But such reassurances would be hollow. He didn't *know* how things were going to turn out. The odds were that they would all die in the hellish storm, either from being suffocated or from the Apaches coming back and killing them. He would do Catherine more good in the long run by finding some place where they could hole up and get some shelter from the storm . . . as well as a place they could defend if the Apaches attacked them again.

He supposed she wished her cavalry officer fiancé were there. He would take care of her. Some shotgun guard who risked his life for wages he could barely scrape by on couldn't really compete with an officer and a gentleman. Anyway, even though she had been polite and even sort of friendly to him, Mike told himself not to mistake that for anything else. She was just a nice young woman who'd treated him kindly, that's all.

She sure was pretty, though. He couldn't get her face out of his mind. Her image seemed to float in front of him, clear despite the blowing sand, and it drew him on.

Abruptly and with no warning, the image was replaced by a visage twisted with hate that lunged at him.

The Apache attacked in silence, no shrill war cries. He swung some sort of war club at Mike's head. Mike brought the rifle up in time to block the blow, but the impact shivered all the way up his arms and knocked him back a step. While he was already off balance, the Apache thrust a moccasined foot between his ankles and jerked.

Mike fell backwards as his legs were swept out from under him.

The Apache couldn't restrain his excitement at the prospect of killing a white man. He let out a little yip as he sprang after Mike and raised the club. It flashed downward.

Mike threw himself to the side in a desperate roll, hanging on tightly to the rifle. The club swept past his ear and hit the ground. He lashed out with a kick that landed on the raider's left knee. The Apache staggered back a step and fell.

Mike swung the rifle around, but his finger didn't tighten on the trigger. He hadn't seen or heard any other Apaches, but that didn't mean they weren't out there close by, unseen in the flying sand. The sound of a shot would bring them running.

He thrust the Winchester's barrel forward like a spear, aiming for the Apache's throat, hoping to crush the man's windpipe.

The Apache jerked aside. The rifle barrel jabbed him in the left shoulder. The blow had to be painful, judging by his grunt, but it hardly incapacitated him. He twisted and slashed at the rifle with his club, striking it on the breech with such force that the weapon was jolted out of Mike's hands.

Both men scrambled up at the same second. Mike could have grabbed the Colt still in its holster, but he still wanted to avoid a shot if he could.

The Apache came at him, swiping back and forth with the club. The man was limping, Mike noticed. He figured his kick to the knee had done some damage, but it wasn't enough to slow down the Apache very much. Mike had to retreat from the flailing club.

He realized an instant later that was exactly what the Apache wanted him to do. By backing up, he had given the man room enough for his next move. The Apache snatched a knife from the sash tied around his waist and flung it at Mike's chest.

Mike dived to the side, but not quickly enough to completely avoid the flying blade. Its keen edge ripped across the outside of his upper left arm and felt like fire as it sliced through the duster and the shirtsleeve and bit into his flesh. Mike ignored the pain as best he could and ducked as the Apache renewed his attack with the club. It went over Mike's head, missing by only a couple inches.

Taller and heavier, Mike dived forward, tackling the raider around the waist and bulling him off his feet. The man had such wiry strength trying to subdue him was like wrestling a wildcat. They rolled back and forth on the ground, struggling for control of the club as Mike wrapped his hands around the weapon.

The Apache tried to knee him in the groin. Mike writhed away from the blow and took it on his thigh. The Apache lunged against him and bit him on the shoulder. The duster was enough to protect him from the man's teeth. Throwing the Apache toward the ground, Mike let go of the club, slammed his hand against the side of the Apache's head, and forced his face into the sand drifting up along the bluff.

He bucked hard and threw Mike off. Mike caught himself and lunged back to the attack almost instantly. Having lost the club, the Apache reached for it with his left hand. Mike dived over the Indian's back, grabbed his wrist, and rolled, twisting the man's arm until he heard a sudden pop and the Apache yelled in pain. Mike knew he had just pulled a bone out of its socket somewhere in the man's arm.

The Apache wasn't going to let that stop him. His left arm hung uselessly at his side, but he used his right fist to slam a punch against Mike's jaw. The blow jolted Mike's head back and made his vision blur for a second, even more than the flying sand had already obscured his sight.

The Apache rammed into Mike with both knees and that right fist. Mike rolled onto his back and tried to grab hold of the man so he could fling him off. The Apache was bare from the waist up, though, and even in this sandstorm he was too slick with sweat for Mike's hands to get any purchase. The sweat and sand had combined to coat his skin with a layer of slippery mud.

A knee dug into Mike's midsection and made him gasp for air as he tried to double over. He struck out desperately, blindly, but most of his punches missed and the Apache shrugged off the ones that didn't. Mike's head was spinning, and he knew he was on the verge of losing consciousness. He had to risk a shot or the Apache was going to overpower him.

If that happened, it would be a death sentence. Mike had no doubt of that.

He fumbled for his gun. His holster was empty.

The Colt had slipped out sometime during the fight.

As that horrifying realization made Mike's insides turn cold and hollow, the fingers of the Apache's good hand clamped around his throat like bands of iron and began to squeeze the life out of him.

CHAPTER 29

When Smoke first came in sight of the coach, it was just a dark hulk up ahead, visible and then gone again as the swirling clouds of sand shifted. Figuring he was within earshot, he lifted his voice and hailed the others, not wanting Preacher and Scratchy to get itchy trigger fingers as he walked up. "Hello, the coach! Preacher, it's me! Hello!"

Smoke's jaw tightened when there was no response. Was it possible that the Apaches had found the stagecoach and slaughtered everyone on it without him knowing? That seemed unlikely. He couldn't bring himself to believe that anybody could sneak up on Preacher and kill him without Preacher at least getting a shot off.

Then he heard the familiar voice calling, "Howdy out there, Smoke! Come on in! Ever'thing is fine!"

A wave of relief went through Smoke. He hurried on toward the vehicle where Preacher and Scratchy were waiting outside. Preacher had taken his Winchester from the boot and held it in his hands.

"Find anything?" Scratchy asked. The question sounded casual, but the tightness of the jehu's voice made it clear how much strain he was under.

"There's a cave back that way," Smoke said, half-turning to point back along the bluff. "It's not big enough to drive the stagecoach inside, but all of us and the horses will fit in it."

"Thank the Lord," Scratchy said with obviously heartfelt gratitude. "That's really all we need."

"Unless Mike has found something better. Is he back yet?"

"Ain't seen the boy since the two o' you left," Preacher replied.

"Well, I'll wait here for him. Scratchy, you get the coach on down to that cave, and Mike and I will join you later. I reckon the two of you and Tom can handle unhitching the horses once you get there?"

"Sure. Don't worry about that."

Preacher cocked his head to the side. "I ain't sure about leavin' you here all by your lonesome, Smoke. Some o' them 'Paches might come along."

"Yeah, and that's all the more reason for you to go with Scratchy and the coach," Smoke pointed out. "I'd rather have you along to help protect the others in case of an attack."

The old mountain man shrugged. "Reckon you got a point there. All right, Scratchy, let's get her a-rollin'."

Both older men climbed onto the box. Preacher sat with the Winchester across his knees, ready for trouble.

Smoke stepped to the coach's open door and told the passengers, "In case you didn't hear me telling Scratchy and Preacher, I found a cave not too far away where we can all take shelter. The coach is heading there now."

"Aren't you coming along, Smoke?" Sally reached out and rested her hand on Smoke's where it gripped the edge of the door.

"No, Mike's not back yet, so I'm going to wait here for him."

Catherine asked, "You don't think anything has happened to him, do you?"

"Not at all. I came back as soon as I located some shelter for us. I reckon Mike's still looking. He knew not to go too far, so he'll turn around before much longer. Fact is, he may already be on his way back here. In this storm, we'd never know until he got here."

Sally squeezed Smoke's hand. "Don't be too long."

"I'll try not to," Smoke promised.

From the box, Scratchy called to his short-handed team. "Get along there!"

Smoke stepped back from the stagecoach as it lurched into motion.

Scratchy turned the team and drove slowly along the base of the bluff. Smoke watched the coach go until it was out of sight. That didn't take long as the wind lifted a curtain of sand into the air and still howled like a banshee.

Mike knew he had only seconds to save his life. He flailed around him with both arms, pawing through the sand with desperate fingers. The touch of cool, smooth metal sent a shock through him. He closed his hand around it and knew he had just grasped the barrel of his fallen gun.

Through the red haze that had fallen over his eyes as the Apache choked him, he saw a blurred image of the raider's face hovering over him. The Apache's lips were drawn back from his teeth in a grimace as he bore down on Mike's throat.

Mike would be damned if the bastard's ugly face was the last thing he ever saw on this earth!

Smoke moved over and leaned his back against the bluff. A bone-deep weariness gripped him. He hadn't given in to it until that moment because he knew the others needed him . . . and anyway, they were probably more tired than he was. But he had to admit, at least to himself, that it felt good to stop and rest for a minute.

With a spasm of effort, Mike brought the gun up and slammed the butt into the side of the Apache's head. The terrible pressure on Mike's throat disappeared, and he dragged a huge gulp of blessed air through his tortured windpipe. The Apache had fallen to the side, and even as Mike tried to fill his lungs, he rolled after his enemy and struck again, the gun rising and then falling with a thud.

Mike hit him again and again, until the Apache's head was battered into a grotesque shape that barely looked human anymore. The skull was cracked open in places, with brains showing through. Mike finally stopped and rolled away from the dead man. He sprawled on his back with his chest rising and falling raggedly.

A voice in the back of his brain shouted a warning that he couldn't stay there, no matter how bad a shape he was in. Where there was one Apache, there could easily be another . . . or more. It was possible the man he had encountered was a lone scout, but Mike knew he couldn't count on that.

He pushed himself up into a sitting position and looked at the gun he still held by the barrel. The butt was smeared with blood and gray matter. A few hairs and bits of bone were stuck to it. He shuddered and began wiping the gun butt in the sand to clean it off.

It was amazing how quickly a civilized man reverted to savagery when his life was threatened, he thought. He figured the layer of civilization was pretty thin, and pure barbarian lurked underneath.

He reeled to his feet and stood swaying for a moment as he looked around, disoriented by the brutal fight and the sandstorm. His hat was gone, knocked off in the battle even though he'd had it tied on. Once it was loose, the wind had blown it away in the blink of an eye.

He spotted the bluff, and that made him feel better. He'd had it on his left before, so he holstered his gun and turned, keeping the sandstone wall on his right. That would take him back toward the stagecoach. He had been gone long enough. He needed to get back and find out if Smoke had had any better luck.

Mike stumbled along, his pulse still hammering

inside his head. Earlier, he had touched the face of the bluff to help him keep his bearings. Now, he stopped to lean on it every few yards because he was so worn out. He hoped Smoke had found some shelter. If not, they might well be doomed. Guilt gnawed at him because his mission had been a failure.

Smoke's rest stretched out, became several minutes and then a quarter of an hour. He looked down at his feet and saw that he'd been standing there long enough for a little sand to drift up around his boots.

The thought that Mike should have been back already brought a frown to Smoke's face. He had expected Mike to show up within a few minutes of his own return. He'd waited, thinking maybe Mike was moving slower or had gone farther than a half-mile before turning back.

Enough time had passed that Smoke began to wonder if something had happened to the young shotgun guard.

With only one way to find out, Smoke started along the bluff. The way the wind was whipping around, it still blew in his face part of the time, but at least going in that direction it was behind him for the most part.

He hadn't gone very far, maybe a hundred yards, when a figure suddenly loomed up out of the gloom in front of him. Smoke's hand flashed to his gun.

* * *

Mike's head was down, so he didn't realize anyone was in front of him until a voice barked, "Hold it!"

Mike looked up and peered through the murk at the broad-shouldered figure. "Smoke?"

"Is that you, Mike?" Smoke asked as he stepped closer. He lowered the gun in his hand. "Are you all right?"

"Yeah, I reckon. Tangled with another of those . . . damned Apaches. He's dead."

"I didn't hear any shots."

"I didn't shoot him," Mike said. He didn't offer any explanations for the bleak pronouncement, and Smoke didn't ask for any. They could hash that out later, if necessary.

Mike went on. "Where's the stagecoach? Did you find any cover?"

"There's a cave back that way." Smoke pointed over his shoulder. "I sent Scratchy and Preacher on with the coach and waited for you. When you didn't show up, I came to look for you." He paused. "Sounds like you were a mite busy."

"Yeah, you could say that. What about . . . the other passengers?" Mike wanted to ask about Catherine in particular, but he didn't figure he had any right to do that.

"They're all fine . . . including Miss Bradshaw."

"Thank God! I mean—"

"I know what you mean, son. Let's go." Smoke put a hand on Mike's shoulder and they turned in the direction the stagecoach had gone.

CHAPTER 30

Preacher could see the exhaustion in the horses as they plodded along the base of the bluff with their heads drooping. Next to him on the seat, Scratchy was pretty much the same way, worn out by the day's dangers and exertions.

The old mountain man felt the strain as well, although he was blessed with an almost supernatural vitality that kept him young far beyond his years. He attributed that to all the time he had spent outdoors as a young man, first on the family farm back in the Midwest but mostly from the years he had spent as a fur trapper in the Rockies.

He shrugged, thinking that sort of life toughened an hombre up, that was for damn sure.

Preacher looked back but could no longer see Smoke. He didn't worry, though. Smoke was the best and toughest man Preacher had ever known, including himself. Thing of it was, Smoke's natural modesty sometimes prevented him from realizing just how much of a legend he really was. To Smoke's way of thinking, he was just a fella trying to get by and do the right things in life.

Lord help anybody who threatened Smoke Jensen or his loved ones, though. *Especially* his loved ones.

"How far do you reckon it is to that cave?" Scratchy asked.

"Smoke didn't say, but considerin' how long he was gone, it shouldn't take us too long to get there. Fifteen or twenty minutes, maybe."

"I'm sure ready to get outta all this blowin' sand. I been around Arizona Territory, man and boy, near on to forty years, and I ain't sure I've ever seen a storm as bad as this one. Usually the weather's pretty quiet around Christmastime, and it ain't blisterin' hot then, either."

"It ain't all that hot now," Preacher pointed out.

"Warmer than usual . . . and drier, too. That's how come we got all this sand blowin' around."

Preacher snorted. "Hot and dry in Arizona Territory. Imagine that."

"Don't go talkin' bad about Arizona. There's times when it's plumb heaven on earth."

"And times when it's hell . . . sort of like now."

Scratchy's eloquent shrug said that he couldn't argue with that.

Preacher kept an eye out for the cave, but they hadn't reached it yet when he spotted something else that made him stiffen on the seat and tighten his grip on the Winchester. "I thought I just seen somethin' out there," he said quietly to Scratchy. "Somethin' movin'."

"Out in the sand, you mean?"

"Yeah. Off to the left, maybe fifty yards."

"You can't see fifty yards in this mess, Preacher. Sometimes you can't even see fifty *feet.*"

"There are little breaks in it, now and then. That's when I saw it, whatever it was."

"Man or animal?"

"Too big for an animal, I reckon. Ain't nothin' around here but lizards and rats, is there?"

"Not to speak of," Scratchy admitted. "What do you reckon we should do?"

"Nothin' we *can* do except push on. We got to get out of this storm to have any chance of makin' it."

"That's true. I'll see if I can't get a little more speed outta these horses—Ahhh," Scratchy called out as he rocked sharply to the side, banging his shoulder against Preacher's and bellowing in pain.

Preacher looked over and saw the shaft of an arrow protruding from Scratchy's upper left arm.

Not exactly sure where the arrow had come from, Preacher knew the Apache who had fired it had to be somewhere to their left. He twisted on the seat, put one knee on it to raise himself higher, and smoothly brought the rifle to his shoulder as Scratchy bent forward to get out of the line of fire. Preacher cranked off five rounds as fast as he could, swinging the Winchester from left to right to spray the bullets through the clouds of dust.

As the deafening roar of the shots faded a little, Preacher asked, "How bad are you hit?"

"Not bad enough to keep me from drivin' this stagecoach!" Scratchy replied. His wounded left arm wasn't much use to him, but with his right hand he lashed the reins against the rumps of the horses closest to the coach as he yelled at them. The animals surged forward in their traces as rifle shots blasted from the sandstorm.

As they headed toward the stagecoach and the cave, Smoke and Mike heard something that made them stiffen in alarm. The wind tried to snatch away any sound, but several distant pops made it through to their ears.

Gunfire.

Preacher heard the rifle shots from within the sandstorm and caught sight of the little winks of muzzle flame. He fired back at them but had no way of knowing if any of his shots hit their targets.

"Up ahead!" Scratchy shouted. "I think I see the cave!"

Preacher darted a glance in that direction and spotted the dark, irregular patch in the sandstone wall to their right. That could be the mouth of a cave, all right, he thought.

The question was whether or not they could reach it before the Apaches stopped them.

The way the coach was jolting along, Preacher almost didn't notice when it bounced suddenly, but it was just enough of a warning to make him whirl around at the same moment an Apache warrior clambered over the rear boot and scrambled onto the roof. He had a six-gun, no doubt taken off the body of some white man he had murdered, stuck behind the sash around his waist.

The Apache made a grab for the gun, but he never had a chance. Flame spouted from the muzzle of Preacher's Winchester as the old mountain man fired the rifle. The slug blew a hole all the way through the Apache's chest and flung him backwards off the coach.

No sooner had Preacher disposed of that threat than another raider raced out of the storm and leaped onto the rear boot. He clung to it with one hand while he used the other to thrust a revolver over the roof and start jerking the trigger. He got off a couple shots before Preacher calmly blew his brains out.

"You hit?" Preacher asked Scratchy.

"No, just this arrow in my arm. I think those bullets went between us. It was pretty damn close, though."

"Too close." Preacher kept moving the rifle from side to side, ready to fire at the first sign of a target.

About twenty yards from the cave, Preacher could see the mouth of it fairly well. He was starting to think they were going to make it when another shot blasted. One of the leaders squealed in agony. The horse's legs buckled. As it went down, the other members of the team stopped short, and the coach slewed to a halt.

An instant later, the other leader threw its head up and screamed, then collapsed next to the fallen horse. An arrow was buried in its throat. The Apaches had given up on trying to kill Preacher and Scratchy and had gone after the horses in a last-ditch attempt to stop the stagecoach before it reached the shelter of the cave.

They had succeeded, too. The coach wasn't going to roll anywhere without a new team.

The gunfire continued in the distance as Smoke and Mike ran through the sand, moving as fast as they could in the stuff. Smoke's heart hammered just as loud as those shots, or at least it seemed that way to him. He had known Sally might wind up in danger when the stagecoach rolled away into the storm, but he also knew she was tough as nails and could take care of herself.

Knowing all that didn't make his heart stop slugging so hard it seemed like it was about to burst out of his chest.

He could tell the shooting came from the direction of the cave and figured the Apaches had either ambushed the stagecoach on its way to that shelter or they had come across the cave after he had and were waiting there for the coach to show up. Either way, the passengers would be in deadly danger.

"We gotta get those folks to the cave!" Preacher told Scratchy as he spotted several shadowy figures flitting through the sandstorm. He leaped down from the box and jerked the coach door open. "Run!" he told the passengers. "Run for the cave!"

Sally scrambled out first. "Give me a gun!"

Knowing she could use a Colt, Preacher pulled his from its holster and held it out to her, butt first.

She took it and said, "Catherine! Mrs. Bates! George! Come on, I'll cover you!"

Catherine jumped down from the coach, followed by George, but Mrs. Bates stayed inside, shaking her head. "I can't, I just can't."

"Grandma!" George yelled at her. "Come on! You got to!" He held out his hand to her. "Come on! I won't let anything happen to you!"

The older woman still hesitated, and just when Preacher thought he would have to reach in and drag her out, she swallowed hard, grasped her grandson's hand, and slid out of the coach.

Ballard was right behind her, the little pistol clutched in his hand. "I'll take the other side, Mrs. Jensen. Let's go!"

Scratchy's pistol boomed from the other side of the coach. The jehu shouted, "Here they come!"

Stumbling because of the sand, the little group of passengers ran toward the cave. Preacher brought up the rear. Scratchy came around the front of the coach to join him. They kept up a steady fire toward the darting shapes trying to close in. More shots came from the Apaches. Over the howl of the wind, Preacher heard slugs whining close past his head.

The borrowed Colt in Sally's hand roared. Preacher glanced in that direction and saw an Apache who had managed to get close on her side spin off his feet from the slug's impact.

Ballard's pistol cracked, too, as one of the raiders tried to angle in and cut them off from the cave. That man faded back. Preacher didn't think the hombre was hit, but Ballard's shot had come close enough to make him duck away.

Preacher wondered fleetingly if they would find some of the Apaches waiting for them inside the cave.

If they were, then it was all over. Preacher and the others had put up a good fight, although that would be scant comfort as they were massacred.

But if the cave was still empty, as it had been when Smoke found it, they could fort up in there and hold off the Apaches. The situation would still be bad, mighty bad, but not hopeless. Not yet.

A warrior popped up and lunged at Preacher with a knife. Preacher batted the blade aside with the rifle barrel, then used the stock to stove in the varmint's skull. From the corner of his eye, he saw Sally, Ballard, and the other three disappear into the cave.

Still triggering shots toward the Apaches, Sally reappeared, crying, "Come on, Preacher!"

He grabbed Scratchy's arm. The jehu didn't seem too steady on his feet. He'd lost a lot of blood from the arrow wound. Pounding toward the cave mouth, Preacher kept him moving, and a few seconds later they reached the cave and ducked through the entrance.

Sally backed away from the cave mouth, the Colt still level in her hand but no longer firing. The cave was wider on the inside than the mouth of it was, and in the dim light Preacher saw that the passengers had taken cover along one of the walls where shots from outside couldn't reach them. He and Scratchy hugged the other wall, with Sally sliding along it, still covering them in case any of the Apaches tried to get into the cave.

For the moment, all the shooting seemed to have stopped. They were safe enough to at least catch their breath.

Safe . . . but still trapped.

CHAPTER 31

"Damn it," Mike panted as he slogged through the sand beside Smoke. "How much farther is it?"

"Not far," Smoke said, and then added as he slowed down, "Wait a minute."

Mike came to an obviously reluctant halt beside him. "Why are we stopping? We have to find the others—"

"Listen."

Nothing could be heard but the howling and droning of the wind.

"The shooting has stopped." Mike's voice sounded hollow.

"Yeah. I reckon the fight's over."

"But that means—"

"We don't know what it means. They could have made it to the cave and driven the Apaches off."

"Or the Apaches could have—"

"We both know damn well what the Apaches could've done," Smoke interrupted again. "But there's only one way to find out what actually happened."

Mike nodded grimly. "You're right. Come on." He started off again with Smoke beside him.

Both men kept close watch for any sign of the Apaches. If the raiders had been driven off, they might flee in the opposite direction . . . right toward Smoke and Mike. With all the sand flying around, they could be almost on top of the two white men before either was aware of the threat.

They didn't see anything, though, and after a quarter of an hour that seemed much longer, Smoke touched Mike's shoulder and said, "There."

"I see it." Mike peered through squinted eyes at the dark shape up ahead. "That's the stagecoach, isn't it?"

"I'm pretty sure it is. We'll check it out, but be careful. The Apaches could have left it there as bait."

Mike held his Winchester ready and Smoke's Colt was in his hand as they approached the motionless stagecoach. As Smoke swung out to the side a little, he understood why he didn't see the horses.

All four animals were down, lying in their traces, dead as far as he could tell.

"They killed the rest of the team," he said quietly to Mike.

"Did they . . . do you see any . . . bodies?"

"Nope. Just the coach and the horses."

Caution made them crouch as they crept up closer to the apparently abandoned vehicle. The broken door was still flapping in the wind. Smoke caught hold of it and looked inside, not knowing what he was going to see.

The stagecoach was empty. Smoke searched for blood on the floorboards and seats but thankfully didn't find any.

"Is that the cave?" Mike asked.

Smoke looked past the coach and saw the dark mouth of the cave some twenty yards away. "It is. They must've taken cover in there. With any luck, nobody's wounded." He knew that would be a lot to ask for, but it never hurt to hope.

Until they knew what was in there, Smoke didn't want to just barge in. It might be a trap waiting for them. He motioned for Mike to keep the stagecoach between him and the cave. Smoke did likewise as he retrieved his Winchester from the boot, then he lifted his voice and called, "Hello, the cave! Anybody in there?"

"Smoke!"

The instant response in the voice of the woman he loved made Smoke's heart jump. He leaned around the stagecoach and shouted, "Sally! Are you all right?"

"Yes! Come on in!"

Smoke knew he didn't have to worry that the Apaches were forcing Sally to lure them into a trap. She would have died before she did that. He nodded to Mike, and they trotted quickly to the cave.

Sally met them at the entrance, throwing her arms around Smoke and holding him tightly. "I was afraid the Apaches might have gotten you," she said in a half-whisper that was husky with emotion.

"I was worried about them getting you. Especially after all the shooting we heard."

"They tried. Preacher and Scratchy were able to hold them off until we were close enough to make a run for this cave when the Indians started killing the horses."

Mike was looking rather desperately around the cave. Smoke knew he was searching for Catherine Bradshaw.

She came out of the shadows, covered with grime and with her hair disheveled, but there was a smile on her face as she said, "There you are, Mike. Are you all right?"

"Fine." He looked like he was having to hold himself back to keep from taking her in his arms. "How about you?"

"I wasn't hurt. Just very, very scared."

Preacher said, "Scratchy's the only one who got elected." He stood up from where he had been kneeling beside the old jehu, who sat with his back propped against the cave wall. The bloody rag tied around Scratchy's upper arm as a makeshift bandage showed what Preacher had been doing.

Smoke went over and hunkered on his heels in front of Scratchy. "How bad is it?"

"I been hurt worse. Caught an arrow in the arm, but Preacher got it out and tied up the wound once we were in here."

"Mighty lucky that Scratchy had a flash o' rye whiskey in that duster o' his," Preacher added. "Used some of it to clean up them arrow holes."

"Reckon I'll live," Scratchy went on. "Considerin' everything that's happened, to have just one of us wounded is pretty darned lucky, if you ask me."

"It sure is," Smoke agreed, wondering how long that luck was going to last.

He stood up and looked around the cave. The gloom was thick, but he was able to make out Mrs.

Bates and George sitting beside the wall, and Tom Ballard standing not far away with a worried expression on his face. Smoke wondered if the newspaperman was thinking about that trunk in the stagecoach's boot.

Whatever was in there, to Smoke's way of thinking they had bigger problems to worry about.

He caught Preacher's eye and inclined his head toward the cave mouth. They drifted in that direction as if to check on what was happening outside, if anything. In the close quarters, they couldn't get completely out of earshot of the others.

Preacher kept his voice low enough that only Smoke was liable to understand him. "We still got a heap o' trouble, don't we?"

"All the horses are dead and we're a long way from the closest way station."

"Yep. Not to mention the storm and all them 'Paches out there." Preacher sucked a tooth for a second, then added, "We keep killin' 'em, but it seems like ever' one we blow to hell, half a dozen more pop up to take his place."

"You could be right about the war party growing. It could have been a small group that crossed the border from Mexico a few days ago, but more warriors could be leaving the agencies as they hear about what's going on."

"Yeah, it don't take much to get them bucks stirred up. Even the ones that pretend to be peaceful got killin' in their blood." Preacher grunted. "Sorta like me. Live wild for long enough, and it's mighty hard to tame down and stay that way."

"Well, in your case, I'm glad. We may have to be as savage as they are before this is over." Smoke changed the subject a little by asking, "Is Scratchy really going to be all right?"

"I think so. His arm got skewered pretty good, but he can drive a coach and shoot one-handed if he has to. Come to think of it, he ain't gonna be drivin' that coach, is he?"

"Not unless a new team sprouts wings and flies down out of the sky."

"Yeah, that'd be a plumb Christmas miracle, wouldn't it?"

"Don't discount miracles. We've made it this far and we're still alive."

"Maybe so, but I ain't gonna rely on 'em, neither. We got to start thinkin' about food and water."

"There may be a few provisions on the coach. Some jerky and hardtack, anyway. Some drivers carry a little food for emergencies. Scratchy can tell us about that. Food's not as pressing a need as water."

"The water barrel attached to the stagecoach is full, I reckon. They filled it from the well at the last place we stopped, didn't they?"

Smoke nodded. "They did. There are a couple canteens we can use, too. But the water barrel is out there, and we're in here."

"Then we'd best go fetch it while we got the chance."

"Just what I was thinking," Smoke said. "Mike and I can get it and carry it in here while you keep an eye out for trouble."

"Sounds good." Preacher patted the breech of the Winchester he held.

Smoke turned and went deeper into the cave, where Mike was reassuring Catherine and Mrs. Bates that everything was going to be all right. "Mike, you and I need to fetch the water barrel from the coach while we still can. There's enough water in it to keep us going for a while, but will take both of us to lift it and carry it back to the cave."

"I was just thinking the same thing," the young man said.

"Be careful," Catherine said.

"I intend to be," Mike told her. "But we've got to have water."

Sally intercepted them on the way to the cave mouth, the look on her face telling Smoke she wanted to know what he was up to. He explained quickly.

She nodded and held up the Colt. "I'll help Preacher cover you."

Smoke opened his mouth to say something, then closed it, realizing that he was doomed to lose the argument. Anyway, having another good shot watching their backs wasn't a bad idea.

They paused just inside the cave and looked around as far as they could see in the blowing sand and fading light. Night wasn't far off, and it would fall suddenly, as it always did on the desert.

Smoke didn't spot any movement or suspicious shapes around the coach, so he nodded and told Mike, "Let's go."

They stepped out and started toward the stagecoach. Preacher and Sally moved into the cave mouth behind them and lifted their guns, ready to fire.

Nothing happened as Smoke and Mike walked quickly toward the stagecoach.

Halfway there, guns blasted, muzzle flame bloomed in the gathering dusk, and bullets began to kick up dirt around their feet and whine past their heads.

CHAPTER 32

Preacher and Sally opened fire from the cave while Smoke and Mike stopped short and returned the shots with their rifles. It took only a couple heartbeats for Smoke to realize that he and Mike were too exposed. They could make a run for the coach, but even if they reached it, they would be cut off from the others.

"Back to the cave!" he shouted as he levered the Winchester and slammed another round into the clouds of sand.

They turned and dashed for the cave mouth as Sally and Preacher kept up the covering fire. Retreating stuck in Smoke's craw; he had always been the sort to go straight ahead into trouble.

But it wasn't only his life at stake. And anyway, only an idiot would be in favor of charging blindly ahead into a situation that could only get him killed.

In fact, he and Mike would be doing good to get back to the cave alive.

Preacher and Sally kept the Apaches ducking enough for Smoke and Mike to cover the ground in long-legged bounds. They darted through the opening and veered to the side, out of the line of fire.

"Get out of there!" Smoke barked at his wife and his old friend.

They whirled away from the cave mouth and pressed themselves to the wall. Bullets screamed into the cave and smacked into the rear wall.

Smoke called, "Everybody stay down!"

Since the cave had been hollowed out of sandstone instead of granite or some other, harder rock, the slugs didn't ricochet. They blasted craters in the cave wall and stayed there. After a moment, the shooting stopped. The raiders must have figured out they were just wasting ammunition.

Preacher said, "Looks like you and Mike got here just in time a while ago, Smoke. Them 'Paches must've been regroupin' when the two o' you came in the first time."

"Yeah, but now they're back," Smoke said. "And they plan to keep us bottled up in here."

Here was twenty yards away from the water they needed to survive. The water they could get only by running a gauntlet of hot lead . . . and back.

Not the sort to sit around and brood, Smoke paced. If he couldn't do something about one problem, he often turned his attention to another and tried to solve it.

He knew they would need a fire for warmth before morning. Earlier, he had noted some branches and other bits of dried brush that must have been dragged inside by animals or maybe even by other people who had taken shelter there. He had a plentiful supply of matches, so he lit one and used it for light as he searched around the walls of the cave for fuel.

George saw what he was doing and offered, "I can help you with that, Mr. Jensen."

"That's a good idea, George. Watch where you grab, though. Could be lizards or spiders around."

Mrs. Bates began, "Oh, George, I don't think you should—"

"It's all right, Grandma. I'll be careful."

Smoke tossed the sticks he had gathered into a pile then walked to Sally on the left side of the cave opening where she sat alone. Suggesting it was a good idea to have everybody on the same side of the cave, he pulled her up then asked, "Ready to make a run for it?"

"With you?" She smiled. "Any time."

"Hold on, you two," Preacher said. "Let me fling a few ounces o' lead out there, just in case those varmints are watchin'."

"Save your bullets," Smoke said. "As dark as it's getting, I don't think they can see in here anymore. Just to be on the safe side, though, Sally and I won't waste any time."

They dashed across the opening. Sure enough, no shots sounded.

Smoke felt a little better now that they were all together again. George had put together a neat little pile of brush. Smoke picked out some of it and arranged it for a fire. It wouldn't be a big blaze—they didn't have enough fuel for that—but he thought they could keep it going through the night . . . perhaps two. The walls of the cave would hoard the heat the flames gave off and reflect it back. The air would be chilly by morning, but not downright cold.

And just having a fire would lift the spirits of the pilgrims trapped there, Smoke knew. Instinct led humans to huddle around a fire in the hope that it would ward off the darkness and all the terrors it contained.

It didn't take him long to get some small flames leaping up. He would feed the fire carefully and make the brush last as long as possible.

Mrs. Bates surprised him a little by saying, "I . . . I have a bit of food in my bag . . . some jerky and a couple cookies I've been saving for George in case he got too cranky—"

"Grandma! I ain't a baby, you know."

"You're *not* a baby," Sally corrected him. Her smile took any sting out of the words. "Sorry. I used to be a schoolteacher, so it's just habit."

"Aw, that's all right, Miz Jensen. My ma was always tellin' me to talk right, too, so I reckon I ought to try."

"To talk correctly, you mean."

"Yeah. That's what I said, ain't it? I mean, isn't it?"

"We'll talk about that later, George," Sally said. "Mrs. Bates, that's a very generous offer."

"Well, like I said, it's not much," the older woman replied. "I could break the cookies up into smaller pieces. I don't know about the jerky . . ."

Smoke said, "Jerky's salty enough it'd be liable to make us thirstier, and since we don't have any water right now, we'd better hold off on that. Reckon the other will be much appreciated, though."

Scratchy said, "There are a few supplies on the coach . . . once we can get to it without gettin' killed."

"When is that going to be?" Catherine asked. "How long can those savages possibly wait out there for us?"

"They'll get bored and wander off," Preacher said confidently. "Injuns is plumb notional critters. Can't keep their minds on one thing for too long at a time."

Smoke knew better, and he knew Preacher did, too. The old mountain man was just trying to make the others feel better, to give them some hope.

The volume of the wind outside rose even higher as they ate their meager supper.

Tom Ballard commented, "I didn't think it could blow any harder out there, but it sounds like it is."

"Yep, the storm's picking up," Smoke said. "But there's not a lot of sand blowing in here, and it might just make those Apaches decide to put this part of the country behind them. I'll bet we have the only good shelter around here."

Scratchy said, "It can't keep on howlin' like that forever. The storm's bound to blow itself out. Might even do it by mornin'. If those savages are gone by then, we'll get the water and provisions from the coach, and we'll be sittin' pretty."

Yeah, dozens of miles from anywhere. No one knew where they were, and even if the Apaches were gone, they might come back at any time. If that was sitting pretty, Smoke thought with a faint, grim smile, he'd hate to see what it was like if they were in a really bad fix.

* * *

Someone had to stand guard all night to make sure the Apaches didn't sneak into the cave, as well as push another branch into the fire every now and then and keep it going. Smoke assumed he and Preacher and Mike would split the duty. Scratchy was too weak from loss of blood and needed his rest.

Tom Ballard offered to pitch in and take a turn. "I know I'm not a Westerner by birth, but I've been out here for a while. I can do what I need to do."

Smoke was about to nod in agreement, but changed his mind and leaned his head toward the cave mouth. "Come on over there and talk to me for a minute, Tom."

Ballard frowned in puzzlement as he followed Smoke. When they were near the entrance, he asked quietly, "Is there something wrong?"

"I just got to wondering if you thought you might sneak out there and get that trunk off the stagecoach," Smoke said, his tone equally soft.

Ballard caught his breath. "I . . . I don't know what you mean—"

"You've been mighty antsy about that trunk ever since we started this trip, Tom. From everything I've seen of you, you're a good man, trustworthy and solid. My gut feeling about a fella isn't wrong very often."

"I'd like to think I *am* a good man," Ballard said stiffly.

"Then tell me . . . were you planning to go after that trunk?"

Ballard hesitated.

Smoke figured he was deciding whether he wanted to lie.

The newspaperman sighed. "All right. The thought did cross my mind . . . but then I realized how crazy it was. I couldn't carry the trunk by myself, and anyway, I'd probably just get my throat cut by some savage if I tried."

"More than likely," Smoke agreed. "Why is it so all-fired important to you?"

"I think that's really my business, Smoke."

"Maybe it started out that way, but now it could affect all of us. If it's something that could put us in even more danger—"

"I don't see how it could," Ballard said. "Anyway, how can we be in more danger than we already are? Let's face it. What are the chances that any of us will make it to Tucson alive? Really?"

"I figure as long as a man's still alive, he's got a fighting chance." Smoke shrugged. "And if we're all going to die anyway, what'll it hurt to indulge my curiosity?"

Ballard looked at him intently for a long moment, then said, "You're right. I suppose it doesn't really matter anymore. That trunk is full of money, Smoke. A lot of money."

CHAPTER 33

Only a few things could make a man as nervous as Tom Ballard had been, and women and money were the main ones.

Not surprised, Smoke drawled, "I reckon the next question is if it's stolen."

"What? No! Of course not." Ballard took off his hat and scrubbed a weary hand over his face. "I suppose I should tell you the whole story. I said I'm a newspaperman, and that's the truth. I went up to the capital to talk to the governor on behalf of myself and a number of other honest businessmen in Tucson. I asked him to use his influence to help us arrange a loan."

"That's where the money came from?"

"Yes. It's all legal and aboveboard."

"Well . . . you *did* ask the governor to put in a word with the bankers who loaned you the money."

"It's not like we bribed him to do anything," Ballard snapped. "I appealed to his sense of fairness and justice. My friends and I are faced with a threat not only to our businesses but the safety of Tucson itself. If Tuttle gets his way and takes over everything—"

"Tuttle?"

"Avery Tuttle. A man who came in a few years ago and started building himself his own little empire."

"A man's got a right to succeed in his business," Smoke pointed out.

"Through hard work, yes, certainly. By hiring killers like Smiler Coe to intimidate his competition and make the stubborn ones disappear . . ." Ballard shrugged.

Smoke's interest had perked up more at the mention of Smiler Coe. He had never crossed trails with the man, but he'd heard of him. Nothing good, either. "Coe works for this Tuttle hombre?"

"That's right. You know him?"

Smoke shook his head. "No, but I've heard enough to know he's bad medicine."

"I'm convinced he's killed several men who stood up to Tuttle. They're supposed to have left town, but no one actually saw them go. They just . . . disappeared."

Smoke nodded slowly. He had no reason not to believe Ballard, and given Smiler Coe's reputation, it was entirely possible the newspaperman was right about him murdering Avery Tuttle's enemies.

"Tuttle either owns outright or controls through notes about half the businesses in town," Ballard went on. "He's got his sights set on all the others. He had some of his hired guns beat up my assistant at the newspaper. I wasn't able to prove it, but I know Tuttle was responsible for what happened."

"Are you sure you're not just suspicious of him because he's a business rival?"

"That's insulting, Mr. Jensen."

"No, it's plain talk."

"It's my honest belief that Avery Tuttle is a criminal and a murderer. He may not have pulled the trigger, but he gave the orders."

"All right, then. I'll take your word for it, Tom. I just wanted to be sure. And this money you're taking back to Tucson . . . it's intended to shore up the other businesses so Tuttle can't gobble them up, too?"

"Exactly. It's really the only thing we can do."

Smoke rubbed his chin. "You could hire some gun-wolves of your own and fight Tuttle on his own terms."

"Are you volunteering for the job?"

"My gun's not for hire," Smoke said with an edge of steel in his voice. "But there are plenty of others out there that are."

Ballard shook his head. "No. My friends and I are honest men. We won't descend to Tuttle's level. Even if we won, that would be just trading one evil for another."

Smoke thought that attitude was idealistic but a mite naïve. Some threats in the world were dangerous enough and evil enough that they could only be met with violence. Talking was fine, but sometimes hot lead was the only answer that truly worked.

Ballard shook his head. "This whole discussion is meaningless, isn't it? We're not going to make it out of here alive. After they've killed us, the Apaches will loot the stagecoach and find the money. They're smart enough to know what it is and how to use it.

They'll probably take it into Mexico and use it to buy more guns and ammunition."

"Maybe," Smoke said. "But I'm not counting on them getting their hands on it. I still plan on making it to Tucson. Have you thought about what'll happen if we do?"

Ballard frowned. "What do you mean?"

"If Tuttle's willing to have people killed to satisfy his ambitions, you reckon he's going to let you just waltz into town with enough money to ruin his plans?"

"He doesn't know about it. Only a handful of people do. I was very careful to keep my plans a secret."

"The governor knows about it, and so do the bankers you borrowed the money from. So do fellas who work for them. It's hard to keep a secret when there's a lot of money involved."

Ballard shook his head stubbornly. "No, it's not possible." He hesitated. "But if Tuttle *did* find out somehow . . ."

"He'd try to stop you, wouldn't he?"

"By any means necessary. Good Lord," Ballard muttered. "You've given me something *else* to worry about now. Even if we get away from the Apaches, plenty of danger could still be waiting for us. But that's insane. We have no horses, we're too far out in the middle of nowhere to walk to civilization, and those Indians show no sign of giving up and going away. Tuttle won't have to kill me." Ballard laughed, and there was a note of hysteria in the sound. "I'll be dead long before I can ever reach Tucson."

"Like I said, I don't believe in giving up as long as I'm alive. You shouldn't, either."

"But how are we going to get out of here?"

"Now, that, I haven't figured out yet."

"Looked like you and Ballard were havin' your-selves quite a palaver a while ago," Preacher said to Smoke later when they were both standing near the cave mouth. "He happen to mention what's got him actin' like a long-tailed cat on a porch full o' rockin' chairs?"

"As a matter of fact, he did." Smoke's eyes swept over the shadowy cave lit only by the flickering, red-dish glow from the tiny fire.

Everyone else appeared to be asleep, although Catherine and Mrs. Bates were restless, no doubt due to the uncomfortableness of stretching out on the ground. With Preacher to stand the first watch, Smoke would be turning in soon.

Quietly, he told the old mountain man what Tom Ballard had explained to him. Preacher listened in silence, nodding every now and then.

"I've heard o' that hombre Coe. Supposed to be snake-quick with a gun, and mean as a snake, too, even with that grin he wears all the time."

"That matches what I know about him," Smoke agreed.

"You reckon Tuttle knows about the money Tom's bringin' back to Tucson with him?"

"No way of being sure. He could, though. I don't doubt that for a second. Men like that usually have eyes and ears everywhere, especially where power and influence are."

"Yeah, that's what I was thinkin'."

"Tom doesn't believe he has to worry about it, though. He's convinced we won't make it out of here alive."

Preacher chuckled. "That's the way the smart money would be bettin', I reckon."

"I've never minded playing long odds," Smoke said with a smile.

"Hell, I know that! You was just a younker when you went up against . . . how many was it? Twenty or thirty or forty gunmen, all at once?"

"Not quite that many," Smoke said, still smiling.

"Still, it was a whole heap, and you charged right into that mess. You ain't changed much over the years, neither." Preacher shook his head. "I don't figure you ever will."

"Right now let's just concentrate on getting through the night. You're still up to standing the first watch?"

"Damn straight. Get some rest. Mike can take the next shift and you'll finish up. Early in the mornin', when dawn ain't far off, that's the time them 'Paches are most likely to come skulkin' around."

Smoke nodded in agreement and left Preacher near the cave's entrance. He went over to where Sally was sleeping with her head pillowed on her arms and lay down beside her. The light was dim enough he could barely make out her features, but that didn't matter. He knew every inch of her beautiful face.

He went to sleep with that image in his mind.

Smoke woke up for his turn on guard duty without Tom Ballard having to rouse him. As he sat up, he could tell that although the wind was still blowing, it wasn't howling madly as it had been earlier.

Maybe that meant the storm was finally coming to an end.

The fire was flickering more than ever and in danger of going out. Smoke stood up and moved over to the fire, hunkering on his heels beside it to feed a few more twigs into the flames. They caught and the glow strengthened.

Smoke was a little annoyed as he went to the cave mouth. Ballard was supposed to have been watching the fire as part of his duties, and he had almost let it go out. That wouldn't have been a catastrophe—they had more matches—but it showed that Ballard had fallen down on the job.

That wasn't surprising, Smoke realized. Ballard wasn't really a frontiersman, he reminded himself.

At least the newspaperman wasn't asleep. As Smoke came up, Ballard turned to look at him and said, "Oh, you're up already. I thought it was about time." He had Mike Olmsted's Winchester in his hands.

"Any sign of trouble?"

"No, and there's a good reason why." Ballard nodded toward the entrance. "Take a look."

The light from the tiny fire barely reached that far, but Smoke could tell something was different. He took a step closer to the cave mouth and realized what it was. The opening was almost completely closed off by a wall of sand that protruded a couple feet into the cave. "It's drifted up like snow. I've seen that up in the mountains during the winter, but I never thought I'd see sand do the same thing."

"That's how sand dunes are formed," Ballard said.

"The wind constantly shifts them around. That's why they're sometimes called walking hills. Usually it just takes a lot longer because the wind isn't blowing as hard as it did last night." A look of worry came over his face. "We can dig out, can't we?"

"We should be able to. There's a more important question, though."

"What's that?"

"When we dig out, what are we going to find waiting for us on the other side?"

CHAPTER 34

Ballard went to get a little more sleep while Smoke waited at the sand-blocked entrance for dawn. The wind outside diminished more and more, and as a gray light appeared in the narrow slice of sky visible above the wall of sand, it stopped blowing entirely, leaving an eerie silence in its wake.

Smoke wished for some coffee, but that wasn't going to happen any time soon. He let the others sleep as long as they could. Exhaustion had drained them, so they needed their rest. Not surprising, it was Preacher, with his iron constitution, who woke first.

The old mountain man climbed to his feet, stretched, and then ambled over to Smoke. He squinted at the sand drift and muttered, "What in blazes?"

"It kept the Apaches from trying to sneak up on us, I guess."

"Yeah, but what're we gonna do now? Burrow out like rats?"

"We can clear away enough at the top to be able to climb out."

"I reckon. Sounds like the derned ol' wind quit blowin', anyway."

George Bates woke up next. He went over and peered up at the mound. "Lordy!"

"Best not let your grandma hear you talkin' like that, youngun," Preacher advised.

George pointed to the top of the mound. "I'll bet I could climb up there and wiggle through that opening, Mr. Jensen."

"You probably could, but you won't be doing that, George. It's too dangerous."

"Oh, yeah. There could be Apaches waiting out there, I guess." George brightened. "But you could gimme a gun—"

"We'll handle the fightin'," Preacher said.

"You can help us dig out, though," Smoke added.

"Sure! That'll be a change—not gettin' in trouble for digging in dirt and getting it all over me!"

One by one, the others woke up and greeted the new day with varying degrees of enthusiasm. Since there was no food except the jerky that Mrs. Bates had—and since they were all thirsty already—they skipped breakfast and got to work clearing away the sand that blocked the cave mouth.

With his wounded arm, Scratchy did what he could. "Smoke, I been thinkin' about what we ought to do if those Apaches are gone."

"That's a mighty big *if*."

"Yeah, but there's a chance some of us can walk outta here and make it back to the stage road. It's got to be somewhere south of us. If you could get there, somebody would come along, I'll bet."

"Some of us, you said."

"I ain't goin'," Scratchy declared. "I lost too much blood, and I'd have to drink up too much of the water from the stagecoach if I was along. I'll stay here and protect the coach. That's part o' my job, anyway. You could send some help back to me, once you got to the next way station."

"You'd be long since dead by the time anybody could get back here," Smoke said.

Scratchy's burly shoulders rose and fell. "Shoot, I never really expected to live as long as I have. Drivin' a stagecoach back and forth across this part of Arizona Territory is a pretty good way to live, as far as I'm concerned, but it ain't exactly what you'd call safe."

Smoke shook his head. "Abandoning my friends doesn't sit well with me."

"Then don't think of it as abandonin' anybody. Think of it as savin' them that you can."

The old jehu might have a point there, Smoke thought, but he wasn't ready to accept such a drastic solution. Besides, trying to walk out of the arid wilderness would hold plenty of dangers of its own.

"I've got something else in mind. It'll be Christmas in just a few days. My brothers are supposed to meet us in Tucson. When Sally and I don't show up, they're liable to come looking for us. They'll retrace the stagecoach's route."

Scratchy shook his head. "That storm won't have left any tracks for them to follow."

"Don't underestimate Matt and Luke. They're pretty good at tracking people down."

That was Luke's job as a bounty hunter, after all, and Matt had ridden as a member of numerous posses on the trail of outlaws, as well as working as a civilian scout for the army.

"So you're sayin' we just squat here and wait for help?"

"I don't like it," Smoke admitted, "but I'm not sure there's a better option."

"None of it matters if we can't get that water off the coach."

"That's right. We have to have it to save our lives."

"So it's sorta up to the Apaches, and we won't know if they're still waitin' for us until we go outside and see."

Preacher, who was working nearby, turned his head toward Smoke and Scratchy. "Hell of a gamble, ain't it?"

Because of hunger and thirst, the members of the group didn't have as much strength as they would have had under normal conditions, but they worked steadily that morning without complaining too much. The mountain of sand that blocked the cave mouth gradually shrank.

Sally paused in her efforts and used the back of her hand to wipe dark hair away from her sweaty forehead. She glanced over at Smoke. "I must look a sight."

"A mighty pretty sight," he told her.

"Oh, don't even attempt any flattery, Smoke Jensen. I know better."

"Wasn't flattery. Just the plain, honest truth. I've never seen you when you didn't look absolutely beautiful to me."

She laughed. "You know, for a man with such a reputation as a gunfighter, you must have mighty poor eyesight sometimes."

A few feet away, Mike and Catherine were working side by side, too, using their hands to scoop away the sand.

"You can take it easy and rest for a little while, Miss Bradshaw."

"I thought you agreed to call me Catherine. And anyway, I can do my part. I'm all right. Just a little tired and hot and thirsty . . . and hungry. Well, maybe I'm not exactly *all right* . . . but I can keep going for a while."

"Your lieutenant is a lucky man to be gettin' himself such a fine wife." At the sudden frown on Catherine's face, Mike added quickly, "I'm sorry, I shouldn't have been so bold—"

"No, that's all right. I'm just not sure Lieutenant Preston is getting himself such a good deal."

That was an odd way to put it, Mike thought. *A good deal.* Folks didn't usually refer to a marriage that way, at least not in his experience. Catherine was from back east somewhere and Lieutenant Harrison Preston was in the army. Mike didn't know all that much about either of those things.

As they all cleared away the drift from lower down, the sand on top slid and spread out, causing the gap to widen.

Finally, Smoke said, "I reckon that hole's big enough for me to climb up there and get through."

"I'll go," Mike said immediately. "I'm an employee of the Saxon Stage Line, Mr. Jensen. It's my job to go check on the coach and bring that water back."

"It'll take two men to carry that barrel, remember?"

Tom Ballard said, "I'll be the second man." When Smoke opened his mouth to argue, Ballard held up a hand to stop him. "Everyone else in this group is going to have a lot better chance to survive in the long run if you're still alive, Smoke. You know that. I'm just a newspaperman." He smiled. "I'm expendable."

Smoke didn't like anybody else stepping up and doing a job he thought he ought to do himself, but it was true that he had more experience in staying alive under extreme circumstances. He and Preacher had come through some pretty harrowing experiences in their lives. With Scratchy wounded, and the women and George out of the question, what Ballard said made sense.

"All right, Tom," Smoke said. "But Preacher and I are snaking our way out there, too, to cover you and Mike while you're fetching the water."

Ballard nodded. "That sounds fine to me."

"I'll go first," Mike announced. He took off his duster and left his Winchester in the cave. Climbing to the top of the sand heap that remained in the entrance wasn't easy, but he managed without sliding down and having to start over. Sand cascaded down from his efforts.

When Mike reached the opening, Smoke said, "Take

a look first. You want to be sure you're not diving right into trouble."

Mike paused, balanced precariously on top of the sand, and twisted his head back and forth. "I don't see a thing. The stagecoach is buried up to its hubs in sand, but there's nobody around it."

"Anybody hiding inside it?"

"Not that I can see. The dead horses are gone, too. Do you think the Apaches dragged them off?"

"Nothing Apaches like much better than horse meat," Smoke said. "All right, Mike. Slide on down outside. I'll come next, then Tom, then Preacher."

No one objected to the way Smoke had taken command. He was a natural-born leader, and the others all knew he was their best chance of getting out alive. He took his rifle with him as he climbed the drift, bellied through the opening, and slid headfirst down the far side.

It felt good to be out of the cave and in the sunlight again. The dust floating in the air in the storm's aftermath gave the sky a brown tinge, but it was clear enough for Smoke to see for hundreds of yards over the arid landscape dotted with scrub brush. Nothing was moving out there.

In short order, Ballard and Preacher joined them. Ballard said, "Let's go get that water. I'm sure ready for it."

"Reckon we all are," Mike said. With Ballard at his side, he strode toward the stagecoach.

They had gone only a few steps when an arrow seemed to come out of nowhere and smacked into Mike's thigh with a meaty thud.

CHAPTER 35

With a hoarse cry of pain, Mike stumbled and clutched at his wounded thigh but managed to stay on his feet. With his left hand, Ballard grabbed Mike's arm and steadied him. At the same time, he used his right hand to yank the pistol from his pocket. Eyes wide, he searched for something to shoot at.

Smoke and Preacher lifted their rifles to their shoulders and looked around, too. Smoke caught just the faintest flicker of movement at the top of a dune about fifty yards away and instantly snapped a shot at it. Sand flew, and a startled yelp told him he had either hit the ambusher hiding out there or had come mighty close to him.

Mike and Ballard were still too far from the coach to reach it safely and use it for cover, especially with Mike having to hobble along on an injured leg. Smoke fired again in the general direction of his first shot, as did Preacher.

As he levered the Winchester, Smoke called, "You two get back here! We'll cover you!"

Smoke and Preacher kept up a steady fire, spraying slugs around the area in front of the cave as Mike and Ballard hurried toward them. Mike limped heavily, leaning on the newspaperman helping him stay on his feet. Despite the covering fire, more arrows flew around the two fleeing men. The Apaches were masters at concealing themselves in the smallest possible spaces.

As Mike and Ballard stumbled past Smoke and Preacher, Mike looked up and cried, "No, Catherine! Get back in the cave!"

Smoke couldn't look around, but he heard Catherine sliding down the mound of sand.

"I'll help you!" she said.

Mike groaned, either from pain or fear . . . or both . . . that she would be hurt. It was no use arguing with a stubborn woman, though. With Ballard on one side and Catherine on the other, all three struggled toward the opening at the top of the drift.

"You next, Preacher," Smoke said as he peered through powder smoke.

"Naw, I'll bring up the rear. Get your carcass back in there, boy."

Smoke didn't waste time arguing. He started up the sand, twisting to fire his Colt toward where the arrows were coming from. One of the shafts whipped past his head, missing him by about a foot, but that was the closest they came.

When he reached the top, he holstered the Colt and lifted the Winchester again as he called, "Preacher, come on!"

Preacher retreated to the drift's base and began climbing. It was tough going. The sand slid underfoot with each lunge upward, but the old-timer was built of rawhide and whang leather and kept going. As he struggled to reach the opening, Smoke's bullets continued kicking up dirt in the area where the Apaches were hidden.

When Preacher was close enough, Smoke stopped firing and extended a hand down to him. Preacher grasped it, and Smoke hauled him up. Both of them toppled through the gap and tumbled down into the chamber the elements had carved out of the sandstone bluff.

"Lord have mercy!" Preacher exclaimed when they reached the bottom and came to a stop.

Smoke sat up and looked around. Enough sunlight came through the opening that he could see the entire cave. Mike sat with his back against the wall, not far from Scratchy. Sally had cut his trouser leg away from the wound and was examining it, along with Catherine, to see how bad it was. Ballard, Mrs. Bates, and George stood by, watching them tend to the wounded man.

"You all right?" Smoke asked Preacher.

"Yeah, I reckon. That arrow's gonna have to go on through the young feller's leg."

"I know." Smoke got to his feet. "Keep an eye on that opening up there. Make sure no Apaches try to sneak through it."

"They'll get a bullet in the face if they do," Preacher declared.

Smoke went over to join Sally and Catherine.

Sally glanced at him. "The arrow's lodged pretty deeply."

"I know," he said with a nod. "Mike, I reckon I don't have to tell you what has to be done."

Mike's face was a little washed out under its deep tan. He swallowed. "Yeah, I know. Best get it over with."

"Turn on your side a little more. You want a bullet to bite . . . or a belt?"

"No"—Mike looked at Catherine—"but maybe if you'd hang on to my hand . . ."

"Of course," she said without hesitation. She caught hold of his left hand in both of hers.

Then he clasped his right hand over hers.

He nodded to Smoke and then looked away, fastening his gaze on Catherine's face.

Smoke grasped the arrow, set himself, and with a quick bunching of corded muscles under his shirt, he shoved the arrowhead the rest of the way through Mike's leg.

Mike tipped his head back and showed his teeth in agony, but he didn't make a sound other than a faint growl from deep in his throat. His hands gripped harder on Catherine's. Pain showed on her face, but she didn't pull away.

Now that he could reach the bloody arrowhead, Smoke took hold of it and snapped the shaft. Then he pulled what was left of the shaft back through the hole in Mike's leg.

Mike took a deep, shuddery breath, and then his head fell to the side. He had passed out. Probably the best thing, considering that the wound still had to be cleaned.

"Scratchy, we'll need that flash of rye," Smoke said.

"Ain't much of it left, but there ought to be enough," Scratchy said as he handed over the silver flask. He sighed. "Better not anybody else get wounded."

Smoke unscrewed the cap from the flask and dribbled the fiery liquor into the entrance wound on the front of Mike's thigh. Mike stirred a little as the whiskey bit into raw flesh, but he didn't regain consciousness. Smoke turned the young shotgun guard's leg so he could do the same thing with the exit wound.

He started to hand the flask to Sally then changed his mind and passed it over to Catherine. "You saw what I just did. Can you do that every couple hours and keep fresh bandages on the wounds?"

She nodded, none too confidently. "I think I can. Is it all right to use strips from my petticoat for dressings?"

"Yep. I think that would do just fine." Smoke stood up and moved back over to where Preacher had an eye cocked on the partially blocked entrance.

Sally followed him, smiled, and said quietly, "Are we going to have to change your name to Cupid Jensen?"

"It's not that at all," Smoke said gruffly. "I was going to get you to take care of him, but then I figured we might need you more for shooting instead of nursing." Then he smiled, too. "Of course, Mike's a fine young man, and I don't reckon it'll bother him to learn that he had such a pretty gal taking care of him."

"A pretty girl who's engaged to another man," Sally pointed out.

"Well, Lieutenant Preston's not here, although I wouldn't mind seeing him right about now, especially if he was leading a company of cavalry." Smoke grew more solemn as he looked at the mound of sand. "So we're still bottled up in here with no food or water and no way to get away from the Apaches."

"I wouldn't worry about it," Preacher drawled. "We'll all die o' thirst a long time before we'll ever starve. That is, if them damn stubborn redskins don't get us first."

Smoke and Preacher climbed to the opening and lay there with their heads just above the sandy crest as they peered out.

"I don't see a blamed thing movin' anywhere," Preacher said after a few moments.

"Neither do I, but if we were to try to get to that stagecoach, I reckon our friends would announce themselves."

Preacher grunted. "Them 'Paches ain't no friends o' mine. You know, I never had anything in partic'lar against the Injuns, despite how many of 'em tried to kill me over the years. Well, the Blackfeet, maybe. For pure cussedness, there ain't nobody in the world who tops 'em. But anyway, I had some mighty fine friends among the tribes in my earlier days. Truth be told, probably fathered a good number o' younguns, too, and like I told you that first time we met, I prob'ly got more grandkids and great-grandkids scattered around the frontier than I can count. So can't nobody say I ain't been a friend to the Injuns who been friends to me."

He spat out through the opening, made a face, and went on. "Dang, a man can't hardly work up no spit when he's this dry. As I was sayin', there's been plenty o' times when the red man got a raw deal in this country, especially from the crooked politicians and the damn paper pushers they've paid off. Like that blasted Injun Ring in Washington we've tussled with a few times."

"You're not saying anything I don't agree with, Preacher," Smoke told him. "I reckon you'll get to a point sooner or later?"

"The point's this. I might have some sympathy for anybody who's fightin' for his land and the way he wants to live, but them 'Paches ain't just fightin' for that. They're crazy mean and cruel. Torture's just a sport with them. I can't abide that. Killin' an enemy in battle is one thing. Makin' him take a day or two to die while he's screamin' for mercy . . . well, that's another. I could put a bullet in the head of ever' one o' them varmints out there and never lose a second's sleep over it."

"I reckon you'll get a chance to try."

Preacher's weathered old face was grim as he said, "You know what's happenin' out there right now, don't you?"

"The Apaches are waiting for us to show our faces?"

"More than that. They've sent out word that they got a bunch of white folks trapped here. Might not 've been more 'n a couple dozen in the bunch that jumped us first. But I'll bet you a fancy new hat more o' them bucks been slippin' off the reservation ever' night since the trouble started. Could be two hundred or more renegades roamin' around by now, and once they hear what's goin' on, they'll be headin' for this place to get in on the fun."

"So you're saying the odds against us are just going to get worse."

"That's what I'm a-sayin'," Preacher declared.

"You think we should try to bust out of here now, before we're outnumbered twenty to one?"

Preacher rasped a hand over the silvery stubble that dotted his lean jaws. "Might be too late to make a break. If there was any way to get that stagecoach rollin', I'd say we ought to give it a try. Some of us wouldn't make it, but we'd have more of a fightin' chance. On foot—" He shook his head. "That'd just be throwin' our lives away." Preacher sighed. "It'd sure be nice to see ol' Matt and Luke come a-gallopin' over the horizon right now. Maybe even with them two hell-raisin' younkers with 'em . . . what do you call 'em? Ace and Chance?"

"That would make a difference, all right," Smoke agreed. "But it would take a miracle for something like that to happen."

"Well . . . it's the right time o' year for it, ain't it? And if you're gonna wish for a miracle, you might as well make it a good one."

Smoke couldn't argue with that, but he commented, "I'm a little surprised to hear talk of miracles coming from a hardheaded old coot like you."

"Oh, I've seen some things in my life," Preacher said. "Things there ain't no reasonable explanation for . . . in this world or any other."

While they were talking to pass the time, they had continued scanning the apparently empty terrain in front of the cave. Both men knew better, however. There were probably dozens of their enemies lurking out there, watching the cave.

Smoke heard someone clambering up the sand hill behind them. He turned his head to look and saw Tom Ballard. "Come to help us keep watch?"

The newspaperman flopped down beside them. "I came to talk to you because I have an idea. Those Apaches want to kill us, but what they really want to do is capture us, right?"

Preacher said, "They could get a lot more sport out of it that way, yeah."

"Do you think they'd be satisfied with *one* captive?"

Smoke frowned. "What the hell are you talking about, Tom?"

"I'd be willing to strike a bargain with them. I would surrender myself, and in turn they'd let the rest of you go."

Preacher let out a harsh laugh.

Smoke shook his head. "You'd be throwing your life away. The Apaches don't make deals. Even if they did, they'd just kill you—probably taking their time about it and making sure we could hear you scream—and then come after the rest of us, anyway. It was a noble thought, Tom, but it won't work." Smoke smiled. "Anyway, you have work to do in Tucson when you get back."

"When I get back," Ballard repeated with a bitter edge in his voice. "You don't really think—"

"Smoke," Preacher said suddenly, "there's somethin' movin' 'way out yonder—and it ain't them blasted 'Paches."

CHAPTER 36

Smoke and Ballard immediately turned their attention toward the opening and peered out. Ballard's noble but futile idea was forgotten. Preacher pointed, and the other two men followed his finger.

Smoke's eyes were at least as keen as those of the old mountain man. He spotted a dark speck about a mile out on the desert. It moved in and out of sight as it climbed and descended the slight rises that rolled across the arid landscape. "Is that a wagon of some sort?"

"I think it is," Preacher said.

Ballard shook his head. "Your eyes must be a lot better than mine. I can't see a thing out there."

"Watch for movement," Smoke said. "See that clump of cactus a couple hundred yards out. Look just to the right and a little above it."

"I still don't—wait! I *did* see something! But it's gone now."

Preacher said, "Most times, the desert ain't near as

flat as you think it is. It rises and falls, but you don't notice it as much close up. That wagon's droppin' down as it comes toward us, and then—"

"You're right," Ballard said excitedly. "I see it again. You say it's coming this way."

"That's the way it looks to me," Smoke said, "which means we've got to get busy."

"I don't understand."

"If that's a wagon, horses are pulling it. Horses that can take us out of here."

"But the Apaches . . ." Ballard's expression fell as bleak despair overcame him again. "They'll just kill the horses and whoever's on the wagon. Maybe we should start shooting to warn them to keep away."

"If we didn't have women and a kid with us, I might agree with you," Smoke said. "But we've got to put that man's life at risk to try to save them."

"One man? You can see well enough to know that?"

Preacher said, "That's how it looks to me, too."

"Come on," Smoke said as he started to slide down the mound of sand to inside the cave. "We have a lot of work to do." Reaching the bottom, he gathered everyone around Mike and Scratchy, who were still sitting with their backs propped against the cave wall.

"There's a wagon coming with a team of horses hitched to it," Smoke explained. "I don't know who the driver is or what he's doing here, but we have to get enough of that sand cleared away that the horses can get inside. Our lives probably depend on it."

"How's the fella gonna even get here?" Scratchy said. "Those heathens are still waitin' out there to kill anybody who comes along, ain't they?"

Smoke gave a grim nod. "More than likely. I reckon we'll just have to keep them distracted. Make them keep their heads down while the wagon's coming in. If we can do that, we've got a chance—but only if we can get the horses inside where they'll be safe."

"Prop me up," Mike said. "I can dig."

"So can I," Scratchy added. "It'll be one-handed, but I can do a heap with one arm if I put my mind to it."

George said, "I like digging."

Sally put a hand on his shoulder and smiled down at him. "It looks like you'll get a chance to do plenty of it."

Catherine bent to take hold of Mike's arm. "Let me help you up."

He smiled at her and nodded.

Within minutes, all nine people trapped in the cave were at the sand drift, digging at it with their hands, slinging the sand behind them into the cave. Dust rose and created a haze in the air. Millions of motes floated in the rays of sunlight slanting into the cave.

They looked a little like a pack of dogs digging holes, Smoke thought wryly. But if that was what it was going to take, he was all for it.

The top of the drift lowered as they spread the sand. The driver of the wagon hadn't seemed to be in a hurry. The man probably had no idea what was going on ahead of him. He was rolling along across what had to look to him like empty desert.

Smoke found himself listening for shots that would tell him the Apaches had noticed the approaching wagon. He heard only the grunts of effort and the panting breath of his companions as they worked at the sandy barrier in the cave mouth. The Apaches probably had all their attention concentrated on the cave. They might not see the wagon coming up behind them until it was almost there.

Smoke was hoping that, anyway.

With all of them working doggedly at the task, it wasn't long before he could peer over the top of the sand pile. He paused and searched the landscape for the unexpected sight that might be their salvation.

There had been talk about a Christmas miracle. Maybe one was about to happen.

"The wagon's still there, less than a mile away and steadily coming closer." Smoke thought eight horses were hitched to it, although from his angle it was difficult to be sure. "Let's go! We've got to get this drift down a little more."

The level of the sand continued to fall. Mike and Scratchy, weakened by their wounds, were beginning to slow down. So was Mrs. Bates, who lacked the stamina of the younger people. The others kept at it until Smoke saw that the opening was big enough for the horses to be led over the sand and into the cave.

No sooner did that happen than rifles began to crack outside.

"Apaches spotted the wagon! Preacher, grab your rifle and come on!" Smoke snatched up his Winchester leaning against the cave wall and bounded over the much smaller pile of sand.

Preacher was right behind him.

"I'm coming with you!" Mike looked around. "Cat, hand me my rifle!"

Catherine either didn't notice the nickname he

had called her or didn't care. She grabbed the Winchester and thrust it into his hands, then slid her arm around his waist. "I'll help you get out there."

"Not hardly," he told her as he shrugged out of her grip. "Stay in here where it's safe."

"I'll come," Tom Ballard said as he gripped Mike's arm to steady him. "I've still got my pistol and quite a few rounds for it."

They clambered over the sand and out of the cave.

Sally moved up next to Catherine as the younger woman said, "He should have let me help him!"

"He just wants to keep you from getting hurt," Sally said. "I've dealt with the same thing from Smoke for years. Men don't change easily." She smiled. "It may be hard to believe, but sometimes that's a good thing."

Outside the cave, Smoke saw plumes of powder smoke where the hidden Apaches were firing at the wagon. He and Preacher sprayed shots around those areas as fast as they could to force the raiders to duck and hold their fire. Smoke knew the man on the wagon might turn tail and try to flee. That wouldn't work. Some of the Apaches would just chase him down and kill him.

Now that the stranger was only a few hundred yards from the cave, his best chance for survival was to charge ahead and try to reach shelter.

Smoke wanted to make sure the man realized that. Instinctively, he reached for his hat to signal the driver. "Damn! Preacher! Wave your hat over your head to signal the driver that he should come on. Hurry!"

The stranger seemed to understand Preacher's frantic waving. He whipped up his team and sent them galloping toward the cave.

Smoke went back to shooting at the Apaches. Mike and Ballard added their guns to the covering fire from Smoke and Preacher.

The stranger was hunched low on the wagon seat, making a smaller target of himself, not an easy task. He was a large man. He was close enough now for Smoke to make out the burly form, the wide-brimmed black hat, and the long white beard that blew back in the wind. As the man drove, he took the reins in his left hand and used his right to pull a long-barreled pistol from a cross-draw rig on his left hip.

Just in time, too. One of the Apaches suddenly appeared, bounding up to the wagon and leaping onto the side of the driver's box. He clung to it with one hand while wielding a knife with the other. The white-bearded stranger thrust the revolver toward the raider and pulled the trigger. Flame spouted from the muzzle and touched the Apache's bare chest for an instant before the heavy slug's impact sent him flying backwards away from the wagon.

More Indians sprang from their hiding places in little hollows and tried to get in the wagon's way. Smoke and Preacher cut down a couple, and their bullets came close enough to make the others fling themselves back into hiding.

With the wagon less than a hundred yards away, Smoke lowered his rifle. "Tom, Mike, you'll have to unhitch those horses and get them inside the cave as fast as you can. The driver can help you. Preacher and I will keep the Apaches off of you while you're doing it."

"Count on us, Smoke," Ballard said.

"We all are." Smoke's rifle began to roar as he brought it to his shoulder again.

With a rumble of wheels and thunder of hoof-beats, the wagon swept past him a moment later. He caught just a glimpse, enough to see it was a long freight wagon with what appeared to be a cargo of some sort heaped underneath a large, tied-down canvas cover. He didn't know what the teamster was hauling and didn't care. He was busy keeping the Apaches' heads down long enough for the other men to complete their task.

Smoke and Preacher didn't fire wildly, they just did it quicker than any normal man could do. They picked their shots and aimed at where they knew Apaches were. Only the near-supernatural fighting abilities of those two men kept the savages at bay while the other three unhitched the team and half-led, half-dragged the frightened horses into the cave.

Ballard came up to Smoke and shouted over the gun-thunder, "The horses are in the cave!"

Smoke jerked a nod and called, "Preacher! I'm going for the water!" He had already decided to make a try for the barrel lashed to the stagecoach since they were out in the open, anyway.

The old mountain man's rifle continued to boom as he yelled, "Go!"

Smoke turned and flung his Winchester through the cave mouth, then sprinted toward the stage-coach. He was a little surprised to realize that Tom Ballard was right behind him.

"You'll need help!" the newspaperman said.

It was too late to tell Ballard to go back. Smoke

had figured with his massive strength, he might be able to carry the water barrel by himself, but it would be easier—and faster—with two men.

They reached the coach. Smoke's knife came out and flashed in the sun as he slashed the ropes holding the water barrel. He stuffed a piece of rope into his pocket along with the knife and threw his arms around the barrel. Ballard helped lift the barrel and awkwardly but still swiftly, they ran toward the cave.

Smoke heard bullets whipping around them. An arrow flew past his ear. Ballard stumbled but didn't fall and recovered quickly. Smoke hoped it really had been a stumble and that Ballard wasn't hit.

Preacher angled closer to them. His rifle had run dry and he had his Colt out, blazing away with it. They reached the sand drift, which was still a couple feet high, and struggled through and over it, into the cave. Preacher ducked in behind them.

"The barrel's leaking!" Sally cried.

Smoke looked down. Sure enough, a small stream of water was spouting from the barrel's side, from a bullet hole Smoke hadn't even realized was there. In the chaos, he hadn't felt the slug strike the barrel.

They had to plug that hole somehow, or all the precious liquid might be lost.

Before Smoke could do anything, George said, "I've got it!" and jumped forward to shove his finger into the bullet hole. The water stopped flowing.

"Can you keep your finger there until we think of something else?" Smoke asked as he and Ballard lowered the barrel to the ground.

"Sure. And look, Mr. Jensen. It's Santa Claus!"

CHAPTER 37

Their thirst momentarily forgotten, everyone turned to look at the stranger and thought for a second the boy was right.

The man stood there in the center of the cave next to his horses with his fists propped on his hips and a big grin on his bearded face. In addition to the broad-brimmed black hat, he wore a bright red flannel shirt over black whipcord trousers and high-topped boots. With his round, florid face and long white beard, he bore a distinct resemblance to the figure Smoke had seen in paintings depicting Christmas scenes.

"I been called a lot of things, sonny," the stranger said in a booming voice, "but I don't recollect Santy Claus bein' one of 'em." He took off the hat, revealing thick, snowy hair that matched his beard, and bowed slightly to Sally, Catherine, and Mrs. Bates. "Ladies. It's a pleasure and an honor to make your acquaintance. At least, it would be if the circumstances of our meetin' hadn't been marred by gunplay." A thunderous laugh came from his barrel chest following that declaration.

"I'm Smoke Jensen," Smoke introduced himself.

"Call me Nick Kendall," the stranger said.

"Saint Nick," Tom Ballard murmured.

"What was that?" Kendall shook his head. "I ain't exactly what anybody would call a saint, neither!"

"And I ain't a preacher, neither," the old mountain man said, "but that's the handle I've gone by all these years."

"You're Preacher? I've heard of you." Kendall stuck out his hand. "This really is an honor." He shook hands with all the men as Smoke performed the rest of the introductions.

George looked up at him. "You're not really Santa Claus?"

"Why would you think I was, son?" Kendall stroked his beard. "Because of this?"

George pointed through the cave's entrance. "You've got a wagon out there. That's sort of like a sleigh. And there were eight horses hitched to it. *Eight.* That's the number of reindeer Santa had pulling his sleigh in the poem my ma used to read to me."

" 'The Night Before Christmas,' " Ballard said. "I remember it, too. You have to admit, Mr. Kendall, you bear a certain resemblance to the jolly old elf in Clement Clarke Moore's poem."

"Maybe. I seem to recall hearin' somethin' about it, although I ain't the sort to read poetry. If I recollect right, ol' Saint Nick had toys in his sleigh that he delivered to boys and girls all over the world on

Christmas Eve. It ain't quite Christmas Eve, and what I got on my wagon sure ain't toys."

"What is it?" Smoke asked.

"Guns."

They all stared at him for a couple seconds before Preacher drawled, "What sort o' guns?"

"Winchester repeaters, Colt and Remington and Smith & Wesson revolvers, and boxes of ammunition for all of 'em. And one other thing . . . a Gatling gun."

Mike let out an impressed whistle. "Sounds like you've got a whole arsenal out there, Mr. Kendall."

"Close to it," Kendall admitted. "I'm a travelin' gun salesman. That load is bound for Tucson."

"Who's buying that many guns in Tucson?" Ballard asked with a sudden frown.

"Fella name of Peabody. Has a store there."

Ballard shook his head. "Avery Tuttle really owns that store. Luther Peabody is just a figurehead."

"I wouldn't know nothin' about that. I just sell my goods, deliver 'em, and move on."

Ballard looked like he wanted to say more in response to that, but he controlled the impulse.

Kendall went on. "I reckon I can look around outside and see how you folks come to be trapped here. I heard Apaches were hellin' around these parts, but I figured I could dodge 'em. Wouldn't be the first time I did."

"We would have tried to warn you off," Smoke said, "but as you can see, we have women and a youngster here. We need your horses if we're going to have any chance of getting away."

"My horses and my wagon, you mean? You figure on pilin' on top of my cargo?"

Smoke shook his head. "No, we're going to hitch your team to the stagecoach. They can pull it a lot faster than they can that heavily loaded wagon, especially if all of us were on it, too."

Kendall's cheerful expression hardened slightly. "I reckon it'd be up to me what's done or not done with my horses."

"No offense, Mr. Kendall, but getting these folks to safety matters more to me right now than anything else."

For a moment, Smoke and Kendall locked stares.

Then Kendall shrugged. "I reckon you're right about that. I got a heap of money tied up in those weapons, though, and you're askin' me to abandon them out here in the middle of nowhere. What you figure the chances are they'll still be here when I come back for 'em?"

"I don't know, but I'll make good your losses, whatever they are."

Kendall cocked his head a little to the side. "You can do that?"

The Sugarloaf was one of the most successful and lucrative ranches in Colorado. In addition, Smoke had a gold claim he had located as a young man that he still worked from time to time. Although he didn't believe in living in any sort of fancy, ostentatious manner, Smoke was one of the richest men in that part of the country.

"I can do that." The utter conviction in his voice was enough to make Kendall nod.

"All right, then. Let's start thinkin' about how we're all gonna get out of here. First, hadn't you better do somethin' about that water barrel so the youngster can take his finger out of it?"

Preacher grabbed one of the branches they had gathered to feed the fire, cut a piece off, and quickly whittled it into a plug for the hole in the water barrel. They each had a drink of the life-sustaining water, then the men stepped away and held a council of war to figure out their plans.

Smoke said, "The Apaches aren't going to just let us hitch up those horses without trying to stop us. We were able to unhitch them and lead them into the cave while Preacher and I kept the Apaches busy, but I doubt if that's going to work again."

"What you need is somethin' that'll really force 'em to keep their heads down." Kendall laughed. "It so happens I got just the thing."

"The Gatling gun," Smoke said.

"Yep. If we can get it set up on top o' that stagecoach, I can cover all the ground hereabouts. Once that devil gun starts spewin' out a couple hundred rounds a minute, those heathens'll be huggin' the dirt and prayin' to whatever god they pray to. I guarantee it!"

Smoke nodded. "While you're doing that, the rest of us can get the team hitched, load everybody in the coach, and throw in as many guns and as much ammunition as we can. Then we'll be ready to light a shuck out of here."

"Sounds like it might work," Preacher said, "*if* we can get that Gatlin' gun set up."

"How about if we move it from the wagon to the stagecoach in the dark?" Mike suggested. "After the moon sets tonight, it'll be pretty dark."

"The Apaches are liable to have guards around the stagecoach," Scratchy said.

"If they do, they'll need to be tooken care of," Preacher said. "Quietlike."

Smoke knew what he meant. In his younger days, Preacher had had the reputation of being able to slip into a Blackfoot camp, slit the throats of several of his enemies, and then get back out again without anyone even knowing he'd been there until the bodies of his victims were discovered the next morning. That grim talent had led the Blackfeet to dub the mountain man "Ghost Killer."

That was a story George Bates would probably enjoy, Smoke thought . . . but the boy's grandmother might not appreciate anyone telling it to him.

"Preacher can handle the guards," Smoke said, never doubting that the old mountain man still had the skills necessary to do the job. "Nick, Tom, and I can move the Gatling and get it set up. By the time we do, it won't be long until dawn. That's when we'll bust out of this trap." He looked over at Scratchy. "You can't handle the team with one arm."

"Mike can take the reins," the jehu said. "He's got two good arms, and he's drove a coach a few times."

"I'd rather be fighting," Mike said, "but I reckon that makes sense."

"I can handle my pistol with one hand," Scratchy said. "I'll try to plug one o' the varmints for you."

"Let's just all get out of here safely," Mike said with a glance toward Catherine on the other side of the cave. "That's all that matters."

* * *

The day dragged by. Now that the wind had died down, it was hot in the cave. The food was gone and everyone's belly was empty, but at least they had water and the deadly, energy-sapping thirst had been relieved.

Everyone knew the plan. Everyone had a job to do once they went into action, even George. He would carry boxes of ammunition from Kendall's wagon to the stagecoach. All would be at risk, but at least they would be fighting to get away, rather than just waiting for death to claim them.

It would take a couple men to carry the Gatling gun and lift it onto the stagecoach's roof. Smoke and Kendall would handle that. Ballard would carry a crate filled with the long belts of ammunition that fed the weapon. Preacher, once he had disposed of the Apache sentries—if there were any—would stand guard while the other men worked.

Everything would have to go right for the plan to work, but taking a chance was better than doing nothing.

A fighting chance was all Smoke Jensen had ever asked out of life.

He had never liked waiting around, so he was glad when the sun set and night crashed down with its usual abruptness in the desert. It was still hours until they would put the plan into action, but darkness meant the showdown was that much closer.

"Everybody get some rest if you can," Smoke told the others. "I'll wake you when it's time to get ready."

He didn't mention that it might be the last night's sleep some of them would ever get.

CHAPTER 38

The horses were restless during the night and so were some of the people inside the cave, but everyone managed to get at least a little rest. At some point, Preacher relieved Smoke and stood guard so Smoke was able to stretch out beside Sally and get an hour or so of sleep. Like any good fighting frontiersman, he had the knack of being able to doze off quickly whenever he had the chance.

He woke up on his own, without Preacher having to rouse him. The fire had burned out—all the fuel had been consumed—but that was in accordance with Smoke's plan. The cave was pitch dark, and the night outside was almost as impenetrable. The cave mouth was just a slightly lighter shade of black.

Smoke stood up and moved toward it. Preacher's whispered greeting reached his ears.

"Everything quiet out there?" Smoke asked.

"Quiet as the grave," Preacher replied. "Although

maybe that ain't really such a good thing to say right now."

"How long until sunup?"

"Couple hours, I'd say."

Smoke nodded. "Time for you to go see if anybody's lurking around that stagecoach. I'll wake up the others."

The idea that Preacher might not be able to handle the Apache guards never occurred to Smoke. The old-timer might be a hair slower and less deadly than he once was—but that meant he was still more than a match for just about any enemy he would ever encounter.

Preacher left his rifle with Smoke and disappeared into the shadows outside the cave. Smoke woke everyone else and told them get ready.

"I've handled a Gatling gun in the past," Smoke told Nick Kendall, "but I reckon you've got more experience with one than I do. You'll be on top of the coach with it. That'll make you more of a target."

"I'm not worried about that," Kendall said. Even in the darkness, Smoke could see the big, bearded man's teeth as he grinned. "Put me behind one of those devil guns and I'll match my chances against anybody else's."

"That's what we're counting on." Smoke moved on over to Sally. "You'll be in charge here in the cave. Everybody stays put until the gun is mounted on the coach. Then you and Catherine get Mike out there as quickly as you can. Scratchy will come, too, and Mrs. Bates and George will bring guns and ammunition from Nick's wagon. Once Scratchy and Mike are on the driver's box, you and Catherine come back in here and get the water barrel. We're liable to need it before we get to Tucson. Oh, the water barrel. I have a piece of rope you can use to tie the door shut. Keep it from banging open when we ride away." Smoke pulled it from his pocket, handed it to her, and put his hand on his wife's shoulder. "That barrel will be heavy, but I think the two of you can manage it."

"We have to, so we will," she said without hesitation. "Don't worry, Smoke. We won't let you down."

He smiled. "You've never let me down for a second in all the time I've known you." He bent forward and kissed her, a sweet kiss that lasted only a moment but still packed considerable punch for both of them. It was a passion that would never go away.

He went back to the cave mouth where Tom Ballard and Nick Kendall waited.

Ballard said, "We're ready, Smoke."

"Yep. Just waiting for—" Smoke stopped short as he heard what sounded like the faint cry of a night bird from somewhere up on the bluff above them. That was Preacher's signal. "That's it," he said softly. "Let's go."

Crouching, the three men ran out of the cave. As quietly as possible, they hurried to Kendall's wagon. The sand crunched a little under their boot soles, but that couldn't be avoided.

Kendall didn't take the time to untie the ropes that fastened the canvas over his cargo. He used his knife to cut the ropes and threw the canvas back. He lowered the tailgate, climbed into the wagon, and picked up one of the wooden crates. Leaning over the side, he thrust it into Tom Ballard's waiting arms.

The newspaperman staggered a little under the weight, but managed to keep his feet and steady himself. He turned and started toward the stagecoach while Kendall picked up one end of a larger crate and swung it around to set it on the wagon's sideboards.

Smoke grasped that end of the crate. Kendall vaulted out of the wagon and took hold of the crate as well. Wood rasped on wood as they pulled it out until Kendall could position himself at the other end. Smoke figured some of the Apaches waiting out there in the darkness might have heard the sound.

If time hadn't already started running out on them, it would now.

Carrying the long, heavy crate between them, Smoke and Kendall headed for the stagecoach as fast as they could. When they got there, they set the crate on the ground on the side between the coach and the bluff.

From out in the shadows, a shrill yip sounded— one of the Apaches signaling to the guards stationed around the stagecoach. There was no response.

Of course there wasn't. Preacher had seen to that.

Kendall rammed his knife blade under the crate's lid and levered it up. Nails squealed as they came free. About a hundred yards out on the desert, orange muzzle flame winked in a couple places. Instantly, shots blasted from the front of the coach as Preacher returned the fire. The sharp cracks told Smoke that the old mountain man was using a Winchester he must have taken from one of the dead sentries.

Kendall threw the crate's lid aside and reached in

to wrap his long, powerful arms around the Gatling gun. He heaved it upward. Smoke helped him, then Ballard stepped in to take some of the weight while Smoke scrambled up onto the driver's box. He reached back down to help the other two men raise the weapon toward the roof.

Then it was up to Smoke's incredibly powerful muscles to hoist the Gatling gun into position. Kendall was already clambering up the rear of the coach with a couple belts of ammunition slung over his shoulder. He helped Smoke open the legs of the tripod that supported the gun and maneuvered it into place where he could swing the barrel back and forth and cover most of the landscape in front of the cave.

More shots came from the Apaches out on the desert, but Preacher's steady fire and deadly accurate bullets had them spooked and none of their slugs came close.

Suddenly, just as Kendall was loading one of the belts into the gun, a shot rang out from somewhere above and behind them and a bullet whined off the brass rail only inches from Smoke. His Colt flashed from its holster to his hand as he whirled around, instinct telling him that at least one of the Apaches had climbed to the top of the bluff. A second shot blasted that gave him a target. He fired, then heard a cry of pain followed by a heavy thud as a body plummeted from the top of the bluff and landed at its base. No more shots came from up there, so he figured the Apache had been alone.

"Ready!" Kendall sang out. "I've been watchin' where those shots are comin' from. Time to chew 'em up!" He turned the Gatling's crank. Fire flickered from the weapon's muzzle as .44 caliber slugs exploded from it in a torrent of lead.

Smoke jumped from the top of the stagecoach to the ground, landed lightly, and called, "Sally! Now!"

Sally and Catherine emerged from the cave with Mike between them, leaning on them as they all half-ran, half-stumbled toward the stagecoach. Mrs. Bates and George were right behind them, heading for Kendall's wagon. The older woman was terrified, Smoke knew, but she was willing to fight to save her grandson's life.

Scratchy hurried out toward the stagecoach.

Smoke and Ballard ran past them going the other way, and into the cave to get the horses. Behind them, the stuttering roar of the Gatling continued from the top of the coach. Smoke didn't know if Kendall was actually hitting anything other than the ground, but with that death storm raging around them, the Apaches would be staying as low as possible and wouldn't have a chance to do much shooting of their own.

Smoke and Ballard led the horses out. Ballard held the other animals while Smoke backed them two at a time into their places and hooked up the harness. He wasn't as quick about it as an experienced hostler would have been, but he didn't waste any time, either.

The Gatling abruptly fell silent. Kendall had emptied the first belt and had to reload. Preacher and Mike—who had climbed onto the box with help from Sally and Catherine—tried to take up the slack with their Winchesters. It wasn't as terrific an assault as the Gatling gun, but it was quite a barrage.

The devil gun began chattering again.

"Sally!" Smoke called. "Get some more ammo belts from that crate and toss them up on the roof!"

Mrs. Bates toddled toward the stagecoach with her arms full of rifles and several pistols. George was right behind her, staggering a little under the weight of the two ammunition boxes he carried. They reached the coach and dumped their loads inside through the broken door.

"That's good!" Smoke told them. He didn't want them running the risk of another trip. "Climb in and start loading those guns!"

Kendall had told Smoke that all the weapons in his cargo were chambered for .44 caliber rounds, so it wouldn't matter which bullets went into which guns. Smoke just wanted all of them fully loaded and ready to deal out death.

He finished hitching up the last two horses. Sally and Catherine were on their way back to the coach with the water barrel. They obviously struggled under its weight, but they were determined to make it. Smoke and Ballard hurried to meet them and take the burden from them.

"No time to tie it on," Smoke snapped. "We'll just put it inside." The interior of the coach was going to be mighty crowded with seven people, a bunch of guns, and the water barrel, but it couldn't be helped.

Once the water barrel was inside the coach, Sally and Catherine climbed in, joining Mrs. Bates and George. Ballard went next. Smoke called, "Preacher, come on!"

"I'll hang on the back!" the old mountain man replied.

That was actually a good idea, Smoke thought, but he would do it instead of Preacher. "No, get in!"

Preacher pulled himself up into the coach, muttering something about blamed, high-handed youngsters.

Smoke realized there was enough gray light in the eastern sky for him to see his surroundings. He spotted a couple sprawled Apache bodies, their heads surrounded by dark pools of blood that had welled from their slit throats. Preacher still had that deadly skill.

Smoke swung up onto the boot, standing on the bags under the canvas cover and hanging on to that cover with his left hand. He had the Colt in his right again. "Mike, get us out of here!" he shouted.

With Scratchy to his right for a change, Mike was sitting in the driver's spot. He slapped the reins against the team and called out to them. The coach lurched forward.

Nick Kendall shoved a fresh belt of ammunition into place and got the Gatling singing its deadly song again as the coach began to pick up speed. Mike swung the vehicle around so they were heading toward the low orange crescent on the eastern horizon. Kendall swept .44 rounds across the landscape like a scythe as the stagecoach wheeled in its new direction. He had to hold his fire for a second as he realigned the barrel, then he opened fire again.

The Apaches, seeing their quarry about to get away, threw caution to the winds and charged out of their hiding places. Dozens, no, scores of them, Smoke realized to his astonishment.

The bullets from the Gatling gun slashed through them and mowed them down, shredding flesh, shattering bone, and knocking them off their feet. Smoke added to the carnage, drilling a couple raiders who came within range of his Colt. Shots blasted from inside the coach as well, as Preacher, Sally, Ballard, Catherine, and Mrs. Bates opened fire.

For the most part, though, it was Nick Kendall, long white beard whipping back over his shoulder, who dealt most of the destruction. The stagecoach was a rolling arsenal of death.

Over the thunderous roar of gunfire, Smoke heard a shout of pain and looked past Kendall to see Scratchy slumping over on the seat. The old jehu was hit again. Smoke didn't know how bad it was, but Scratchy appeared to be out of the fight.

An instant later, Mike rocked to the side. Smoke saw an arrow protruding from the young man's right arm. Mike couldn't handle the team one-handed, so Smoke slid his Colt back in its holster and grasped the rail around the coach's roof to pull himself up.

He crawled past Kendall, who was still firing the Gatling gun at the Apaches, and leaned down between the two wounded men on the box. "Mike! Hand me the reins!"

Mike was bleeding badly, but he twisted around on the seat, grimacing in pain, and passed the reins over. Smoke sat on the front edge of the roof and drove from there, slashing the reins against the horses' backs to keep them galloping. From the corner of his eye, he saw Apaches on horseback, racing their ponies alongside the coach. Kendall blasted away the raiders on his side, but more were closing in from the other side.

Mike leaned over, fumbling with his left hand for

something at his feet, and came up with the coach gun. He thrust it out and fired it one-handed, triggering both barrels. The recoil tore the Greener from his grip, but the double load of buckshot smashed into the Apaches and blasted several of them off their ponies. A couple mounts fell, too, and tripped up the others. All of them went down in a welter of flailing horseflesh and smashed humanity.

The Gatling ran dry again. Rather than trying to reload once more, Kendall hauled out his long-barreled revolver and began picking off some of the remaining raiders. He was an expert shot and had a good vantage point from the top of the stagecoach.

Smoke glanced back, saw the bluff receding in the distance. Between where they were and the cave where they had taken shelter a couple days earlier, the ground was littered with corpses, a bloody trail of the dead that showed where the coach had passed. Not many of the raiders were still alive, and those who were had peeled off and were getting away as fast as they could. Ultimately, the pilgrims had been outnumbered by more than ten to one, but had fought their way through, anyway.

The coach rolled toward the spot where the sun would soon peek above the horizon as Smoke kept the team moving at a fast pace. He believed the Apaches had given up for good, but he and his companions still needed to put as much distance as they could between them and the surviving renegades.

"Ho, ho!" Nick Kendall boomed. "Left 'em in the dust, we did! Dash away, Smoke, dash away!"

Unless Smoke had gotten confused, it was Christmas Eve.

CHAPTER 39

"Still no word?" Matt Jensen asked as he stood in the Tucson office of the Saxon Stage Line.

"No, sir," the nervous-looking clerk replied. "And now we can't even communicate with Casa Grande anymore. The storm that passed through yesterday must've blown down some of the telegraph wires between here and there."

Matt shook his head in disgust. The stagecoach carrying Smoke, Sally, and Preacher should have arrived a couple days earlier. He knew that from the information that had been wired from Casa Grande about the railroad trestle being out. According to the stationmaster in Tucson, several people had chosen to take the stagecoach on a roundabout route, rather than waiting until after Christmas when the bridge was repaired.

That stagecoach hadn't shown up when it was supposed to, and no one seemed to have any idea what had happened to it.

Except . . . rumors had been floating around of Apache raiders from across the border helling in southern Arizona Territory. If the coach had come across some of those renegades . . . no one seemed to think the passengers had any chance of surviving.

That might well have been true sometimes, Matt knew, but Smoke and Preacher had been on that stagecoach. If anybody could survive, in any sort of dangerous situation, it was those two.

So Matt kept checking at the stage line office, hoping to hear something, but his patience was running out. If the wait lasted much longer, he was going to saddle his horse, pack some supplies, and set out to find his brother.

The door opened behind him. Matt looked over his shoulder and saw a young, fair-haired man in the uniform of an army lieutenant.

He strode up to the counter and slapped a hand on it. "I've tolerated your impertinence long enough, sir! I demand to know where that stagecoach is!"

Matt lazily lifted an eyebrow and leaned his left elbow on the counter. "You're waiting for the stagecoach to get here, too?"

The lieutenant cast an annoyed glance in his direction. "I don't think that's any business of yours."

"I reckon it is," Matt drawled. "My brother and sister-in-law and an old friend are on it. I was just thinking about going out to look for it. If you've got a detail with you, Lieutenant, we could organize a search party."

"I don't have a detail," the officer snapped. "I'm here on temporary leave to meet my fiancée and escort her back to the fort, where we'll be married." He scowled. "By the time I get back, the entire company will be out pursuing those damned renegades. I'll have missed my chance to be part of it."

"Anxious to chase Apaches, are you?"

"A victorious engagement with the hostiles would look very good on my record . . . not that it's any of your affair, mister."

Matt suppressed an instinctive dislike for the lieutenant. During some of his stints working as a scout for the Army, he had run into officers like that one—men who cared only about advancing their careers, men who were willing to endanger the soldiers under their command if that would "look good on the record." As far as Matt was concerned, men like that weren't worthy of wearing the uniform, but a depressingly large number of them could be found.

However, it wouldn't do any good to express his feelings to the arrogant young lieutenant—although handing him a whipping held a lot of appeal—so Matt turned back to the clerk. "I'll be around town. Let me know if you hear anything, all right?"

"Of course, Mr. Jensen."

Matt gave the lieutenant a curt nod and walked out of the office into the December sunshine. It was warm and didn't feel much like winter. A terrible sandstorm had blown through the day before, leaving the air hazy, but the wind had died down completely and that haze was starting to settle.

As he crossed the street to the hotel where he was staying, he was startled to hear his name called. He looked to see who had hailed him, and a grin broke out on his face as he recognized the man riding toward him.

Luke wasn't alone. Two younger men rode with him—a dark-haired hombre in a buckskin shirt and jeans, with a flat-crowned brown hat pushed back on his head; and a gent with sandy hair, dressed fancier in a Western-cut brown suit and a cream-colored Stetson with a tightly curled brim.

Matt recognized the two younger men as well, having met them in Texas a couple years earlier. Ace and Chance Jensen—no relation as far as anybody knew—but they shared gun speed, quick fists, and a knack for getting in trouble with the more notorious Jensens.

Seeing the three of them lined up like that—Luke, Ace, and Chance—made the smile disappear from Matt's face, replaced by a puzzled frown. Even though at first glance they were very dissimilar, there was something about them . . . a resemblance that might go unnoticed unless a person happened to see them that way.

They might have to reconsider the idea that Ace and Chance weren't related to the rest of them, Matt thought. Distant cousins, maybe.

"Hello, Luke," he said as his oldest brother reined in. "Smoke's letter said you might show up, too, but I didn't know if you would."

"Yeah, and I ran into these two hellions on the way," Luke said with a chuckle as he pointed his thumb at Ace and Chance.

"Was there gunplay involved?" Matt asked, smiling again.

Ace said, "No, for a change things were nice and peaceful."

"Then Luke walked in," Chance added.

Matt said, "I reckon all hell broke loose after that?"

Luke snorted. "I think I resent that. You're implying that violence occurs wherever I happen to be."

"Isn't that usually the case?"

"Well . . . usually," Luke admitted with feigned reluctance. "But not always."

The three newcomers swung down from their saddles and tied the horses at one of the hitch rails in front of the hotel.

Ace said, "Luke told us you were getting together with Smoke and Sally and Preacher for Christmas here in Tucson. I'm afraid we sort of invited ourselves along for the ride, but we won't interfere in your family get-together if you want—"

"If it's up to me, I sure don't care. Jensens are bound together by more than blood and a last name. I'd say hot lead and powder smoke play a part in it, too, and you fellas have shared in that right with us. As far as I'm concerned, you're part of the family already."

Matt paused, thinking about what he had noticed a few moments earlier. He was wondering if he ought to bring it up when he noticed that Luke had stiffened and moved his right hand closer to the butt of one of the Remington revolvers he carried.

"What's wrong?" Matt asked quietly.

"Fella over there moseying along the boardwalk," Luke replied. "That's Smiler Coe."

Matt looked across the street and saw a lean, dark-featured man sauntering along in front of the stores. He looked like a hardcase, which wasn't surprising considering Luke's reaction to him.

"Don't reckon I know him . . . but you obviously do. Is he wanted?"

"Not that I know of, but only because he's always worked for powerful, important men who managed to keep his face off the reward dodgers. He's a cold-blooded killer, though, no doubt about that."

"But you can't collect a bounty on him," Chance said.

Luke shook his head.

"I wouldn't risk my life trying to arrest him, then," Chance said.

"I'm not going to, but I'm sure going to keep my eyes open. Coe may know me by reputation just like I know him. He might decide I was after him and figure he'd be better off gunning for me first."

"I'm sure it won't come to that," Ace said.

"But if it does, we'll back your play," Matt said. "You know that, Luke."

Luke nodded slowly, then, as Smiler Coe disappeared into one of the buildings across the street, he turned to Matt. "Where are Smoke and Sally and Preacher?"

"That's something I'd sure like to know," Matt said as a grim, worried expression settled over his face.

Luke looked surprised. "It's Christmas Eve. They're not here yet?"

"Come on in the hotel," Matt said. "We can get some coffee in the dining room and I'll tell you what I know . . . but it's sure as hell not much."

Smiler Coe paused in Avery Tuttle's outer office and nodded toward the closed door on the other side of the desk. "He's in there?"

"Yes, he is," Amy Perkins said as she got up from her chair. "But he's upset."

"Yeah, and I reckon I know why," Coe muttered.

"Still no sign of the stagecoach?"

"I've got men ridin' back and forth between here and Sahuarita Ranch several times a day, bringin' me word. The coach ain't shown up yet. When it does, they'll be waitin' to jump it as soon as it's far enough away from the way station."

"Something's happened to it," Amy said, a little breathlessly. "The Apaches got it, or it was lost in that sandstorm . . ."

"If that's true, then Tuttle gets what he wants. That money's gone, and so is Tom Ballard."

"But *we* don't get the money," Amy practically wailed. "I was counting on that—"

"Never count on money until it's in your pocket," the gunfighter told her. "Folks can always try to double-cross you, and sometimes fate just ain't on your side." He put his hands on her shoulders. "But believe this, darlin' . . . if there's any way to get hold of that cash, I'm gonna do it. And for anybody who gets in my way, it's just too damn bad."

"Oh, Smiler . . ." Amy leaned in, came up on her toes, and pressed her mouth hungrily against his.

Was she hungry for *him*, Coe asked himself . . . or just for the money?

He couldn't answer that but figured it would all play out the way nature intended. So far, nature seemed to intend that he wind up on top. He broke the kiss and stepped back. "Reckon I'd better go talk to him."

"Don't lose your temper with him."

"I don't intend to." Coe moved to the door and grasped the knob.

"Maybe you'd better knock first," Amy suggested.

He gave her a look that said he didn't like being subservient to anybody, even the man he worked for, but then he shrugged and rapped a couple times on the door with the knuckles of his left hand.

"Come in," Avery Tuttle called.

Smirking, Coe twisted the knob and went in.

Tuttle stood by the window, half-turned away from it as if he had been looking through the glass before Coe knocked. His hands were clasped together behind his back. "Is there any news?" he asked briskly.

"Nope," Coe said as he propped a hip on a front corner of the big desk.

"Tomorrow is Christmas. That stagecoach should have arrived yesterday."

"You mean it should have started up the river trail and ran right into the ambush I've got waitin' for it."

"It's the same thing," Tuttle snapped. "Do you think it's lost somewhere out in the desert west of here? Could the driver have strayed from the road during that storm and not been able to find his way back?"

"Can't rule that out," Coe said with a shrug. "Or the Apaches, either."

"I suppose I should be happy." Tuttle stepped away from the window and went behind the desk. "Tom Ballard is no longer a thorn in my side, and the money he was bringing back will never help my enemies. I'll take over the bank, call in all the notes, and by the first of the year, nearly all of Tucson will belong to me."

"Yeah, you'll be a rich man. A *richer* man, I reckon I ought to say."

"But I want to *know*," Tuttle said. "The uncertainty is tormenting me. Ballard could still be out there somewhere, heading this way to ruin all my plans. I can never be sure that he isn't."

"I can take care of that for you," Coe said as a plan formed in his mind. "If I don't get word by tomorrow morning that the stagecoach showed up and our boys stopped it, I'll ride down there, gather 'em up, and we'll retrace the route until we find it. If Ballard and that loot don't come to us, we'll go to him."

Tuttle frowned in thought for a moment and then nodded. "All right. That's a good idea. Just make sure that whatever happens, none of it will ever come back to threaten me."

"Sure, boss."

Yeah, that was like Tuttle, all right. Making sure his own hide was safe, no matter what happened to anybody else. Things might be different, Coe told himself, once he had his hands on that money. Amy knew all the details of Tuttle's business enterprises. No reason the two of them couldn't run things just as well or better than Tuttle had been doing. All it would take was not being afraid to seize power . . .

"Is there anything else?" Tuttle snapped, interrupting Coe's thoughts.

"Nope." Coe's lips pulled back in a grin, exposing the gold tooth. "I reckon I've got plenty to think about."

CHAPTER 40

Smoke brought the coach to a stop when the remaining Apaches were far out of sight behind them then called to the passengers, "Need some help up here!"

As they piled out, Smoke spewed orders. "Preacher, keep an eye on our back trail. Tom, give me a hand with Scratchy."

Ballard hurried to assist Smoke in lowering the old jehu to the ground. The front of Scratchy's shirt was dark with blood.

Mike's face was pale and drawn. His shirtsleeve below the arrow shaft was bloody, too, but at least he was conscious. "Scratchy's hit bad." His voice was choked with emotion. "You've got to help him."

"We'll do everything we can," Smoke said as he and Ballard propped Scratchy up against one of the coach's front wheels.

Scratchy was still breathing, but raggedly.

Sally knelt at Smoke's side as he tore the shirt back

to reveal the bullet hole in Scratchy's chest. Both of them heard the faint whistling from the wound and saw the bloody froth on Scratchy's lips. They glanced at each other, knowing he was shot through the lungs and was done for.

"Tom, help Mike down," Smoke said quietly. "Sally, see what you can do for his arm."

"Don't worry about me," Mike protested. "Just tend to . . ." His voice trailed off as he realized what Smoke's words meant. "Aw, hell no! He can't . . ."

Scratchy's eyelids fluttered open. His eyes were unfocused for a moment, then his gaze settled on Smoke. "The passengers . . . ?" he said in a weak, raspy voice.

"I think everybody's all right."

"We are," Mrs. Bates said from the coach's open door. "No one was hurt."

"That . . . Kendall fella . . . ?"

"I'm still up here on top of the coach," Kendall said, "keepin' an eye out for any more hostiles."

"I don't think any of them will be bothering us again," Smoke said. "Not after the damage we did to them. There's a good chance the ones who are left are lighting a shuck back to the border as fast as they can."

"Hope . . . so," Scratchy managed. "Smoke . . . listen to me . . ."

"You ought to take it easy."

"Wouldn't do . . . a derned bit o' good. I know I'm . . . a goner . . . but I'd be obliged . . . if you'd get the coach through."

"I'll do it," Smoke promised.

"Mike . . ."

With Ballard's help, the young man had gotten down from the driver's box. Sally was looking at his wounded arm, but she stepped back and nodded to him as Scratchy called his name. The wound appeared to be a clean one, not too deep, and a few minutes wouldn't hurt.

Mike moved over and knelt beside Scratchy. "I'm right here, partner."

"You gonna be . . . all right?"

"Yeah, don't worry about me."

"You help . . . Smoke and the others . . . get where they're goin' . . ."

"You can count on that."

"We're a good ways . . . north of the road . . . head southeast . . . that'll take you . . . toward Sahuarita Ranch . . ."

"I know it," Mike said, nodding. "I can find it."

"Then I reckon I can . . . head on across the divide . . . without worryin'—" Scratchy straightened suddenly, his eyes opening wider. "Get on there!" he called, his voice strengthening as if he were calling out to his team. "Run, you blamed varmints! Run—" He fell back against the wheel and more blood bubbled from his lips. His chest rose, fell, and then didn't move again.

Smoke reached up and gently closed the wide, staring eyes.

Catherine and Mrs. Bates were crying. A tear ran down Sally's sun-bronzed cheek, too. Mike muttered something under his breath, a curse or a prayer . . . or both.

Smoke said, "Mike, can we make it to Tucson today?"

The young man swallowed his grief and nodded. "Ought to be able to by tonight, if we don't run into any more trouble."

"We'll wrap Scratchy up in a blanket, then, and take him with us, instead of burying him out here."

"Might be better to lay him to rest at Sahuarita Ranch," Mike suggested. "He'd be happier at a way station than in town."

"Then that's what we'll do," Smoke said. "Now, let's see about getting that arrow out of your arm. It's going to hurt like hell."

Preacher took Mike's usual seat, riding next to Smoke as Smoke handled the team. Nick Kendall continued riding on top of the coach, with Ballard and George joining him to make room inside the vehicle for Scratchy's blanket-shrouded body. A few days earlier, Catherine and Mrs. Bates probably would have complained about being forced to share the coach with a corpse, but they were just grateful to be alive . . . and grateful to Scratchy for everything he had done to help keep them that way.

The coach rolled into the way station at Sahuarita Ranch late that afternoon. Mike, with his wounded arm bandaged, had helped navigate from inside the coach, calling up to Smoke whenever he spotted a familiar landmark. Several men hurried out of the station when the coach rattled up.

The one in charge exclaimed, "We were starting to think we'd never see you folks!" Then he frowned. "Where are Stevenson and Olmsted?"

"We're in here, Joe," Mike said from the coach window. "Scratchy's dead."

"Good Lord! And what the devil is that up on the roof?"

"Devil's right," Kendall said with a laugh as he slapped the Gatling gun's barrels. "This is what some folks call a devil gun."

"Well, come on inside, all of you. We'll take care of the team. You look like you've been through hell, so I reckon you can all use some rest."

Smoke dropped to the ground and shook his head. "We're pushing on to Tucson."

"Now?" the stationmaster said in amazement. "But you won't get there until after dark."

"Doesn't matter. This is Christmas Eve, isn't it?"

The stationmaster scratched his head. "Yeah, I think so."

"We're going to spend Christmas Day with our families if we can."

"That's up to you, I reckon."

Mike said, "We'd like to lay Scratchy to rest in that little cemetery in the village, Joe."

"Sure. I reckon he'd probably like that."

There had been a village at this spot along the Santa Cruz River since ancient Indian times. Water was rare and precious in Arizona Territory, but the banks along the Santa Cruz were green with vegetation and the stream had attracted settlers for a long time. Tucson was some fifteen miles north, and as soon as a fresh team had been hitched up, Smoke intended to push on without stopping again.

First, was the matter of the burial. People from the village of Sahuarita pitched in to help. The local blacksmith also served as the undertaker and had several coffins on hand. The padre at the mission conducted the service and prayed over Scratchy as the old jehu's body was lowered into a hastily dug grave. The occasion was solemn and a little out of place on the day before the celebration of a famous birth.

Birth and death had always gone hand in hand, Smoke mused as he stood next to Sally, holding her hand.

When the prayers had all been said, everyone climbed back onto the stagecoach. Nick Kendall had taken the Gatling gun off the roof, folded up the tripod, and stowed the deadly apparatus in the rear boot. He was going to ride inside for the rest of the trip. George stared at him, still not completely convinced that the jovial, white-bearded giant wasn't really Santa Claus.

Smoke took up the reins and sent the coach rolling northward toward Tucson. The journey was almost over.

The river ran fairly straight between Sahuarita Ranch and Tucson, and the stage road followed it closely. The river bed was about twenty feet deep, with steep, rocky bluffs along its sides in places. In other places, the banks were shallow and had clumps of trees growing along them, since the water was close enough for the roots to reach it.

Five men and their horses waited in one of those clumps of trees, smoking and talking idly as the time dragged by. Nelse Andersen was one of them, but the other four were new men, recruited by Smiler Coe from the steady stream of hardcases and saddle tramps that passed through Tucson. They were good enough for ambushing a stagecoach, Andersen supposed, but he would have felt better about things if Smiler and Sam Brant and Phil Deere had been there.

It didn't really matter, Andersen thought as he flicked the butt of the quirley he'd been smoking. It landed in the river. That stagecoach wasn't ever going to show up. It had been buried in the sandstorm, or the Apaches had massacred everybody on it, or maybe it had fallen into a ravine somewhere. Andersen was convinced that he and the other men were wasting their time.

Then he heard the swift drumming of hoofbeats from the south.

He stalked to the edge of the trees and looked in that direction. The sun was low in the western sky, but he spotted the rider galloping along the river trail. He recognized the man as a hardcase named Cardwell, who had been left behind in the village of Sahuarita to watch for the stagecoach.

At that thought, Andersen's heart jumped a little in his chest. The only explanation for Cardwell being in such a hurry was that the coach had finally arrived.

Andersen turned to the other men and snapped, "Get ready. Looks like we may have work to do in a little while."

The men who'd been sitting scrambled to their feet. Guns slid out of holsters and cylinders were checked. Andersen stepped out of the trees and raised a hand in greeting as Cardwell reined in.

"They're here," the hardcase said. "I mean, they're there." He heaved a breath. "I mean, they're on their way. They left the way station a while ago."

"Did they see you ride out ahead of them?" Andersen asked sharply.

Cardwell shook his head. "No, I moseyed on out of town when I saw the stagecoach roll in, and then I waited behind a ridge where I could watch the road. As soon as I saw the coach leaving the village and heading this way, I circled around and lit a shuck to warn you, Nelse. I figure they're about a mile behind me."

Andersen turned his head to look at the others. "You heard the man. Get ready! Find some good places to bushwhack that coach and take cover." He turned back to Cardwell. "Do you know what happened to delay them?"

"No idea, really," Cardwell replied with a shake of his head. "But I saw some of 'em takin' what looked like a body out of the stage. It was wrapped up in a blanket, so I can't be sure. Looked like a carcass to me, though. Might've been the driver. Some cowboy I never saw before was handling the reins, and he had an old man on the seat beside him."

Andersen frowned. "They must've run into some Apaches. They're probably pretty lucky to have made it as far as they have." An ugly grin stretched his hatchetlike face. "Too bad their luck's about to run out."

CHAPTER 41

The final leg of the journey from Sahuarita Ranch to Tucson would take them a couple of hours, Smoke estimated. They wouldn't arrive until after dark, but he didn't think he would have any trouble following the river trail, even at night. "It's been quite a trip," he said to Preacher as the coach rocked along, approaching a grove of trees beside the Santa Cruz. "There was a time or two I didn't know if we'd make it this far."

"Fiddlesticks. I don't believe that for a second. You always knew we'd make it if we kept fightin' and didn't give up."

"Well . . . I figured we'd have a lot better chance that way. But one of these days, Preacher, we're liable to come up against odds that are too much even for us."

The old mountain man snorted dismissively. "I'll believe *that* when I see it," he declared.

The words were barely out of his mouth when a muzzle flash spurted orange fire in the shadows under the trees. Smoke felt the wind-rip of the bullet's passage as it whipped past his left ear. More tongues of flame licked from hidden guns and slugs slashed the air around the coach. One of the horses screamed and reared up in its harness.

"Ambush!" Smoke shouted as he hauled back on the reins.

Preacher flung the Winchester to his shoulder and opened fire, peppering the grove with bullets. Smoke drew his Colt and joined the battle. Inside the coach, shots blasted from the guns belonging to Tom Ballard and Nick Kendall.

Kendall exclaimed, "Blast it! I knew I shoulda kept that Gatlin' gun out! I'd 've made short work of those bushwhacking varmints!"

Next to Catherine, Mike turned and put his good arm around her, drawing her against him so he could shield her with his own body. Mrs. Bates had already pushed George to the floor and was hovering over him, protecting him the same way Mike was doing with Catherine. Sally stayed low, too. She didn't have a gun at the moment, or else she would have gotten in the fight, too.

Bullets stormed back and forth for a few seconds that seemed longer. Another horse screamed as it was hit. The men in the trees had better cover, but the speed and deadly accuracy of Smoke and Preacher helped even the odds. The ambushers were getting a lot stiffer fight than they had expected, more than likely. Trying to bushwhack Smoke Jensen and the old mountain man called Preacher was one of the dumbest things a man could do.

One by one, the muzzle flashes in the trees died

away. Smoke set the stagecoach's brake and dropped behind it. Preacher was already on the ground.

"I'll circle around," Preacher said as the guns fell silent. "Could be we got all the durn bushwhackin' buzzards."

"I'll cover you," Smoke said.

Preacher disappeared into the dusk, seeming to fade away with uncanny stealth.

Smoke pouched his iron and picked up the other Winchester from the floorboards of the driver's box, leveled the repeater at the trees, and waited. "Everybody all right in there?" he asked quietly.

"We're fine," Sally replied. "Nobody caught a bullet . . . although quite a few were flying around."

Smoke couldn't be certain why they had been attacked, but he had a pretty good idea it had to do with that trunk of Tom Ballard's—the one back in the boot. The one full of money intended to save Tucson from being swallowed up by Avery Tuttle's greed and ambition. Ballard didn't think Tuttle knew about the money, but Smoke had a hunch he did.

After a few minutes that seemed longer, Preacher strolled out of the trees and called, "Four dead hombres over here, shot to pieces. Look like typical range trash. Their horses are still tied up."

"That's good," Smoke said as he came around the front of the team. Two of the horses hitched to the stagecoach were down, killed by the hail of bullets. "We can use a couple of them. They may not be used to pulling in harness, but they can learn."

"Another thing, Smoke," Preacher said when he had walked back over to the stagecoach. "Looked to me like there were *five* horses here before the shootin' started."

Smoke's mouth tightened into a grim line. "So one man got away."

"Could be. And if he did, you know what he's gonna do next."

"Head straight back to the man who hired him and warn him that this ambush didn't stop us. And that means we may find more trouble waiting for us in Tucson."

Smiler Coe, Sam Brant, and Phil Deere were sitting in the saloon they frequented, nursing beers and playing a desultory game of three-handed, penny-ante poker, when the batwings swung open and Nelse Andersen came in. Coe sat up straighter when he saw the tense look on Andersen's face and noticed that the pale gunman was holding himself rather stiffly.

Andersen stalked toward the table. As he came closer, Coe saw how he had his left arm pressed tightly against his side. A small bloodstain was visible on Andersen's shirt.

"Oh, hell," Coe said quietly.

Brant and Deere hadn't noticed Andersen's arrival, but they looked up at hearing Coe's curse. Brant cursed, too.

Deere said, "Looks like something's wrong, Smiler."

Coe ignored that stupidly obvious comment and signaled the bartender for a bottle of whiskey. Andersen pulled back one of the empty chairs and slumped into it. "That damn stagecoach got past us," he said, getting right down to it.

"Was Ballard on it?"

"Yeah, along with a couple gunslinging sons of bitches up on the box. Don't know who they were, but they weren't the usual driver and guard, that's for sure." Andersen paused, then added grimly, "They shot the hell out of us. I'm the only one who made it, and I got nicked."

Coe frowned, wondering if Andersen had abandoned the other bushwhackers and got out of there in a hurry once he was wounded. It didn't really matter, he supposed. Either way, the stagecoach had gotten through and was on its way to Tucson. "How bad are you hit?"

"I'll be all right," Andersen said. "Hurts like blazes, though."

Coe grunted. One of the girls who worked there placed a bottle on the table. He nodded toward it and told Andersen, "There's some medicine for you." He scraped his chair back. "I've got things to do."

"Going to see the boss?" Brant asked.

"You just let me worry about that," Coe snapped. He didn't like letting his men in on his plans too much. He told them what they needed to know, and that was enough.

Andersen said, "We need to get more men together. We can give those bastards a welcome they're not expecting when the stage rolls in."

"I told you, let me worry about that." Jaw clenched to restrain his temper, and his usual grin nowhere in sight, Coe strode out of the saloon.

*　*　*

Avery Tuttle could often be found in his office even at a late hour. Coe checked there first and saw a light burning in the window. Tuttle was there, all right. He went to the front door, found it locked, and banged a fist on it.

A few moments later, Tuttle opened the door and glared out at him. The businessman wasn't wearing his coat, but his collar and tie were still in place. "What is it? This had better be important."

"It is. You might want to hear it inside, though."

Tuttle squinted angrily at him for a second, then stepped back.

Coe went inside and heeled the door closed behind him. He glanced around the outer office. No sign of Amy Perkins. She had gone home for the day. Well, it *was* Christmas Eve, after all. Anyway, Tuttle had no interest in any after-hours shenanigans with his pretty secretary. Amy had told Coe she'd tried to flirt with Tuttle, only to have him steadfastly ignore her efforts.

"That stagecoach got through," Coe said bluntly. "Ballard and the money are on the way here. Probably won't be long until the coach shows up."

Tuttle drew in a deep breath and his clean-shaven face tightened. "You told me your men could stop it."

"I figured they could. Nelse Andersen was the only one who got away, and he said a couple men on the coach are good with their guns. They shot up my bunch." Coe shrugged. "Maybe Ballard hired himself some guards."

"I don't care what he did. You were told to stop that money from getting here. You failed. Failed miserably."

The words lashed at Coe.

Fury welled up inside him at being talked to like that. In an instant, he could put a bullet in Tuttle. It would be even more satisfying to beat the life out of the man. Coe knew that wouldn't really accomplish anything, though.

"What do you want us to do now? We can jump the coach as soon as it rolls in."

"And do what? Steal the money and murder Tom Ballard? Everyone in town knows you work for me. I'd be arrested, even if you got away."

"I don't see any other way to keep Ballard from putting that money in the bank."

For a moment, Tuttle just stood there with the wheels of his brain obviously spinning in his head. Then he said, "We'll let him put it in the bank. Tomorrow's Christmas. He can't put any plans into action until after that, so the money will stay there for a few days. That will give you and your men time to steal it."

"Rob the bank, you mean?" Coe said.

"That's exactly what I mean."

Coe frowned. "We'll have to go on the run."

"The border's not far, and there'll be enough money in the safe to let you and your friends live like kings in Mexico for a long time. Maybe from now on."

Coe rubbed his beard-stubbled chin as he thought. He pointed out, "That won't solve your problem with Ballard."

"I'll handle Tom Ballard. Anyway, without that loan, his business won't stay afloat for much longer, and neither will the others I've set my sights on. I wouldn't have mourned Ballard's death, but in the long run he's no threat to me. That money is."

"I don't much cotton to the idea of spending the rest of my life as a wanted bank robber."

"You'll be well paid for it."

Coe shrugged. "I reckon you're right about that. So we don't do anything when the stagecoach gets here?"

"That's right. Let Ballard believe that he's won." Tuttle's smile was cold and vicious. "He'll soon find out just how wrong he is."

CHAPTER 42

Smoke steered toward the lights of Tucson—a welcome sight in the darkness. Two of the bushwhackers' horses were in harness, and the other two saddle mounts were tied behind the stagecoach.

"You reckon they'll hit us again when we get to town?" Preacher said.

"Wouldn't be surprised."

The old mountain man patted the stock of the Winchester he held. "We'll be ready for 'em if they do."

However, as the coach rolled into the settlement and Smoke headed for the stage line's local office and barn, the street appeared peaceful. Only a few people were in sight, most of them around the brightly lit saloons. It was Christmas Eve, and he supposed most folks were at home with their families—if they *had* homes and families.

The stage line office was dark.

Preacher said, "By now they've probably given up on us ever gettin' here."

"We can unhitch the team ourselves," Smoke said as he drove past the office. "For now, let's go up to the hotel. I don't know where Tom and Mrs. Bates live, or where Catherine's lieutenant might be, if he's still here."

"I ain't sure Miss Bradshaw's real anxious to see that lieutenant anymore," Preacher said with a chuckle. "She seems a mite more interested in ol' Mike."

"Well, that's none of our business . . . thank goodness."

Smoke brought the stagecoach to a halt in front of the hotel. Before he and Preacher could climb down, the double doors of the hotel's front entrance swung open and several figures appeared on the porch.

"Smoke!" a familiar voice called.

Smoke grinned as he recognized Matt and Luke. A couple men followed them, and to Smoke's surprise, he knew them, too. He hadn't sent letters to Ace and Chance, but the Jensen boys were there and Smoke was glad. He had grown fond of the two young drifters and adventurers who shared the family name.

"You fellas don't know how good it is to see you," Smoke said as he set the brake and wrapped the reins around the lever.

"Had some trouble getting here, did you?" Luke asked.

"A mite. We'll tell you all about it, but right now, we need to get this coach unloaded."

Ace had already stepped down off the porch and pulled on the coach's door. "Let me give you folks a hand."

Catherine tugged on the rope latch and emerged first. The sight of a pretty girl made Chance perk up. He hurried forward, too, evidently bent on shouldering his brother aside so he could be the one to help Catherine.

She ignored both of them, however, and turned back to assist a burly young man with a bandaged arm and thigh. "You two, help me with Mr. Olmsted." It was the only attention she gave them.

As Mike was climbing awkwardly out of the coach, another figure emerged from the hotel. Lieutenant Preston said, "The stagecoach is here? My God, why didn't someone tell me? Miss Bradshaw? Catherine Bradshaw?"

Smoke frowned. Preston was looking right at Catherine. Didn't he know her?

Startled, she stepped away from Mike and said, "Lieutenant Preston?"

Ace and Chance grabbed on to Mike's arms and kept him from falling.

Preacher muttered, "What in blazes? I thought they was engaged to get hitched."

Smoke was beginning to understand. "Yeah, but I think they're just meeting for the first time." He grunted. "She's a mail-order bride."

"Thank heavens you're here," Preston went on as he stepped closer to her. "Now we can get back to the fort and be married—assuming everyone isn't off chasing the Apaches! What delayed you?"

"I got here as quickly as I could . . . Harrison." The name sounded stiff and clumsy coming from her mouth.

"Very well, I forgive you." He took hold of her arm. "Come along. I've engaged a room for you in the hotel. Tomorrow we can start for the fort."

"But Harrison . . . aren't you glad to see me? Are you . . . pleased to meet me?"

"Of course I'm pleased. I've made a thorough and extensive study of the situation, and a married officer is significantly more likely to be promoted than an unmarried one."

"Aw, hell," Preacher muttered to Smoke. "That boy ain't got a brain in his head."

Catherine was staring at him. "But . . . but your letters were so charming . . ."

"I wished to win you over. Now that I have—"

"Mister, I just laid eyes on you, but you're already the biggest jackass I've ever seen in my life!" Mike interrupted.

Preston stiffened "How dare you!" He took a step toward Mike, only to have Matt and Luke edge partially into his path. Preston stopped short as they looked grimly at him. "Ah . . . I don't know who you are, my good man," he said to Mike, "but since I can see that you're injured, I'll overlook your rudeness."

"Rude, hell!" Mike said. "Let go of me, boys. Even with one arm and one leg, I can whip this stuffed shirt!"

"Hold on . . ." Smoke started

But Catherine stepped in. "It's all right, Mike. Lieutenant Preston has been laboring under the assumption that I'm going to marry him, but I see now that he's very much mistaken."

Preston stared at her in anger and confusion. "We had an arrangement—"

"Here's what I think of our arrangement." Catherine's hand came up and cracked across his cheek in a sharp slap.

Preston stepped back in shock.

"In case you're too stupid to understand, our engagement is off." She turned to the Jensen boys. "Let's get Mike into the hotel. He needs to rest." As they started up the steps, Catherine looked back over her shoulder and added, "By the way, Lieutenant, I think you're the biggest jackass I've ever laid eyes on, too."

Preacher chortled and slapped his leg in amusement.

The rest of the passengers had climbed out during the confrontation between Catherine and Preston.

With a hand on George's shoulder, Mrs. Bates turned to Smoke and Sally. "Mr. and Mrs. Jensen, I can't ever thank you enough for what you've done—"

"No thanks necessary," Sally told her with a smile. "We were all just trying to make it through. And we were happy to help, weren't we, Smoke?"

"We sure were." Smoke held his hand out to George. "Put 'er there, son. You've got the makings of a mighty decent hombre."

"You really think so, Mr. Jensen?" George asked as he shook hands.

"I sure do."

George looked at Sally, and when she opened her arms, he put his arms around her waist and hugged her. "Gee, Mrs. Jensen, I . . . I'm sure gonna miss you."

"We'll be around for a few days," Sally told him. "Maybe we'll see you again."

Mrs. Bates said, "You certainly will. You're all coming to dinner at my house before you leave Tucson."

Smoke nodded. "We'll sure take you up on that offer, ma'am."

Ace and Chance came back out of the hotel.

Ace grinned. "I think we left that fella in good hands. That lady seems like she plans to fuss over him for a long time."

"Maybe from now on . . . drat the luck," Chance added.

"I'm glad you fellas are here," Smoke told them. "There are plenty of bags to unload and carry."

"Why us?" Chance asked.

"Well . . . you're the youngest, aren't you?" Smoke said with a smile.

Chance sighed, but Ace laughed and slapped his brother on the back. "Come on. Let's get this chore done. And Merry Christmas!"

"Yeah, Merry Christmas," Chance said.

Tom Ballard stepped over to Smoke. "I need to get that trunk over to the bank and what's inside it locked up in the safe."

"Figured as much," Smoke said, nodding. "You'll have to roust out the banker first, won't you?"

"I'll go and get him right now. I was hoping maybe you could keep an eye on the trunk . . ."

Smoke nodded toward Preacher, Matt, and Luke, who all stood with him. "I don't reckon anybody will bother it."

By the time an hour had passed, the money Tom Ballard had brought from the territorial capital was locked up in the bank's safe and Ballard had returned home to be reunited with his family for Christmas Eve. Mike was resting in a comfortable hotel bed with Catherine sharing the meal she had brought up on a tray. The coach was in the stage line barn and the weary horses in the attached corral. Smoke had spoken to the local sheriff and explained about the ambush and where the extra horses had come from.

The lawman looked over the mounts in the light from a lantern Preacher held and then said, "I don't recognize any of 'em, but that doesn't mean anything. Plenty of men drifting through here all the time, and some of them aren't exactly what you'd call solid citizens."

"These four sure weren't," Smoke said. "We left the bodies where they were. You'll need to send somebody down there with a wagon to fetch them . . . if the scavengers have left anything."

The sheriff nodded. "I'll do that. We'll let our undertaker enjoy Christmas morning first, though. I don't reckon there's all that much hurry."

Smoke didn't argue about that. He wasn't going to waste any time worrying about what happened to the bodies of men who had tried to kill him and his loved ones.

With all that taken care of, the Jensens and Preacher went into the hotel dining room. Smoke sat with Sally on his right, Preacher on his left, and Matt, Luke, Ace, and Chance around the rest of the table as they enjoyed coffee and a late supper. It was a celebration of the Savior's birth and a Jensen family reunion at the same time.

Funny how it often seemed to work out that way, Smoke mused.

He looked at Luke, Ace, and Chance sitting together and thought about something Matt had said to him earlier in a brief, private moment. It was true. There was more of a resemblance than Smoke had ever noticed before, maybe because Ace and Chance were getting a little older and time had refined their features a little. When he had first met them, during a saloon brawl up in Wyoming, they hadn't even told him their last name was Jensen, but later on, Chance had mentioned jokingly that Ace sometimes speculated about them being long-lost relatives.

Maybe there was something to that. Smoke had never really asked Ace and Chance about their family history. He would have to do that, one of these days.

In the meantime, there wasn't anything better than sitting in a comfortable chair with a full belly and a hot cup of coffee in hand, surrounded by friends and family. Smoke should have been content. He wished he was.

Sally leaned her head on his shoulder for a moment. "I'm glad all the trouble is over."

"Me, too," Smoke said.

But he couldn't quite bring himself to believe it.

CHAPTER 43

Christmas Day dawned clear and cool in Tucson. Although it wasn't Sunday, Christmas services were being held at the mission, as well as at the Baptist and Methodist churches. Most of the businesses in town were closed, but the saloons were open, of course, and so were a couple cafés.

Around midmorning, Smoke, Luke, and Matt were sitting on the hotel's front porch, enjoying the nice weather, when Preacher came walking up the street.

Smoke hailed him. "I wondered where you'd gotten off to, Preacher."

"I went to hunt up Lije Connolly."

"Your old friend you came here to see before he passed away," Smoke recalled. "Did you find him? Or was it . . . too late?"

"I found him, all right. Sure wasn't what I'd expected, though."

Matt said, "He'd already passed on?"

Preacher let out a snort. "Passed on? He ain't even sick!"

"Isn't that a good thing?" Smoke asked, frowning.

"Well, I reckon it is," Preacher admitted. "Seems Lije was in a pretty bad way when he come out here, but the climate hereabouts was good for him. He's hale and hearty now, says he expects to live a long time. But here's the disgustifyin' part. The ol' goat went and got hisself married to some little Mexican gal who's young enough to be his granddaughter! Not only that, her belly's all swole up with a baby! Lije is gonna have hisself a youngun runnin' around. Wouldn't surprise me if even more of 'em come along later."

Matt laughed. "Preacher, I think you're jealous."

"Jealous!" The old mountain man squinted at him. "Why in tarnation would I ever be jealous of a feller who went and got hisself tied down so he can't go a-roamin' around no more? Lord have mercy, that'd be plumb torture!"

Smoke said, "It sounds to me like your friend's made a good life for himself."

"Aw, I reckon he has. And I'm happy for him, I s'pose. 'Tain't for me, though. I might settle down one o' these days . . . when I get old."

Smoke and Matt laughed again, but when Smoke glanced over at Luke, he saw that his older brother had a wary look on his craggy face. Luke was gazing down the street as if something had caught his interest.

"Something wrong?" Smoke asked quietly.

"About ten minutes ago I saw Smiler Coe lead a horse down an alley over yonder," Luke said.

"Smiler Coe," Matt repeated. "He's that gunman you mentioned a while back."

"That's right. A few minutes after Coe did that, another man did the same thing. I didn't recognize him by name, but I sure knew the type."

"A hardcase, you mean," Smoke said.

"Exactly. Then another one came along, and unless I miss my guess, it's about to happen again." Luke nodded toward a man leading a horse along the street. As they watched, the man turned and disappeared into an alley, taking the mount with him.

"Well, that's downright suspicious," Matt said as he sat up straighter.

Luke nodded "That's just what I was thinking."

"That alley runs between a hardware store and a milliner's," Smoke pointed out.

"Yeah. And two doors down from the hardware store is the bank."

Preacher cocked his head to the side. "You think they're a-fixin' to rob it?"

"I don't recall hearing about Coe going in for bank robbery," Luke said, "but there's always a first time for everything."

Smoke got easily to his feet. "Maybe we ought to mosey down that direction ourselves."

Luke nodded. "That's just what I was about to suggest." He glanced around. "Where are those two youngsters?"

Smoke looked at Luke. "Ace and Chance? They were upstairs keeping Mike company the last time I saw them. I don't reckon we need their help with something like this, though. There's only four men back there."

"That we know of," Luke said. "No telling whether any more came skulking around before I noticed Coe. But I agree, there's no need to disturb the boys." He hitched his gunbelt a little. "Let's go."

The four men stepped down from the hotel porch and began walking along the street toward the bank. From one of the churches came the sound of an organ playing and the congregation singing a Christmas hymn. At the other end of the street, the mission bell began to ring. The street was empty except for Smoke, Matt, Luke, and Preacher as peace reigned over Tucson.

Peace that was abruptly shattered by the dull boom of an explosion.

Hands flashed toward guns.

Smoke called, "They blew the safe in the bank! Come on!"

The four of them ran toward the alley, knowing they would have to move fast to stop the robbers from fleeing with their loot. As they rounded the corner of the hardware store and pounded into the alley, shots blasted from the passage's far end. A bullet whined past Smoke's head.

Instinctively, he returned the fire, and so did the other three. The outlaw who'd been posted at the back end of the alley to stand guard had already ducked out of sight and hightailed it away. Through the echoes of the shots, Smoke heard him shouting a warning to his companions.

A couple heartbeats later, they stepped into the alley behind the buildings and saw two men and half a dozen horses. The outlaws tried to hide behind their mounts as they opened fire, but they were exposed a little in order to shoot.

It didn't take much of an opening for men as deadly accurate with their guns as the Jensens and Preacher. Colts and Remingtons roared. One of the outlaws in the alley flew backwards as a slug slammed into his forehead, bored through his brain, and exploded out the back of his skull. The other man reeled into the open with a bullet-shattered shoulder but was too stubborn to give up. As his gun came up, four shots crashed in unison and he staggered back as four bullets drove into his chest. He flopped into a limp sprawl.

Smoke and the others spread out as the rest of the gang emerged from the back door of the bank carrying bags of money and shooting wildly.

Clouds of powder smoke rolled through the air and the thunder of guns drowned out the mission bell and the Christmas carol. It was a holy day, but those outlaws had profaned it. And they wouldn't get away with the money that Tucson needed.

Crouching, Matt felt a bullet tug at the buckskin jacket he wore. The next instant, flame spouted from the muzzle of his Colt and the man who had almost winged him doubled over as Matt's slug punched into his belly. The outlaw folded up as his finger jerked the trigger again, sending a bullet into the ground at his feet.

A few yards away, Preacher squinted down the barrel of his revolver and squeezed off a swift but steady pair of shots that ripped through the torso of another outlaw. The man stumbled and pitched forward to lie facedown as his life leaked out into the dust.

One of the outlaws vaulted into the saddle. Smoke's quick shot caught him just as he landed. The bag of currency he was carrying flew into the air and came open, scattering money. The man's horse, spooked by all the shooting, reared up and dumped him off backwards. He hit hard, rolled, and wound up on his belly. He clawed a gun from its holster on his hip and fired once at Smoke, who ended the threat by planting a couple slugs in his face and turning it into a red smear.

That left Luke to tackle the last outlaw. The man was fast, throwing lead around with such speed it was all Luke could do to weave out of the bullets' paths. His pair of Remingtons came up and boomed. The outlaw cried out in shock and pain and staggered back. He tried to raise his gun, but his arms wouldn't obey him. Both were drilled cleanly, bones broken and leaking blood. The man's gun slipped from nerveless fingers and thudded to the ground. He dropped to his knees beside it.

An echoing silence settled over the area behind the bank. Smoke, Matt, and Preacher checked the men they had shot.

Luke kept the last man covered and strode toward him. "Smiler Coe. You should have stuck to back shooting and bushwhacking, Smiler, instead of robbing banks. You're not good at it."

"You . . . you . . ." Obscenities spewed from Coe's mouth.

"It's Christmas," Luke snarled. "Shut that up or I'll bust your head open." A grim smile tugged at the bounty hunter's mouth. "Looks like all you'll be getting for Christmas is a prison term."

"I won't be locked up alone," Coe raved. "It was all Tuttle's idea, every damned bit of it! Avery Tuttle! He's the one who wanted that stagecoach stopped and Tom Ballard killed! He wanted that money gone so it wouldn't interfere with his plans! His damned plans!" Coe's head sagged forward and he moaned. "You've ruined me. These arms will never be the same. I can't handle a gun anymore!"

"Where you're going it won't matter," Luke said. "They won't let you have one in prison."

Smoke heard hasty footsteps and looked around to see Tom Ballard hurrying toward them.

"Did I hear him right?" Ballard asked excitedly. "Did Coe just admit that Tuttle ordered him to rob the bank?"

"That's right," Smoke said. "We all heard it, and I reckon Coe will be willing to testify in court, too. That'll end Tuttle's efforts to take over the whole town, won't it?"

"I heard the shots and came running to find out what the story was going to be," Ballard said. "I didn't dream it would be Avery Tuttle's downfall!"

The sheriff and a couple deputies showed up a few minutes later. Smoke, Matt, Luke, and Preacher holstered their guns and stepped back to let the law take over. It was obvious what had happened, with the back door of the bank open, the door on the safe inside blown off with dynamite, and bags of money scattered around, including the one that had come open and spilled its contents. All the would-be bank robbers were dead except for Smiler Coe, who in his pain and shock was still babbling about everything being Avery Tuttle's fault.

A short time later, Smoke walked into the hotel and found Sally waiting for him. She looked calm and composed, but he saw concern lurking in her eyes.

Even after so much time together, she was a little worried about him whenever all hell broke loose. She knew that Smoke Jensen was probably right in the middle of it. "What's happened now? Are all of you all right?"

"We're fine." Quickly, he explained what had gone on behind the bank.

"Then it really is all over now? We can relax and enjoy the rest of the holiday with our family and our new friends?"

"I think so. We're going to dinner at Mrs. Bates's house tonight, right?"

"That's the plan. Try not to get mixed up in any more shoot-outs between now and then, all right, Smoke?"

"I'll sure try," he said as he put his arms around her and drew her to him. "Thing of it is, you never know—"

Somewhere else in Tucson, a gun went off just then. Sally stiffened, but Smoke's arms tightened around her. He brushed his lips against her dark hair and said, "Nothing to do with us."

Sally looked up at him. "You promise?"

Smoke's kiss was answer enough.

Belgium, December 1944

"As it turned out, Smoke was wrong for one of the few times in his life," Sarge said. "That gunshot was Avery Tuttle taking the easy way out when the sheriff came to arrest him. Tuttle would have just gone to prison for a few years, since he hadn't killed anybody and Smiler Coe never confessed to anything except bank robbery and setting up that ambush on the stagecoach. But Tuttle couldn't bear the thought of even that and put a bullet in his brain."

"Ho, ho, ho. Merry Christmas," Private Bexley said. "Sarge, don't you know Christmas stories are supposed to be full o' warmth and good cheer, not all that shootin' and killin' and stuff?"

Corporal Wallace grunted. "Tell that to the Krauts. It don't seem like they're takin' a holiday, does it?"

Despite his fears, Private Mitchell had gotten caught up in the story. "What happened to that gunfighter? Smiler Coe?"

"Well, my grandpa kept up with everybody, of course, since that was sort of his job, and he told me Coe lived through his prison term and went on to raise more hell," Sarge said. "He even met up with Luke Jensen again and caused some pretty bad trouble for him. I don't think we've got time for that story tonight, though."

"Wait a minute," Private Thorp said. "What about the girl? The one who worked for Tuttle."

Private Hogan nudged him in the ribs. "You always got the pretty girls on your mind, don't you, Thorp?"

"Amy Perkins dropped out of sight and was never seen in Tucson again. Maybe she reformed after that or maybe she got mixed up in some other crooked scheme." Sarge shrugged. "I don't reckon we'll ever know."

Bexley said, "It was a good story. I guess you're sayin' that those people bein' caught in that storm and then surrounded by Apaches is sorta like us, right, Sarge? The odds were against them, but they came through all right." He patted the .30 caliber. "We don't have Santa Claus comin' outta nowhere with a Gatling gun, but we got this baby."

"What about that fella Kendall?" Wallace asked. "He wasn't really . . ."

"Santa Claus?" the sarge asked with a grin. "I don't know, Wallace. A guy has to make up his own mind about that stuff, doesn't he?"

The dogfaces were silent for a few moments. The German artillery barrage had stopped, and the night was unusually quiet.

The sound of combat boots tromping through the thin layer of snow made all the soldiers swing around and lift their rifles. The sergeant's hands tightened on his Thompson submachine gun.

"Sergeant Ballard?" a man called softly.

Sergeant Thomas Ballard III heaved a sigh of relief and answered, "Here, Lieutenant."

An officer slipped up to the machine gun post and knelt as the men gathered around him. "I'm making the rounds, checking on all the outposts personally. How are you holding up?"

"We're fine, sir," Ballard said. "A little cold, but fine. Isn't that right, boys?"

A chorus of agreement came from the men, even from Mitchell.

Bexley said, "The sarge has been tellin' us cowboy stories to pass the time, sir."

"Is that so?" The lieutenant chuckled. "Maybe after the war you can write for those pulp magazines, Sergeant. I hear a lot of newspapermen write fiction on the side."

"Yes, sir, I'll give that some thought," Ballard said. "Right now I'd rather just concentrate on getting through this fight."

"I'm sure we all feel the same way. The Germans sent a surrender demand, you know. What answer do you think General McAuliffe sent back to them?"

Bexley said, "I hope he told 'em to go to hell."

The lieutenant laughed. "Not quite, Private, but close. He told them, 'Nuts!' Can you imagine the looks on the faces of those Kraut generals? 'Nuts!'"

"Sounds like something Smoke Jensen might have told them if he was here," Ballard said.

The lieutenant shook his head. "I don't know who that is, Sergeant."

"Just an old friend of the family, sir. Just an old friend of the family."

Keep reading for a special preview of the next Smoke Jensen adventure!

VENOM OF THE MOUNTAIN MAN

When Smoke Jensen sees a gang of outlaws holding up a stagecoach, his gunfighter instincts take over and he storms in with guns blazing. He kills one of the gunmen—the rest scatter like the rats they are. But the dead man is the brother of the notorious outlaw Gabe Briggs, and Briggs will want revenge . . .

Tired of the savagery of the lawless countryside, Smoke's wife, Sally, heads back east for a spell, only to find the big city choking in filth, violence, and corruption. Before Sally can return home, though, she's snatched right off the street.

When Smoke gets word that Sally's been kidnapped, he hops the first train east. But Gabe Briggs and his ruthless band of badmen are along for the ride. Unless Smoke can punch their tickets to hell first, they'll blow this train sky high . . .

**Coming in December, wherever
Pinnacle Books are sold.**

Salcedo, Wyoming

The hooves of Smoke Jensen's horse, Seven, made a dry clatter on the rocks as Smoke made a rather steep descent down from a seldom used trail. Seeing the road below, he felt a sense of relief.

"There it is, Seven, there's the road. Taking the cutoff wasn't all that good of an idea. I was beginning to think we never would see that road again."

Seven whickered.

"No, I wasn't lost. You know I don't get lost. I just get a little disoriented every now and then."

Seven whickered again.

"Ah, so now you're making fun of me, are you?"

On long rides, Smoke often talked to his horse, because he wanted to hear a voice, even if it was his own. And talking to his horse seemed a step above talking to himself.

Smoke dismounted, and reached up to squeeze Seven's ear. Seven dipped his head in appreciation of the gesture.

"Yeah, I know you like this. Tell you what, why don't I walk the rest of the way down this hill, that way you won't have to be working as hard. And when we get on the road, we'll have a little breather.

A few minutes later, before they reached the road, Seven suddenly let out an anxious whiney, and using his head, pushed Smoke aside so violently that Smoke fell, painfully, onto the rocks.

"What was that all about?" Smoke said, angrily.

Seven whinnied again, and began backing away, lifting his forelegs high, and bobbing his head up and down. That was when Smoke saw the rattler, coiled, and bobbing its head, ready to strike.

Smoke drew his pistol and fired. There was a mist of blood where the snake's head had been, the head now at least five feet away from the reptile's still coiled but decapitated body.

"Are you all right?" Smoke asked, anxiously, as he began examining Seven's forelegs and feet. He found no indication that the snake had bitten him.

Smoke wrapped his arms around Seven's neck "Good boy," he said. "Oh, wait, I know what you really want." Again, Smoke began squeezing Seven's ear.

"Well, as much as you like this, we can't hang around here all day. We need to get going."

Smoke led Seven on down the rocky incline then, just before he reached the road, his foot slipped off a rock, and he felt the heel break off.

"Damn," he said, picking up the heel. "Don't worry," he said. "I'm not going to remount right away, but probably a little earlier than I previously intended."

Smoked limped along for at least two more miles then, when he was certain Seven was well rested, he swung back into the saddle. "All right boy, let's go," he said.

Smoke started forward at a trot that was comfortable for both of them.

"We'll be coming into Salcedo soon. Tell me, Seven, do you think this bustling community will have a shoe store?"

Seven dipped his head.

"Oh, yeah, you would say that. You always are the optimist."

Salcedo was the result of what had once been a trading post, then a saloon, then a couple of houses, a general store until, gradually it became a town along the banks of the Platte River. The river was not navigable for steamboats, and even flatboats had a difficult time because of the shallowness of the water and the many sandbars and rocks long the route.

An overly optimistic sign at the town limits read:

SALCEDO
POP. 210

Smoke had been to Rawlins, and was on his way back to his ranch, Sugarloaf, when he broke the heel. He found a boot and shoe store on Main Street, and heard the cobbler's optimistic account that he could fix it. He was now standing in the window of the shoe repair shop, his attention drawn to a stagecoach parked at the depot just across the street.

"Swan, Mule Gap, and Douglass!" the driver shouted. "If you're goin' to Swan, Mule Gap, or Douglass, get aboard now!"

Five passengers responded to the driver's call: two men, and a woman with two children. The coach had a shotgun guard, and as soon as he was in position, the driver popped his whip, the six horses strained in their harness, and the coach pulled away.

"Your boot is ready," George Friegh, the shoemaker, said as he stepped up beside Smoke. When he saw that Smoke had been watching the coach leave, he added to his comment. "It's carryin' five thousand dollars in cash money."

"You mean that's common knowledge?" Smoke replied. "I thought stagecoach companies didn't want it known when they were carrying a sizeable cash shipment."

"Yeah, most of the time they do try 'n keep it quiet. But you can't do that with Emile Taylor."

"Who is Emile Taylor?" Smoke asked.

"Taylor's the shotgun guard. He's an old soldier and like a lot of old soldiers, he's a drinkin' man. I heard him carryin' on last night while he was gettin' hisself snockered at the Trail's End."

Trail's End was the only saloon in Salcedo.

"He started talkin' about the money shipment they're takin' down to Douglass. Five thousand dollars he said it was."

"He told you that?"

"Not just me. Hell, mister, he was talkin' loud enough that ever' one in the saloon heard him."

Smoke examined the boot, then paid for the work.

"You did a good job," he said, slipping the boot back on. "I'd better be getting back on the road."

Five miles south of Salcedo, on the Douglass Pike

Four men were waiting on the side of the road, their horses ground hobbled behind them.

"You're sure it's carryin' five thousand dollars?" one of them asked.

"Yeah, I'm sure. I heard the shotgun guard braggin' about it."

"The reason I ask if you're sure is, the last time we held up a stage we didn't get nothin' but thirty-seven dollars, 'n that's what we got from the passengers. Hell, you could get shot holdin' up a stage, and thirty-seven dollars ain't worth it."

"This here stagecoach has five thousand dollars, you can trust me on this."

"Here it comes," one of the other men said as the coach crested the hill to come into view.

"All right, you three get mounted and get your guns out. Gabe, you hold my horse. I'll have 'em throw the money bag down to me. Get your hoods on," he added, as he pulled a hood down over his own head.

Smoke heard the unmistakable sound of a gunshot in the distance before him. There was only one shot, and it could have been a hunter, but he didn't think so. There was a sharp flatness to the sound, more like that of a pistol, rather than a rifle. He wondered about it, but there was only one shot, and it could have been anything, so he didn't give it that much of a thought.

Then, when Smoke reached the top of the hill he saw the stagecoach stopped on the road in front of him. This was the same stagecoach he had watched leave Salcedo and the passengers, including the woman and children, were standing outside the coach with their hands up. The driver had his hands up as well. For just a second he wondered about the shotgun guard, then he saw a body lying in the road beside the front wheel of the coach.

There were four armed men, all but one mounted, and all wearing hoods that covered their faces. There was no doubt but that he had come upon a robbery.

Pulling his pistol, Smoke urged Seven into a gallop, and quickly closed the distance between himself and the stagecoach robbers.

"Drop your guns!" Smoke shouted.

"What the hell?" one of the robbers yelled, and all four of them shot at Smoke.

Smoke shot back, and the dismounted robber went down. There was another exchange of gunfire, and one of the mounted robbers went down as well.

"Let's get out of here!" one of the two remaining robbers shouted, and they galloped off.

Smoke reached the coach then dismounted to check on the two fallen robbers to make certain they presented no further danger to the coach. They didn't, because both were dead.

A quick exam of the shotgun guard determined that he, too, was dead.

"Mister, I don't know who you are," the driver said. "But you sure come along in time to save our bacon."

"The name is Jensen. Smoke Jensen. Are all of you all right? Was anyone hurt?"

"We're fine, Mr. Jensen, thanks to you," the woman passenger said.

From the *Douglas Budget:*

> Smoke Jensen is best known as the owner of Sugarloaf, a successful ranch near Big Rock, Colorado. He is also well known as a paladin, a man whose skillful employment of a pistol has, on many occasions, defended the endangered from harm being visited upon them by evil doers.
>
> Such was the case a few days ago when fate, in the form of the fortuitous arrival of Mr. Jensen, foiled an attempted stage coach robbery, and perhaps saved the lives of the driver and passengers. The incident occurred on Douglas Pike Road, some five miles south of Salcedo, and five miles north of Mule Gap.
>
> Although Mr. Jensen called out to the road gents, offering them the opportunity to drop their guns, the four outlaws refused to do so, choosing instead to engage Jensen in a gunfight. This was a fatal decision for Lucas Monroe and Asa Briggs, both of whom were killed in the ensuing gunplay. Two of the men, already mounted, were able to escape.

Although the bandits were wearing hoods during the entire exchange, it is widely believed that one of the men who got away was Gabe Briggs, as he and his brother, Asa, like the James, Dalton, brothers, rode the outlaw trail together.

Wiregrass Ranch, adjacent to Sugarloaf

Wiregrass Ranch had once belonged to Ned and Molly Condon. When they were murdered, Sam Condon, Ned's brother, came west from St. Louis. Sam had been a successful lawyer in that city, and everyone thought he was coming to arrange for the sale of the ranch. Instead, he decided to stay, and he brought his wife, Sara Sue, and their then-twelve-year-old son, Thad, with him. Both Sara Sue and Thad adjusted to their new surroundings quickly, and easily. Thad not only adjusted, he thrived in the new environment.

Sam had made the conscious decision to sell off all the cattle Ned had owned, and replaced them with two highly regarded registered Hereford bulls, and ten registered Hereford cows. Within two years after he started his operation, he had a herd of fifty, composed of ten bulls and forty cows. By keeping his herd so small, he was able to keep down expenses by having no permanent cowboys. Thad, who was now thirteen years old, had become a very good hand.

Sam Condon's approach to ranching paid off well, and he earned a rather substantial income by selling registered cattle, both bulls and cows, to ranchers who wanted to improve their stock.

Sam and Sara Sue were celebrating their seventeenth wedding anniversary, and they had invited Smoke and Sally, their neighbors from the adjacent ranch, to have a celebratory dinner with them.

"Chicken and dumplin's, Missouri style," Sara Sue said.

"Oh, you don't have to educate me, Sara Sue," Smoke said as his hostess spooned the pastry onto his plate. "It's been a while, but I'm a Missouri boy, too."

"Well, I'm from the Northeast, but I've learned to enjoy chicken and dumplings as well," Sally said. "Smoke loves them so, that I had to learn how to make the flat dumplings."

"She learned how to make them all right," Smoke said. "She just hasn't learned how to say 'dumplin's' without adding that last g," he teased.

The others laughed.

"Mr. Jensen, I read about you in the paper," Thad said.

"Oh?"

"Yes, sir, I read how you stopped a stagecoach holdup, 'n how you kilt two men."

"Thad," Sam said. "That's hardly a subject fit for discussion over the dinner table."

"But that is what you done, ain't it? You kilt two men?"

"That's what you did, isn't it?" Sally Sue said, correcting Thad's grammar.

"See, Pa, even Ma is talking about it," Thad said.

The others at the table laughed.

"I'll tell you what," Sam said. "We'll talk about it after dinner. That is, if Smoke is amenable to it."

"Amenable, oh, a good lawyer's word," Sally said with a smile.

After dinner, Smoke, Sam, and Thad sat out on the front porch while Sally helped Sara Sue clean up from the meal. In the west, Red Table Mountain was living up to its name by glowing red in the setting sun.

"The newspaper said that one of the men who got away was Gabe Briggs," Sam said.

"He probably was, but they never removed their masks, so there is no way of saying," Smoke replied.

"Would you have recognized him, if he hadn't been wearing a mask?"

Smoke shook his head. "No, I don't think I would have. I've heard of the Briggs Brothers, but then, who in this part of the country hasn't? But I've never seen either of them before that little fracas on the road."

"But he did see you," Sam said.

"Yes."

"Doesn't that worry you a little? I mean, he knows what you look like, but you don't know what he looks like. If he is bent upon revenging his brother you could be in serious danger."

"I appreciate your concern," Smoke said. "But my life has been such that I have made as many enemies, as I have friends. And I never know when some unknown enemy is going to call me out or, even worse, try and shoot me from ambush. I've lived with that for many years. Gabe Briggs will be just one more."

"How many men have you kilt, Mr. Jensen?" Thad asked.

"Thad! That's not a question you should ever ask anyone!" Sam scolded.

"I'm sorry," Thad said, contritely. "I didn't mean it in a bad way. I think Mr. Jensen is a hero."

Smoke chuckled, softly. "I'm not a hero, Thad. But I have always tried to do the right thing. I'm not proud of the number of men I've killed—no one should ever kill someone as a matter of pride. But I will tell you this. I've never killed anyone who wasn't trying to kill me."

Connect with

Us

Visit us online at
KensingtonBooks.com
to read more from your favorite authors, see books
by series, view reading group guides, and more.

Join us on social media

for sneak peeks, chances to win books and prize packs,
and to share your thoughts with other readers.

**facebook.com/kensingtonpublishing
twitter.com/kensingtonbooks**

Tell us what you think!

To share your thoughts, submit a review,
or sign up for our eNewsletters, please visit:
KensingtonBooks.com/TellUs.